PRAISE FOR ELEANOR HERMAN
AND THE BLOOD OF GODS AND ROYALS SERIES

"Herman mixes real history with magic, mystery and intrigue, putting the 'epic' in epic fantasy!"
—Maria V. Snyder, *New York Times* bestselling author of the Study series, on *Legacy of Kings*

"Thoroughly researched and absolutely modern…. Just right for today's audience."
—*Kirkus Reviews* on *Legacy of Kings*

"Action and fantasy lovers will gobble it up."
—*School Library Journal* on *Legacy of Kings*

"A cast of dozens, with eight narrative perspectives…full of reawakening magic, sex, and lots and lots of violence: it's the formula behind George R.R. Martin's bestselling A Song of Ice and Fire, and there's no doubt it has appeal."
—*Kirkus Reviews* on *Empire of Dust*

"Sexy and full of secret plans, *Legacy of Kings* has a lot of elements coming together to make an unputdownable story with many memorable characters. Written for teens, the book will cross over to adults as well. This could easily be the next big saga."
—Jackie Blem, Tattered Cover Book Store

"With its intriguing blend of history, political intrigue and mystery, *Legacy of Kings* reminds me of *Outlander*. I can't wait to find out what happens next."
—Anne Allin, Lake Forest Book Store

"An intricately woven tale of magic, romance, and deception, *Legacy of Kings* has something for every reader. Once you start it, you won't be able to put it down. Fantasy fans will truly adore this one."
—Katie, *Katie's Book Blog*

"*Legacy of Kings* is a stunning, imaginative and spellbinding saga that will send readers back to a time of magic and myth, prophecy and fate, bloodshed and brutality, dishonesty and deceit. It is a tale that will capture readers' interest from the start, will ensnare them as the story unfolds, and won't let go until the very end."
—Rachel, *Fiktshun* blog

Books by Eleanor Herman
available from Harlequin TEEN

Blood of Gods and Royals series
(in reading order)

ELEANOR HERMAN

EMPIRE OF DUST

HARLEQUIN TEEN

Recycling programs
for this product may
not exist in your area.

ISBN-13: 978-0-373-21235-4

Empire of Dust

Copyright © 2016 by Paper Lantern Lit LLC and Eleanor Herman

This edition published by arrangement with Harlequin Books S.A.

For questions and comments about the quality of this book, please contact us at CustomerService@Harlequin.com.

Printed in U.S.A.

To my stepson Sam Dyment and his bride, Crisy Meschieri Dyment
May your marriage remain an enchanted adventure forever.

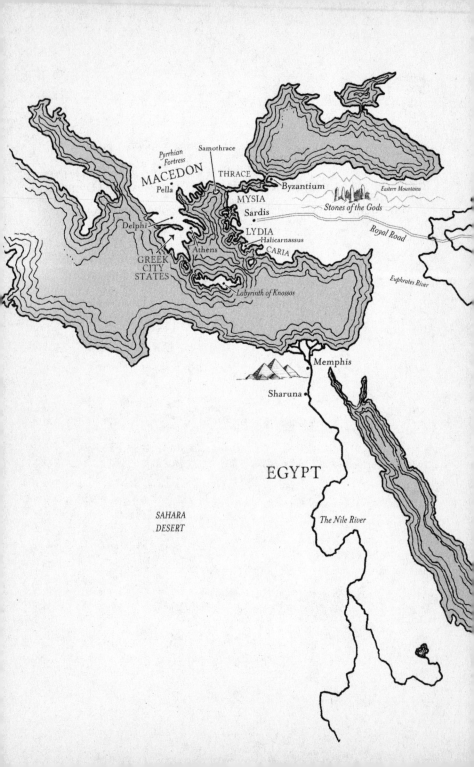

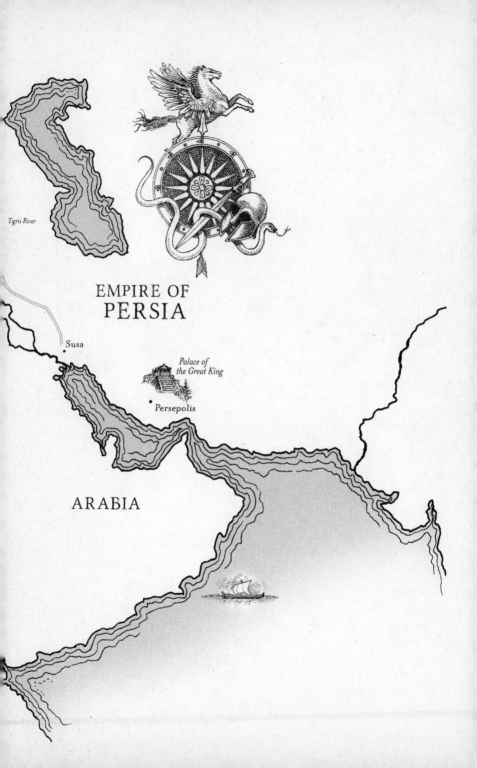

Tigris River

EMPIRE OF
PERSIA

Susa

Palace of
the Great King

• Persepolis

ARABIA

ACT ONE:
CAPTIVE

From the deepest desires often comes the deadliest hate.
—Socrates

CHAPTER ONE

LEAVES RUSTLING. BRANCHES CREAKING.

The tinkle of tiny bells and cymbals creeps toward her on the wind. Olympias—queen of Macedon, mother of Prince Regent Alexander—knows she is close.

She keeps walking through the trees of the sacred trail—where horses are forbidden—even though her legs ache and a dull pain in her lower back throbs from long hours in the saddle. She needs answers.

Finally, she sees the sacred oak in the clearing ahead, a tree that was already ancient when Troy burned. Its weighty lower limbs, thick as a man's body, rest on the ground, gray and gnarled, before curling up again.

The afternoon air is thick and warm, and a trickle of sweat drips down her neck. Her long, silver-blond hair has come undone, wisps blowing into her face as they did so often when she was young and preferred to wear it loose.

An eternity ago, on just such a summer afternoon full of birdsong and sunshine, she lay with *him* here, wrapped in his strong arms under these wide, whispering boughs. Then her heart was alive with love, and she truly believed she could feel the presence of the goddess who was said to dwell within the tree. Now her pulse is no more than a beating drum, counting the hours, months, years that have been lost. The emptiness of her life eats at her organs like the arsenic she has feared ever since she became queen. For all know that arsenic is the king of poisons, the poison of kings. And queens.

She feels the unquenchable hunger rising in her blood again, the insistent need for something—anything—to stop the torment. Watching as flames consumed the potter's house three days ago—hearing the screams of the family as her guards dragged them outside—satisfied her need for action for a few beautiful hours…but then the bright, warm blaze of vengeance quickly turned cold as ashes.

Frustration gnawing at her, she pushes her way into the sanctuary of the branches. The world under the tree is like a spacious villa, with countless rooms on many floors—long-empty—divided by diaphanous curtains of green. Golden light pours through dozens of windowlike partings. She approaches the trunk and runs a hand over the rough edges of the lumpy bark. How many warriors joining hands would it take to surround the trunk? Twelve? Fifteen?

A man's voice startles her and she inhales sharply. "I received your message, my queen."

Lord Bastian steps out from behind the trunk and gives her a mocking bow—not quite low enough and far too fast. She lets herself take in the burning dark eyes and tall form, a bit sorry he isn't wearing the black leather uniform and horned helmet of an Aesarian Lord, although his mulberry-colored tunic shows off his lean muscles. His dark hair hangs in thick waves to his shoulders.

Olympias fingers the dagger in her cloak pocket and feels the sharpness of its tip. "You survived the battle," she says archly. "My guards told me that my son performed brilliantly as general."

The scar on Bastian's cheek twitches a bit, puckering. "Yes. It was an impressive performance. Still, I don't know that Alexander would have won if the girl hadn't helped him."

The girl.

Olympias should be grateful to the wretch for saving Alexander's life, but all she can feel is a bright, hard anger pulsing through her veins. "My messengers have brought me stories that Katerina used a catapult to shoot amphorae full of scorpions and snakes at your army. That she unleashed the hellion—"

Bastian winces and waves a hand to stop her. "Speak no more of the battle," he says, taking a step toward her. "The Lords have been humiliated. Despite our superior numbers, despite the fact that we are the best fighting force in the world, we were vanquished by a boy leading an untested army—and a girl tossing pots."

He steps even closer, and she can feel his breath on her forehead. "Where have you been the past few days?" he asks. "Our spies say you left the palace before the battle."

Her heart beats faster as he nears. It's not just that he's young and handsome and slender while her husband, King Philip, is middle-aged, stocky, and missing an eye. What draws her irresistibly to this Lord is the sense of danger that wafts about him like an Egyptian perfume. Intoxicating.

This man knows no loyalty—he is capable of doing anything, killing anyone. Even her. He's already tried once.

When her taster had fallen unconscious after sipping the queen's wine, Olympias learned from her guard that the Aesarian Lord Bastian, a guest at the palace, had been flirting with the serving maid while she was carrying the queen's tray to the royal rooms. It was not hard to conclude that he had poured poison into the cup while the silly fool was staring love-struck into his dark eyes.

She could have called her guards and had Bastian imprisoned, tortured, and executed—but that would have been the impetuous solution. Olympias has always prided herself on seeing the larger stage and possessing the patience to allow plots to unfold. She suspected the Lord would make a useful tool, and she had been right.

At her request, he had framed her long-lost daughter, Katerina, for his own misdeeds, keeping the queen free from Alexander's blame when his friend was flung into the dungeons. Bastian had whispered to her the Lords' plans to break into the palace, so she had had time to hide from the attackers in her hidden altar. Bastian had proven very useful—until the Aesarian Lords left the palace to prepare for battle against Macedon while King Philip was away in Byzantium.

With war declared between Macedon and the Lords, Bastian could obviously no longer serve as her spy in the palace. As easily as he'd become her minion for a brief time, his loyalties shifted.

But they are *always* shifting, she realizes now. She can see it in his eyes, the way self-interest and opportunity ripple across his vision like waves in a pond. He is more of a threat than ever before. He knows too much about her plots, her fears, and her needs.

She cannot allow him to live.

But she needs one last thing.

"What are you hiding?" he asks, tracing a finger across her jaw.

"All mortals have their weaknesses," she says, refusing to answer his question. "That girl—Katerina…" The name tastes like acid on her tongue. "She happens to be mine. And yours, well…" She removes her cloak and unclasps the jeweled brooches at her shoulders, letting her gown slip down slowly until it pools around her ankles. Streaks of sunlight sway through the curtain of leaves and tickle her skin. "We all know yours."

A man's eyes are the best mirror for a woman's beauty. When she gazes into his, a thrill of satisfaction, of power, moves through her. He closes the distance between them, unable to contain his hands, which weave themselves into her waist-length hair. He grabs on—a bit too hard—and draws her to him, his mouth pressing on hers. For a moment, she *wants* to be overpowered. Wants to forget.

She kisses him back, tasting the sweetness of his youth, his energy, his belief in his own invulnerability. Olympias was like that once, too. Long ago, when the world shimmered like a gem in the palm of her hand and anything seemed possible. Before the curse that ground the gem into dust.

But now, at least for a while, she can be young and free again as the wind rises around them, and the giant oak whispers restlessly, urging them on.

Olympias adjusts her gown as Bastian pulls on his boots. The sun is low on the horizon, its rays filtering in through the branches and turning the trunk bright red in patches.

"I won't make it back to the fortress until the day after tomorrow," he says. "And you? You, too, have a long ride back to Pella, or are you returning to Erissa? What were soldiers doing there—looking for the girl?"

When she doesn't respond, he picks up his sword belt and buckles it around his slim hips. "Why does that girl matter so much? What is she to you?"

"*She* is nothing," Olympias says. "But she is the key to freeing someone infinitely more important."

He tilts his head and stares at her. "Who can be that important to the queen of Macedon?" His eyes narrow. "A lover, perhaps?" He laughs as she looks quickly away from him. "What—you think I don't know you're imagining someone else when we're together? I don't care. I'm not in love with you. Zeus help the man who is."

Olympias pretends to focus on tying her sandal strap, but she is angry. Not with Bastian, but with herself. Has she gotten so soft that she can't mask her feelings? Philip never knew. But then, Philip is a fool.

"You spoke of freeing him. Is this lover a slave, then? I would like to see the man who has such an effect on you," he says, taking a step toward her. He towers over her, his long shadow swallowing her. "More of an effect, even," he says slowly, "than me."

"A slave? No," she says sharply, standing and slapping the dirt from her robe. *I am not afraid of you,* she thinks as she flings the cloak over her shoulders, aware of her dagger's weight in the right pocket. "No *man* could ever have a hold on me." She's tired of his arrogance. He speaks to her as if he owns her—and she is no toy.

He grabs her wrist hard and leans in to her, his breath hot on her cheek. "A woman, then," he says, his eyes lighting up with sensual amusement.

"A *god!*" she spits at him, her patience done. She hasn't spoken the word in years, but it doesn't matter that he knows because after today he will cease to exist. Bastian thinks he knows what power is—but what he knows is only a poor imitation of true majesty.

It takes Bastian a moment to comprehend what she's saying, but she can see the instant he understands. His eyes burn, sharp as flints.

Suddenly, his expression softens, and he puts a hand on her arm. "In that case, I can't be jealous of my rival, Olympias," he says, his voice oddly gentle. "Indeed, you have my sympathy. It's ruinous for a mortal to love a god."

She says nothing, though his words unsettle her. She doesn't want his pity.

The wind moans. All around them, the chimes tied to the branches—offerings to the goddess—clang like harsh laughter, the ribbons dance, the branches pop and wheeze.

He plucks a leaf off her robe. "Wouldn't you rather have a companion of flesh and bone?"

Olympias smiles, more to herself than to the scarred Lord. He would never understand the sensation of being next to the burning soul of a being made from the same stuff as the stars, who has wind in his blood, and fire for a heart.

"You have been a most amusing companion of flesh and bone," she purrs, placing a small white hand on his chest, feeling the hardness of muscles. She runs her hand down to his abdomen, lingering a moment on his rib cage and feeling the tendons alternate with bone. The best place in which to slide a dagger.

He stops her hand from dipping lower. "Let's toast to that." He pulls a goatskin from his pack, and she observes as he puts it to his lips, drinking deeply. She watches carefully, noting when he swallows. "Ah, Chian wine," he says. "Even better than the gods' nectar." He passes the goatskin to her.

It's strong and sweet, and she feels it warming her chest. She tries to hand the goatskin back to him, but he shoos her hand away.

"Have more," he says, studying her intently.

A red-hot spike of fear shoots up her spine. "No," she replies, pushing the goatskin away too hard. "I don't...don't..." Her words slur, and her head is suddenly crushed by dizziness.

Poison.

Impossible. She *saw* him sip it, too...

The wind whips angrily through the tree; the huge boughs seem to rise up like arms and drop down again with a groan as the bells and cymbals jangle. The world reels diagonally, and Olympias drops to the ground, facing the tree trunk. She hears Bastian's footsteps crunch over the leaves as he walks away. She tries to turn her head to see, but she can't.

Her blood turns to ice, slowing and hardening in her veins. Her breathing slows, too—she can't get air. Blackness descends all around her, muffling the swishing leaves, the creaking branches, and the sound of her heartbeat, faltering.

CHAPTER TWO

HEPHAESTION STARES AS THE VEIN ON THE farmer's sunburned forehead begins to pulse. It seems he's not the only one with a headache this morning.

"I brought two barrels of olives with me, and I won't leave until you either pay me for them or give me two barrels of olives back," the farmer insists, crossing his arms.

If he keeps talking, will the vein eventually pop? Heph wonders as the farmer continues his tirade. He stopped listening two peasants back. This task Alexander assigned him—to make sure the peasants returning to their homes after the battle received proper payment for the provisions they provided—is by far the worst punishment the prince could have given him. He is—he *used* to be—Alexander's best friend. He should be at the prince's side, not here in this mess.

None of the peasants can read, and they each claim that the receipts they were given are for a lesser amount than what they brought to the palace. Who's scamming whom here? The palace officials who wrote the receipts, or the peasants themselves?

This little office of a low-level palace clerk has one window facing the stables, and the smell of manure rises in the humid air. Heph glances down at his desk, covered with lists, receipts, and accounts.

As the farmer drones on, his voice morphs into another voice: Alex's. The voice that Heph has heard again and again over the past two days, ever since the prince called all surviving soldiers into the main palace courtyard to congratulate them on the casualties they inflicted in the battle with the Aesarian Lords.

"Jason, son of Alfio, for killing five Aesarian Lords!" He clapped the soldier's shoulder as the others around cheered. "Ander, son of Maarku, for killing three Aesarian Lords!" Then he was standing in front of Heph. "Hephaestion, son of Hipparchus," he said loudly, "for killing at least eleven Aesarian Lords." As cheers went up, Alex added under his breath, "And that's one more than he should have."

Heat rushed to his neck, and Heph dropped his eyes. Then, even though it seemed it couldn't get any worse, it did. Alex walked over to Kadmus, smiling broadly. "Finally, our greatest praise of all for General Kadmus, who estimates he killed fourteen Aesarian Lords, the most of any of us!"

Kadmus. He is several years older than Heph and, as a general in King Philip's army, far more experienced in battle. As Kadmus seems to gain Alex's trust, Heph can't help but feel Alex lose just a little more faith in him. Heph's entire relationship with Alex is built on trust. Without Alex, he has nothing. *Is* nothing. He is a—

"…disgrace to the prince's name."

Heph's attention snaps back to the farmer, whose forehead has turned a magnificent shade of puce. "What?"

"You heard me," the farmer says. "A disgrace to the prince's name. Alexander saved us from the Lords, but *you*— his ill-bred puppy—can't even get a man his rightful possessions from the palace cellars! No wonder he put you down here with the manure smell."

The pounding in Heph's head becomes unbearable. What does it mean that even the peasants in the village know he has fallen out of favor? He has to get out of here before he says anything—does anything—he cannot fix. He pushes back from the desk with such force that the chair clatters to the floor. The farmer jumps back as Heph strides past him and the dozen other grumbling peasants crammed onto benches against the walls waiting in line.

"What about my olives?" the farmer calls to Heph's re-treating back, but he ignores him. Head throbbing, Heph walks down the marble corridors, past the frescoes and painted statues, toward the residential wing of the palace. He quickens his pace, trying to outrun his anger. But no matter where he goes, he still feels its heat on his neck. It's not just *what* the farmer said—it's the *truth* of what the farmer said.

Dealing with the refugees should be the work of a mid-level palace bureaucrat, not the prince's right-hand man and best friend. Or is it now *former* right-hand man and *former* best friend? Heph has no idea where he stands anymore.

Before the battle, Alex had given every Macedonian sol-dier a horn to blow if they spotted the Aesarian High Lord Mordecai, and specific instructions to capture—not *kill*—him. Heph had found Mordecai on the battlefield. He had lowered his sword and brushed his thumb against the smooth, cool surface of the horn dangling from his belt. He was about to bring the horn to his lips, signaling the other soldiers to help him capture the Lord, but the old man had spoken first. Smiling cruelly, Mordecai mocked him, stirring up all Heph's old feelings of being an orphaned outlaw who belongs no-where—least of all at a prince's side.

His injured pride flamed into rage, and Heph didn't blow

his horn. Instead, he let the red mist engulf him, and when it cleared, the High Lord was a tangle of blood and bone that didn't even look human.

This wasn't the first time fury had overtaken him. And the first episode had lost him his home, family, and position. Alex had found him and given Heph his life back.

But how many times can he depend on Alex to rescue him from himself?

He finally reaches his room and enters. It's small and simply furnished, but for five years it has felt like home. Safe. Until now.

He slams the door behind him, pours water from a pitcher into a basin, and splashes it on his face, hoping it will cool the heat pulsing through his veins. Hoping it will reduce the pressure behind his forehead. But it doesn't. The anger—and fear—remain.

Before the Battle of Pellan Fields, as they now call it, Heph and Alex had dreams together. They were to go on a quest to the Eastern Mountains of Persia to find the legendary Fountain of Youth. Heph doesn't really care one way or the other about sipping from the rumored magical waters himself. But Alex has wanted to ever since they found the map in the cave last spring, and that was enough for Heph to prepare for a dangerous, possibly suicidal, mission.

Alex says he wants the waters to heal his weak, scarred leg, but Heph knows that the prince's need to find the Fountain is deeper than that. He knows Alex feels it is the only way he can prove to King Philip, and to the world, that he is not limited by his weakness, that he can do great deeds like his hero, Achilles. Heph understands all too well the lengths one is willing to go to prove oneself.

He and Alex haven't discussed the Fountain in many weeks now. Maybe it's time. Maybe Heph can remind him of everything they had planned together, everything they've been through so far.

He kneels on the floor and counts four tiles from the foot of his bed, feeling for their special hiding place. The tile is cracked. He never noticed a crack before. Removing the tile, he carefully lowers his hand into the hole beneath. There's nothing there.

The map is gone.

His heart sinks as he tries to comprehend this twist. Either Alex has purposefully removed the map without telling him—or someone else has. He sits back on his legs. No one else knew about the map. No one else knew Heph had hidden it under the tile. It could only be Alex who took it. Perhaps Alex is planning to leave for the Fountain of Youth… *without* Heph.

There's a soft tap at his door, and a teenage girl slips in. Katerina. "I'm looking for Alexander," she says, her long fingers tapping the bejeweled Carian scabbard hanging from her hip. "Is he here?"

She watches as Heph hastily pushes the tile back in place and stands, smoothing his tangled dark curls and adjusting the silver torque that hangs heavy around his neck. He can't help but notice how the emerald of her robe brings out the green of her eyes, and the way her golden-brown hair shines as brightly as the polished bronze diadem on her head. Today, it's clearer than ever before what her lineage is: Katerina, the secret princess of Macedon, daughter of King Philip and Queen Olympias, and Alexander's own twin sister.

"He's not here," he says, more harshly than he intended.

"I see that. Do you know where I might find him?" she asks. Standing in his doorway, she looks so much like Heph's best friend and yet so, so different.

"No. I haven't seen him." *In days*, he silently adds.

"Oh. All right, then," Kat says. Heph expects her to leave, but she lingers in the doorway.

He needs her to go. He needs to get out of the palace. Trying to ignore Kat, he walks over to his weapons hanging on wall hooks and removes his short sword, the best one to carry when on a horse.

"I…I wanted to talk to you, too," she finally says. "About the battle."

"I don't want to talk about the battle," he says over his shoulder, buckling his sword belt so that it fits snugly around his hips.

"I'm not going to let you ignore me," she says stubbornly. He tries not to look at the way the robe clings to her body, which is just inches from him.

"Now is not a good time," he says, turning to face her. "I'm busy."

"Are you avoiding me?" she asks, crossing her arms and barring his exit. "Have I offended you in some way? Each time I try to ask you what happened on the battlefield, you run away."

He *has* been avoiding her, but not for the reasons she seems to be thinking. Her smiles chase him during the day and at night, and images of her long legs and firm arms have appeared in more of his dreams than they should. She and her legs are just more complications in his relationship with Alexander. He got into enough trouble when he let Alex's half sister, Princess Cynane, distract him for a time. He can't let it happen again.

"I can't remember what happened," Kat continues. "One moment, I felt the blade slicing into my side, and I was certain it was all over, that I would never breathe again… And then the next moment…" She trails off, and Heph notices a rising pink in her cheeks. "What did I do? Why won't you speak with me?" She places her hands on her hips, and he notices their gentle curve.

"I'm busy," he says again, pushing himself out of his stupor and walking toward the door. He takes a step to move past her, but she remains firmly planted in front of him. "Please stand aside."

She crosses her arms. "Make me."

Heph is done with these games. In one motion, he wraps his hands around her small waist.

"What are you doing?" she says in surprise.

He picks her up and lifts her to the side. But as he sets her down, she stumbles and grabs at the front of his tunic to stop herself from falling backward. With a bang, she hits the wall, pulling him toward her. Only by quickly bracing his hands against the wall on either side of her head is Heph able to stop himself from crashing into her.

Taking deep breaths to steady himself, he inhales Katerina's sweet scent. It's not the cloying perfume the other palace women wear, but something fresh and wholly of herself. He looks down and sees that she's looking up at him from between his arms, her mouth open in surprise, her pink lips tantalizingly close to his.

They stand there staring at each other; the air pulses between them. And suddenly, Heph knows: he's going to lose control again.

In a different way from the battlefield, but just as forbidden.

He's going to kiss her.

And either she will be angry and run to tell Alex, or she will like it and…that will be even worse. Because when it comes to killing a man or kissing a girl, Heph is weak. His pride and desire are too strong.

And he's so tired of fighting his emotions. All he wants to

do is surrender. From the way Kat tilts her head, her breath coming fast as she leans in, it seems she wants him to surrender, too. The temptation of someone who wants him, someone who sees the value in him, is too much.

He bends closer to her—

And just then, Alex bursts through the door, closely followed by General Kadmus.

Heph hurls himself away from Kat as Alexander stares at them in bewilderment.

"Alex!" Kat says a bit too loudly, pushing past Heph. "I was just looking for you. Buthos wants to put down a wounded horse even though I explicitly told him that the horse will survive."

"Tell Buthos to do as you say, Katerina," Alex says, nodding. "If he dismisses you, tell him he is free to come see me, but that he might not like what he hears."

Kat flashes a smile at Alex, then finally leaves Heph's room, though her fresh scent continues to linger. Alex turns his unsettling eyes—one pale blue, the other dark brown—on Heph. "Kadmus," he says, his gaze never leaving Heph, "would you oversee the northern wall? Please tell Captain Krisos I shall be there shortly."

"Yes, my lord." The general bows, and Heph can't help but notice the many scars that crisscross his deeply tanned body, physical proof of his courage for all to see. An image flashes in front of him of Alex and Kadmus kicking their horses into a gallop as they ride east, toward Persia and the Fountain of Youth.

Alexander waits until the door shuts behind Kadmus. "There's a crowd of angry farmers saying that you left them with nothing," he says, and Heph can hear the barely controlled irritation in his voice. "Why did you leave your post? Can't you follow *any* instructions?"

"I needed a break," Heph says, forcing himself to meet Alex's gaze. At least the moment with Katerina dissolved his earlier anger, draining him, leaving him empty—empty enough not to do something rash in front of Alex. "I have no idea who stole the olives and figs, the honey and amphorae."

Alex's eyes take in the short sword hanging at Heph's side. "And so you decided to go out for a ride and ignore your responsibilities? Can't I even trust you with the simplest assignments? Is that too much to ask?"

"Why are you wasting me there when I could be training your men and organizing the city's defenses?" Heph fires back. "You yourself said the Aesarian Lords might return with reinforcements. You know I can help you. I'm good at that—not handling whiny farmers!"

Alex's mouth becomes a hard line. "You know you're banned from anything to do with the military until further notice. Kadmus is helping me with the defense."

"Give me another chance," Heph demands.

Alex shakes his head. "I can't trust you, Heph. Not in war. You don't follow orders."

Heph unbuckles his sword belt and places it on the table, feeling as he had the time they were fording a particularly violent river and he fell off his horse. He'd struggled against the heavy armor weighing him down, unable to breathe, until another soldier pulled him out. Everything he has built and dreamed of and hoped for is slipping away from him, and he doesn't know how to get it back. He takes a deep breath. "All right," he says, his voice flat and professional. "I'll return now."

"No need," Alex says. "I put Ortinos in charge of it. He's a farmer's son himself, and I think the farmers will heed him. But you can help Achaus supervise the restoration of the library."

Heph winces. Another administrative role, nearly as insulting as the last. But he nods curtly. "Yes, my lord." He exits quickly before he can see Alex's response to his formality. Heph hasn't used Alexander's title since his first days at the palace, and the words burn his throat. He swallows hard.

The smell of smoke and charred wood still lingers from the Aesarian Lords' fire, though it was a full week ago, as Heph approaches the blackened façade of the royal library. Only the far west section of the gold marble building collapsed—the secret archives and a section of the main reading room next door. Overseeing the crumbling building is another menial job, well beneath Heph's rank and skill, but at least with this one, he can be outside, away from the stuffy little office. As in battle, he will be directing men, even if it's only where to move a ladder.

"We have cleared enough debris to make a thorough examination of the foundations," Achaus, the royal architect, says, wiping sweat and ashes from his bald, domelike head with a strip of linen cloth.

"Good," Heph says. "There's no point in repairing the upper levels if the entire structure is going to collapse. Would you show me the most damaged areas?"

Achaus nods and hands Heph a cloth, which he immediately ties around his nose and mouth. The architect leads him to the far end of the building where they descend a small winding staircase into darkness, coolness, and ashes. The air, still heavy with smoke, stings Heph's eyes. He holds his torch high. "Where are the weight-bearing walls?" he asks, voice muffled.

"This is one," the architect says, striding down the corridor and pointing with his torch. "Some of the blocks are scorched but…" The man continues to talk, but something itches Heph's nose, and he stops listening. There's a smell, something that lurks under the scent of smoke, soot, and charred wood. Heph pulls the cloth off his face.

"What is it?"

"A moment," Heph says and takes a deep breath. The smell is still there. It reminds him of the time he accompanied King Philip and Alex on a mission to ferret out cattle raiders in the hills and they came across the decayed bodies of their advance team, swarming with flies.

Achaus takes off his own cloth and sniffs the air. They walk down the hallway, looking right and left, carefully studying the walls by the light of their torches. He and Achaus enter a large room directly under the main reading room, shafts of daylight pouring through holes in the half-burnt floor of the devastated room above. The smell seems to be stronger in here, but all he sees is a jumble of old desks and bookshelves.

"Where is it coming from?" he asks, stopping before a wall decorated with patterns of cemented-on scallop shells.

"I think it's coming from behind this wall," Achaus says. "There's a secret chamber built here."

Heph nods. Everyone knows that Philip has a rabbit warren of hidden rooms and passageways throughout the palace. Years ago, he and Alex found several during their explorations. The architect twists a large scallop shell as if it were a door handle. A small door, cleverly concealed in the decoration, pops open.

The smell that escapes hits Heph with the force of a mace, knocking him back as he retches. It's as if a living thing with a thousand legs crawled up his nostrils and lodged itself inside him. Covering his nose and mouth with the cloth, he stoops to enter the small, windowless room.

On the floor is a decomposing body.

Heph lowers himself on one knee and holds the torch close to what had been the face. There, underneath a coating of soot, is Leonidas, the palace librarian. Heph's stomach lurches and bitter bile rises in his throat. Leonidas had been missing since the fire a week ago, and Alex, suspecting a traitor on the Royal Council, speculated that he'd been an Aesarian spy.

It seems even princes can be wrong.

Leonidas wasn't just the guardian of the library. He had also been both Heph's and Alex's teacher for years until they turned thirteen and went to Aristotle's school at Mieza. Though he was strict and as likable as a burr in a saddle, the old man did not deserve this fate.

"Achaus," Heph calls over his shoulder, "tell the men to bring a stretcher. And a blanket to put over him."

Holding his breath, Heph moves the torch across the body. It's not burned. Nothing in this small room is burned, not the table, chair, or lamps. Leonidas crept in here and died from breathing in the smoke. But why come in here at all? He squints in the flickering torchlight and notices something in the right hand of the corpse. A scroll.

He pries the stiff dead fingers off the tattered parchment and carefully unrolls it. The heading identifies it as one of the Cassandra scrolls, a list of prophecies supposedly uttered by the doomed Trojan princess hundreds of years ago.

Squinting at the writing, he tries to decipher the archaic letters. A few words jump out at him immediately: *Age*, *Man*, and *Monster*. His frown deepens. The scroll seemed to be describing the end of the Age of Gods and the coming of a new age—something philosophers have written about and spoken of for many years now. He himself knows nothing of it, but ever since the eclipse of the full moon a few weeks ago, murmurs have been circulating the palace that the time has come. Some whisper that the eclipse heralded a transitional time when seemingly insignificant decisions would have un-expectedly large consequences. But Heph never thought that Leonidas was one to put his faith in the stars. He preferred knowledge and action over an oracle's song.

Heph decides to take the prophecy upstairs to the main reading room, where the assistant librarians sorting out the mess of smoke- and water-damaged scrolls can reshelve it. But then he spots something in the margins. Contemporary Greek, written in a familiar scrawl. It's Leonidas's handwriting. In the dim light, it's hard to make out his teacher's notes. Holding the parchment as close as he can to the torch's light without scorching the hide, Heph scans the words.

As the message sinks in, blood begins to pump in his ears. For a moment, he feels as though he's at the edge of a cliff, that one brush of air will send him over and down into Tartarus.

Quickly, he stuffs the scroll into his tunic, feeling the stiff, cracked parchment rub against his skin.

Alexander must never see this scroll.

No one can.

CHAPTER THREE

KATERINA CLINGS TIGHTLY TO THE BROWN mare as she races across the wide fields behind the palace walls. She has never ridden like this before, as if she is astride a lightning bolt. Back in Erissa, before she knew she was a princess stolen at birth—back when she was an innocent child—she and Jacob used to play around on the family donkey. But that was a far cry from sleek Kokkymo, who tears through the grass with the speed of a lion and the grace of a doe. Despite her lack of formal riding training, it's as if Kat has become one with the horse, an unstoppable force of nature in perfect harmony with air and sky, earth and water.

A part of Kat's mind slides beneath the tickling mane and smooth, sweat-slick hide, and she inhales the smells of green summer grass and the rich earth of the riverbanks. Soon, it is Kat herself who switches her tail and gallops ahead, stretching her four long legs and pounding the ground hard. If only she could keep going, never return to the palace with its confusing dark-haired boys, its baffling mysteries, and all its dangers. She wants to eat sweet grass and drink cool river water and smell a thousand subtle scents on the wind.

She's always known she has a way with animals, that she can communicate with them in a manner that others cannot. It was a gift that Helen—the woman she thought was her mother—warned her to keep hidden. But she assumed her ability to understand animals came from the fact that she paid attention to them, that she took the time to listen to them while most humans didn't.

Then she met the great sorceress, Ada of Caria, and everything changed.

Ada told her of the magic flowing in her veins—Snake Blood, one of the two ancient Blood Magics—and trained her to use her abilities. Kat learned to fall into trances, experiencing what it was like to be a bird soaring through the air, a worm pushing through moist earth, and a fish darting through cold, deep water. But Snake Blood, she learned, is far more than just a connection with the minds of animals—it is a connection to the power of human thought, too.

In her last trance at Ada's palace, Kat sank into forgotten memories of her own life, all the way back to her birth. These lost memories are what led her to realize that she is Prince Alexander's sister, and that Queen Olympias, the coldhearted murderess, is her real mother. Kat can't shake the details of that memory from her mind.

Kill the girl, Olympias had said as she held her newborn twins, thrusting baby Kat toward her handmaiden, Helen. But Helen didn't kill the baby. She started a new life in a little village called Erissa and raised Kat as her own.

Suddenly, Kokkymo stumbles and Kat's mind is jolted from the horse's body as she flies through the air and lands hard on her side. She's aware of dirt in her mouth and the gilded sword Ada gave her pressing into her leg. When she finally catches her breath, she stands up shakily and sees her mount galloping away, truly free now, whinnying in delight.

She rubs her arm and notices something glint in the grass: her Flower of Life pendant, a silver lotus blossom on a leather thong she always wears around her neck.

Kat picks it up and holds it to her heart. This belonged to Helen, whom Kat will always consider her real mother. She ties the thong behind her neck and feels the cool slippery metal just below the base of her throat. She remembers Helen's smile, her beauty, the sweet scent of her skin as if it were yesterday she last saw her. But it has been ten years since Kat, hiding in the wool box, witnessed Olympias ordering her soldiers to kill Helen.

Kat never told anyone who killed her mother, not even Jacob's family, who took her in and promised to care for her until she was of age to marry. But vengeance has long since become the blood that pumps through her heart and the air that fills her lungs. It was the reason she came to Pella with Jacob, hoping for an opportunity to get near the queen. It was also the obstacle to marrying Jacob—a quest she had to accomplish before her heart would be free to love.

But now she knows that her sworn enemy is in fact her real mother, that she had, unknowingly, plotted for years to kill the very woman who gave her life. *And* that for some unknown reason, Olympias wants her dead. In the beat of a dragonfly's wings, Kat has gone from predator to prey.

Kat looks for Kokkymo—it's unlike the mare to startle, and now she is nowhere in sight. Stiffly, Kat begins her walk home. The tall grass waves eerily, and a scent she can't name causes her to shiver. The sky has taken on a sickening gray-green color.

A surge of foreboding sweeps through her chest with the suddenness of a spear thrust, knocking the breath out of her.

Something terrible, she knows, has happened.

There's movement in the trees ahead. The strange sorrow that beats in her heart has turned Kat's legs to lead.

The pebbles on the ground jump, and she hears a strange buzz in the air.

A herd of gazelles breaks from the forest, all of them kicking up their hind legs in panic.

Stampede.

They race toward her like a surging tide, and Kat can do nothing to outpace them. Instead she stands, bracing for the impact of fur against her flesh. But it never comes. They veer slightly away from her at the last moment and wash around her, spraying her with clods of dirt.

She sucks in a sharp breath as one of the gazelles skids to a stop directly in front of her, its flanks heaving, its straight black horns trembling.

What? she asks silently, feeling the animal's terror so keenly that now she is trembling, too. *What has happened?*

She stares into the gazelle's dark liquid eyes...and then she sees it.

A house in flames. Smoke. Murder. Screams. She sees bodies in the courtyard.

It's Sotiria, lying next to the well, her dark hair streaming into a widening puddle of blood. Jacob's mother. For many years, practically Kat's own.

She can't breathe. In the gazelle's eyes she sees Cleon, too, next to the gate, an ax head in his broad back.

Jacob's younger brothers, broken and lifeless, lie in the dirt.

And in front of the flames is a flash of white-gold against burning red. Silvery hair. A slender, petite figure: Olympias.

Kat's knees buckle and she sinks slowly into the grass.

So that is where the queen has been these past few days: looking for Kat. And when she couldn't find her, she killed the closest thing Kat has to a family—Jacob's.

Her chest seizes and she can't breathe.

This is all her fault.

If Jacob's parents hadn't taken her in, raised her as their own, the queen would have had no reason to hurt them.

The children…

She clutches at thick tufts of grass with her hands, holding on because around her the world is reeling. Just like that day when she was six and the queen's men murdered her mother and then came looking for her. She climbed out the upstairs window and clung mutely to the thatched roof.

Kat's lungs don't seem to be working, and golden spots dance in the blackness forming around her. Maybe she will pass out, die here, even, in the sweet summer grass… She gasps and air floods her chest.

More hooves race toward her, but she doesn't look up, not until she feels strong hands on her back. "Are you all right?" She hears Heph's voice, and then she's aware that he's knelt down beside her and is holding her hands. "Were you thrown? I was looking for you. The stable hand said…"

She stares at him speechless, unblinking, barely understanding the words tumbling from his lips.

"Here, stand up so I can see you," Heph says, pulling her up. He brushes dirt off her head and rubs both thumbs over her cheeks. "What is it?" he asks urgently. "For godssakes, Katerina, what has happened?"

Kat tilts her head back and closes her eyes. The sun feels warm on her face, the same sun that Cleon, Sotiria and the children will never feel again. "They're all dead." The words slide out more like an animal howl of pain than a sentence.

"Who?" Heph asks, taking her by the shoulders, gently rubbing the top of her arms. "Who is dead?"

"My family. Jacob's parents and his little brothers. The people who raised me." Kat grabs her stomach, rocking herself back and forth, wishing they were Sotiria's arms rocking her back and forth, comforting her after she'd skinned a knee or missed Helen too much to sleep. "Olympias killed them all. She couldn't find me, so she killed them."

Heph looks around the field in puzzlement. "Did a messenger just come—"

Kat inhales sharply and rubs her eyes. "The gazelles saw it," she says simply.

Heph frowns, but understanding quickly comes to his eyes. Kat can almost see him come to accept again, as he had in battle, that she is something more than just an average potter's daughter.

"After what I saw on the battlefield, Kat, I would believe anything you say."

At the kind words, Kat begins to cry, her body shuddering. "I know she wants me dead—has always wanted me dead since the moment I was born," she says between aching sobs. "I just don't...know...why."

Heph's arms tighten around her, and she leans against his hard chest. "Because of reasons known only to the queen and the gods," Heph murmurs into her hair. He gives her another squeeze, and Kat stays there, tucked against him.

How can she live with herself, knowing she shares the blood of that evil woman? She wants to take a knife and drain every drop of Olympias's blood from inside her. She sees again the pitiful bodies of the children. She hears the queen's cruel laughter and smells the acrid smoke. She needs to cry until she empties herself completely, until there is nothing left except a shell made of cold, hard revenge.

Another sob tears through her body. Her thirst for vengeance—did she inherit that, too, from the queen, along with her green eyes?

She aches for Jacob. For the sight of his wide grin, his broad, friendly face. For his goodness and undying belief in her. Jacob was always there for her when she was sad or lonely. He didn't even need to say a word, just put a strong arm around her. But Jacob is lost forever now—an Aesarian Lord. Her brother's enemy.

And, if she believes Heph's report from the battle, her own enemy now, too. Heph claims Jacob tried to kill her, but Kat doesn't believe it. Can't believe it. He doesn't even *know* that the prince is Katerina's brother. There's so much Jacob doesn't know. But he can't hate her. If he did, she wouldn't be able to live with herself.

Heph holds her tightly, and she feels his beating heart against her back, his chin stubble rubbing slightly against her cheek, and for a moment she pretends he's Jacob. She inhales deeply and smells an expensive citrus cologne, a tunic fresh from the palace laundry, and a whiff of horse and leather. Jacob smelled like wood smoke and clay dust.

It's Hephaestion she's clinging to now—the impolite, vain boy she disliked at first sight when he tried to have her arrested for cheating on bets at the Blood Tournament. The brave, clever boy who got her out of the deepest, foulest dungeon in the palace when she had been imprisoned on false charges.

The boy whose kiss may have saved her life on the battlefield.

Or was the kiss only a dream, and her miraculous recovery just an effect of Snake Blood? For a moment, the face hovering above hers seemed to belong to Jacob, but then it had morphed into Heph, and she passed out. She's been trying to ask Hephaestion about it, but he has been busy after the battle, helping Alex with the refugees and rebuilding the library. And now, well, it doesn't seem to matter so much anymore if she'd died out there. Maybe none of this would have happened. Maybe Jacob's family would still be alive.

"Kat," Heph says gently. He brushes the hair out of her face. "If Olympias has done what you say, then she must know who you are. And if she finds you here when she returns to the palace, even Alex and I won't be able to keep you safe every moment of the day and night. We must get you out of here. Far away from the queen. She will return."

Kat nods, but she doesn't move from his arms—not yet. Tomorrow, she can plan. Tomorrow, she can be brave. Her tear-stained cheeks are cold as the wind brushes them, its touch as light as a ghost's caress. She shivers and stares out over the swaying grass.

Silently, she says: *Goodbye*.

CHAPTER FOUR

FROM THE WINDOW OF THE COUNCIL CHAMBER, Prince Alexander observes a hunched figure riding a donkey across the palace courtyard toward the main gate. Six peasants accompany the boy. One leads his swaybacked mount while the others follow in a ramshackle cart laden with turnips. But if anyone were to examine these peasants closely, he would quickly see that they are too well-fed—and too well-muscled—to be anything other than royal guards. And that the boy is none other than the prince's younger, slow-minded brother.

Even though Alex knows he must send Arridheus away for his own safety, his heart twists as he watches his little brother pass through the gates and out of view. An hour ago, he watched Arri's nursemaid, Sarina, fill his saddlebags with a change of clothes and a travel blanket. She even remembered to pack his favorite shiny buttons while Arri cried about leaving his pet rat behind. Even though he is twelve years old, the age at which most Macedonian boys would be training with the militia, Alex knows that Arri will always have the interests of a five-year-old.

Worry gnaws on Alex's heart. He is sure that the Aesarian Lords kidnapped Cynane—despite their heralds' vehement denials during negotiations for a treaty after the battle of Pellan Fields. As King Philip's son, Arri would make an even more valuable hostage than his half sister. And despite—or better said, because of—his brother's slowness, the Lords could set him up as a puppet king, ruling through him.

It was Kadmus who suggested to the council that they fake a kidnapping. Arri and several royal guards, all disguised as peasants, would ride to Mieza to stay with a family of farmers known for their loyalty to the crown. Once the young prince was safe, the palace and council would announce that the prince had been stolen. Most people would assume the Aesarian Lords kidnapped him, while the Lords would think one of Macedon's other enemies or so-called allies—the Thracians, the Byzantines, the Persians, or Athenians—had snuck inside during this time of confusion and stolen the young prince.

"He's safe now," Alexander says, more to himself than the council as he turns to face them. Still feeling the pulsing energy of secrets, he begins to pace. "A good suggestion, Kadmus. Thank you."

Alex feels Heph's glower before he sees it, like the burning, prickling rays of a summer noontime sun on the back of his head. He fights the urge to roll his eyes. Heph is acting like a jealous child. He knows that Alex must listen to *all* suggestions and act on only the best, regardless of whom they come from. Ever since the battle, the distance between him and Heph has pained Alex, but he is a prince acting as a king to protect his people.

"May the gods go with him," the minister of religion, Gordias, intones and raises both gnarled, spotted hands.

"May the gods go with him," echoes Theopompus, minister of provisions, settling himself on a chair that squeaks ominously under his bulk. The other men in the room take their places with a scraping of chairs. Except for Alex.

He can't sit still. Pacing helps him think, helps calm the worry. "What of the Aesarian Lords?" he asks.

Theopompus tugs thoughtfully at his blond beard, woven with turquoise beads, and says, "The Aesarians seem to be keeping their side of our treaty. They wait quietly at Pyrrhia for their Supreme Lord to send them the compensation they owe us and word on where to deploy next."

After the battle, the new High Lord Gideon asked Alex for peace terms, a prisoner exchange, and a safe place to tend to their wounded, promising to pay damages for the unprovoked attack on Macedon. Alex permitted them to retreat to an abandoned fortress a day's ride from Pella. It is a place they visited from time to time in the past when King Philip allowed them to stay here for mountain warfare training and hunting.

He doesn't trust them. Not about Cynane—if Alex and his men arrived at the fortress to search for her, they would probably just hide her—not about paying the ten talents of gold they promised as reparations, and not about leaving peacefully. Thousands of Lords from all over the known world could attack Macedon like swarms of angry bees. There are rumors of a device the Lords created that breathes fire like a dragon and can incinerate city gates. And the best part of the Macedonian army is with King Philip attacking Byzantium. When Alex asked his father to send some men back to defend the homeland, he refused, sarcastically pointing out that Alex and the Lords had made peace.

"Have our spies and scouts reported any Aesarian ships near our waters?" Alex asks. The fizz in his blood still won't shake loose, and he continues to pace in short, quick strides.

"Are any Aesarian troops marching toward Macedon over land?"

Kadmus shakes his head gravely, his gray eyes like chunks of ice in his thin, tan face. "None. But the first reinforcements from Macedonian forts arrived this morning, and they should be enough to protect Pella if the Lords are hatching some plot."

Theopompus drinks deeply from a black-and-red glazed cup and sets it down heavily, wiping red droplets from his blond beard. "The Chians, the Euboeans, and the Megarans are willing to part with some of their soldiers, if we can pay their price."

"We don't have the money for this!" sputters Hagnon, minister of finance. "King Philip's march on Byzantium has greatly depleted the royal treasury. And we've signed a treaty with the Aesarian Lords! I shall not sign off on such wasted expenses…"

Alex feels a spike of irritation. Hagnon wouldn't dare talk to King Philip like this. It's because Alex is young that the minister is treating him so disrespectfully. As he studies the man who holds the keys to his father's gold, he tries not to let his dislike show in his face.

Not only is the man miserly, but he clearly enjoys wielding such power over the prince regent. Alexander, like everyone else, is forbidden from touching the royal coffers. If only there was a way of convincing the man that this is more important than petty power struggles. Suddenly, Alex stops pacing. Perhaps, there *is* a way…

Pulling out a chair from across Hagnon, Alexander sits and folds his hands on the priceless ebony table. Some slave has polished it to a reflective gleam, and it smells of beeswax and lemon. Alex steadies his breathing as Hagnon rambles on about frivolous spending, empty coffers, and foolish decisions.

"You are right to be concerned," Alex interrupts the man, remembering what Katerina told him about getting in touch with her Snake Blood. *Relax. Calm yourself. Think of nothing, at first. Be an empty vessel with no thought. Then think of something that makes you happy.*

It's hard to think of nothing. That's like having no heart to beat in your chest, no guts in your belly. He pushes away his thoughts as if they were cobwebs, though he is aware of a few shreds dangling. Then he thinks of clouds soft with rain, the warm smell of leather, and the wind in his hair as he rides Bucephalus. He almost floats inside himself.

"And you are admirably dutiful in your responsibilities to my father," Alex continues, locking his eyes with Hagnon's beady ones. "We are deeply indebted to you." He speaks slowly, trying to make each word a long, golden drop of honey.

Alex has never chosen when and where he sees flashes of men's hearts; the unknown force that pulls him into people's memories—often at the most inopportune moments—has always come unbidden. But in the days since Kat told him that she was Snake Blood—that she has the ability to enter the bodies of animals and become one with them—he has been realizing that his own gift may in fact have been a form of the same ability. Though he can't quite fathom the idea of possessing magic blood, he's been interested in finding out if he can do what Kat does. Not with animals so much—except for Bucephalus, with whom he has always felt an extraordinary kinship—but with people. If he has the ability to see a man's strength, weakness, and past, could he also have the ability to persuade?

Judging by the way Hagnon's chest swells and bright pink spots bloom on his cheeks, it seems he does.

The white tunnel that usually appears and drags Alexander into a man's mind does not form this time. Instead, the white light hangs low, misting over his vision. Alex becomes intensely aware of his heartbeat—or perhaps, it is Hagnon's heartbeat.

Alexander suddenly feels the smoothness of pride, the sharpness of fear, and the ragged hunger for power. The disjointed swirls of thought tangle like ribbons as Alex searches for a thin thread that can be used to convince Hagnon to come over to his side. And then he finds it: the slipperiness of self-doubt.

"That is why," Alex says, slowly and calmly, his voice seeming to echo from someplace very far, "I know you will find the way to collect the funds for our military needs. You have my complete faith in your abilities." Finally, Hagnon's decision slices down on the mesh of thoughts and emotions, knocking Alex unceremoniously from his mind. Back inside himself, he feels shaky, weak.

The minister smiles and nods. "My lord, I am grateful for your praise and will do as you wish, despite the difficulties that might arise."

Alexander nods as a bead of sweat drops into his eyes. He brings his hand up to wipe it away and hopes that no one has noticed his uneven breath. He did what he needed to do, but it has a physical cost. And the meeting isn't over yet, no matter how tired he is. "The next order of business, if you please."

Theopompus shuffles some scrolls in front of him. "I received word last night that the Persian bride chosen for you has unexpectedly died. There is, however, no need to trouble yourself." He looks toward Alex and peers down his fleshy nose. "The Great King himself is seeing to her replacement."

Hagnon sighs. "It's a shame she didn't die after she arrived here. We could have kept the bride price."

Alex lowers his head, but it is only a polite gesture of respect for the dead. He is sorry for the girl and her family, but he didn't know her...or even her name. It's just as well, really, that she will not be coming to Pella, as an entire retinue of Persian girls and eunuchs would be a distraction in this time of war.

Besides, he wonders how desirous Artaxerxes really is for an alliance, remembering the finely chiseled agate cameo of the king he found under the council table last month. The cameo was set in a frame of shining gold studded with gems—it had to be worth a fortune. He told himself at the time that if someone had obtained it honestly, he would post a reward for its discovery and make every effort to find it. Yet no one has come forward. It was, Alex realized, a bribe.

He looks at his council members now. Is one of them a spy for Persia? The thought makes his whole body itch. He can't afford a traitor. It's both a danger and an insult.

After the Aesarian Lords set the library on fire, Leonidas disappeared, and Alex assumed his former tutor had been the spy. But now Leonidas's body has been recovered. He had wronged his former tutor by thinking he was the traitor in the council.

His glance falls on Theopompus, his full rosy cheeks, his hair sparkling with gold dust. A man who lives well, swirling in bejeweled robes, enjoying the finest food and wine, the owner of luxurious estates... And yet the origin of his wealth is a mystery. He was an actor's son with winning ways who worked his way up in Philip's diplomatic service.

Alex's gaze slides to Hagnon's pursed lips and darting eyes. He's a known miser reputed to have hoards of treasure hidden in the walls of his houses even though he was born a sandal-maker's son. If he is hiding treasure, where did it come from?

He studies Gordias, his thin eyelids fluttering a bit as he

naps. The ancient minister of religion is known to live frugally and devote himself to honoring the gods. But wouldn't that be the best cover of all?

A memory comes to him. A rumor. A story that Philip had forced Gordias's beloved granddaughter to go to bed with him and when she discovered she was pregnant, Olympias poisoned and killed her. It could be possible the old priest seeks revenge…

If only he could figure out how to enter someone's mind at will to see their past the way he just entered Hagnon's thoughts to persuade him. But the Sight has always come at random moments and it isn't coming now. Perhaps he could try to make it come… But no, he is too exhausted from his experience with the finance minister to try anything else.

Kadmus brings the conversation back to reinforcing the defense of Pella, and Alex is glad to hear the general speak so sensibly. Lean, alert, and serious, Kadmus has been the only council member to take Alex's side again and again since he was appointed regent. But how much does Alex know about him? He's…what? Twenty-five? He rose quickly in Philip's army to become the youngest general. But the king snubbed him by taking an older general, Parmenion, to Byzantium. Would he want to avenge himself on Philip for that? And didn't Alex hear some story about Kadmus visiting family members in Persian territory a few years ago?

Who is the traitor? The idea of a betrayer so close at hand is deeply unsettling. But equally disturbing is the simple fact of not knowing. It undermines everything. It leaves him reeling with distraction and uncertainty, when he should be focused and fierce. The question doesn't leave Alex's mind even after the council adjourns for the day.

As the men amble out of the chamber, Heph approaches him, his face cold. "May I have a word."

A wave of irritation floods Alex—he doesn't have the patience for another one of Heph's jealous complaints. But the look on Heph's face erases that annoyance instantly. Something terrible has happened. He doesn't need the ability to see into men's minds to know that.

Fury roils in Alex like white foam on a violent river as he thunders across a field on Bucephalus's back. After Heph finished what he had to say, Alex wished fervently it *had* been a jealous accusation instead of the murder of Kat's entire foster family in Erissa. At the hands of his own mother. He wanted to see Kat right away, but Heph told him he'd given her some poppy juice in wine to make her sleep. And of course he couldn't confront his mother, because she has yet to return to the palace. He *had* been concerned about her disappearance—now he knows where she went, but not why.

High up on his favorite stallion, Alex feels strong and perfectly formed; he doesn't have to worry that his limp is showing. On and on he rides, muscle and sweat and wind, hoping to drive away all the worry and frustration. But they don't leave him.

By the time he's finished cooling down and currying the huge black stallion, he's as agitated as ever and his left leg has begun to ache. He knows a bath is always waiting for him upon his return and pictures the steaming, fragrant water, and his bath attendant, Hestia, clucking over him in her motherly way. Though he should go to Philip's office and review the peasant reports that Ortinos has left him, his head feels like it is on fire and he wonders briefly if he might have strained himself earlier by trying to influence Hagnon's mind. Perhaps his suspicions of a spy lurking among his council are overblown. He has no actual proof of a traitor, only a vague discomfort, his own swirling questions, the Persian cameo…

Can he trust his own misgivings, or is he allowing doubts to distract him from the more important issues at hand?

Whatever the cause, all he can think of now is submerging himself in hot water and drowning out his racing thoughts. He jogs up a flight of stairs and down a long corridor, and enters the private bathing chamber reserved for him.

It's a small room with a copper tub over a drain that leads the bathwater outside. Beside the tub, a fire pit, now cold and dark, keeps the room warm on winter days and heats up extra cauldrons of water. All four walls are painted with frescoes of blue-bearded Poseidon, god of the sea, cavorting with sirens and stabbing ships with his giant trident.

To his surprise, Hestia is not there, but Arri's former nursemaid, Sarina, is. She sits with perfect posture in a chair next to the window, her slender hands clasped on her glistening white gown, but jumps up the moment she sees him. She looks at him with large dark eyes fringed by thick black lashes.

For a moment Alex is struck by her beauty. She's so different from anyone he has ever seen before, with skin the color of burnished bronze and waist-length hair that shimmers like blue-black silk. He had first seen her early in the summer when he returned from his three years at Aristotle's school, and he'd been intrigued…but then came the Blood Tournament, Katerina, the Aesarian Lords, and he forgot about Sarina until she joined the palace women on the battlefield in full armor. So, not just beautiful. Brave, too.

"What are you doing here?" he asks, running a hand through his sweat-soaked hair. He's suddenly very conscious of how he must look. Clumps of dirt on his legs. Sweat stains on a tunic that sticks to his back.

"Forgive me, my Lord Prince," Sarina says in her accented

voice, "but with Arridheus gone, I have been reassigned here. Hestia has left to stay on her grandson's farm."

Old long before Alex was even born, Hestia is the only person who has ever attended to him in this most intimate of settings. Painters and sculptors glorify the physically perfect—the young, the beautiful, and the athletic—to be sure. But Alex is not physically perfect, not quite. He was born with a hideous scar snaking around his left thigh, and all the muscles in the leg are weaker than those of his right even after years of pushing himself through shattering pain to strengthen it.

It wouldn't have been such a tragedy if he wasn't a future king. But if the people of Macedon knew of his deformity, they might see him as an ill-starred monarch, believing that the gods must have disliked him even in the womb. So Philip, Olympias, and Alexander himself agreed to hide his shameful leg.

As Sarina walks up to him—half a pace too close for Macedonian protocol, but then again, she is Egyptian—he gets a whiff of her scent. It conjures up images of a glowing red sun setting behind enormous triangles of stone. Of soft perfumed beds and a cerulean blue river growing, spreading as far as the eye can see.

"My lord, if I may?" She gestures, and Alex clearly understands that she's waiting for him to remove his clothes.

"Why has Timandra reassigned you here?" he asks, stalling. "This seems like a demotion."

The girl bows her head. "Prince Arridheus is gone, my lord. So I must do something else. And caring for the prince regent is not a demotion, but an honor."

Alex spies a finely woven linen towel on the table in front of the window and walks over to it. "Is this where you believe your talents will be most useful?" he asks, his words coming out more harshly than he intended.

Sarina flinches as if he's slapped her. "In my former house, I was trained to rid a man or woman's jinns away through massaging the hands and feet with essential oils. However..." She hesitates a moment, as though wondering if she should continue. "I have many skills that can serve you better, my lord. I can read and write. I can prepare financial accounts."

Alex is both surprised and not surprised. He has heard her play the lyre and flute at palace gatherings and speak in several foreign languages to important visitors. Those skills— and her queenly deportment—point to the fact that she came from a noble house before she was a slave.

"We will find something suited to your skills," he says, pulling his tunic over his head and quickly wrapping the towel around his waist. As he steps into the hot pool of water, he makes sure that the towel continues to cover his leg even as he sinks into the tub. The linen forms to him, concealing the snake-shape scar and outlining the contours of his calves. "I shall personally look into it."

Sarina curtsies. "Thank you, my lord." She hurries over to the corner and lights the bronze perfume burners. Soon, incense rises and mixes with the steam of the bath.

Alex closes his eyes, inhales deeply, and sinks farther into the water, feeling his tight muscles relaxing and his head clearing as Sarina pours in fragrant oils and sprinkles flower petals. She cups his right foot in her hands and massages it.

He opens his eyes lazily and sees Sarina flashing him a smile, her big eyes shining. How can eyes so dark— almost black—also be so bright? They are emotive eyes, hard with concern when he first entered, and now sparkling with warm, gentle humor.

"It's a lovely name, Sarina," he says, and she blushes.

"It's the name given to every firstborn daughter in my family," she replies.

He seizes the moment—and the small tease of information—to allow himself to be drawn into those eyes, swirling disembodied a moment in their liquid blackness and then hurtling through a tunnel of overpowering silence and blinding white light.

As always when this happens, he's suddenly powerless, drawn forward by an unseen force. At the end of the tunnel he emerges, a being of invisible thought, in a courtyard of tall whispering palm trees and brightly painted mud brick buildings.

Soldiers—Persians, by the looks of them—are pushing a family into two different groups. A priestly family, Alex knows, serving strange and ancient gods. Sarina, wearing heavy gold jewelry and a pleated robe of fine white linen, is in a group of women and young children, clinging to a boy of about eight, perhaps her brother, and pleading that he remain with her even as a soldier tears the boy away.

"What troubles you, my lord?" Sarina's voice pulls Alex out of her memory, and he hastily blinks away the haze that has obscured his vision.

A better question would have been what *doesn't* trouble him. His father's stubbornness in besieging Byzantium when so much is going wrong at home. Kat's horrific story about their mother's cold-blooded killing of her foster family. He needs to find out how to protect his newfound sister. For when the queen returns, her life won't be worth an obol. And then there's…"My council."

He doesn't even realize he's spoken aloud until he hears Sarina's sigh. "Every king's problem," she says, moving behind him and massaging the spots behind his ears. "Who is telling the truth? Whom can you trust? Long ago, when

Egypt and the world were young, there was a great god-king who gave the people a choice: they could choose truth and die with honor or live lives of base dishonesty. One by one his people chose truth. One by one he slaughtered them."

She slides her fingers to the back of his neck. "But then, when he had no people left, he resurrected them all as a reward for their regard for truth. The moral of the story is this, my lord: truth and trust are more important to kings than anything else. Those who would die for truth are the only advisors you can trust."

Yes, Alex thinks. How could this slave girl know more about what's in his heart than his council? She is a paradox. Young, but brimming with ancient wisdom. Feminine, but with the courage of a seasoned warrior. A slave, yet born a noblewoman. Ethio-Egyptian, working for the Macedonian royal family.

"Was this god-king the one your family served?" he asks, feeling her warm breath on his left ear as she digs deeply into his shoulders.

Her fingers slip, and Alexander can tell he's startled her. Then her fingers find his skin again and continue working at the knots.

"You see many things, my prince," she says. "My mother's family served many gods who walked the earth thousands of years ago. Our civilization was already ancient when Greeks lived in caves and foraged for acorns. I learned much wisdom from my mother. In Egypt many wise women are unofficial advisors to pharaohs. My father hoped one day I would be one of them, but it was not to be."

"And if you were advising a prince regent of Macedon, what would you say?"

Alex feels her push him forward so he is leaning into the tub. Then she pours water down his back as she says, "I would tell the prince regent my favorite story about Princess Laila of Sharuna."

"Who was she?"

Sarina kneads and pushes the taut muscles of his shoulders and back. He can feel the knots pop and release under the pressure, which is both exquisitely painful and pleasurable at the same time.

"Who *is* she is the more accurate question," she says. "She's still alive, as far as I know, though she doesn't age. My uncle saw her fortress city shining in the sun, though he dared not try to enter. The princess lives in the cliff country below Akhetaton on the Nile and worships the sun god, Re-Harakhte, by bathing in his light every day."

Hunting out tension with her fingertips, Sarina leans in, and for a moment, Alexander feels her breasts brush against his wet back.

Suddenly, water pours onto his face as she empties a basin of lightly perfumed water into his hair. "Laila is richer than the Persian Great King Artaxerxes," Sarina continues, "and has a powerful army of warriors. Many suitors have sought her hand. But she is the mistress of many enchantments, and all have failed."

Alex has an idea, a seed at first, growing, blossoming... Perhaps his father wasn't so far off course when he negotiated for Alex to marry the Persian princess of Sardis. After all, there was a reason, besides lust and love, when Philip himself married so many chieftains' wives. A royal marriage brings military alliances. It brings power. And power brings victory.

And he has two perfect ambassadors in mind. A girl who needs to disappear and a warrior not allowed to fight.

Almost as if he had summoned him by thought, the door bursts open and Heph appears in the doorway, breathless and ashen-faced. Alex instinctively springs up from the tub, towel forgotten. "What is it?" he asks. "What's wrong?"

As Sarina hastily ties a dry towel around Alex's waist, Heph strides toward him. "Your brother's party has been attacked," he says, voice hard. "All the guards were killed except one who is gravely wounded. He's in the barracks infirmary."

"Is he conscious?" Alex asks, stepping out of the tub.

"No," Heph says, his dark eyes flashing with emotion. "Or, at least, he's not in any fit state to speak. He arrived with a deep gash to his wrist. He lost a lot of blood on his ride back here, and the doctor wanted to amputate his hand immediately. But I got a few things out of him."

"What?" Alex asks, throwing his tunic over his head.

"Two hours' ride north of here, men on horses swarmed out of the woods," Heph says through gritted teeth as he hands Alex his sword belt. "The guards were greatly out-numbered. The attackers wore armor but no recognizable uniform. They grabbed Arri and carried him off, scream-ing." Heph slaps the wall in frustration. "The survivor, real-izing he couldn't get the prince back by himself, raced back here as fast as he could."

Numbness begins to spread throughout Alex, but his mind remains agile and a plan forms quickly.

"How many men attacked?"

"The guard thinks about fifteen."

"Send Diodotus with twenty soldiers and a team of track-ers after them immediately," Alex says. Diodotus, the fear-less military trainer, is the best man to plan a rescue if the trackers find the group holding Arri. "And make sure to in-clude Phrixos and Telekles." Two of Alex's good friends from Mieza, both men are excellent warriors with the tracking skills of seasoned hunters.

Heph nods and departs while Alex casts a glance out the window. The statue of Poseidon casts a long shadow across the flower beds. Daylight is almost gone.

"Arri," Sarina whispers, leaning against the wall as if she needs its support. "Poor little Arri. He will be so afraid. He won't understand..."

Alex takes her gently by the shoulders and turns her toward him. Her eyes are brimming with tears, and all at once they spill down her cheeks. "A spy," she says softly. "My lord prince, you have a spy. Only your council, Hephaestion, and I knew of this secret plan."

And then she says something he has already figured out: "One of those closest to you has betrayed you."

CHAPTER FIVE

"THIS IS IT," OCHUS SAYS AS HE PULLS HIS HORSE up and gestures to the wide valley below, lush grasslands bisected by a sinuous river that reminds Zofia of a silver snake. In the distance, she sees white, columnlike rocks—or are they leafless birch trees?—scattered across the flat expanse of green.

"Katpatuka," he continues, "the land of beautiful horses. The perfect place to find a Pegasus. And only a few days' journey to the Flaming Cliffs." He looks at Zo, raises an eyebrow, and grins. "You'd better hope your old nurse's stories are correct."

What he leaves unsaid is that she will be sold like a sack of turnips at the nearest slave market if they don't find one. She kicks her mount in the sides and races down the hill, trying hard to ignore the smirk that she can practically feel chasing her.

When Zo was little, Mandana *did* tell her tales of flying horses that lived in the Eastern Mountains. Zo never believed them, of course, and judging by the way her old nurse would smile through her crooked teeth, she doubted that Mandana did either. How could horses fly? How could cliffs be on fire? But then last week, lying in her bed in a posting house, Zo saw a huge white wing brush against her window frame. She crept silently out of bed, trying not to wake Ochus, and peered into the golden-pink air of dawn. There, in the distance, she thought she saw a white horse flying just above the tree line. But it couldn't have been.

The question is, how long can she keep her captor convinced of her story? How long can she hide the fact that she is not the lost daughter of a horse trainer but in fact the runaway princess of Sardis, betrothed to the Prince of Macedon?

Her horse's hooves pound the dirt. Her long dark auburn hair—hennaed and combed with scented oils during her other life in the palace—flies behind her, a mass of tangles and probably faded, by what she has seen of the ends. But the afternoon sky is an impossibly bright powder-blue. For a moment she can pretend she's riding west, back home to find Cosmas, not east to find a winged horse that died out centuries ago, if indeed it ever existed.

For an instant, she allows herself to imagine that Commander Ochus of the Persian Fifteenth Cavalry—sarcastic, insulting, and proud—is a thousand miles away. That she is riding instead toward her true love: a soldier as brave as he is tall, whose kind eyes lit up the dark that one fateful night they spent together, the night she imagined would bind them forever… Cosmas's hands in her loose hair, tracing the curves of her body…his soft voice in her ear…

But as her captor rides up alongside her, she hears metal clatter in his saddlebag and knows it's the shackles he uses to chain her hands whenever she's not riding, so that she won't try to escape again.

She grits her teeth, and now the pounding of the horse's hooves seems to say, *I hate I hate I hate Ochus.* As the chains clink each time his horse's hooves touch the ground, her resentment builds and her cheeks burn.

When Zo looks up from the road, she sees that they have entered a forest of stone, tall white pinnacles rising from the ground like giants' spears with pointed caps on top. They gleam in the sun, taking her breath away, and the wind whistles around them like voices chattering in a thousand ancient tongues. Instinctively, she and Ochus slow their horses to a walk and look around in wonder.

"What is this?" she asks in a hushed, reverent voice, bringing her horse closer to his.

The wind blows Ochus's wavy golden-brown hair behind him. "It is called Korama, the Stones of the Gods," he says. "It goes on for hundreds of miles. These are the foothills of the Eastern Mountains."

The Eastern Mountains. Her heart leaps. That is where she needs to go to find the magical beings she is searching for, the ones who can free her from her fate.

Kohinoor—an old soothsayer—told Zo that her blood is destined to unite with that of Macedon—Prince Alexander's, to be specific. That the only way she might alter her destiny and marry Cosmas instead would be to seek help from the Spirit Eaters of the Eastern Mountains, a sprawling region, but last week the posting station waitress told her they were rumored to live north of Korama, the very region where she finds herself right now.

Kohinoor told her something else, too, something that chilled her unshakably: that if she ever were to see Cosmas again, it is fated he would die.

So she knows, she *must* change her fate. She *must* see him again.

After all, she is carrying his child.

She looks around now, and every hair on Zo's body stands

on end, alive with the knowledge that they are in an enchanted land of jinns and fairies. She is, at this very moment, in a place carved by the hands of the gods themselves, a place where myth and reality meet.

Perhaps the Spirit Eaters themselves formed these strange rocks.

"Was it a god who turned these trees to stone?" she asks.

"No one knows how it came to be," he says, looking up at a particularly tall stone as they ride past. "But some say that long ago, the earth goddess ate and drank too much at a feast and vomited all these rocks up, and the wind god took pleasure in sculpting them. Since then, the shades of the dead wander here, blown this way and that by the wind." Zo finds herself sinking into the stunning magic of the place, torn between awe and fear.

"My great-grandfather told me all that," Ochus adds smugly.

The mysterious moment snaps like a too-tight sandal strap.

"Every day I've had to listen to you bragging about your royal blood," Zo says. "My great-grandfather this and my great-grandfather that. But everyone knows that the Great King Artaxerxes has *thirty* wives and concubines. And more than *ninety* surviving children. So he probably has *thousands* of great-grandchildren. And somehow I can't imagine three thousand children crowding around his throne while he tells a story. I bet he wouldn't even know who you were if you bumped into him."

Ochus focuses his intense golden-brown eyes on her. "You don't know anything about my childhood," he says. "Some of those children—"

Even as Ochus is speaking, Zo smells something wrong. A whiff of latrine and sour body odor and rotten flesh.

With a loud shriek, a filthy, wild-haired man emerges

from a cluster of pillars and grabs the reins of Zo's horse, which rears, nearly throwing her. She screams, clinging to the horse as she's jostled roughly, thinking her attacker must be an ogre or a troll.

"The age of gods is ending!" the creature cries, his pale eyes crazed, as she steadies her horse. "The monsters have been loosed! They will devour the world!"

"Get away!" Ochus commands, unsheathing his sword.

The man lets go of Zo's reins but doesn't run. "The age ends!" he shouts again.

A chill goes up Zo's spine. The Persian magi, consulting the stars, have all predicted a new age. But a new age of what? No one seems to know.

"Come," Ochus says sternly to Zofia. "We should ride faster. This place is haunted by both the living and the dead." He spurs his horse forward and she follows.

As much as she dislikes Ochus, Zo has to admit it's good having him by her side in times of danger. The first time she saw him, she was curled up in a filthy cage in the camp of the brutal rogue slave traders who had captured her, the old soothsayer—Kohinoor—and several others. Ochus and his men swooped in on horses, fired arrows and threw spears until all her captors were dead. As she climbed weakly out of the cage, she thought he was the most beautiful sight she had ever seen.

But when he asked who she was, she couldn't exactly tell him she was a princess of Sardis who had run away from the palace to avoid a marriage with the crippled prince of Macedon, to marry the man she loved, a common soldier and the father of her unborn child. If Ochus returned her to the palace, what would her uncle, King Shershah, do to her?

So she wove a web of lies about being a horse breeder's daughter who had seen a map of where the last of the Pegasi lived. With a greedy gleam in his eye, Ochus agreed to her suggestion to find the last of the winged horses to give to the Great King, and Zo had chalked him up for a fool. But throughout this interminable journey, Ochus has proven himself clever and resourceful. Surely he should have guessed by now that she's been lying to him. But if he *has* guessed, why would he put up with the sweat, dirt, heat and ache of riding east? Of course he *must* believe her, and she should not let doubt get in her way, not when she's come this far.

Her thoughts are interrupted by an imperial courier thundering from behind, calling loudly to clear the way for the king's post as the horse's hooves kick up clods of dirt. She and Ochus edge to the side. The purpose of the Royal Road is to deliver mail, taxes, and armies throughout the Great King's far-flung empire. The well-maintained highway runs sixteen hundred miles from Sardis in the breezy west, near the Aegean Sea, across deserts, mountains, and swamps all the way to the dusty capital of Persepolis in the east.

Once the courier passes, she and Ochus nudge their horses back to the middle of the road, only to be edged off again when several merchant carts packed with goods trundle toward them. The passengers cheerfully call out greetings, and one, a little freckle-faced girl, waves at Zo.

Zo quickly turns her head away, unable to wave. *Roxana*, she thinks. Her six-year-old half sister, who followed her out of the palace and down the Royal Road, only to be killed by the slave traders. At night, she still hears the screams.

No, Zo can never go home. It wouldn't be the same without Roxana. Who would she tell bedtime stories to, the old tales of valiant heroes rescuing beautiful princesses? Zo told Roxana only the happy stories she learned from Mandana, not the ones that kept her up all night when she was small; really Mandana should have known better. Corpses cracking open their tombs to eat the living. Evil jinns flying into people's mouths and possessing their bodies. A group of murderers called the Assassins' Guild who always slashed the chests of their victims with a bloody X.

Zo starts to laugh at the memories of herself sleeping under the bed rather than on it to fool the corpses, jinns, and Assassins when they came for her. But her laugh turns into a little sob. Roxana will never be old enough to hear those stories. Never. A dull ache courses through her and she tries to stop all thought, to concentrate on the horse's rhythm.

After a couple of hours, the landscape changes into crumpled white cliffs that look like wet laundry thrown in a heap. And beyond them, gray cones of stone rise up. As the sun slides low on the horizon, they enter a town of towering pointed houses, four and five stories tall, each carved out of rock formations and leaning toward the west as if pushed there by the wind. Rooms have been dug out of the stone, and Zo sees an intricate series of wooden ladders and stairs that connects them all.

"This is our last posting house along the Royal Road," Ochus says, pointing to several rock-cut dwellings with high walls in between and a courtyard in the center. Creaking in the wind over the main gate is the usual wooden sign of a running horse carrying a blue sack of mail and the posting house's number; this one is 374. The comfortable posting houses—located every fifteen miles or so—were built for the couriers to sleep, eat, and get fresh horses, though soldiers and other travelers can use them, too.

"Tomorrow we head northeast," Ochus says, wiping the road dust off his face, "on a smaller road."

Zo nods carelessly, but her thoughts are racing. She will miss the comforts of the posting houses—the clean beds, water to wash with, and delicious tavern food—but their barricades slam shut at dusk and open at dawn. She could never run away even without the manacles, which, she knows, Ochus uses only to humiliate her. But perhaps—if he gets careless or starts to trust her off the Royal Road—she could escape.

When they turn their horses into the stables and try to arrange for new ones the following morning, the horse master shakes his head sadly. "We don't have any to offer," he says. "We keep getting reports that horses—and their riders—are meeting with…accidents in the east. Even royal couriers have…gone missing."

"What accidents?" Ochus asks in irritation. The man shrugs. Ochus runs his hands through his tangled brown hair. "But our horses are exhausted," he says, "and one of them is favoring his right leg."

But there are no fresh horses to be had.

With Ochus grumbling by her side, they enter the tavern and she immediately knows it's very different from the other posting house taverns they have dined in. This one has been dug out of stone. It's smaller and cooler, and Zo feels the crushing weight of rock all around her. She smells roasted meat, fresh bread, spilled beer, and the smoke of resin-soaked torches. It seems that lately her sense of smell has increased dramatically, not always a good thing.

A cheerful girl shows Zo and Ochus to a low table, and Zo sinks gratefully onto the cushions. The first ten days of riding on the Royal Road were agony, with blisters blossoming on her rear end and thighs, and pains shooting up her back and legs. Now, she is just tired and sore.

"It is time, my darling love," Ochus says, jingling the manacles.

Biting back the embarrassment, she holds out her hands, and he snaps a heavy iron bracelet on her right wrist and another on her left, the chain dangling between them. She feels a weight, greater even than the rock all around them, pulling her down.

The waitress's eyes widen when she sees Zo's manacles, but she says nothing as she plunks down a basket of fresh bread, a bowl of olives, and two mugs of frothy beer. Ochus asks her about the food, but Zo isn't paying attention. She is looking at a group of five imperial couriers in bright blue uniforms at the next table who are drinking deeply and talking loudly.

"What news from the east?" asks one, smooth-faced and hardly more than a boy. "You come from Persepolis, don't you?"

An older man with gray-streaked hair smiles broadly. "Good news and bad news," he replies.

"Tell us the good news first," the teenaged rider says.

"Our Great King Artaxerxes has another son at the age of eighty-five! The mother is twenty-five. Such vigor at his age!"

"Or her eunuch is not really a eunuch," says a third, stroking his pointed chin thoughtfully as the entire group guffaws. "Well, Kurush, what is the bad news?"

Kurush leans in as if telling a secret, and Zo strains to hear above the buzz of conversation, Ochus's questions about how the meat is cooked, and the clanking of mugs.

"Entire villages have been reduced to ashes and bone," the man says. "Peasants are panicking and wandering the roads with all their possessions in carts or on their backs. I have spoken with some. They told me when they went to visit the next village no one was there. Just a heap of bones. Even couriers have gone missing. Horses have disappeared out of paddocks, their bones discovered later, chewed and drained of marrow."

Zo shudders. Kurush's report echoes what the stable master said. Will it be dangerous for them to continue? Though when she thinks how Ochus killed the mountain lion early in their journey, she would put her money on him rather than whatever is killing villagers and horses.

The man with the pointed chin laughs and slaps the table. "A wonderful ghost story, Kurush!" he says, raising his mug. "I will be awake all night, shaking with fear. You, Davood," he says to a good-looking one with a trim black beard, "you rode in from the west, didn't you? What news there? Skeletons walking the road, perhaps? The dead climbing out of graves to eat babies?"

"Ah," says Davood, "nothing quite so dramatic. But Prince Alexander has won a great battle in his father's absence."

Zo stiffens. Alexander. The boy she would have married if she hadn't run away from the palace.

"How old is the prince now? Eighteen? Twenty?" the older man asks.

"Only sixteen," the one called Davood responds.

"Any word of his upcoming nuptials?" asks the gray-haired courier. "Who has Philip decided will be his bride?"

Davood waves his hand dismissively. "There are many rumors that Philip chose a bride for his son. Some say she's from Samos, and some say Crete…but I know for a fact they are both wrong."

The youngest leans forward, "How do you know?"

"I know that the prince was set to marry a princess of Sardis, but that she mysteriously disappeared days before she was supposed to leave."

The jokester with the pointed chin nods. "More likely she was poisoned by a rival princess."

The waitress has bustled off, and now Ochus's head twists in Zo's direction and his golden eyes gleam. He, too, is listening.

"Who knows? Either way, the lost princess is probably dead." The gray-haired man nods knowingly. "That's what everyone's saying. But other princesses must be lining up. Alexander might just be a boy—and there's something wrong with his leg, isn't there?—but Macedon is a prize."

Zo sits back. She can't listen anymore.

Dead. Everyone in Sardis thinks she's dead. Is her mother sorry for trying to force her to marry Alexander instead of the man she loved? Perhaps Attoosheh is finally remorseful for ignoring her all these years. And her uncle? King Shershah was always kind to her in a distant, brisk way. Will he grieve for her? No, she decides. He will see it as an irritating strategic setback, preventing a Sardisian alliance with Macedon. The only one who will truly mourn is Mandana, who always did everything in her power to make Zo happy, including helping her leave the palace to join Cosmas.

Then a terrible thought makes panic rise in her chest. Has *Cosmas* heard she's dead, too? What would he do? Would he risk his life foolishly in battle in a noble and desperate effort to join her in death? Or worse, would he soothe his grief in the arms of another girl?

She must let him know that she's alive and that he must wait for her—especially now that she's carrying his child, and he doesn't even know. He needs to know. But how can she reach him, hundreds of miles from his barracks and under the constant watch of Ochus? Unless... Couriers are allowed to deliver the letters of Persian subjects if they are inclined to take on extra jobs. But this is the last posting house she and Ochus will visit. Tonight is her last chance to find an imperial courier.

Zo stares listlessly at the steaming bowl of goat stew the waitress places in front of her and answers Ochus's questions mechanically. Yes, she's tired. No, she's not really hungry. Yes, the beer is fine.

Her mind is whirling. Because even if she could sneak away to find a courier, she has nothing to write Cosmas a message *on*. At the palace, she used wax tablets to write notes to her friends. They would read her message, rub it off, and write their response. Royal archives are written on clay tablets. Couriers usually carry letters on papyrus. Though terribly expensive, it's light in their saddlebags.

And then there's the issue of her shackles. No courier would accept a message from a chained slave. A horrible thought nibbles at the back of her mind, but she pushes it away. She's not that desperate, is she? But as the meal progresses and she sees the couriers retire one by one, her sense of despair rises until she's left with only one thought: yes, she is.

She doesn't touch the rest of her meal. Ochus doesn't comment, but she can feel his eyes on her, and she supposes she should be grateful when he settles their payment quickly and announces they shall retire early tonight, but Zo isn't. Gods help her, she isn't.

In their small room, Ochus locks the door and slips the key into his coin pouch, which he places on the scarred wooden table with a little clink. Two basins of water are set out. Without a word, she takes one of them and heads to the corner for a bit of privacy.

With a clinking of chains, Zo splashes water on her face and arms, rinsing away the dust from the road. For a moment, her resolve weakens—her skin, once white from baths of milk, is now brown as a nut. And though she hasn't seen a mirror since she left the palace, she can only assume she has dark roots above her carefully hennaed auburn hair. If only she had some perfume. Some kohl eyeliner. A sheer, spangled veil to hide behind.

Her hand trembles as she rubs her arm with the towel, and she steals a glance at Ochus, who has removed his tunic and stands in his baggy checkered trousers and boots. He has an incredible physique. His shoulders are broad, his biceps enormous, his stomach flat as an anvil and chiseled like a temple statue. If he wasn't so obnoxious, and if she didn't love Cosmas, maybe she wouldn't feel so revolted.

She swallows hard. She has to do this as she is. Now. *For Cosmas.*

"Ochus," she says, approaching him. But she's chosen the wrong moment; he ducks his head into the basin, and then resurfaces, water droplets dripping down his face. He reaches for a towel.

"Ochus," she says again, trying to keep her voice low and throaty.

"Uh-huh," he grunts, the sound muffled by the towel.

She stands and puts her hand gently on his arm. He stops drying and looks at her in expectation. "Well, what is it?" he asks.

"So…so many nights we have spent together on this long journey…" She falters, not knowing what to say next as he tosses the towel, crosses his arms, and looks at her. It's not coming out right. She sounds stupid.

Cosmas always told her that her lashes, thick and long and black, were extremely beautiful against her dark blue eyes, and now she tries to peer up at him through them, blinking slowly.

"Do you have dust in your eyes?"

"I feel fine," she snaps back. By all the gods, why did she think it would be a good idea to try to seduce this impossible man?

"I...I just wanted to—to—" What should she do next? Panicking, she reaches out to try to flirtatiously touch him. Her hand now on his shoulder, she doesn't know what to do with it, and so she just stares at her small and helpless hand against the audacious curve of his bicep. One second drags on. Then two.

Suddenly, she realizes his shoulder is shaking, and she looks up to find Ochus laughing silently. As soon as he sees her looking, his laughter bursts out like an ox's bellow.

"You are amazingly awkward at seduction, Zotasha," he says, using the fake name she gave him. "But then, I suppose all virgins are."

Flushing, Zo looks down at the floor, caught off guard by the word *virgin*. What will he do if they are together long enough that he realizes she's with child? But they'll never be together that long. It is so early that Zo wouldn't be sure of it herself if the soothsayer in the cage next to hers on the slave cart hadn't told her.

He hasn't even seemed to notice she hasn't bled over the weeks they've been together. But then again, men usually don't want to know such things, Mandana told her. They are more afraid of a woman's monthly blood than seeing their own gushing out on the battlefield.

As Ochus's laughter continues, she grinds the knuckles of her right hand into the palm of her left, wishing she could just disappear. She's never been so mortified in her life. She's too embarrassed to even yell at him. Finally the laughter stops, but Zo keeps her eyes on the floor. She can't look at him.

"No reply, little temptress?" Ochus says. When she's silent, he sighs. "It's no fun if you don't rise to the bait." Zo hears him walk across the room. Then he's back in front of her.

"Since I can't believe you really want to seduce me, I can only assume you want me to take off your chains," Ochus says, his voice kinder. "All you need do is ask. Hold out your hands."

Startled, Zo obeys. She looks up to see him pull the key from his pocket, unlock the shackles, and remove them. She has a sudden image of a sweating, trembling ox when its owner removes the heavy yoke from its shoulders. This must be what it feels like. Lightness. Freedom. Kindness.

He takes her hands in his and turns them upside down, examining the pink marks on her wrists. His hands are calloused and hard, and a ragged purple scar runs across his left hand from the base of his thumb to his pinky. Yet these strong warrior's fingers are gentle now, and she can feel their heat as he enfolds her small ones.

"Perhaps we won't need those chains anymore," he says, pulling away from her. "It would be nice to sleep without hearing you clink as you toss and turn."

Zo still holds her hands out in front of her, palms up, and they feel awkward, cold, exposed. She hastily pulls them back and follows him into bed.

He turns away from her, blows out the lamp, and falls asleep.

She wishes he hadn't been so nice to her. It's much easier to plot against him when he's being obnoxious…but, she has to admit to herself that his action was kind. For a captor, anyway.

After waiting what seems like an eternity, she slowly gets out of bed, hoping the ropes below the mattress don't creak with the shift in weight. They do, but his heavy breathing doesn't change. Then, like the comic pantomime actors who performed at the Sardis palace, she pads in slow motion across the tiny room to the table where she feels around for the pouch, opens it, and removes the room key and one of the big coins.

Unlocking the door is the tricky thing. She feels for the keyhole, turns the key, and stifles a gasp as the rusty lock screeches in protest, but Ochus remains sound asleep.

Zo doesn't dare take a lamp, and walking down the corridor she feels drowned in darkness. She runs her hand along the wall to find the opening for the stairs and walks down the twisting staircase until finally, in the courtyard, she sees some light—sputtering torches on the buildings, lanterns held by guards watching the merchants' wagons, and gold light spilling from the window slats of the tavern.

Goddess Anahita, she pleads, *let there still be an imperial courier inside.*

Three merchants are playing knucklebones. One of them has scattered the four bones across the table and laughs at his successful throw as the others groan and push coins his way.

A weary waitress stacks chairs on a table and sweeps beneath. And in the corner, two imperial couriers sit quietly, hands clasped around their mugs and heads bowed, almost as if in prayer. She recognizes them from dinner.

Zo marches up to them, her heart pounding. "I beg your pardon, sir, but are you headed east or west?" she asks the handsome bearded one called Davood.

He raises dark eyes that look at her appraisingly, and she wishes she had thrown her cloak over her tunic and trousers before she left the room.

"Why do you ask?" he says, his slow grin revealing white teeth. "Would you like to join me? We ride fast, you know. I doubt you could keep up."

"I... My master wants me to send an important message west."

The grin fades. "I am headed east. To Persepolis."

Zo can't help but groan. "No," she says. "I'm afraid that won't do."

The other one, the older man with gray hair and a gentle face, says, "I'm headed west, girl. All the way to Sardis. I have dispatches for the royal garrisons there."

Relief floods her. "Can you take a letter to the Ninth Regiment outside Sardis?" she asks.

He nods. "For a gold daric," he says.

"And..." she shuffles her feet, embarrassed to ask the next question. But after her humiliation earlier this evening, this feels like such a small task. "Do you have anything I can write on?" she asks.

Both men laugh. The older one raises a bushy gray eyebrow and asks, "You know how to write?"

Zo pulls herself up to her full height and says, "I was trained to keep my master's household accounts."

"And yet you don't have papyrus or ink with you?" asks the younger one. She finds herself tongue-tied.

"It just so happens I have something in my pouch," the kind one says. He picks up a blue bag on the floor and brings out a small scroll. "A Sharm merchant gave me a list of merchandise he agreed to pay in taxes to deliver to the satrap of Gordium, but there was a mistake so he wrote a second one. I planned to soak the ink out of the first list, but you may use it."

Now she needs to ask for ink. She's almost prepared to cut herself with a meat knife and dip her fingernail in her own blood to write, if that's what it takes, but the courier brings a bronze cylinder out of his bag without asking, and opens it into two halves. In the top half he unlatches a little door and removes a sharp pointed stylus. From a lower compartment he takes out a cake of ink and a small stone container of water.

Zo thanks him and seats herself at another table, trying to collect her thoughts. She should put the date and location at the top so Cosmas will know when she was here. She pours a few drops of water onto the cake of ink and dips the sty-lus into it, scratching into the softening ink. *The Royal Road Inn 374 in Korama*, then stops. "What is today's date?" she asks, looking up.

"The twelfth of Mordad," says the gray-haired courier.

The twelfth of Mordad? How could that be? She ran away from Sardis on the...on the... It must have been the twenty-first of Tir. Only three weeks, but it seems more like a year at least. She writes the date and looks in dismay at the list of merchandise. Will Cosmas understand that she wrote in between the lines of someone else's list? She has no choice but to hope.

When she is finished, she reads the letter:

Taxes To Be Paid by Arash of Sharm
Cosmas, I am alive
Sixteen fat sheep
I ran away to be with you
Four barrels of beer
But was captured by slavers
Three large amphorae of wine
I was freed, but am heading east
Five barrels of black olives
My dearest love, I wish I had
Nineteen sturdy goats
Space to tell you everything
Two large brown and white bulls
I will return to you soon
Two barrels of peas
Wait for me, my love.

She blows on the ink, and when it is dry, turns the papy-rus over and writes on the top *Cosmas, son of Borzin, Captain,*

Ninth Regiment, near the village of Hamda, a full day's ride east of Sardis. Then she rolls it back up and hands it to the courier along with a gold daric, which glints in the lamplight.

"Very well," he says.

Returning across the courtyard, she feels as if a boulder has been removed from her shoulders. Cosmas will get the message in a week at most, given that imperial couriers ride almost as fast as lightning. She did it. Against all odds, she sent the message. And against all odds, she finds herself in Korama. As she and Ochus head north up the mountain paths to find a flying horse, they are sure to find villages. And in those villages, there should be some wise man or woman who knows more about the mysterious Spirit Eaters. She *will* find one. She *will* change her fate.

She will escape Ochus. She will marry Cosmas and together they will raise their child, without the interference of kings, or queens, or crippled princes of Macedon.

Hope rises as she climbs the pitch-black staircase. For the first time in ages, she feels that everything is going to be all right. But a moment later, she knows she celebrated too soon.

At the top of the stairs, blocking the narrow corridor, a man holds a lamp, the light making it appear as if his angry eyes glow like carnelians.

Ochus.

CHAPTER SIX

JACOB EXAMINES THE EDGE OF HIS SWORD, scrapes it over the whetstone again, and lays it on the wobbly corner table. He stands up and looks out the arrow slit window for the source of the smell wafting into the little room. Black smoke billowing from a pyre in the far courtyard of the old fortress makes him want to shudder. But he fights the urge.

He knows it's the duty of the Aesarian Lords to burn magic from the world, but as a new recruit, he doesn't know any of their secrets. And sometimes he wonders if—when he eventually does learn them—he will like them.

Too late for that now. He is sworn to the Aesarian Lords. For life.

He runs a hand over a flaking, water-stained fresco, so damaged he can't even tell what the faded strokes of paint once represented. This abandoned fortress must have been built in the time of Achilles. As the bruised and battered Aesarian army approached it after losing the battle with Alexander, it seemed to Jacob that Pyrrhia was like a vicious animal crouching high on a hill, its back against a cliff, suspicious, angry, and ready to pounce.

The Lords chose the fortress not for comfort, he realizes, but for defensibility: a single, steep path leads up to the only entrance where, immediately after their arrival, the men built a new gate of thick oak sheathed with bronze and iron. Since then, they have also reinforced the walls and dug the wells deeper to help withstand a siege as they await the Aesarian regiment from Nekrana, sent by Supreme Lord Gulzar himself. Jacob has learned that the power of the Aesarian Lords spreads farther than he ever suspected, with growing regiments throughout all of the known world.

There's a good reason for the Lords to strengthen Pyrrhia's defenses, Jacob knows. Over the past several days since the battle, Alexander's envoys asked repeatedly if the Lords had captured Princess Cynane the night of the library fire. He was willing to pay a large ransom for her return, but the Lords responded by categorically denying that they had ever even seen her. If Alexander learns that they lied about having Princess Cynane, the treaty is void. Alex will attack to rescue his sister. He will have to. Family honor will demand it.

A groan interrupts his thoughts, and he turns to see that the princess is coming back to consciousness. She lies chained to a table, bruised and filthy, her long black hair matted.

"Water," she whispers, her voice as scraping as his sword on the whetstone.

Jacob hesitates a moment—he's not supposed to help her—but then he pours water from an *oenochoe* into a clay cup, and brings it to her lips. She raises her head to drink greedily, then shuts her eyes before lying back down with a heavy sigh.

It doesn't seem right to do this to Cynane. She's just a girl, even though she is tall and strong and trained as a warrior—and killed two Aesarian Lords when they infiltrated Pella, before Lord Bastian kidnapped her and smuggled her out of the ancient drainage tunnels below the palace to their military camp.

When Jacob lived in the palace of Pella, first as a royal guard and then as an Aesarian Lord in training, he saw Princess Cynane striding about in her breastplate, sword, and boots. He wouldn't have dreamed of talking to her then, but the limp form in front of him is a far cry from the lonely princess who hid behind her barbed tongue.

"Princess, you should tell them what you know. They will be back soon," he says, setting the *oenochoe* back on the table with a hard click. "Why did the fire in the library not harm you? Why do you heal almost immediately when they torture you? What kind of *magic* do you possess?"

Her eyelids flutter, and it takes a moment for the onyx eyes to focus on his face. But when they do, she smiles. "I know you," she says hoarsely. "The victor of the Blood Tournament."

"Yes," he says. That was only four weeks ago, and yet it seems like centuries.

She shifts her weight and grimaces. "You brought your lover, Katerina, to Pella with you from that village—what was it, Trissa?"

"Erissa," he corrects her automatically, but he doesn't bother to correct Kat's relationship to him. He and Kat grew up together practically as family. He knows she considers his brothers to be her brothers, too, and that she loves his parents as if they were her own. But his relationship with her began to change in the last year. Though they only kissed three times, he'd be lying if he said he doesn't think of her that way. But he is no longer that peasant boy with time on his hands to pine for his childhood love.

He returns to the window and looks out. White ash floats on the air, along with a heavy odor of strange sulfur.

He hears a low, gurgling sound from across the room. It's laughter. Cyn's laughter. "You may have won the gold Alex so desperately wanted, but he took your lover. Oh, didn't you know?" she says, correctly interpreting Jacob's quick turn to face her. "They were *always* in bed together."

"That's a lie," he croaks, his mouth suddenly dry as sawdust. Kat insisted many times that her bond with Alexander was not a romantic one, that it was something very different.

"You saw them together, did you not? You wanted her, did everything to get her, but lost her. It's not your fault, though," she says, her simulated sympathy dripping like honey from her words. "How can an oaf like you compete against a prince?"

Jacob doesn't say anything. Because he can't. It's like the time he was hunting in the woods and a whirlwind hit. Suddenly trees were falling, lightning crashing, leaves and dirt flying up from the ground to hit his face. The screaming wind tore at his tunic like talons. He didn't know what was happening, where to go, or how to save himself—and he feels the same way now.

He has denied to himself—a hundred times, a thousand times—the possibility of Kat being intimate with Alexander. He tried to push the ugly thought to the back of his mind and slam the door on it. But now the lock from that door has been ripped away, and Cyn's forbidden words have crashed through his defenses.

Cynane laughs weakly before her mirth erodes into a cough, and she has to turn her head away. Her weakness infuriates Jacob—how dare she become silent and leave him with these thoughts? He wants to fight her, to force her to take back what she has said. He knows she can fight. He saw her practice against the king's men many times, and now she just lies there, a lost princess no one really wants to find.

He fights the urge to shake her into action and instead sits back down at the small corner table and draws his sword against the whetstone—long, slow motions to sharpen the iron blade. The sound is excruciating, just like the pain in his chest, but the action makes him feel better somehow.

Maybe not everything Cynane said is true, but at least a portion is. Jacob *did* do everything to win Kat. He wanted to offer her something more than life on the farm making pots and, more selfishly, he wanted her to be proud of him. He risked his life in the Blood Tournament battling twenty-four of the best warriors from across the known world, and he won—for her.

And still Kat wouldn't have him, so he joined the most powerful—both politically and physically—fighting force in the world: the Aesarian Lords. Then, before he could speak with her, the Aesarians' sacred Hemlock Torch exploded, and with it, the chance to be with Kat as well. For Macedon was no longer a tentative ally, but now an enemy who had hidden magic from the Lords.

The last time Jacob saw Kat was on the battlefield. In the midst of war, he had wondered if the recent sword blow to his helmet had addled his brains, because he saw Kat—Kat, the weaver's daughter—fighting a Lord more than twice her size and ably defending herself with a shield and sword. Kat had never trained with weapons in Erissa—so how was she able to fight a Lord? Had she hidden this talent from him their whole life together? But even as a sense of betrayal crept into his heart, he was racing toward her—to help. Because even in battle, even though he had sworn himself to the Lords, his heart had sworn him to Kat long ago, and he could not fight it. Helping Kat was instinct, like breathing air or feeling heat.

And then Lord Bastian had appeared, and Jacob watched

in horror as he pushed his sword into her side as easily as one would spit a rabbit.

The spray of crimson blood on her white tunic would linger in his memory forever.

Kat dropped her shield and sword, and held her wound with both hands, as if she could keep the blood inside. She fell at Bastian's feet, and the Lord spat on her body before diving back into the melee.

Jacob knelt beside her in the red dirt, stroking her hair and promising her that when all this was over, they would return to Erissa, and hunt in the meadow and swim in the pond, and that he would never, ever let her get hurt again.

Something glimmered on her cheek, and Jacob was surprised to realize it was a tear. His tear. He had only kissed her twice: that magical evening in the pond before they left for Pella, and that day in the palace when he visited her room, before they got in a fight and he stormed out saying things he would now never be able to take back.

They would have three kisses. This would be the last one.

He bent to kiss the soft lips, so warm and tender against his. At that moment, with death and pain all around him, he felt his sorrow lift. Joy infused him with an inexpressible delight. His arm and shoulder, exhausted from carrying the huge shield, stopped aching. The bloody scrape on his neck from an arrow whizzing past and taking a sliver of flesh with it no longer throbbed. He had the ridiculous feeling that despite everything, it would all somehow be all right. Even now, her breath seemed to strengthen.

"I love you, Kat," he whispered, as he raised his head. There was movement behind him and the spell was broken. He looked around and saw Hephaestion, Prince Alexander's top lieutenant and right-hand man, running at him with a sword. Jacob leaped up to face him, and their swords rang out again and again until the Aesarians sounded the signal for retreat.

At first Jacob ignored the signal. There was no way he was going to leave Kat there, bleeding. But then he realized she would continue to bleed as long as he and Hephaestion continued to fight. If Jacob retreated, Hephaestion would surely help her immediately. He turned and ran, casting a backward glance. Hephaestion hesitated a moment, looking angry that Jacob had run off, looking like he might chase after him. But then he ran to Kat and knelt beside her.

Later, in the days following the battle, Jacob heard reports that the prince's warrior girlfriend had been seen at the palace. There were whispers that she was an enchantress—how else did she catch the prince's eye the moment he first saw her? How else had she helped defeat the Aesarian Army and survived what was surely a fatal wound? Jacob was confused by the reports of Katerina's supposed magical abilities, but the relief that she had lived overshadowed any other feeling—except for one.

Jacob would never forgive Bastian.

He vowed to pay him back one day, a promise he means to keep. He will train, he will become strong so that he can take Bastian down in whatever way possible. He will look for opportunities for advancement. He will become the best Aesarian Lord there ever was. Hundreds of years from now, people will talk about him. His name will be inscribed on the Wall of Heroes in the Lords' capital of Nekrana in the Eastern Mountains. And most important, he will forget about Kat—or die trying. Because above all he knows he cannot live with the torture of his thoughts. When he joined the Aesarians, they were still loyal to King Philip of Macedon. But that quickly and violently changed. And now Kat is on the opposite side of war. He originally became a Lord to try and impress Kat. It had all been for Kat. But it didn't work. And now, knowing she doesn't want him, he can't risk losing everything he has gained by their protection and training.

The ancient door creaks open and Lord Turshu enters. He has the heavily tattooed arms of all Scythians and the badly bowed legs from being raised on the back of a horse.

"The warrior woman has spirit," he observes in his melodic accent.

Jacob looks up from the whetstone and grunts. "I suppose you could call it that," he says.

"Back home, we have many such women trained to fight as warriors. Lord Jacob, don't you find the average Greek woman…boring? Not muscular. Not strong. Not exciting. This one, however, is like a tiger. This one," he says, picking up a long lock of Cyn's hair and curling it around his finger, "I would very much like to have."

"Not on your life," Cyn says, twisting her head as she tries to bite him. Turshu yanks back his hand and bursts into loud laughter.

"Spirit," Jacob says, nodding. He runs a finger lightly over the sword edge and feels it bite into his flesh. It is ready.

Turshu's eyes crinkle in amusement as he looks at Jacob. "I am come to relieve your watch, Lord Jacob. High Lord Gideon has had to leave the forge for an emergency and wishes you to help Lord Timaeus with his task." He takes a step closer and adds in a low voice, his broad face serious now, "Have you heard? The Elder Council believes there is a traitor among us."

Traitor. The word echoes in Jacob's mind as he thinks of the faces of his Aesarian brothers. Who would possibly—and then he has it. Bastian. Arrogant. Smirking. Self-serving.

"No, sir," Jacob says, his mind racing. "But thank you for telling me. I'll certainly keep my eyes and ears open. And, sir," he adds, his spirits lifting at the thought of leaving this torture room and Cynane's tormenting words. "I wouldn't get too friendly with the prisoner. She bites." And then he strides down the winding stairs and toward the portable military forge set up in an abandoned room off the stables.

The moment Jacob enters he's struck by a wave of heat. He sees thick black smoke rising through a hole in the roof as a wiry figure the size of a twelve-year-old girl shovels coals in the bottom of the forge.

"Lord Timaeus," Jacob says, bowing as one would to a king.

"Lord Jacob. I am most honored." Timaeus's monkeylike face breaks into a grin, showing his amusement at the false formality. They had first met as competitors in the Blood Tournament, ready to slice and cut into each other as the crowd cheered, but when King Philip chose both of them to join the Royal Guard, the new recruits quickly became best friends. Jacob isn't sure if he would have survived the rigorous training of both the palace and the Aesarian Lords without his friend's biting humor.

"I've been told to help you," Jacob says, going to the old wooden table in the center of the room and eyeing the black iron objects spread across. "How is it?"

Tim wipes his sweaty brown hair from his brow. "I'll tell you how it is—it's hotter in here than an Egyptian shithole in mid-summer."

"I mean, how is the torch?" Jacob asks. The black iron torch, almost three feet long, lies on the table, its pointed arms thrusting out jaggedly like cruel thorns. In the center is a basket of what looks like long, wicked nails. He sees thin iron medallions lying near the torch: a lightning bolt, a group of five flames, and a crescent moon, Aesarian symbols. "Looks almost finished."

"Nearly," Timaeus says. "There's just some decoration left. Want to hold it?"

"After what happened to the last man?" Jacobs asks, backing away. "I tripped over his charred skull in the odeon!"

Timaeus smiles and shovels more coal into the forge. "I admit, I was worried, too, when the High Lord first assigned me to help him forge the new one, but I'm not anymore. The torch is simply a detector of magic. If the torch burns white, there's no magic around. If it burns red, there is. And since I'm about as magical as the High Lord's dog, there's nothing to fear."

"But when it burns black, sucks all the air out of an arena, extinguishes the torches, disintegrates the bearer..."

"Then there's some highly powerful magic in the palace and you're in deep trouble," Tim says, leaning on his shovel and panting slightly. "But the High Lord has strengthened the torch. It should now be able to withstand even the powers of Zeus himself."

Jacob reaches out a finger and taps it. Nothing happens.

"Stop acting like a little girl," Tim says scornfully. "Really, you're making me embarrassed to be your friend."

Jacob takes a breath and picks up the torch. It's heavy, which he expected, but ice-cold, which he did not expect in a room of such stifling heat. It's already decorated with twisting garlands of flame that remind him of a lopsided sneer. Of Lord Bastian's scarred and puckered sneer, come to think of it.

"Tim, I wanted to ask you," Jacob says, turning the torch and examining it closely, "have you seen Bastian sneaking around? I noticed it even when we were still at the palace. Coming and going at all hours, not wearing his uniform. Very mysterious. He snuck out of here a few days ago in a hooded cloak and hasn't come back yet. I think he might be a spy for the enemy."

"Isn't it more likely that the Elder Council is sending him to spy *on* the enemy?" Tim asks, poking the coals with a long iron rod.

Suddenly, a pure white flame flicks out of the top of the torch, and Jacob almost drops the heavy instrument.

"Your face!" Tim crows. "You'd think that you'd never seen fire be—" But suddenly, his mirth is cut short, and he grabs Jacob's arm, pushing it down. "Drop the torch," he orders harshly.

Jacob is surprised at his friend's demeanor, and he looks at the torch, where the white flame has sunk into a deep red the color of sunset.

Shocked, Jacob stares dumbly at the torch in his hand. How could it be red? There are no magic wielders in the Aesarian Lords' ranks. Tim yanks the torch out of his hand and throws it into a bucket of water that is always kept near the forge. It is extinguished immediately, and the hissing sound of water-turned-hot fills the small space.

"It's still malfunctioning," Tim says, looking straight into Jacob's eyes. "Progress has not been smooth. I shall let the High Lord know."

"Know what?" Jacob hears the silky voice of the Aesarian Lord he despises the most. Turning, he sees that bastard, Bastian, slouching against one side of the doorway, his arms crossed. His dark eyes flicker as he studies first Jacob, then Tim.

"I was told High Lord Gideon would be here," he says, his face unreadable.

Jacob's heart pounds. How much did Bastian hear? How much did he see? Did he see the torch flame red? Did he *cause* it to?

"The High Lord will return in a few minutes," Tim says, turning away from Bastian and picking up an anvil.

"I need to speak with him now," Bastian snaps, dark eyes smoldering.

"Well then, you'd best go out and find him," Tim says. "Because no matter how much you bark at me, he's still not here."

Bastian looks as if he's about to say something but must think better of it because he spits onto the dirt floor of the smithy and leaves. Jacob waits until he's sure that Bastian is gone before he asks the question that has been burning in his mind, "How long was he standing there?" he says in a low voice. "Did he hear me call him a spy?"

"I don't know," Tim says, his face twisting into a mask of worry. "I don't think he saw anything either. You were blocking it."

"You mean the torch?" Jacob says, and Tim nods his head silently. Jacob lets out a breath. It's all starting to make sense…

"Lord Bastian must be a sorcerer," Jacob says, excitement rising in his voice. "Or maybe he possesses Blood Magic. Turshu just told me that there is a traitor in our ranks. That's why High Lord Gideon had to run off. Don't you see, Tim? The torch is proof that Bastian is a spy for our enemies! We need to figure out some way for the council to see the torch turn red around him."

Tim begins to hit a sheet of metal rhythmically, smoothing out dents to make it workable. "I'm not sure that's the best idea, Lord Jacob. The torch obviously isn't fixed yet."

"But you said it was working!"

"I did," his friend replies, his watery blue eyes troubled. "But, well, just drop it, will you? Just be patient and wait."

"I'm done with patience!" Jacob explodes. "Waiting only means missing out. I'm tired of sitting on the sidelines. I know I'm right. I know Lord Bastian is betraying us, and if you don't believe me, I'll find proof!"

Clang, clang, clang, the hammer beats. "Are you going to help me with this?" the short man asks, ignoring Jacob's declaration. "I'm more sweat at this point than I am flesh and bone."

Jacob looks at the door through narrowed eyes. If Bastian heard him call him a spy, good. He wants him to know he's watching him. That whatever he's up to, he won't get away with it.

"I will," he says. "But…I have to do something first."

"Fine." Tim sighs. "But if you find a greasy puddle on the floor when you come back, that will be me."

Bastian is gone from the stable yard, but Jacob hears his boots clattering on stone. He runs after him, through the large room where the men store their weapons. Thinking he lost him, he picks up his pace. He's so intent on catching up with the Lord that he almost clatters into the middle of the main fortress courtyard, and it's only at the last moment that Jacob realizes he has caught up with his prey. Two cloaked figures stand in the courtyard talking: the new High Lord Gideon and Lord Bastian.

Quickly, Jacob ducks behind one of the short, wide pillars and listens.

"…do not believe what you tell me is possible," Gideon is saying. "No one has heard of him or his brother in years. They have, most likely, found a way to return to the surviving gods—" The new High Lord has the deepest, most melodic voice Jacob has ever heard. Whenever he talks, everyone stands riveted. Even now, hiding behind the pillar, Jacob feels himself slipping into the voice, ready to curl up and fall asleep.

An Ethiopian by birth with skin the color of rich, fertile

soil, Gideon is admired for his unruffled composure even in the worst of circumstances. Tall and imposing, he was fearless in the battle of Pellan Fields, rallying the men, racing with raised sword into the thick of the fighting to skewer the enemy. It was Gideon who called the retreat and calmly shepherded the remainder of the army to the safety of this fortress. When the Lords learned that High Lord Mordecai was killed, it seemed natural that they would choose Gideon to replace him. Yet Jacob wonders if fierce passions boil just below this cool veneer. Sometimes—especially when Gideon supervises Cynane's torture sessions—he has seen something flash in Gideon's eyes that makes his blood run cold.

"...not waste time on investigating the silly fireside tales of old women," Gideon concludes.

In a clipped voice, Bastian argues, "No one has heard of Riel for years because he has been hiding in the Pellan palace. That witch-queen, Olympias, was protecting him, perhaps in return for magical assistance in some way."

Was? Why the past tense for Queen Olympias? Jacob wonders. Wouldn't the queen still be protecting this Riel in the Pellan palace?

"Who knows what powers Riel granted her in return for his safety?" Bastian continues.

Jacob hears the crunch of gravel underfoot as one of them starts walking. "It would explain what happened to the Hemlock Torch," Gideon says, as the crunch stops. "What kind of magic could have an effect like that on Socrates' torch? Perhaps only the magic of one of the primal gods."

They are now very near the column Jacob is hiding behind. If he darts toward the door, they will surely see him. He holds his breath and keeps his arms tightly at his sides.

"But why do you believe Riel is in the Pellan palace?" Gideon asks. "And hidden by the queen? Where have you been? You asked for time to complete a secret mission and bring us back information. Now that I know the information, tell me, what was the mission? Where did you go?"

Jacob hears a boot kicking gravel. "I regret, High Lord, that I cannot say at the moment. But I swear I will find the last god, in whatever form he takes, and bring him to the Lords."

"If you do, you will be the best of the Aesarians," comes the resonant voice. "Rest assured, your name will be inscribed at Nekrana. Never before have we…" Gideon's voice fades as the two men leave the courtyard. Jacob peers around the column at their retreating forms and sees no way of following them without being seen.

Questions churn in his mind like a river in spring flood. What does it mean, the last god? The gods are asleep—they have not come in contact with men for hundreds of years now. Is Bastian trying to waken them? Why was he on a secret mission? But another thought grows larger and larger until it pushes all others from his mind: the best of the Aesarians. High Lord Gideon said find Riel and become the best.

Now Jacob knows what to do. Now he has a new star guiding him toward his new goal, the goal meant to replace the green-eyed girl in his heart.

Jacob will beat Bastian to the last god. Jacob will bring this Riel to the Elder Council. Jacob will be the best of the Aesarians.

CHAPTER SEVEN

ABOVE THE CRUMBLING STONE COURTYARD of the ancient fortress, the sky spins wildly as the men turn the wheel to which Cynane, princess of Macedon, half sister to Alexander, is chained. The spinning alone makes her nauseated, but she knows that what's coming next will be worse.

The iron bars crash down on her arms and legs and ribs, smashing her bones. Her shrieks are so piercingly terrifying that the pounding stops for a moment as the men take a step back from the wheel and wait.

Sweat rolls off her face. Tears stream down her cheeks. She is no longer human. She is pain.

Then the smashing starts again.

By the time the wheel stops spinning, she feels the agony slip away like water running out of a drain, along with the dizziness as the bones and skin and muscle mend in a gentle warmth. When she feels thick, muscular hands examining her arms and legs and chest, she is too exhausted to open her eyes.

"And so, once again, within moments, all injuries are healed," says a deep voice that is unthinkably beautiful to hear even in this horror. "Can you imagine, Ambiorix, if we had soldiers like this? We would be invincible on the battlefield. Within a few years, we would rule the world."

"Through *magic*, High Lord?"

"It is no dishonor when warriors use the enemy's weapons to conquer them."

She feels huge hands on her cheeks and opens her eyes. Above her looms the face as dark as night. The large eyes—glittering like faceted obsidian—study her as if she is an interesting object he found on the beach. Because that's all she is—jetsam coughed up from the sea of fate and spat in front of this man's feet. The humiliation is worse than any physical torture.

"Tell us what you are," the man says, "and this torture can stop. We only wish to understand the type of magic you possess. It is neither Snake nor Earth…so what is it?" There is something so coaxing, so persuasive in the voice that she considers telling him that she's nothing as weak as Snake and Earth Blood, the kind of magic handed to people at birth. She is *Smoke* Blood, the only Blood Magic to be earned rather than inherited. The only magic so rare that none know of it except for the royal house of Illyria, her mother's line. She has never found any mention of it in scrolls, and she's heard about it only once, when she was eight. She stood in the hallway outside her mother's room listening to Audata arguing with someone, begging for help against mortal danger coming her way.

Sobbing in desperation, Audata wanted to know what act of true betrayal was vicious enough to reward her with Smoke Blood. When Cyn entered, she found her mother alone, and Audata angrily refused to talk about her solitary conversation.

The next day, Cyn found her mother dead in her bath,

eyes and lips open, skin white as milk, black hair floating in bloodred water. She had been stabbed in the heart, the gaping wound like a ragged scarlet mouth.

Though Audata had not found the blood of true betrayal in time, Cyn vowed to earn it herself. She had plotted and schemed to have Alexander's best friend Hephaestion betray his master. When he had proved loyal, in desperation Cyn had killed a beggar thief and used his blood in the ancient ritual, hoping to seal his betrayal to her soul so that she might use its power.

At first, she didn't think it worked, but when the flames licked her body in the library fire, her wounds healed almost immediately—though the magic did nothing to stop the pain. She'd never had an injury so grave before—only scratches and bruises that were fleeting at most. Some did leave scars...but these burns should have killed her. At that moment, in the midst of her capture, she knew: she was Smoke Blood.

When she escapes the Aesarian Lords, she will be an invincible general leading armies, and she will chop off the Lords' heads, one by one, starting with this giant black man who speaks to her of betraying her secret inheritance.

"Tell me," the High Lord coaxes again. "Tell me what you are." Again, some part of her wants to tell him everything, to please the being behind the deep ringing richness of those words.

Then something inside her hardens, and Cyn feels a flicker of white-hot rage in a stagnant sea of limp exhaustion.

With the last of her strength, she spits at him. She's too weak and too dehydrated to call up any saliva, so she only succeeds in blowing air at the man. But it is enough. He gets the message. He slaps her across the face with an enormous paw, and her right cheek smarts in pain.

"Why don't we just prepare her for the ritual?" asks the huge Gaul with long blond braids and burning blue eyes. Lord Ambiorix, they call him. He's one of the Lords who breaks her bones with an iron rod. "Her blood might buy us some time."

"Not until we know what she is," High Lord Gideon replies, his voice carrying all the warning of a sword slowly scraping out of its hilt. "She is not Earth Blood, nor is she Snake Blood. Nor is she a witch or sorceress or oracle. She is nothing we have ever found before. And because of that, she is far more valuable than any of King Philip's treasures or even the most priceless artifact in King Artaxerxes's hoard."

"I understand, my lord," Lord Ambiorix replies.

The dark one crosses his powerful arms and says, "Very well. Phaedron, Gaius, unchain her and put her in the trough."

Cynane's body is too tired to curl in horror. Once she would have screamed her fury, but now she can barely muster the strength to rail against them in her own mind. For the first time, she fears that she will actually give in. That she will betray Audata and her own future of leading a nation as the sole possessor of Smoke Blood.

The Lords place her in an old stone horse trough filled with water. She is too weak to struggle much, and when they set the huge stones across her flat abdomen, she sinks to the bottom. She holds her breath for as long as she can, her lungs burning, and then they explode, exhaling air and then inhaling water. The pain in her chest is unbearable. Her heart is hammering, her head splitting. And then she sinks into blackness.

She wakes to find herself folded in strong arms covered in thick blond hair. She glimpses mildewed gray walls curving around her. They are in the small spiral staircase that leads up to her room in the tower.

"Two hours," the High Lord says. "This time she was under water for two hours."

"High Lord, why don't you behead her and see if she can heal that?" asks the one called Gaius in his Roman-accented Greek. "Perhaps she will reach up with both hands and set her head back on her shoulders."

"That is something I'd like to see," one Lord sniggers over the clatter of boots on stairs. "Like how the cook cuts a chicken—a fowl princess." Though the other men laugh, Cyn does not hear Gideon's dark laugh among them. She opens her eyes and sees him standing before the door to the tower room, staring at her, a bitter smile on his broad face. "I suspect that might be impossible for her," the High Lord says. "Though we might use that as punishment if she fails to tell us what we want to know." He kicks the door open with his black boot.

She is dropped on the table and chained, too helpless to move. She hears boots on stairs again, and then the sound fades. Outside the little window in Cyn's shabby room, a gentle afternoon rain begins to murmur a soothing lullaby. The window slats have long ago rotted and fallen off, and a steady patter hits the cracked stone floor. The breeze is fresh, clean, and she gulps it in. She is alone for once. She closes her eyes and tries to sleep.

Soon it seems that there are voices in the rain. Whispers, really, mixed with sighs.

Cy...na...ne, they say.

Cy...na...ne.

A dream. Sometimes she thinks everything that has happened to her since her abduction has been a dream, and that she will wake in her soft palace bed, morning light streaming through her windows, and laugh out loud at the dream's intricacy.

Cynane!

She opens her eyes and sees a figure of smoke and mist bending over her. Tiny droplets of rain dance in the form.

She tries to rub her eyes, but remembers too late that her wrists are chained down on the table. The heavy metal clanks against rough wood. "Who are you?" she asks, her voice cracking from the screams that have scraped her throat.

The figure stands up straight. She believes it to be a man from its height and wide shoulders, but she can't be sure. The outline shifts, coming in and out of focus like someone emerging from thick fog.

"I am one who knows you well." The voice is made of mist and smoke, like the figure itself, but this time, Cyn is sure that it is a male voice—though she could not have sworn it was entirely human.

"I am relieved to see my work has kept you safe from harm," he says. The rain beats harder, almost drowning out the soft words.

"Work?" she whispers. "What work?"

"The spell of protection I placed on you the day your mother was killed. A very difficult spell, although I've had to put all my power into strengthening it against the Aesarians or you never would have survived this." Cyn thinks she can hear something like ridicule in the wafting voice. "Still, you need all the help you can get, my girl," the figure continues. "Beheading will indeed be the end of you. Even my incantations have their limits."

Cyn shakes her head, wishing this dream of mist and rain would leave her in peace, but also scared of when it evaporates under the illuminating rays of the sun. Then she will be friendless again, and she is so, so tired.

"I don't need help," she says, and pride gives her voice. Her defiance gives her strength. She needs no one. "I have Smoke Blood."

Then the apparition begins to laugh in earnest, and as his humor travels through his body, his form begins to dispel. "You do *not* have Smoke Blood, my darling," he says. "Nor should you desire it, ever. You have a glorious destiny to fulfill. But be wary of Smoke Blood. It is a greater curse than it is a gift."

The flattering words give her strength, and Cynane lifts her head. "Tell me what I must do," she says hoarsely.

"Escape, of course."

"Can you not just release me?"

The being raises its wide-sleeved smoky arms in a gesture of helplessness. "No," he says. "I cannot move matter, break shackles, or open doors."

"Then it is impossible," she says, her voice raw with frustration.

The smoke fluctuates now, scattering like light through a prism. "You are powerful," he whispers with the subtlety of the softest breeze. "You are a princess of Illyria. You will think of something, blood of my blood…" And then his words melt into the rain, and she cannot hear them anymore.

The last trail of smoke floats out the window, and with it, the last of Cynane's strength. She slips into a sleep so deep that she can see death's door.

ACT TWO:
FUGITIVE

*The greatest way to live with honor in this world
is to be what we pretend to be.*
—Socrates

CHAPTER EIGHT

"WE'RE IN FOR ROUGH WEATHER," CAPTAIN Zeno says, gesturing out to sea where Hephaestion can see towering dark clouds that seem to be growing by the minute. "I want everyone to pack up their tents and go below deck."

"I understand. Thank you, sir," Heph says to the captain of the *Prometheus*, ardently hoping the storm doesn't interfere with his mission for Alex in Egypt. Bad weather can sink a ship, damage it, or blow it off course for weeks. *Don't fail me*, Alex had said when he told him of his request: Heph and Kat are to seek out the famed Princess Laila and bring her back to Macedon to wed the prince, securing her military alliance. The journey will also keep Kat far from Olympias's grasp.

Alexander's words keep echoing in Heph's head. *Don't fail me*. The implication, he knows, is that this might be his last chance.

The captain nods at him before hurrying over to some of the mercenaries on deck. This merchant vessel isn't only carrying timber, but more than twenty soldiers who have hired themselves out to help the Persian satrap of Egypt stamp out rebellion among their new Egyptian subjects. Their tents cram the deck; the smell of unwashed soldiers baking in the sun wafts over it, and their belches intrude on the calming sounds of wind and waves.

Heph looks sideways at Kat, who leans on the railing and stares out at the endless water as if she hasn't heard the captain. Her eyes are pink and swollen, and she's hardly eaten since learning of the murder of her family. Still, she was willing to go on this mission to Egypt to help Alexander—and glad to get away from the palace before the queen returns.

He's still haunted by the scroll he ripped from Leonidas's dead hand. As soon as he got to his room, he cut a slit in his mattress ticking, thrust the scroll deep into the mounds of feathers, and sewed up the slit. Still, the words are forever singed into his memory.

In the womb of the night
Twin stars struggle to shine their light
The moon with great joy will blot out the sun
When the girl kills the boy and the world comes undone.

Above the word *girl* Leonidas had written *Katerina*. Above *boy, Alexander.* And in the margin: *The night the queen gave birth to the prince, she cried out a prophecy given to her by her handmaiden, a secret oracle, and issued a command as cruel as it was necessary.*

Olympias obviously believed the prophecy—believed her daughter would kill her son, unless her daughter was killed first. But it is as clear as day that Kat and Alex have a bond that others could not begin to imagine. Heph *knows* that Katerina would never harm Alexander, at least not on purpose. So why does his stomach squirm at the thought of Leonidas's spidery scrawl? *Because Leonidas was never one to set store in prophecy,* Heph answers himself. And neither is Heph, but still…it must have meant something that the man died to protect this piece of parchment.

It is best to be cautious. Watchful. Leonidas indicated that Olympias tried to kill Kat to prevent the prophecy from coming true, and that is probably the reason she is still trying to kill Kat now. Heph knows the power of prophecies is not always in what they say, but in the fact that people go to such extremes to either avoid or fulfill them. Prophecies, real or false, are incredibly dangerous.

And there's something else… A sense of urgency eats away at him from the inside at the idea that the person he holds dearest in the world—the prince—could be in danger. And worse, that the girl who has come to occupy his thoughts relentlessly, the girl whose voice he thrills to hear even when she is insulting him, the girl whose gaze causes his pride to falter and his heart to beat faster—this girl could be destined to ruin Alexander…and ruin him, too. He doesn't want to believe it—*can't* believe it. And yet some part of him feels the truth in it.

Aristotle always taught Heph to distrust his passions. Taught him to be wary of desire—it is the downfall of many men. Could it be so with Kat?

Even now, the way the increasing wind sets Kat's hair flowing all around her face makes Heph's heart leap and his body sweat. Luckily, a soldier's voice cuts into the turmoil of his thoughts.

"If we can draw Persia's attention back down to Egypt," the soldier says to another, leaning on the ship's railing not too far from Heph, "then maybe they won't attack Macedon. But we'll probably be too late. I hear things are in motion in Persia."

Heph and Kat look at each other in alarm, then gaze out to sea again, pretending they are not listening.

"Why Macedon?" his companion inquires. "Why not Athens or Sparta if Persia's Great King is thirsty for Greek blood?"

"Because King Philip has taken so many Greek lands that Persia is certain to be next on his list. And Caria, Lydia, and most of the Persian islands used to be Greek. Maybe they want to be Greek again, especially if Philip promises them reduced taxes. Easier to kill a lion cub than a lion, right?"

"I wouldn't exactly call Philip a cub," the second soldier says doubtfully. "Maybe twenty years ago, but not now."

"Not Philip—his son, Alexander," the first one explains. "Even now Philip is attacking Byzantium in the north. The Persians have already sent some troops to fight him and keep him busy there. But I've heard the bulk of their army will swing to the south, perhaps with help from Athens, and attack Macedon." He pauses, looks at the sea, and rubs his forehead. "Holy gods, look at those waves. Come on, time to go below, I think."

The men's voices are whipped away by the rising wind as they walk toward the hatch.

Heph's head pounds. He needs to stop wasting his energy fantasizing about Kat and pondering the prophecy in Leonidas's charred hands. He needs to arrange the marriage with Princess Laila. And fast. Alex is going to need a much bigger army if Persia is planning an attack.

Wind whips up spray into his eyes as he reaches out to gently touch Kat's shoulder, feeling the rough fabric of her disguise beneath his fingers. Their mission must remain secret. They are not only traveling to secure a bride but also to secure her armies. There's no need for Alex's enemies to know that Macedon's defenses are about to swell. Heph and Kat are dressed as peasants, but even in the ill-fitting, dun-colored tunic, it is hard to mask Kat's beauty. For a second, he thinks how soft her skin must be under the coarse material.

"Katerina?" he says. "We should go below."

"One moment more," she says, so faintly he can barely make out her voice above the rising wind. "The fresh air, the wind...helps. Like it's sweeping away the hurt."

Of course. On top of his own worries, Kat's grief weighs heavily on Heph, not least because there's simply nothing he can do to assuage it. She has lost those closest to her. Her entire family.

Heph knows what that feels like.

And he cannot fix it.

As though to echo her pain, the sky seems to be hanging lower and grayer. The wind continues to pick up speed. He resists the urge to brush Kat's long wild hair out of her face.

A low rumble of thunder comes from the west, and two Macedonian mercenaries mumble apologies and squeeze by them. The soldiers are packing up their tents as the sailors tie down everything on deck so that it will not be blown into the storm-boiling waters. A gentle rain begins to fall.

Captain Zeno returns, his dark hair already slick against his face. "You need to move below. *Now*," he says. "No more lingering."

"Yes, Captain," Heph says as he eyes rising waves the color of iron. A jagged bolt of lightning illuminates the black clouds on the horizon. Wind rips at the sails as crew members pull on ropes to bring them down to stow. The rain begins to fall harder, angrily. Another sailor pulls down the Macedonian flag of the sixteen-pointed gold star on a light blue background, while three more check the ropes holding the huge timbers in place on deck. The ship bucks in the waves and Kat suddenly grabs onto Heph's arm, nearly losing her balance.

"Come on," he says, trying to keep the urgency from his voice. "Let's pack up."

As Heph, Kat, and the others quickly roll up their tents and sleeping mats and shove their belongings into sacks, a sailor in the rigging calls down, "Captain! Ship approaching!"

The captain holds on to the mast to steady himself as the ship rocks. "What kind?" he calls up, his words almost swept away by the wind. "Merchant vessel? Military trireme? What flag does she wave?"

Everyone cranes to hear what the sailor in the rigging says but he says nothing.

"What flag, you fool?" cries the captain, almost shrieking to be heard above a strong gust of wind.

"Black, sir!"

Black. Heph's arms prickle. No. It can't be. First the storm, now this. How can he win Alex's trust back when the Furies themselves seem to be dogging this mission? He kneels and takes his sword belt out of his pack and buckles it on, his hands slippery in the rain. A peasant wearing a rough-spun tunic would never own a sword like this, and Heph has probably ruined their careful disguise. But now is not the time to worry about it. He reaches again into his bag and removes his bow and a quiver full of rattling arrows.

"Arm yourselves!" the captain cries, striding down the deck. "Get your weapons ready."

"What is it?" Kat asks, eyes wide, looking around at the sudden, deadly serious activity. "What does a black flag mean?"

"Pirates," Heph says, slinging the quiver and bow over his shoulder. "It means pirates. Go hide below deck."

The wave crests above Heph and Kat so suddenly that he

has no time to warn her, only time to open his mouth and grab a rope. It crashes into the ship so hard that Kat flies backward and slams against the far railing. Still clutching the rope, Heph takes her hand and pulls her up.

"Even after all we've been through, you want me to hide among the amphorae like a girl?" she says, eyes blazing.

"Kat, you *are* a girl."

"A *dangerous* girl," she cries hoarsely into the wind, and for a brief, unnerving moment, Heph thinks *if only you knew* how *dangerous*.

Kat stumbles toward her pack but is thrown to her knees by another wave. Undeterred, she crawls forward and brings out her own sword. Heph knows she's good—he's witnessed her on the battlefield himself—but she's not invincible. He's also held her in his arms, her face white as snow while her blood flowed from the gaping hole in her side.

"How can I fight the pirates if I am worried about you getting wounded?" he asks, his desperation rising like the wind.

As she buckles on her sword belt he notices that her eyes are like fiery emeralds, her face flushed. The listless apathy of the past three days has been replaced by a fierce energy, the kind she radiated on the battlefield. "If I am," she says, staring at him steadily, "you'll just have to kiss me again." She turns to face the black-flagged ship bobbing ever closer.

Her words are like a jolt—and even though his heart is already pumping fast, Heph feels heat flood his body. He couldn't have heard her correctly. Kiss her *again*? He's never kissed her in his life, though he can think of little else.

Heph opens his mouth to ask her but the ship rises high on a swell. He grabs hold of Kat with one arm and the rope with the other. The ship slams down into a trough as water crashes in on all sides. Some on deck have managed to grab hold of something while others go flying like rag dolls and hit the rail or deck with heavy thuds.

A man pops his head out of the hatch and passes out armor the mercenaries stowed below to take with them to Egypt. The soldiers, along with Captain Zeno and his crew, quickly strap on breastplates and greaves, buckle on sword belts, and clap on helmets. Next the man tosses out spears, bows, quivers full of arrows, and shields. They laugh as Kat pushes her way into their midst and grabs a helmet, breastplate, shield, and spear.

Heph is furious. If he could tie her up and lock her below deck he would. But there's no time for that. Not with the pirate ship angling up beside them, its grappling plank raised high and ready to slam down on their rail. Now he will have to fight with one eye on the enemy and one on Kat.

As the other men get into formation, Heph puts on a helmet and breastplate. Buffeted by the whistling wind, he climbs up the mid mast. When he reaches a good point to fire arrows, he stops and looks down. Rain falls in his eyes. As the enemy vessel bobs alongside the *Prometheus,* its grappling plank crashes down. Below him, the Macedonian mercenaries and sailors crowd together behind the timber. The men, he is glad to see, have pushed Kat to the far rear.

Heph nocks his arrow and trains it on the first pirate swaying on the grappling plank. A filthy bandana covers the man's forehead and his mud-colored beard is long and matted. There's a crazed look in his eyes as he waves his sword in the air, and the pirates behind him beat their swords on shields and yell at the top of their voices in a language Heph doesn't understand.

Heph fires. The arrow hits the pirate between the eyes. The man stops as if in surprise, then falls into the narrow space between the two heaving ships. Heph fires at the man behind him and hits him in the neck—but the pirate vessel also has an archer.

An arrow flies by Heph and lodges itself deep into the mast only two finger-breadths past his cheek. No matter how quickly Heph launches his arrows, he can't stop the mass of pirates now spilling onto the deck with wild cries. The Macedonian mercenaries crouch behind the timber and launch their spears at the invaders, most of them hitting their mark. Then they bolt forward with swords drawn as more pirates scramble onto the deck.

"Up there!" one of the pirates cries, pointing with his sword to Heph. "Get him!" Heph aims an arrow straight down. As a pirate starts to climb the rigging, a spear embeds itself in his back and he falls off.

Kat looks up at Heph, then unsheathes her sword, and jumps into the melee of waving arms, gleaming swords, and red-crested helmets below. Arrow nocked in the bowstring, he shifts right and left, trying to pick an enemy target. But everyone is moving so fast he is afraid he might shoot one of his own men—or Kat.

Where is Kat? Over the cries and clanging of the battle below, over the moaning wind and creaking ship, Heph hears his own heart beating. His own rapid breathing. *Calm.* He has to stay calm and focused to get through this. To get Kat through this.

Then he sees her again, fighting like Athena on the prow with a man twice her size. The pirate grins, obviously thinking it's a good joke to fight a skinny girl, but Kat holds her ground. She holds it—but doesn't gain. Heph fires at the man, and the arrow sinks deep into his back. Kat doesn't even look up at him as she moves on to the next pirate, her sword a blur of silver.

A pirate pops his head out of the hatch and another one

takes a heavy wood casket from him—gold coins or jewels, Heph assumes, as he tries to take aim. But the ship rolls again, and the men duck behind a Macedonian fighting another pirate and spring onto their ship.

Lightning tears across the sky and thunder booms as rain beats down. Up high on the mast, when the ship rises, Heph feels as if he is riding it into the clouds. When it sinks, he wonders if it will slam into sand. Sometimes the ship rolls so far to either side, he could almost reach out and touch the waves. Below him, soldiers and pirates slide into the rail, somersault across the deck, and slam into the heap of timber tied between the masts. The pirates back on their own vessel are shouting orders Heph can't understand, and those remaining on the ship suddenly retreat, nimbly climbing onto the grappling plank, and jump onto their ship. They row away, oars battling the waves furiously. But why?

The answer comes to Heph in the slight movement in his peripheral vision. Turning to face starboard, he sees another ship flying a black flag, its many white oars beating like birds' wings through the molten seas. Heph's heart stutters when he recognizes what kind of ship this is: a Rhodian battle rammer that the pirates must have captured. This ship has an eight-foot-long spade of sharp bronze on its bow just below the waterline. Now that the pirates have plundered the *Prometheus,* they will destroy it so there is no word of their crimes. Everyone will think the ship went down in the storm.

"Battle ram!" he cries as he scrambles down the rigging, but the wind whips his words into the roiling sea. Does anyone else see it? Or are they all too busy fighting? Kat! Where is Kat? He leaps onto the heaving deck just as she staggers toward him, a bloody sword in her hand. Heph sees a jagged cut on her upper arm and trickles of blood down to her wrist, but she doesn't seem to notice.

"Kat, that second ship is a rammer," he shouts, watching it struggle toward them. "It will try to sink us."

"Heph, I have an idea," she says, her hand cupped to her mouth. "Several of us should climb up the masts and those below should pass up jugs of olive oil. We can throw them down onto the rammer."

"What?" Heph says, wondering if he's heard her correctly over the whistling wind.

"That barrel of tar, over there," she says, pointing with her sword to a barrel lashed to the mast. "Heph, dip your arrows in it, set them on fire, and shoot them onto the oil on the decks of the rammer before it strikes us."

Suddenly he understands. Olive oil—used to light lamps all over the world—is highly flammable. And the tar that sailors use to seal planks and repair small leaks is almost explosive. "It could work," he says, "if the rain doesn't put the fire out."

"And if it doesn't set our own ship ablaze in the process," says a voice behind Heph. He turns to see Captain Zeno with a wild, determined look in his eyes. "I'll issue the orders," the captain says, before turning and lurching down the deck to a group of sailors.

Heph looks at Kat quizzically. "You sure like throwing pots," he says. Kat just smiles at him.

Within moments Heph is high in the rigging next to Kat as she lobs an amphora of olive oil onto the lurching deck of the attacking ship, which is having a hard time picking up ramming speed against the angry waves. Below them and on the other mast, mercenaries and soldiers are also tossing amphorae passed up by men below. Many pots miss as the ships twist and heave, but several hit the rammer's deck. The pirates look up and laugh as the amphorae crack open and oil spills all over the deck.

Heph has a quiver full of arrows dipped in tar. The sailor below her now passes Kat a lantern filled with lit oil lamps. She slides up one of the ox-horn panels and tries to keep it from swinging as Heph dips his first arrow into the flame. It catches immediately despite the rain.

He aims for a slick spot full of broken pottery on the rammer. For a moment a large wave obscures his view, then he spots his target and lets his first arrow fly, quickly followed by two more.

His arrows stick deep into the deck. The flames catch and leap across the ship, sputtering at times from the rain. One of the pirates grabs a rolled-up sail, opens it, and throws it on the flames. It, too, catches fire. The rammer is quite close to the *Prometheus* now and picking up speed. The rowers below deck must be unaware of the fire above because they keep rowing, oars dipping into the churning sea again and again.

"Hold tight!" Heph cries, shouldering his bow and wrapping his arms in the rigging. "They're going to ram!" Kat throws the lantern below and plunges both hands into the tangled ropes.

With a horrifying crunch of splintering wood, the ships collide. Heph and Kat are thrown back from the mast and dangle over the deck before swinging back in. Below them, many men on deck fall, and one man on the other mast loses his grip and flies screaming into the sea. A comrade on deck throws him a rope. Heph sees flailing, foam-flecked arms swim toward it and latch on.

Pushed by wind and waves, the rammer slips back from the *Prometheus*, which is a good thing, as the rammer's top deck is now burning brightly. When a large swell tosses the vessel, several men fall into the flames and catch fire. Screaming, beating at their tunics, they throw themselves overboard and disappear.

Soon the rammer is an inferno, the flames spread by the raging wind, as the pirates leap into the sea. Heph, Kat, and the others up the masts climb down and watch the seas push the burning vessel farther and farther away from the *Prometheus*.

"Now all we have to worry about," Heph says, "is whether this ship is going to sink."

As if in response, Captain Zeno climbs nimbly out the hatch to survey the scene. A grin spreads across his tanned face as he spots the enemy ship going down in flames.

"How is it below, Captain?" asks a gangly young sailor with a badly slashed chin.

"It's not a bad breach," Zeno replies. "They couldn't ram us full speed with the waves interfering. We'll need to take shifts bailing, but we will be able to limp into the nearest port. I'll have to do some calculations to figure out which one."

Heph knows he should be grateful they're not sinking. After all, not many ships survive a Rhodian battle rammer. But all he can think about is the delay. *Don't fail me*, Alex said. Already things have gone terribly wrong.

"Remove this vermin," Zeno says to the young sailor, gesturing to the pirates' bodies littering the deck, before climbing back into the hatch.

Kat stares at a dead pirate with a bloody chest, his bandana half off his head. "Writing," she says. "On his forehead."

Cringing, she pulls the filthy rag off entirely. Heph sees the words *Runaway Slave* tattooed in Greek on the man's tanned skin. She goes to another body and yanks off that bandana. *Paid in Full*, his tattoo reads.

"That's why pirates wear bandanas," he says, as two sailors pick up the body and carry it to the railing. "They're all runaway slaves marked in some way on their foreheads."

"That's horrible," she says. "No wonder they run away and become pirates."

Heph sees the corpse fly over the railing as two large waves like foaming blue-gray lips open wide to swallow it.

Heph, all sweat and seawater, climbs stiffly out of the hatch and gulps in cool night air. This afternoon, after the storm vanished as suddenly as it appeared, a fresh wind filled the sails, pushing them east. But now the *Prometheus* is anchored for the night, rocking gently. A half-moon streams a silver glow through scattered clouds, and creaking lanterns swing on poles, spreading warm arcs of golden light on deck. He plunks down next to Kat, who is sitting against the railing sharing cheese and olives with other men exhausted from bailing. They sit cross-legged looking deeply into wine cups, their flesh orange in the lanterns' glow.

She holds a chunk of cheese up to him.

"Water," he says, his throat hoarse. His back, shoulders, arms, and legs are throbbing from two hours of nonstop bailing. His neck is as stiff as a plank of wood. Even his feet hurt. His arm shakes as he reaches for Kat's proffered goatskin.

"Has the captain said yet where we're heading?" asks the Macedonian mercenary whom Heph recognizes as the one who called King Philip a lion and Alexander the cub.

Drinking deeply, Heph nods, afraid of Kat's reaction. She hasn't told him much about the sorceress, Ada of Caria, who lives in the mountains above Halicarnassus. Only that in the week or so Kat spent there, she learned years' worth of weapons training and can fight battle-hardened warriors with uncanny skill.

And Kat made it clear that she is utterly devoted to Ada.

"Halicarnassus," he says casually, wiping the dribbles off

his chin. "With the water we're taking on, we won't be there until tomorrow afternoon, he thinks, even with a fair wind."

"Halicarnassus!" Kat says, her face brightening just as he feared it would. "We could visit Ada! She doesn't live so far from harbor."

"No, Kat," Heph says firmly. He looks at the sailors and soldiers nearby. Some of them have the musical accents of Lydia and Caria—Persian provinces. Others have the crisp bite of Athenian Greek. They need to be careful, especially after what happened to Arridheus. No one can know they are on a mission for the prince of Macedon. "My...*father* insisted we get to Egypt as quickly as possible. As soon as we dock in Halicarnassus, we will find the next ship south."

A mutinous look settles on her face. But before she can speak, a black-bearded sailor sitting nearby leans forward and asks in a Carian accent, "Are you talking about Princess Ada of Caria? Because if so, she's not there anymore."

"What?" Kat asks, her expression clouding. "Where did she go?"

"No one knows," the sailor replies. "But when I left last week, it was all anyone could talk about. There was a strange fog hanging over the mountains, they said, and when people went up to investigate, they suspected that dark magic had taken place there—the lady was gone. Some say she has a brother still alive, but no one has seen him either. If you don't mind my asking, how would you know the princess? She is said to be a recluse."

"What? The likes of us knowing a princess!" Heph says in the best country accent he can muster, forcing a smile. He shoots Kat a warning look and stands up, stretching. Then he ambles over to the bow and stands behind the painted wooden figurehead of a muscular chained Prometheus, an open-winged eagle pecking at his exposed liver.

A moment later, Kat joins him.

"We need to see what has happened to her, see if we can help her," she says quietly, yet urgency hums in her voice.

He shakes his head. "We are on an urgent mission, Kat," he replies. "We have no time to waste."

She says nothing, and when he turns toward her he can see, even in the moonlight, the stubborn tightening of her jaw. "The gods have sent not only a storm but pirates to take us off our planned course, Heph," she says. "Do you think it is a coincidence that, despite boarding a ship to Egypt, we are now heading for Halicarnassus? If anyone has the power to defeat…our family's enemies, it's my aunt, and it's a short journey to her…farm from port. A few hours at most."

She has a point. The *Prometheus* could have been attacked a few miles away and now be heading to Miletus or Apasa. Could Fate itself be at work here? At Mieza he learned two prevalent viewpoints about destiny. Some modern philosophers insist that everything in life is random and meaningless and that believing anything else is ignorant superstition. But most people believe that there are no coincidences, and if you look closely enough, you can see divine Fate's connecting threads. Is this diversion to Halicarnassus such a thread?

Heph rubs his forehead. To Ada or to Egypt tomorrow? What is the right answer? He can't fail Alex. Not again. If only he could be sure what to—

A pulsating ball of light with a fiery tail streaks across the sky, illuminating the ship, the sea, and the sky as if it were midday. Heph's seen shooting stars before but none that bright or that close. Kat inhales sharply and some of the men shout and jump up, pointing in wonder. A moment later, it's gone.

"It was headed east," Kat whispers. "To Caria."

CHAPTER NINE

ALEXANDER FEELS A TWIST IN HIS GUT AS THE prisoners lurch forward through the crowd. Despite the ovenlike heat, all of Pella seems to have turned out for the trial. The courtyard is packed. Every palace window and balcony is crammed with faces, and dozens of people sit on the orange tiled roofs.

Hagnon, Theopompus, Gordias, and Kadmus—his council—shuffle up the scaffold stairs, their manacles clanking, and stand in a little clump of misery in front of Alex. He slows his breathing and tries to calm the rapid stutter of his heart. Today he needs to show he is worthy to be a king. Today, a member of his council may die.

He's seated ramrod-straight on a throne, his ankles crossed nonchalantly, a studied expression of alert dignity on his face. Behind him stands Sarina, Alex's new personal attendant. Despite rumors that she has become *more* than an attendant— that she's been attending to his needs in the bedroom as well—Alexander has kept their relationship platonic. Though he can't deny the effect her beauty has on him, and the persuasion of her hands against his tight muscles, he is far more moved by her words.

Her sandalwood perfume wafts near him and gives him strength as he rises to stand, a liquid regal move he has practiced for public appearances. He faces his council members.

"At least one of you—maybe more—is a traitor," he says loudly and slowly, projecting his voice the way Aristotle taught him for large audiences. "Each day at noon, I will pick one of your names at random from a pot and I will question that person with all the insight gods give to kings. If treachery is found, the traitor shall be beheaded immediately."

The four counselors look at one another in panic as time stretches out unbearably. "Theopompus," Alex says, "do you have anything to say?"

Theopompus, his turquoise eyes huge, moves his bulky frame forward. The normally exquisitely groomed minister is rumpled, his hair uncombed.

"My lord," he says in his deep rich voice, "is it possible that it was one of the guards who accompanied the young prince Arridheus who sold the secret to our enemies?"

Alex feels mounting irritation, a grinding sensation on the back of his neck. Theopompus's charm and persuasion are legendary in the Greek world, and now he is using them as weapons against him.

"And the traitor arranged to have himself slaughtered or his hand cut off?" he asks harshly. Theopompus lowers his head and steps back. "Gordias," Alex says, "what do you have to say?" Gordias hobbles forward, the manacles almost too heavy for his ancient frame to bear. Alex casts his gaze around the spectators, many of whom wince or shake their heads. No one wants to see a bearded grandfather, beloved of the gods he serves, treated this way. Alex feels a bitter pang of regret, but he steels himself for what must be done. The spy must be rooted out. For the sake of Macedon.

"The gods protect the innocent," the old priest says, spitting on the scaffold. He doesn't look at Alex. His wrinkled face is a mask of disapproval.

"Priests always speak in riddles," Alex says to the muttering crowd. "Though in this case mysterious words could be hiding treason." He turns to the next prisoner. "Hagnon."

"My lord, my prince, I protest my innocence!" Hagnon chirps, lifting plump, manacled hands in supplication. "For many years I have served your father loyally! Write to him! Ask him!"

Alex raises his hand as if to ward off a blow. "Silence," he commands. Do they really think he savors their discomfort any more than they themselves do? He'd rather be anywhere but here. Except that one of them is the rat. One of them has sold him out. One of them has offered up his little brother to the enemy and will do greater damage until he is rooted out. The idea that someone this high in his ranks is using Alex, speaking to him every day in meetings while smugly hiding his true allegiance, is nauseating. *Especially* when Alexander has always prided himself on his ability to detect men's true nature in their eyes. How has this traitor continued to elude him?

He must remind himself of Sarina's story: The god who allowed his people to prove themselves, one by one, in death. He takes a deep breath. "Kadmus," he says.

The young general's calm gray eyes meet his. "I am ready for trial," he says. "I have nothing to hide."

Alex hopes that this is true. Above all, it would pain him to find Kadmus at fault. The general has been nothing but noble. He is young and strong, intelligent and reliable. He has become what Heph was to Alex.

Well, almost.

Alex is unwilling to believe that he has lost a friend—a brother, nearly—in Heph. Only that he needed space from Heph's hotheadedness in order to find his own voice as regent. And Heph needed space, too, to cool down, to be of real service. Alex feels sure that when Heph returns from Egypt, all will be well between them again.

"Sarina," Alex says now, and she walks forward holding a many-handled *hydria*, used for fetching water. On its bulbous glazed exterior, red soldiers clash on a black painted background. Inside are four *ostraca*, pottery shards, on which she has scratched the names of his counselors with a knife.

Alex puts his hand down the vase's neck into its cool, dark belly, and picks up the first *ostracon* he touches. *Not Kadmus. Please not Kadmus.*

It's not, and relief floods him as he calls out loudly, "Hagnon, son of Protis."

Hagnon is trembling like a palsied man, his eyes flitting right and left as if seeking escape. When he doesn't step forward, the guard pushes him hard and he stumbles, awkwardly regaining balance as his chains clatter.

"When my guards searched your palace quarters and your country estate," Alexander says, "do you know what they found?" Hagnon opens his mouth but only a squeak comes out.

"They found heaps of foreign gold coins hidden in the walls," Alex says, walking around the prisoner, his hands clasped tightly behind his back. "Persian darics, Athenian owls, and Phoenician shekels, as well as gold cups and jeweled belts."

The murmurs die away and an eerie silence blankets the crowd. "You do not come from a wealthy family, Hagnon. You worked your way up in the ministry, and your salary, though generous, would never buy such treasure. Did you obtain it from Macedon's enemies as bribes?"

"N-no, my prince," Hagnon says, his entire body shaking as if he has the falling sickness. Sweat pours off his face.

"How much did you receive for selling out my brother?" Alex says, feeling anger flush his face and neck. "How much was Arri worth to you?"

"I never—I swear! I am not a spy!" Hagnon cries.

Alex steps closer and stares directly into the treasurer's brown eyes. He needs to harness his abilities and enter the man's memory himself. What did he do to persuade Hagnon to loosen his purse strings at the council meeting? He must do the same things now. He calms his breathing, relaxes, and tries to empty his mind, though the trying itself must be a thought. After a time, he thinks of swimming in the river behind the palace on hot summer days, splashing his friends. He remembers laughing with Aristotle and the other boys around the fire pit on winter evenings at school in Mieza.

It doesn't work. He's still standing there, staring into frightened, darting little eyes, aware of sweat trickling under his tunic and a general miasma of impatience in the crowd. He wonders if perhaps it's not supposed to work, that no one should be able to enter the memories of others at will. But this is to find a traitor, he reminds himself. To save innocent lives, to keep the entire nation of Macedon strong. He makes a silent vow to himself and any gods who might be listening: he will never trespass on anyone's memories unless it is absolutely necessary. Like now.

Then he relaxes again and clears his mind, experiencing that strange sensation of loss at being human, at being Alex. He replaces the emptiness with thoughts of Kat, her arms around him, flying over the fields with him on Bucephalus. He feels her soft cheek against the back of his neck, the warmth of her against his back, and the wind in his face. He feels that anything is possible.

Around him, the harsh sunlight fades and all sounds are silenced as he's pulled forward. He enters the small dark eyes and travels through a tunnel of white light, emerging in Hagnon's office in the palace.

A tan man, his long beard braided with ivory adornments, slaps down a heavy pouch of coins on the desk, and Hagnon hands him a small scroll. The man takes it, grinning. Alex hovers invisibly, studying him. He wears gold earrings and a red-and-blue checked tunic. Persian.

With a jolt, Alex reels backward through the tunnel. He finds himself once more in his body on the scaffold, his ears ringing. He looks at Hagnon, at the crowded courtyard, at a boy eating a cucumber on the roof, his legs dangling over the side, in wonder and confusion, and then remembers where he is and what he has to do.

"What information have you sold to our enemies? Military secrets?" Alex asks, revolted by the sweat pouring off the man. The minster's limp dark hair is slick with it, his tunic sticking to his paunchy body.

"You have been privy to all of my father's war planning: the number of men we have, the kinds of munitions, and the tactics we devise." He moves closer, the sour stench of fear nearly engulfing him, and whispers, "Are you the reason why King Philip is failing in Byzantium?"

"I would never!" Hagnon says, his voice cracking.

Alex whispers again, "What was on the document you gave the Persian with the long black beard in your office, Hagnon? The one who gave you a sack of gold in return?"

Hagnon steps back as if Alex struck him, his eyes open wide. He shakes his head. "How do you know?" he asks in a shaking voice. "No one was there. But it wasn't what you think, I swear…"

Now tears are falling onto his pale, sagging cheeks. He crumples to his knees and tries to grab Alex's hands to kiss them. Disgusted, Alex turns away. Behind the throne, Sarina looks at him, solemn-faced.

He has killed many men in battle but that is very different. In battle the enemy is trying to kill *him*. Weapons raised, they race toward him, equally matched in strength. There is a fairness about it. He even grieves for his slain enemies afterward, for lives lost with bravery and honor. But this sobbing wreck of a man before him isn't able to defend himself at all. Worse, as Alex turns back to look at him, he sees a puddle forming around his knees. Hagnon has wet himself in fear. The other prisoners share Alex's distaste. They look away, wincing.

Alex straightens his shoulders and reminds himself that traitors deserve death. He has no right to be regent of Macedon—or ever hope to be king—if he doesn't have the strength to go through with this. He tries to imagine himself the brave god of Sarina's stories. He tries to imagine himself the king he is meant to become.

A drop of his own sweat trickles from his eyebrow onto his cheek. He wants to wipe it off with the back of his hand, but the knowledge that hundreds of people are watching him keeps his hand at his side. He doesn't want the people to think he is sweating because he is nervous or indecisive.

His gaze sweeps over the crowd. A pretty woman at a palace window leans out, her eyes wide in expectation. An old man near the scaffold stares at Hagnon, his mouth open. To Alex's left, a group of well-dressed merchants mumble to each other behind their hands. Everyone here is expecting him to be strong, to prove that despite his youth he is a leader.

"Hagnon," Alex says quietly. "This is your last chance. Tell me what you sold to the Persian. Was it our plans to take Arri to safety?"

"No, not that!" Hagnon, still kneeling, shakes his head. "Other things, but never that!"

A spike of anger shoots through Alex's entire body. Arri, his little brother who can't understand what is happening, is still missing. And this man, though perhaps he did not betray this particular secret, cannot be trusted. This man, muttering nonsense, is making Alex look like a weak, indecisive fool.

His father expects more of him. Macedon *needs* more of him. He looks around at the expectant faces of the crowd.

"Kill him," Alex says, almost choking on the words. He swallows hard as a guard steps forward. A sword flashes in the sun and comes down with an awful *thud*, like a knife hitting a melon. Blood sprays over Alex's white tunic as Hagnon's head rolls into the crowd.

He swallows again, praying to all the gods that his face doesn't show the horror and sickness entwined in his gut.

People scream and push backward as the head hits the ground and rolls to their feet. On the scaffold, Hagnon's body is still kneeling, blood pouring from the fountain of a neck, until it falls to the side.

Alex looks back at Sarina, trying to control the faint tremor throughout his body. Sarina nods almost imperceptibly, her eyes steady. As far as he can tell, she did not even wince at the violence. And the people—in the courtyard, in the windows, on the balconies and roofs—wear expressions of grim satisfaction. The prince regent has killed a traitor in his father's council. When the time comes, he will be a strong king.

Alex takes a deep breath and feels his stomach unknot. So

this is what it feels like to be a ruler who is both respected and feared.

He turns to Gordias, Kadmus, and Theopompus. "Tomorrow, one of you will be tried, unless the guilty one admits to betraying my brother." Alex waits for the relief to wash over him. To feel calm now that the deed has been done. But peace eludes him. His trackers have lost Arri's trail—it's as though the earth has opened up and swallowed him. And the traitor is still out there, while the Aesarian Lords, only a day's ride away, probably have Cynane and are planning another attack.

He has always longed to rule, watching his father govern with a mixture of awe and jealousy. But is this what it is like—one catastrophe after another? If only he had someone to talk to, but the people he trusts most in the world are gone. He sent them out himself, and now they are far beyond his reach.

There is stark silence as he turns and leaves the courtyard. He has to remind himself to walk slowly, both to appear self-assured and to hide his limp. In actuality, he just wants to run.

The next day, thunder rumbles from the distant hills, and the clouds look like molten iron, heavy with rain. Birds, eager to be back in their nests before the storm breaks, flitter low and swift across the palace courtyard. Alex is glad the day is cooler than yesterday when the people saw him sweat. Even more spectators, if possible, have crowded into the courtyard today. He studies the three men standing before him in chains.

Theopompus's usually pristine teal robes are now filthy from the dungeon, and his carefully coiffed hair has lost its dazzling sheen of gold dust. White streaks run through it, along with dirt and cobwebs. Gordias's white robes are caked with dirt. His long snowy beard is matted. He is bowed, but only with age. His dark eyes burn bright and hard with anger. But Kadmus looks as if he's just returned from a pleasure hunt or military training, a bit sweaty and rumpled, but perfectly relaxed.

Once again, Sarina proffers the *hydria* and Alex dips his hand into its belly, fingering the three *ostraca* left.

Not Kadmus.

Hiding a swell of relief, Alex says, "Theopompus, son of Nicander, step forward." The golden-haired minister musters his considerable dignity and does so. "When my guards searched your quarters, they found countless jewels and foreign gold."

"Gifts, my lord," Theopompus says, looking Alex straight in the eye. "For many years I have served Macedon as ambassador. Foreign governments give me gifts, just as Macedon gives gifts to visiting dignitaries. It is no secret."

"Your lifestyle goes above and beyond gifts. Does treachery fund your lavish estates?" Alex asks. "In your country houses we found entire harems of slaves for your bed, the most expensive paramours money can buy. A collection of rare gems. Chests of gold. A statue by Praxiteles."

"I have my own businesses, my lord," Theopompus says, lifting his chin. "Profitable and legal."

Alex steps so close to Theopompus that they are almost nose to nose. He stares into eyes of the most exquisite pale blue-green color and does the same thing he did yesterday. First he relaxes, making a silent vow to never use this power except for good. Then he empties his mind for a long moment before thinking—no, *feeling*—one of the happiest times of his life. This time he relives the moment when the Aesarian Lords blew the horn for retreat at the battle of Pellan Fields, when it seemed that the sweet nectar of victory pulsed through his veins instead of blood.

He finds himself disembodied, whipping through the tunnel of light. He emerges in a large, richly furnished parlor, one he's visited before with his father; it is in Theopompus's hillside estate right outside Pella. An Athenian, by the cut of his cloak, snaps his fingers and slaves wheel in a magnificent larger-than-life-sized statue of a nude Aphrodite with blond hair tumbling down her shoulders. Her wide blue eyes seem surprised that someone has come upon her bathing, and her lips are parted as if she is about to speak. Alex is most amazed at how the fingers of her left hand push into the flesh of her thigh in a way that is incredibly lifelike.

Yes, this is the statue by Praxiteles, the most famous sculptor of all time, now retired in Athens, his hands stiff with age, his chisel passed to other, lesser artists.

"The Athenian gave you the Praxiteles in return for... what?" he asks. Theopompus's eyes widen.

"I am the traitor," Gordias says suddenly, stepping forward with clanking manacles and standing between Theopompus and Alex. "I am your spy."

"You?" Alex says incredulously. Theopompus, too, stares at Gordias, his mouth open in shock.

"We searched your rooms," Alex says. "There was nothing. Not even much furniture, no comforts at all."

"Perhaps I've hidden my ill-gotten wealth too well for your men to find," Gordias says, his reedy old voice quavering with anger. "Perhaps I've given Macedonian secrets to our enemies for free out of the loathing I feel for the injustices of unwise rulers."

Alex steps closer and sees raw hostility in those dark and ancient eyes. The granddaughter Philip raped and Olympias may have murdered—that must be it. It has been there all along, concealed by the theatrics of a clever spy. Gordias never fell asleep at all those council meetings. He just pretended so everyone would think him a harmless old fool. Alex steps closer to travel into those contemptuous eyes but Gordias turns his face away.

"Enough of your tricks," the old man whispers.

Alex wonders for a moment if Gordias has guessed that he possesses this power. He must, for no other person has refused to meet Alex's gaze. Evidently Gordias doesn't want Alex to look too closely into his past.

Gordias has confessed to treason in front of hundreds of people, and now Alex will have to execute him, the white-bearded grandfather beloved by Pellans for his intercession with the gods on their behalf. He glances back at Sarina, who is also gauging the mood of the crowd, her face tense. Kadmus's mouth is a hard, thin line, and Theopompus's large features look like a tragic theater mask.

Alex nods once, and a guard takes Gordias by the arm.

"A chief priest of the gods cannot be executed unless permission is granted by the oracle of Delphi," Gordias says loudly, angrily shaking off the guards.

"It is true, my lord," Sarina says hastily, stepping forward. "Gordias belongs to the gods, not to you, and only the gods can decide his fate."

Relief rushes through Alex. It will no longer be his decision to execute Gordias, but the gods'. And if they decide he is guilty, Alex will hold a private execution so the people won't see the silver head go rolling off the withered shoulders.

"Agreed," Alex says, relieved at something else, too. Kadmus isn't the spy. Kadmus can go free. "Kadmus and Theopompus, you are released. Gordias, you will stay in prison until we receive word from Delphi."

Soldiers hustle Gordias off the scaffold, his shackles rattling. Theopompus, sweat trickling off his forehead, holds out his hands for his chains to be removed. Without looking at Alex, he climbs heavily down the steps and hurries off in the direction of the baths. Kadmus stands calmly while the guard removes his shackles. "May I return to the barracks?" he asks.

Alex nods. Then, holding his head high, he climbs down the scaffold and strides back to the palace, feeling as exhausted as if he had fought in an hours-long battle.

In fact, this *was* a battle. One in which he has lost men. And he has lost something else, too, some final shard of his boyhood, an inner peace he once knew and may never know again.

But for now, he has work to do. Of his father's council, two are dead and another in prison. This can mean only one thing: it's time for some replacements.

CHAPTER TEN

DARIUS, BOTH NEPHEW *AND* GRANDSON TO the Great King Artaxerxes, watches patiently as the king stands up from the imperial table on the dais, a tall, slender figure, his enormous diadem making him seem even taller. All the guests in the throne room stand up from their tables with him. Darius notes with a silent sneer that some of them are drunk enough to knock over their stools, even though it is only midday.

The ceremonial hall of the Persepolis palace is crowded with members of the court, feasting at banquet tables placed between countless red columns ten times the height of a man. Smoke from incense burners rises all the way to the golden horns of two-headed bulls that sit atop each column. Bars of slanting light flooding in through high open windows reveal that everyone has worn their most colorful clothing to this meal to honor the Bactrian envoys—red and lapis blue, Tyrian purple and forest-green, spangled with gold and silver—except for Darius, who wears his customary black tunic and trousers of the finest Milesian wool, a single crow in a court of countless peacocks.

The Great King waves, a short, dismissive gesture, the signal for everyone to stay where they are. But Darius rises to join him, the world's most powerful king, ruler of all of the Satrapies of Persia from his envied capital in the center of his three-million-square-mile empire. With a spike of irritation, he notices that Artaxerxes's other favorite advisor, the eunuch general Bagoas, joins them. The womanish general, as he calls him to his friends, always pushes Artaxerxes to do exactly the opposite of what Darius advises.

"Perhaps, sire, we could speak in private," Darius suggests, stroking his well-trimmed beard. When the king nods, Darius notes in satisfaction Bagoas's obvious disappointment and his awkwardness as he returns to the banquet table.

"Oburzus is training the young horses," the old king says. "Let us speak there."

Darius smiles broadly. "Yes, sire, let's!" But he groans inwardly. How could a man so intent on ruling the largest empire the world has ever seen enjoy watching horses gallop in circles?

With the king's guards stomping behind them, the two men walk through jewellike gardens with monkeys chattering in palm trees, past fountains splashing into blue rectangular pools, and across brightly painted courtyards. The king's sequined purple robes billow behind him as he strides forward, and Darius must hurry to follow the taller man, wondering yet again how an eighty-five-year-old can ride horses, race upstairs, and walk for hours on end. The king has none of the weaknesses of age and is never sick. Some members of the court whisper he is, in fact, immortal.

As soon as they enter the racetrack, Artaxerxes waves his hand, and all the spectators stand up and move to benches on the other side.

The king watches a stallion gallop toward them. "Some

say it is harder for horses to qualify for my army than it is for men," he says in a low voice, never taking his eyes off the animal. "And they are correct."

Every angle in the king's sharp, bony face radiates amusement. "Horses are flight creatures, prey in the wild. Their inborn tendency to panic helps them survive. We must train them against their instincts. That is why one well-trained warhorse is worth twenty foot soldiers."

Darius nods and tries to keep an expression of polite interest. "Like a clever horse, we, too, must keep going in the face of obstacles, sire. The disappearance of Princess Zofia of Sardis has still not been solved, but Macedon has accepted our story that she died suddenly. Girls often die of fevers—it is not so unusual."

The king nods. "Though it is unusual when a princess disappears," he says, almost hissing the last words, his dark eyes gliding from the track below to Darius.

Darius starts inwardly, but his well-trained face continues to smile benignly. "I imagine the prince of Macedon will not mind our solution," he says. As soon as word had come thundering over the Royal Road from a sweat-soaked courier that Princess Zofia had vanished, Darius had, with the Great King's approval, personally selected three girls from the royal harem to be Alexander's new brides. They were all dark-haired and doe-eyed, with the smooth skin of women who bathed in milk. Their sparkling eyes smiled at Darius, proof that they found him attractive despite his forty years. His body is as hard as it was two decades ago, and much more muscular. His proud, hawklike face fascinated them almost as much as the aura of power he wears like cologne, a scent that leaves women swooning in his wake.

He watched the girls excitedly climb into the royal *harmanaxa* of bright red cowhide with their eunuchs. This magnificent vehicle would take the brides sixteen hundred miles west along the Royal Road, from Persepolis to the port of Apasa, where the brides would board a ship bound for Macedon.

The thought of what their gauzy robes concealed caused Darius many agonizing hours since then, the needling pinpricks of desire. And then the surge of true power when he refused to give in to what his body demanded.

Artaxerxes's next words seem to echo Darius's thought. "With these new brides, the boy will be spending the next several months in bed. I know I would, if I were sixteen."

Darius needs to move the conversation in another direction. "The point is, Uncle, Philip is trapped in Byzantium now that we are reinforcing the city. When we distract Prince Alexander with the brides, who will be defending Macedon? Now is the time."

"I don't want outright war, grandson," Artaxerxes says as he removes his heavy crown and sets it on the bench beside him, rubbing the deep red mark at the top of his forehead. It irritates Darius like a pebble in his boot that the king refers to him in the more remote relationship—grandson rather than nephew. Darius's mother, Artaxerxes's daughter, married the Great King's much younger half brother in a typical arranged palace union.

"These marriages will help us avoid that," Artaxerxes continues. "We are playing both sides against the middle. Luring Macedon in as our ally through the brides. Defending our other ally, Byzantium, against their attacker, Macedon. We are using diplomacy to sow confusion and uncertainty. No one knows exactly where they stand with us. It is a good plan. A Persian plan." A hot desert breeze blows a wispy silver tendril against his lined cheek.

"Macedon is rising, that is clear, sire," Darius says. "But

they are small as yet. The conquests of which they are so proud are rebellious clans, cattle thieves and raiders. They haven't yet conquered an organized nation with a strong military. Now would be the time to vanquish them. Before Philip returns. Before their prince gains more experience."

"Vanquish? Oh, I think not," Artaxerxes replies. From an ornately jeweled scabbard, he unsheathes his dagger with a slow scrape and holds it up. Darius can't help but admire how the smooth, polished iron glints in the sun. It is a masterpiece that belonged to Cyrus the Great two hundred years ago, its ivory hilt marvelously carved with winged deities and studded with gemstones.

"The last time Persia tried to vanquish the Greek nations, it cost us greatly," the king says, running his fingers over the blade. "You, grandson, were named for the great King Darius who burned Athens and tumbled their Parthenon to the ground. Perhaps you would like to do something similar. But remember that Darius lost our army at Marathon and his son Xerxes lost our navy at Salamis."

Darius sits in silence. No matter how fast Artaxerxes can walk, he is too old to be king. Careful and plodding, the blood in his veins hardly flows at all; it is gelid with age and caution. He can hardly believe this is the same man who, to grab the throne, murdered eighty brothers in a single day, personally strangling the infants in their cribs. "Sire, that was a hundred and fifty years ago."

"A valuable lesson nonetheless," the king says, running a thumb over a protruding sapphire. "We do not want to make an enemy of Macedon. If these brides have children, Alexander's heirs will be half-Persian, raised by Persian mothers. They will be unwilling to attack us and will attack Greek city-states instead: Athens, Sparta, Corinth. These heirs will do our work for us. It spares men, treasure, and resources for us to use elsewhere. It is a brilliant scheme."

Darius nods as if he is truly considering Artaxerxes's nonsense. On the racetrack before them, horses spark up clouds of dust. He says, "Perhaps we should ask ourselves, sire, where Philip will look when he has solidified his gains in Greece. To Judea, that dusty land of goats, sand fleas, and squabbling tribes?"

He swats at something that landed on his cheek and it falls to his lap. A large black sand fly. He flicks it away and continues. "Will he look west to that ambitious village of farmers and shepherds called Rome? North to the wild Scythians and their endless fields of grass? Or will he not look *east*, to Persia, a land rich in gold and manpower? If we rid ourselves of both Philip and Alexander and control that idiot Arridheus, we can marry *him* to a Persian princess *and* rule all of Greece."

The old man looks up at Darius, his small, dark eyes hard. "A good strategy. And one we can implement whenever we wish. But for now, I want Alexander to be wooed by brides, not killed by swords. And, Darius, you would do well to take a new wife. Perhaps it would help you keep your war-hungry sword in its hilt."

Darius takes the dig in stride. Since the death of the mother of his firstborn son, Ochus, Darius has sworn off the touch of a woman. It's a vow that has left him many a frustrated night. But he will not succumb to the gross temptations of the flesh, as the old king has, at the risk of losing mastery of his own mind.

He has woven so many complex plots across this great nation that the web of deceit could engulf and strangle him if he isn't careful at all times.

He watches as the king pushes on the round ivory pommel of his dagger and it springs open, revealing a hollow compartment filled with tiny stone vials. Poison, Darius assumes, used to coat the weapon or drop into someone's wine. The king must think this will impress him. But Darius first used this old trick when he was six and borrowed the vial he found in his older brother's sword to poison the bad-tempered nursemaid who beat him.

"Only barbarians rush in foolishly with swords drawn, young Darius," the king says. He snaps the compartment shut and slides the dagger back into its scabbard. "Tell me. Have you heard more of the Hunor? Have you learned yet what has happened to them?"

Darius hesitates. The latest tales are so horrifying he can't repeat them, at least not until they are confirmed. "I have sent men to investigate the rumors. I should know more soon, Uncle."

The king nods, exhaling deeply. "If it is as they say, then the greatest threat to our empire is not that barbarian one-eyed king of Macedon. Nor any other mortal kingdom, for that matter. We'd be wisest to fear the evil that is as yet unknown."

And for the first time all day, Darius wonders if, for once, the king is right.

Chapter Eleven

IN AN ORB OF LIGHT CAST BY THREE TINY OIL lamps, Jacob wraps a wet rawhide cord tightly around the junction of an iron arrowhead as he tries to ignore Princess Cynane's low moans. Keeping busy is the only way he can stay in the same room as her. Even now, asleep, she makes awful sounds—sounds that remind him of when his family's farm dog lost her litter in a sudden flood, and she whimpered for the lost pups for days.

He would never tell anyone, but when Cynane sleeps, he can't help but feel slightly sorry for the unloved princess. In her dreams, she calls out for her mother and sobs that blood is all around. He often wonders what cruelties she has witnessed.

Jacob dips his fingers into a pot of beeswax and massages the leather cord. When it dries, it will be both tight and supple. For a moment, he considers putting some of the beeswax into his own ears, but as an Aesarian Lord, he knows he needs to show more courage than that.

He sets the arrow in the finished stack and is reaching for another when he hears heavy boots tromping up the north tower stair. The door opens wide and High Lord Gideon enters holding a torch, followed by Bastian and two other Lords. Standing in the gloomy, dark little torture chamber with their horned helmets and black capes, they remind Jacob of the horned god Pan doing penance in the Underworld.

Gideon steps forward, and Jacob knows before he asks what the High Lord will say. It's the same question every night. "Has she told you anything?"

"No, High Lord," Jacob replies. He knows Gideon doesn't want to hear about the curses she's hurled at him or her demands for water.

The High Lord goes over to the girl and, moving his torch over her tangle of limbs, bends to examine her pale face and her skin, unmarked other than the Scythian tattoo on her arm Turshu gave her yesterday as she shrieked. Finally, Gideon shakes his head. "Then there's truly nothing more we can learn from her," he says.

Cynane's groan startles Jacob—he thought she was asleep—and he looks over to see her turn her head away.

"Are we all agreed," Lord Gideon continues, "that she does *not* possess a Blood Magic?"

Bastian and the other Lords nod their assent, though one of them speaks: "She is protected by a powerful spell. A sorcerer's spell."

"And if that is true," Gideon says, tilting his head, "the Hunor will welcome her eagerly, regardless of whether the magic is hers or not."

In two strides Bastian is leaning over Cynane, smiling like a lover, and for a moment Jacob wonders if he's going to kiss her. "Turshu and I can prepare the mixture," Bastian says. He grabs a lock of Cynane's black hair, which, once as shiny as a river pebble, is now listless and dull. He gives it a tug, and she spits in his face.

Swearing, Bastian wipes off the saliva, and Jacob quickly looks away to hide his smirk. How many times he's wanted to spit at him. Watching Cyn do it was almost as good as doing it himself. But he must not have looked away quickly enough, as Bastian's eyes narrow at him.

"I think Lord Jacob is ready for the honor of applying it," the scarred Lord says. Though Bastian grins, Jacob knows that any kind of honor that Bastian wants to bestow upon him is one that must be truly disgusting. Two hours later, Jacob knows that he was right.

Dipping his shovel into the cauldron of warm mud and ashes, Jacob stirs the slightly bubbling mixture. It smells of sulfur and something very ancient, like earth from a forgotten tomb. Once in a while he gets a whiff of something that reminds him of dead fish and human vomit and can hardly stop himself from retching. In Erissa there was a wise woman who healed people by applying mud mixed with herbs to injured or painful body parts. Two years ago, when he and Kat were hunting a deer, Jacob tripped in a rabbit hole and badly sprained his ankle. The wise woman slapped thick, hot mud infused with aromatic herbs on the ankle, and let it harden to rock. Three days later she chipped it off, and his ankle was as good as new.

But he knows this stinking brew can't be intended to heal Cynane, who is now chained to a wooden board on the floor. He is supposed to coat her with the mud up to her neck, let the mixture harden, then turn her over and coat the back of the board. Gideon will give her a drug to render her unconscious and then coat her face, leaving holes over the eyes, nose, and mouth.

Torchlight flickers in the derelict kitchen of the old fortress, and a sliver of moonlight slants through the smoke hole, silvering the fumes rising from the cauldron. Bastian and Turshu left him with a shovel and a warning that if he splashed the mixture on himself he mustn't let it dry or else they'd have to crack him open like a sculptor's plaster mold. Only then did Jacob realize the task at hand: he would be sealing her into a skintight tomb.

Cold sweat breaks out across his back. He doesn't want to do this, but he must follow orders if he's to rise in the ranks. Taking a deep breath, he dips his shovel into the cauldron and drops the mud on Cyn's abdomen. She throws her head back and screams.

"Does it hurt?" he asks, surprised. Bastian instructed him to make sure it was pleasantly warm, not burning hot, and he tested it.

"No," she says, gasping. "But it will before they're done with me. I won't be able to move when you've finished." She claws at Jacob's tunic with filthy manacled hands and stares straight into his eyes. He sees fear there for the first time. More than fear. Desperation.

"If they want to kill me, why can't they let me fight and die like a soldier?" she croaks. "I don't want to die like this. Not like the helpless prey of some evil spider."

Jacob wrenches his gaze away from her, turns to the cauldron, and dips in his shovel. This time he doesn't look at her as he piles the mud on her thighs. It hardens quickly, he notices, becoming something like stone.

"I thought the victor of the Blood Tournament would be more noble than this," she asks, her voice a jagged shard. "I thought you of all people would understand what it means to face death fighting."

Her words pierce his heart as sharply as any sword. He remembers his mother's parting words to him as he left for Pella. "Do what you know is right, Jacob, and we will be proud of you whether you win or not. Act honorably, that's all that we ask." He knows that she would hang her head in shame to see her son help kill a defenseless girl.

No, this is for them! he tells himself fiercely. He has already sent back a large portion of his Blood Tournament winnings for his father to buy more land and improve the farm. But he wants to do more for them. He wants to earn more money so that Cleon can build a second kiln and hire an assistant. He wants to send his mother a finely woven red robe—a color they could never afford—and a pair of real gold earrings. And he wants to hire a private tutor for his younger brothers so that they can learn things Jacob didn't. His hands shake slightly as he dips the shovel into the cauldron again.

Cyn strains against her chains. "I'm a high-born princess with powers you can't even imagine. If you help me get out of here, I can get you whatever you want."

Powers, yes, Jacob thinks. The uncanny power to heal broken bones and burns, and resist drowning. Just to be tortured all over again. Sometimes the ability to die is the greatest gift of the gods.

"I don't want anything," he says flatly, pouring the foul mixture on her knees and patting it gently with the shovel.

"Oh, but I think you do," she says, her voice softening to a caress. "I think you want Katerina. I can make her fall in love with you. Marry you."

As Jacob leans on his shovel, he has a fleeting image of Kat kissing him in the pond and again in her room at the palace. The feel of her slender yet muscular body against his, the sweet smell of her hair. The idea of having her, after everything that has happened, as his wife, jolts him with something fresh and powerful and also painful: hope.

But just as quickly as it soared with spread wings in his chest, he forces it back into oblivion. Because he wants Kat only if she wants him. And she's already told him no. He doesn't want this hard, bitter princess to interfere with Kat's feelings, doesn't want her to put some dark spell on Kat to be anything but herself. He pictures Kat, in an unblinking trance with a smile that doesn't reach her eyes, promising to marry him and love him always. He shudders.

No, he must forget her and concentrate on his new life and new goal—to become the best Aesarian Lord ever. To find Riel and...

Riel. Bastian told Gideon that Riel had been hiding in the Pellan palace. The girl in front of Jacob, so desperate to escape, has spent her entire life in the Pellan palace.

"I don't want you to make Kat love me," he says slowly, crouching beside her. "But perhaps you could tell me something I want to know."

Her eyes become uncertain. "What?" she asks.

Heart beating fast, he whispers, "In Pella, have you ever heard of anyone named Riel, someone protected by a member of the royal family?"

To his surprise, she flinches hard, almost as though she has been slapped. "Yes," she breathes, and the way she clenches her lips shut immediately afterward tells Jacob that she didn't mean to give way so quickly.

Jacob's heart beats faster. "Tell me," he urges.

Her mouth hardens. "Only if you swear by the Kindly Ones on all you hold dear, that if I tell you, you will help me get out of here."

Jacob hesitates. Helping her escape would be treason. And yet...is it really treason if Cyn's information helps the Aesarian Lords capture Riel—a true god?

"I swear by the Kindly Ones..." he says, shuddering as he invokes the euphemism for the Furies, vicious winged goddesses of vengeance on all those who break oaths. For a second, the memory of bright green eyes and light brown hair flashes before his mind, but he forces himself to keep speaking "…and on all I hold dear."

Cynane relaxes back onto the stretcher. "One evening when I was very young—five or six, I think—my mother asked me to borrow some embroidery thread from the queen. I even remember the color: green. When I went into her chambers, no one was there. At least, that's what I thought at first. Then I saw an open trap door, and a ladder going down into darkness. I heard someone moaning. I remember thinking the queen must have fallen and needed help. So I went down there, telling myself not to be afraid, that I was a royal daughter of Illyria, who is afraid of nothing. That's what my mother always told me, you see. May I have a little water, please."

On pins and needles to hear the rest, Jacob hastily pours her a cup and holds her head up as she drinks greedily and then goes on. "At the bottom of the ladder was a little chamber with an altar where she kept her snakes. And there, on the floor, lay the queen, though I could barely see her as only one lamp was lit and its wick faltering. 'Riel! Riel!' the queen cried, writhing on the floor. A large snake was wrapped around her. I thought it was killing her. I called out, 'Stepmother! Are you all right? Should I try to kill it?'"

She pauses, squeezing her eyes tightly shut.

"Then what?" Jacob urges her, impatiently.

"All at once the queen was digging her nails into my arm so deeply, it bled, and holding a snake in my face, a large angry snake, its mouth open, venom dripping from sharp fangs. 'If you tell anyone about this, girl,' she said, 'I will send this snake to kill you in your bed.' I never did tell anyone. Not even my mother. But I have never forgotten."

Jacob's heart beats fast with excitement. The queen knows where the god Riel is. Perhaps she hides him with her snakes in the altar beneath her bedroom. Did she tell Bastian because they are working together somehow? Or did he find out on his own? Is he planning on returning to find Riel and bring him back to High Lord Gideon? Maybe Jacob can beat him to it. Then he will be the best of the Aesarians and his name will be inscribed on the Wall of Honor in Nekrana.

"I've given you what you wanted," Cyn says, her dark eyes glittering eerily orange and silver from fire pit flames and moonlight. "Now help me get out of here."

Green eyes, long hair, soft lips. Once so dear to him, but they cannot be anymore. His heart has been reforged in the dark by Aesarian fire. The Brotherhood has replaced all. How can he betray it by letting Cyn escape?

Yet he took an oath to her, the unloved princess who fulfilled her end of the bargain, giving him what he needed. How can he send her to a horrible death?

Seeing his hesitation, Cyn hisses, "You swore by the Kindly Ones to let me go free."

"I did," Jacob says. He forces himself to lock eyes with her, hating what he is about to say. "But when I joined the Lords, I swore to the Kindly Ones that I would never betray the Brotherhood. So you see, either way I will suffer their wrath."

Jacob braces himself for Cynane's curses, but she stays as silent as a statue. Then she turns her head and stifles a sob. A bubble of sound comes from her, a plea...a prayer... No, he can't understand. "What was that?" He leans closer to hear her.

"I said," she whispers, "that *I* am their wrath!"

He feels a tug on his tunic and suddenly his cheek burns with an all-consuming fire. Clutching his face, Jacob howls with pain. It's only then that he realizes what has happened: with her manacled hands, Cynane tugged the pin on his tunic free, then jabbed up at him with the long, iron pin on the back of the smooth green stone.

She laughs triumphantly, and his blood drips down from the pin onto her neck.

He found that stone long ago, next to the stream in the woods, and paid the village blacksmith to make it into a pin for Kat. For years she wore it proudly, but the night before he left for the Blood Tournament she gave it back to him. It would protect him, she said. He hadn't taken it off since, not even after swearing his oath to the Lords.

A furious anger boils within Jacob. Cynane has defiled what he holds so dear. He lunges for the pin, but she writhes away from him. Even restrained, she is fast. He grabs hold of her chains to keep her still, but Cyn lifts her head, slamming her skull against his.

Jacob's body becomes white-hot. A tingle shoots from her metal cuffs into his fingers, then stings up through his arms like an angry bee. The stinging intensifies until it fills his entire body—overwhelming and controlling him. He has lost all sense of self and has become the furious red of his eyelids. Pain sears across his palm, and a curious odor fills the air—the tang of molten metal that pervades a blacksmith's shop. Fighting through the angry haze, Jacob finally opens his eyes.

Cynane's chains glow red.

And as he watches, a link twists open, followed by another one. The cuffs burn bright, curl open, and fall off.

In a heartbeat Cyn sits up, flings off the chains and throws herself at him, managing to wrench her legs free of the quickly hardening mud. Despite her ordeal, she's strong and scrappy, while he is suddenly filled with an exhaustion as immense as the forests between Erissa and Pella. Jacob feels as if a wild wolf cub has jumped on him, thrashing and biting and scratching.

Wildly, he cries out and pushes Cynane hard against the wall, but she scrambles to her feet and races out the open door into the darkness, leaving behind her chunks of what looks like concrete. Jacob makes a step to follow her, but his body does not respond to his commands. He feels as weak as a newborn foal, his legs shaky and awkward. Time has stopped for Jacob. He just stands there, blood dripping down his cheek.

Last time he felt warm blood on his skin, he was on the battlefield, holding a dying Katerina in his arms. Then, he'd also felt something strange course through his blood. Not the burning sting that just overtook him, but a warm, gentle fizz, like the tiny bubbles of sea foam popping under a summertime sun. Like the time in the palace when Kat touched the wound on his arm and it healed.

Both times before, Kat had been there. But today—today she was not. The only similar things between now and those other times was the blood, the leftover exhaustion…and Jacob. In his still dazed mind the impossible thought comes to him: *Me. I did those things. I did that.*

As the curious thought tumbles and whips through his mind, men's shouts echo in the courtyard. Boots slap against paving stones.

Timaeus arrives first, panting. Taking in the melted chains, his face twists into a mask of shock and horror. Quickly, he scoops them up and throws them into a cracked amphora in the corner just as High Lord Gideon and Bastian enter.

"The watch just saw the prisoner climb over a wall," Lord Bastian says, unsheathing his sword with a ringing sound that echoes throughout the room.

"Lord Jacob, put down your sword," Gideon commands, warning ringing in his voice. Jacob quickly removes his sword belt and throws it on the floor.

Other Lords clamber into the room holding torches and drawn swords, their faces orange in the light of the flames as Bastian speaks loudly for all to hear. "You helped her escape!"

"No!" Jacob says, his heart and head pounding. What must it look like? Cynane, chained and partially embalmed, escaped, and he was the only one watching her. It all happened so fast he is still trying to figure it out. He looks at the men's hard faces, their horned shadows looming monstrously large behind them in the fire's glow. Suddenly he can hardly get his breath. What will they do to him?

"She—she used magic!" he sputters. Standing in front of the cracked amphora, his arms crossed, Tim gives Jacob a nearly imperceptible nod. "She scratched my face and the chains disappeared. She—"

"There is no time for explanations." High Lord Gideon's voice slashes through Jacob's stuttering explanation. "Ambiorix, have every spare man saddle his horse and search for the prisoner. She might get far in the night, but we will find her tracks in daylight."

Jacob feels rough hands grab his arms and yank them behind his back. Though his muscles scream as they are stretched, he doesn't do anything to shake Bastian and Turshu from him. The pain doesn't matter—all that matters is what the High Lord will order next.

Gideon's voice rolls out like thunder. "Take Lord Jacob to the dungeon. In seven days' time, he shall be tried by the Inquisitorial Council. If he is found innocent, he shall be allowed to remain a Lord."

He turns his eyes toward Jacob, who feels the weight of their gaze. "If Lord Jacob is found guilty, he shall face the fate of all traitors: immediate death."

CHAPTER TWELVE

THE HARD WALL OF RUSHING WATER THUN-
ders behind Kat as she stands in the cave behind the waterfall, just below Ada's fortress. The last time she stood here,
the torches on either side of the opening in the back burned
a bright welcome. Now they are dark. A splinter of ice-cold
fear pierces her heart.

She hears an intake of breath as Hephaestion slips beneath the pounding waterfall to join her. The reflections of
silver-blue light dance around the rock walls. Once, she had
thought the fractured light looked like guardian spirits, but
now she thinks it looks ghostly—more like phantoms of the
underworld than protectors of a sorceress queen. She shivers.

A strong hand envelops hers, and Hephaestion squeezes
her fingers. A few weeks ago, Kat would have shaken his
comfort away, but now she is grateful that someone—even
if he is an arrogant aristocrat—is with her.

Her fear melts a little as Heph removes the fire starter kit
from the pouch on his belt. For several long moments, his
sparks don't hit the tinder, and she feels her heart is going to
burst out of her chest if they can't get moving. No sooner has

he lit a torch than she pushes past him into the dark tunnel, knowing he will be right behind her with the light.

Kat walks straight into something warm and sticky that coats her entire body. When she opens her mouth to scream, she inhales something gooey that clings to the back of her throat, making her choke. She has run right into a thick, grayish-white netting blocking the corridor from ceiling to floor.

No, not netting. A giant spiderweb.

"Heph!" she calls, coughing and spitting. When she tries to turn around she finds she's stuck, glued to the spot.

He's there in a heartbeat holding two torches, which he puts in the nearest wall brackets, then starts slicing away at the web with his sword until Kat can wrench herself free. She brushes them out of her face and pulls them off her arms, grunting in disgust.

Heph holds a torch up to the dangling shreds. "I've never seen a spiderweb this big. Almost as though a single giant insect created it."

Panic grips Kat's chest. *Ada.* What has happened to her? Who has done this? Or has Ada done it herself to keep out an enemy, the Aesarian Lords, perhaps? Then she remembers Ada telling her that her own brother spent most of his time in the minds of spiders, so much that it had driven him half-mad. Could he have anything to do with this?

At her silence, Heph adds: "Any spider, small or large, should flee from our torches." He hands her a torch, takes the other one, and keeps his sword in his right hand. "Let's go," he says.

They walk cautiously down the twisting corridors. When they come to forks, Kat remembers the way, and finally they emerge in Ada's throne room.

The room is sunk in darkness, the air hot and oppressive.

Heph and Kat raise their torches, and the flickering light reveals more webs blocking out the windows and hanging from the huge iron chandelier. When Kat approaches one of the windows, hundreds of tiny spiders scuttle away from the light, and for a moment she feels their surprise and fear.

She whips around, casting her light in a wide circle. The floor is littered with feathers—black, tan, and white. But the dozens of silver bars protruding from the walls where Ada's birds used to sit are empty. Where is Ada? Where are her twin servants with the yellow eyes and beaklike noses?

A movement catches her eye, and Katerina sees a solitary spider crawl out from under a feather. It runs haphazardly, as though it's being chased by some unknown prey. Kat bends down and places a finger in its path. As the hairy bristles of its leg brush her skin, she momentarily seems to be wheeling wildly around the room, desperately searching for escape in a whirlwind of shrieks and feathers and fear.

Movement blurs four of her eight eyes, and she can feel the human part of her wish that she still had eyelids to block out the confusion of her two front eyes.

Sticky silk tears and webs shred in the chaotic flight, and she knows she must spin for protection. *Spin to trap. Spin to hide. Spin, spin, spin…*

Suddenly tremors shudder up through her long, spindly legs. Too late! A rush of warm wind—or maybe hot breath—sears the spider's body. She zigzags across the room, not knowing anymore which way is up or which way is down. Lost its home. Lost its siblings. Lost its eyes.

They were afraid. Something evil was coming.

The knowledge jerks Katerina from the spider's brain and she falls hard on the floor, her torch rolling away. The blind spider disappears into the corner shadows.

Loss and dread creep into her veins, and there's an empty

feeling in the pit of her stomach. The mercenary on the ship was right. Ada is truly gone: fled, captured, or dead. And once again, Kat is too late.

Too late. Too late. The knowledge consumes her like a massive tide, taking her breath away.

She's too late to save the Carian sorceress, too late to help the one remaining connection she had to Helen.

She clutches her head as if that might help squeeze out the pain inside it. What's the use of her powers if she can't control them and can only use them to discover, too late, atrocities she is unable to stop? Is she doomed to end up alone—all her loved ones dead—left with just her own mind driving her to madness?

"Katerina, what's wrong?" Heph's voice comes from far away, as if he is speaking through water. Tears sting her eyes, but she doesn't want to cry in front of Heph. Not after he found her in the meadow, reeling from the news about her family in Erissa.

She heaves in a breath, trying to focus her vision on the dark walls around her. *Pull yourself together,* she tells herself, breathing deeply again before looking at Heph. "I'm just... worried about Ada," she says.

She holds out her hand and Heph pulls her to her feet. She picks up her torch and sets it in a wall bracket behind Ada's throne, which she pretends to examine, as if looking for some clue. It is a masterpiece of craftsmanship, the back a spreading peacock tail of green agate, turquoise, and lapis lazuli. The arms are peacock heads with onyx eyes and silver beaks. The golden seat rests on four carved ivory legs, each one ending in long, fingerlike talons. Kat places a hand on the top of it and closes her eyes. *Ada.*

She hears sounds that remind her of her foster mother, Sotiria, ripping old clothing into rags for cleaning. *Sotiria...*

It seems she can't get away from painful memories no matter how hard she tries. Bright light enters the room from one of the windows. Blinking rapidly to clear her eyes, she sees Heph attacking the next web, ripping open the thick spider silk. When all five windows are clear, letting in cool, fresh air, he approaches Kat, sweat running down his cheeks.

"That's better, isn't it?" he asks, and she can hear forced cheerfulness in his voice. "Less...tomblike, anyway."

"She was the only one who understood." Kat's voice sounds brittle, dry like the herbs Helen used to hang upside down from the rafters.

Heph wipes his forehead with the back of his hand. "Understood what?"

Kat walks unsteadily to one of the windows where long shreds of tattered spiderwebs dangle in the breeze. She looks over the green valley below and begins to speak. "My m— Helen, told me never to speak of my strange ability with animals."

She takes a deep breath, then turns away from the window to see Heph, his dark eyes fixed on her. "I can... It's hard to explain, but I can feel what they feel. Hunger. Fear. Curiosity. Pain. Pleasure. I know what it's like to be a fish in cool, dark water, a bird gliding through the air, a goat chewing on weeds." She laughs bitterly. "I can even...talk to them in a way, though not in words."

Heph's face is still, expressionless. She wishes she could understand him as she does birds and horses and even hellions.

"Helen said never to speak of it," she continues. "That the world could be dangerous for people like me. And I didn't. I never even told my best friend." *Jacob*. Her dear, sweet, strong Jacob.

A thought occurs to her: Jacob doesn't know.

It is unlikely he would have heard the news of what the

queen did to his family. Jacob deserves to know the truth and to mourn for them properly. Then again, part of her hopes he'll never have to find out.

She turns back to the window, and her heart sinks again at the sight of an empty sky. No kestrel wings its way toward her with secret messages. Not today. Maybe not ever again.

She suddenly feels Heph standing beside her. "Go on," he says, touching her arm.

"When I came here, Ada told me I have Snake Blood. Like her. Do you know what that is?"

"I heard something, once." She can make out the frown in his voice though she continues to stare out at the sky. "The legend that long ago, gods mated with humans and created two kinds of Blood Magic, Snake and Earth Blood, right?"

She nods. "Yes."

"Then…" There's a silence and Kat imagines all the strange things that have happened since she's arrived in Pella flashing in front of Heph's eyes. Her ability to call the hellion—the vicious flying panther in King Philip's royal menagerie—to battle with the Lords, her sudden lethal prowess with a shield and sword, the gazelles. Finally, he speaks again, "And Alex… Him, too?"

She nods. "Yes, but different from mine, I think. I'm more comfortable with animals and insects while Alex understands people better than me. It's what will make him a great king, one day."

Heph considers this, then nods slowly. "Yes," he says. "Yes, you're right."

"Besides Alex, as far as I know, only Ada shares this gift. She was the first one to explain I wasn't a—a freak. She gave me hope, but now all hope has flown away with her." She puts her head in her hands, feeling the tide of devastation rising inside her, threatening to pour out. She has been holding it in ever since they left the palace, punishing her-self, silencing her emotions.

Pressure on her shoulders turns her from the window, and she lowers her hands to look into Heph's eyes. Sunlight reflects in them, and for the first time Kat notices they are not just a uniform dark brown. Black striations dance through them, with tiny stipples of amber, and they glow with an inner fire. "We still have a mission, Kat. And I need you. *Alex* needs you."

"Everything I touch gets ruined," she says, breaking free of his grip, a tear slipping down her face despite her best efforts not to let it. "Don't you see?" Her voice breaks. "You'd be better off continuing without me."

"That's not how it works," he says firmly. "This is about Alexander. This is about Macedon. It's not about your self-pity."

His words are like a slap. "Self-pity? You don't know anything about how I feel."

"Maybe I know more than you think."

"What's that supposed to mean?"

"It means we all have our losses. But we can't afford to be selfish," he snaps back. "Alex—your *brother*—sent us to help him and you cannot collapse into a puddle of tears because Ada is gone."

Her cheeks burn as the truth of his words becomes shame in her heart. "I love the prince but I have room in here," she says, slamming her hand against her chest, "for more. It seems like you can't understand that. Are you really just Alex's plaything?" She knows the question is a barb. She hopes it stings. "Don't you have any desires of your own?"

For a second, she thinks she's gone too far. Now his eyes are black. Blacker than the sea at midnight, and she can't tell what he's thinking. "I do," he says gruffly, and then he leans forward, closing the gap between them.

His lips touch hers and suddenly he's kissing her, hard and deep.

And she's kissing him back.

Heat floods her, rolling in waves from her head to her toes. She leans in, and his tongue curls around hers even as one of his hands finds her waist. The pain is still inside her, but it pulses now, hot and passionate, surging into her fingers until she can't help but let them run through his hair. His body is taut against hers, lithe and wiry, so unlike Jacob, who felt more like he was carved from a massive piece of stone.

Jacob.

Kat wrenches herself away from Hephaestion, races across the throne room and into the dark corridor, trying to breathe. She reaches the end and pushes open the heavy arched door before hurtling into Ada's room.

The windows are covered here, too, thick with webs and dust. She sinks her hands into the spider silk and pulls, the material tearing apart like unspun wool, the little fibers cutting hairline fissures into her palms.

Jacob flashes before her, his warm brown eyes shining with happiness as he stands with her in his mother's vegetable garden and slips something into her hand. "You see?" he says in the memory, smiling as she examines the brooch he made for her. "It's flecked with gold. Like sunset on the river. Or the gold flecks in your eyes."

Touching her lips, she remembers their first kiss in the pond the day before he left for Pella and their world started to fall apart.

She hears footsteps and her anger flares again. She turns to see Heph standing awkwardly in the doorway, holding a torch. Looking at him, she knows he is the exact opposite of Jacob. Tempestuous, unpredictable, and contradictory, like fire on wind. How could she care for two such different men?

"I'm sorry, Katerina," he says. "I shouldn't have... I won't do it again. I promise." He takes a few halting steps into the room. "But I understand more than you think," he says and stops, keeping distance between them. "I, too, lost my family. I thought I found a new one in Pella, but now even that seems uncertain. I don't..." He pauses, and she notices for the first time that there is a boyishness in his face, the look of someone who is tough because he has had to be, forced to hide the vulnerability inside. "I don't know *where* I belong." The final words come out like a whisper.

Standing in the doorway in his rumpled, travel-stained tunic and disheveled hair, he reminds Kat of the baker's lost dog who came limping and matted back to Erissa. Her anger softens into new awareness: Heph, too, has suffered loss. He, too, has been forced to go on. Was it really so awful for him to reach out and try to find comfort and hope? Maybe she is not angry at him for kissing her, but angry at herself for kissing him. And Jacob... The Jacob she knew is gone now. She saw that for herself on the battlefield as he tore into Macedon's armies with Aesarian iron.

"I don't think we should stay here tonight," Kat says, and she's pleased to hear that her voice sounds closer to normal as she walks to the door. "If it was dangerous for Ada, it could be dangerous for us, too."

Heph nods. "The place feels evil somehow, as if it has been cursed. And cursed things often fear the light of day but gain power in the night."

For a moment, she's back in the spider's mind, moments before it was blinded. "I agree," she says. "We must leave well before sunset."

★ ★ ★

As the sun slides toward the horizon, Kat descends the steep path. *No more breaking down,* she thinks. She is Katerina, daughter of an oracle, sister to a prince, friend to a sorceress. More than that, she is Snake Blood, and the blood of a god pulses in her veins. No more will she be a crying girl brought down by her grief. No more will she let her heart take her this way and that.

They scramble around a twist in the track, and she sees Halicarnassus in the distance, a jewel of a city embraced by thick walls. In the center, the white marble Mausoleum, the tomb of the last king, juts a hundred and fifty feet into the air, the dozens of bronze figures on top shining like pure gold. Below it, the circular harbor bustles with brightly painted ships, and beyond, the sun glistens like fire on patches of the cobalt blue Aegean Sea.

And there are ships, there, one of them waiting for her, ready to take her south into an exotic land of ancient mysteries.

CHAPTER THIRTEEN

THE COARSE MANE WRAPS AROUND ZO'S FIN-gers, making her hands ache. It wouldn't be hard to untangle them, but Zo would rather have her fingers go numb than risk falling off the horse. The scarf drawn tight over her eyes has not only taken away her sight, but also some of her balance.

Ever since she sent the message to Cosmas, Ochus has blindfolded her during their travels, chaining her up at night to a tree, pocketing the key, and sleeping out of her reach. The scarf cuts into the bridge of her nose, but at least it keeps the sweat from dripping into her eyes. The sun hammers the top of her head like a hot fist. Without sight, Zo is forced to sharpen her other senses. She counts the strides of the horse, counts away the seconds, minutes, hours until they reach…what?

The fake Pegasus? The Spirit Eaters?

Will the adventure end when the child in her belly grows bigger than a secret? Or will it end when a gallant Cosmas appears to rescue her? Even if her message did somehow manage to get to him, she wonders how, in all these countless miles of farms and fields, woods and hills, he could ever find her.

And then there's the mysterious evil force out there, said to be killing off, even devouring, people and horses, leaving behind fields of bones—if the gossiping couriers she's overheard along the way are to be believed. Not long ago, Zo's entire life was contained within the gates of Sardis, but in the last few weeks she has grown aware of just how vast the empire beyond her protected city really is—and how deadly. They are maybe a third of the way to Persepolis, but now, with her eyes blindfolded, she feels more than ever that the world is so immense she could travel forever and never reach its end, that she, Princess Zofia of Sardis, is in fact infinitesimally small. The thought is unsettling, silencing.

With a clanking of manacles, Zo lurches forward as her horse, which has been favoring its right front leg the past few days, suddenly stumbles and stops altogether. For a terrifying moment, she fears she'll somersault over her horse's ears, but her hands gripped in the mane root her.

"Ochus?" she calls. From the crunch of his mount's hooves, she knows that her captor must only be a few lengths ahead. "I think my horse has gone totally lame this time."

As he curses, she can almost picture his scowl—his dark brows knitting together over flashing eyes the color of honey—and the beat of the hooves stops and comes back toward her. A second later, she hears the jangle of a bit and feels a tug on her horse. Ochus must have leaped to the ground and taken the reins while he examined the leg, but he'd been so quiet, she hadn't heard him hit the packed earth. It continually astonishes her that a man of such burly strength can move about with such deep silence, like the enormous wildcats of the mountains said to stalk their prey soundlessly.

"Get off," she hears him say gruffly.

Zo lets out a wry chuckle. "Easier said than done. Tell me, have you ever dismounted blindfolded?"

Suddenly she feels hands around her waist and a hard tug pulls her to the ground. She gasps as Ochus catches her an instant before she would have landed in the dirt.

Heart beating wildly, she silently thanks the old eunuch Bagadata for the lessons in diplomacy she received all her life. Though she rarely paid attention to the customs of foreign nations, the one thing she does remember is never to let her face betray her fright.

"So I suppose we are going to walk all the way to the mountains?" she asks sarcastically instead. "Such an easy task with this blindfold."

He snorts. "It's an easier task than trusting you." Then his hands are around her again, and her stomach swoops as he throws her onto the back of what she assumes must be his horse. Awkwardly, she grips the mane and swings her leg around the other side.

"And to answer your question..." Ochus's voice rises up to her from somewhere on the ground. "We are going to buy horses at the next farm and leave these there. My horse needs a full day's rest before going on, and that's a luxury we don't have."

"Buy horses?" she asks. "In that case, you had better take off this blindfold so I can pick good ones."

She's surprised when she hears a bark of laughter come from him, but the scarf remains on.

"Sit back a few handsbreadths so I can mount in front of you."

Zo tries to scoot backward, to the far rear of the saddle, but loses her balance and almost topples off the horse. Strong arms stabilize her.

"Watch what you're doing," he barks.

"How can I watch anything when you have me blind-folded?"

"Quiet," he says. "Or I'll gag you as well."

She opens her mouth to respond, then thinks better of it.

She feels him swoop up in front of her, brushing against her, and hears the creak of the saddle as he settles. She grabs him to steady herself, one arm gripping his biceps, the other clutching at the back of his tunic.

She breathes in his scent: a salty tang of sweat, smoke from last night's campfire, fresh country air, and something all his own. She pulls her head away from his neck.

They are riding more slowly now, the lame horse on her left side, trying to keep up. She hears the warbles of birds, the buzzing of insects, and the murmur of trees. She licks her lips; they taste of sweat and dust.

"There's a farm up ahead with horses in a paddock," he says as they stop. He helps her off the horse and removes the blindfold. The light is so bright, it hurts Zo's eyes. She rubs them, her chains clinking, and sees broad fields and a gated compound of small wooden buildings. On one side, three large horses nibble grass in a paddock.

Ochus digs into his saddlebag and pulls out his cloak, which he throws over Zo to hide her manacles.

As they approach the house leading their horses, two men march out of the gate, one holding a pitchfork, the other a large kitchen knife.

"Can we help you?" asks the tall one with a face like a hatchet.

Ochus spreads his hands to show he's not holding a weapon, though the farmers can't miss the sword hanging by his side. "I mean you no trouble. My wife's mount has gone lame," he says, and the brown mare, as if on cue, holds its right front leg a bit above the ground, "and mine is exhausted. I would like to buy two of yours. I have gold and will pay well. You can keep these horses, too, for your trouble."

The smaller man, tan and wrinkled, shakes his head. "Horses are worth their weight in gold these days," he says. "At night we bring ours into the house with us. And these are farm horses, larger and sturdier than yours. We need them to run the farm. I'm sorry."

He stares at Zo with his beady raisin eyes, a hard gaze that makes the hairs on the back of her neck stand on end, and turns to Ochus. "Do you come from the far west? Sardis, perhaps?"

"No," Ochus barks. "Gordium." He grabs Zo's elbow and says, "Come."

Sardis. How did the farmer know she was from Sardis? Has someone been out here, in the middle of nowhere, asking for her, the lost princess? Impossible, that a farmer—a complete stranger—might suspect her true identity, while the captor who has been escorting her for weeks has no clue. Once again, she wonders how it's possible that Ochus, who claims not to trust her, still believes in her story of being a lost horse breeder's daughter in search of the last Pegasus. She wants to talk to Ochus about the farmer's comment, but she would have to tell him she's been lying to him this whole time, and surely he'd kill her just as easily as he has bound her.

She walks beside him as he leads the two horses to the road and asks, "What are you going to do now?"

"We are going to wait a while behind those trees, and then I'm going to go back and steal two horses."

They sit in patches of dappled sunlight within sight of the farmhouse. After a time, Zo asks, "Why did they ask if we came from the west? Sardis, in particular? That was a strange thing to ask, way out here."

"Who knows? It doesn't matter." But from the tension in his face, she knows it does.

Finally, Ochus takes the saddles and saddlebags off the horses and picks up their halters.

"What are you doing?" she asks.

"Leaving them at the farm. Payment. Also, I don't want you riding away without me."

She peers through the trees as Ochus marches the horses up to the paddock, opens the gate, and leads them inside. But shouts echo from the house, and suddenly six men pour out bearing makeshift weapons and sweep into the paddock. Ochus unsheathes his sword as the horses whinny in terror. Zo hears men's cries and grunts, thumping and thwacking, and sees horses race out of the paddock and into the fields.

"You killed my brother! And my uncle!" one man cries, knocked to the ground but brandishing what looks like a rusty rake. "May the gods punish you!"

Ochus leaps on the sole remaining horse, a bay mare with a white star, and gallops toward Zo. He jumps off and, keeping one eye on the farm—where women are now rushing out of the house and shrieking—throws on the saddle and saddlebags. Without fastening them, he mounts the horse and clumsily pulls Zo up behind him.

"You killed them?" Zo asks, the words like cold spikes in her throat as she's jolted forward.

Ochus kicks the horse hard and they race down the road. "Only the two who saw you," he says.

"Why?" she asks, trying to keep the tremor from her voice.

He does not reply.

"And we still only have one horse…"

"But it's a fresh horse."

"Let me rephrase that," she says, indignation mingling with her fear and turning it into a fire in her gut. "You *murdered* two innocent people and we still have one horse." She's seen him kill before—murderous slave traders—but these were harmless farmers.

"Shut up and pull down your blindfold."

She does. The choice between obedience and death is an automatic one.

After a time, they slow and she feels coolness and shadows. The air is fragrant with pine, soft loam, and sweet decay. Her sense of smell seems to be increasing by the day. She hears birds flapping out of branches and small brown creatures darting out of their path and diving into leaves. Now she can make out a small sliver of light directly under her nose. It's not much, but it's better than total darkness. She looks down and sees her travel-stained blue tunic and, when she leans left, her leg against the horse's belly.

After what seems like hours, she feels the sun on her face again as Ochus pulls up. "Found it," he says. "The road from the ancient city of Hattusa, which will lead us away from the Royal Road and north."

"Away from the Royal Road?" Zo asks. "But we haven't been on it for days."

"We've been on a track paralleling it," he says.

Zo can hardly believe her ears. "Sleeping in the dirt instead of beds? Eating berries and dried leathery meat instead of hot food in the posting house taverns? Are you crazy?"

She feels the muscles of his back tense, but he doesn't answer.

Zo looks down and sees reddish earth and pebbles. "I'm exhausted," she says. "Can I have some water? Do we have any food left? Where are we going to sleep tonight? Can we go back to the Royal Road? Or is there an inn or a farm-house out here where you won't have to kill people to get us a bed?"

Ochus sighs. "May the gods have pity on me."

She feels him slip off and place warm, calloused hands on her waist. She leans into him and he sets her on the ground. She smells something sweet, something that reminds her of... She inhales deeply, but the scent is gone as quickly as it arrived.

Then she feels a goatskin thrust between her shackled hands and drinks, saving some for him, though she wonders why. She hears him drink the rest. "We need to find water," he says.

"And I need a place to...get rid of some," she says. Her bladder is pinching her sharply.

"Again?"

She rolls her eyes, even though he can't see them behind her blindfold. "Yes. Again." The pressure of her belly has started to increase noticeably. Even if she still can't see much of a difference in the shape of her body, she *feels* it changing, and believes more than ever that the old seer Kohinoor was right. There is no doubt in her mind that she is carrying Cosmas's child. "Please remove my blindfold so that I may relieve myself."

"No."

"Oh, for the love of Anahita, why not?"

He yanks the blindfold off her head. She watches as he pulls a long coil of rope from his bag, which he ties to her manacles. "All right," he says. "I'll wait here."

Zo looks in disgust at the makeshift leash, but she's too tired to argue more. Looking around, she sees dark trees spread out on both sides of the track. The road isn't nearly as wide or well-maintained as the Royal Road. It's full of potholes; if the horse goes faster than a walk it will probably break a leg. Vegetation has grown across part of it, making it narrow in spots.

Shaking her hair, she wanders into the trees, prepared to suffer once again the indignity of peeing while attached to Ochus with a rope.

But just before she ducks behind a bush, she spots something shimmering on the ground. She bends over, mystified, and picks it up. It's a solid gold hair comb made of six thick prongs topped by a band studded with garnets. Tiny statues of goddesses stand on top, holding long golden chains in their minuscule hands that loop over one another several inches below.

"By all the gods..." she murmurs.

"What is it?" Ochus growls over his shoulder, tugging on the saddlebags he is fastening to the horse.

"Look what I found," she says, holding it up.

He marches over, scowling. "Where did you find it?" he asks, running a hand through his sweat-damp brown hair. "Did it tumble out of your pants, like the other gold jewelry?" he asks, bemused, reminding her of the moment he discovered that the girl he had freed from slavers had been hiding a small fortune in her garments.

She ignores the comment and points, her chains clinking. "There. In the dirt."

He grabs the comb from her and examines it. Then he looks up, his eyes darting around the thick woods. Just as quickly, his face closes like a tightly rolled-up scroll, inscrutable.

"It will come in handy as we travel," he says shrugging, shoving it into his pouch. "We can pry out the gems and cut up the gold and pay for food and lodging." He looks at the sky. "It's late. Let's move on. Do you want to pee or not?"

"Don't you think it's strange?" she asks, suddenly not needing to go at all, "that I found that valuable ornament here? In the middle of nowhere?"

"Fortune smiles on us," he says. "Some robber must have dropped it in his hurry to escape. Come." He yanks on her rope.

Zo moves with him toward the horse, but a soft breeze brushes her skin, bringing with it the scent of pine, and... She turns back and frowns. There's that sweet, familiar smell again. Something lilting and floral and with it come memories of shimmering pillows, the soothing music of pipes and lyres, and succulent feasts served on silver platters.

She suddenly knows what it is.

"Ochus," she says, her voice catching at the memories that have formed into an aching ball in her throat. The rope yanks her forward again and she stumbles.

"Too late. You had your chance to pee."

"Ochus!" she says more loudly. "Stop a moment. There's palace perfume on the air."

"How do you know what the palace smells like, horse trader's daughter?" he asks, crossing his arms, his eyes taking on a hard, shrewd look.

Zo shakes her head. Now is not the time. She pushes on. "There's something in the trees. Something else."

He looks about to spew another sarcastic insult, but something in her face seems to stop him, for he slowly unsheathes his sword. "Do you hear something?" he asks quietly.

She shakes her head. "I *smell* something."

He lifts his nose and shuts his eyes, inhaling deeply. "I do, too," he says, letting his breath out. His golden eyes dart around again, like a rabbit sensing the nearby presence of an owl. "Look, over there. Those bushes are crushed."

He gives her a warning look, drops the rope, and hands

Zo the reins. Then he walks ahead of her, sword in hand, studying tracks in the ground.

"A large vehicle has been through here recently," he says. "Very large from the depth of those tracks."

Cautiously, they walk into the forest, their eyes scanning the leaf-covered ground. They spot a necklace of cascading flowers, each delicate petal a turquoise, a fat luminous pearl at each blossom's center, and a heavy gold bracelet with huge lions' head terminals. With each step, Zo falls further into the embrace of the perfume. She remembers the panic she and Shirin felt after they drank an amphora of unwatered wine and heard Zo's mother speaking angrily with Mandana, who tried to stall her from entering Zo's room. Zo grabbed a bottle of that perfume, took a swig to cover the smell of wine on her breath, grimaced, and handed it to Shirin, who did the same. It tasted as bad as it smelled good.

Part of her wants to laugh at the memory. Part of her wants to cry at losing her best friend to a fever. But most of her wonders what palace perfume is doing here, in the middle of the woods. With priceless jewelry.

Then, in a small clearing ahead, Zo sees something that shouldn't be there at all. Three bright red wheels high in the air. A vehicle, overturned, its contents strewn about it like raisins on a honey cake.

She drops the reins and walks toward it, stepping over scattered pillows and richly embroidered coverlets. Bright garments spill out of open trunks. One case has a dozen smashed perfume bottles, and the fragrance sweetens the air until she walks a few steps farther. Then she's aware of a new spice that rapidly grows stronger, overpowering the perfume. Her stomach flips. She knows what it is now.

"Zotasha!" Ochus says before she can open her mouth to

call out to him. He ties the horse to a tree. "Don't go any closer."

But she can't stop moving toward it. Now only a few steps away, she can see that it is a *harmanaxa* of bright red cowhide with purple human-headed bulls on the side. The curtains are ripped and hanging into the dark void of the interior. She's seen this *harmanaxa* once before. When the Great King visited Sardis three years ago, she and Shirin watched the procession from the women's viewing chamber atop the main gate of Sardis.

"What's it doing here?" she asks, climbing over a fallen branch. This vehicle should be in Persepolis, hundreds of miles east of here, or at least traveling in comfort on the Royal Road. Why did it leave the road? Was it forced onto this track? Lured here?

Ochus's hand is suddenly on her shoulder. "Stop," he says. "Let me."

She pulls away from him. She has to see what's inside. As she approaches, the sickly smell becomes stronger and she hears the buzzing of flies. She climbs up on the side of the wagon and flips open the torn cowhide curtain.

The stench slams into her face and she bends in half, gagging. A swarm of gorged flies rises, some of them getting tangled in her hair. In her desperate effort to get them out, she scratches her face with her manacles.

Then she looks down inside the *harmanaxa*.

Three girls—no doubt princesses—no older than she, lie at odd angles. Gold jewelry glints on their green, bloated skin. Empty eye sockets stare blindly. And, worst of all, their robes are ripped open, and their chests exposed so that Zo can clearly see the deep, bloody Xs carved directly over their hearts.

The mark of the Assassins' Guild.

Chapter Fourteen

WITH A STRANGLED GASP, OLYMPIAS SITS BOLT upright.

Every organ and muscle in her body is pulsing with pain. She wants to scream but her parched throat feels choked with ashes.

She looks around in panic, expecting to see enemies with drawn swords racing through flames to kill her, but instead she finds herself in a tidy, prosperous-looking cottage. An iron pot hangs over the fire pit, filling the room with the aroma of mouthwatering stew. She's in a clean shift on fresh sheets.

Olympias licks her parched lips. Her trembling hands grasp the *oenochoe* next to her bed, but it's too heavy to lift and she sets it back down shakily. Exhausted, she leans back on her pillow. She needs water or she will faint. And then she will need some of that stew and a cup of wine—

And then she remembers.

Bastian gave her wine under the sacred oak, a diabolically potent vintage that sent the world reeling and fire coursing through her veins.

Bastian poisoned her...and someone must have found her and brought her to this place.

If it wasn't for the theriac her poison master makes for her, she would have died. Every day for years, she has been ingesting a dash of arsenic, a pinch of wolfsbane, a sprinkle of dried jellyfish sting, a drop of deadly yewberry juice, and a dusting of fatal nightshade, combined with trace amounts of cobra, adder and viper venoms. Mixed with the cleansing properties of garlic, myrrh, and cinnamon and with sulfur to neutralize arsenic and charcoal to filter toxins, she has built up her tolerance to even the most deadly of poisons.

Fury at Bastian floods over her like an angry tide, nearly as dizzying as the poison had been. She will send her personal guards to find and kill him, first cutting off the parts he finds most precious. She will—

A black-haired woman enters the cottage, holding a basket of eggs. "Thanks be to the goddess!" she cries, rushing to the bed. "You're awake! The goddess of the sacred oak has been watching over you. She told me what she saw, what that man did to you."

"Water," Olympias croaks, and the woman grabs the *oenochoe* next to the bed and pours some into a clay cup which she holds up to Olympias. She gulps it down, some of the water dribbling onto her chin and splattering on her chest. When she's had her fill, she pushes the cup away and looks up at the woman. She is about forty, with flashing dark eyes, a strong jaw, and a slender, shapely form.

"Who are you?" she croaks. Her voice sounds strange from not speaking for so long.

"I am Nike, priestess of the sacred oak," the woman says. "I found you there, unconscious, when I went to say the evening prayers. I've been taking care of your horse. What is your name? Can I send word to your family?"

Olympias stares at her in disbelief. How can the priestess of the sacred oak not recognize her own queen? Everyone in Macedon has heard of the queen's unique beauty. Who else in the land has long, thick, silver-blond hair? Olympias runs her hand over her head and frowns. Her hair is thin. She has lost a great deal.

Arsenic.

Nike interprets her silence as exhaustion. "But hush, don't speak," she says. "Eat and rest. Here, I've drawn you a basin of water if you'd like to…wash yourself."

Without meeting her eyes, Nike presents the heavy basin to her, placing it beside the bed.

The queen bends to dip her hands in, noticing how bony her pale fingers look. She splashes the cool water onto her face, breathing in a sigh. When she goes to take another splash, though, the reflection in the water causes her to freeze. At first, Olympias cannot register what she sees.

The face looking back at her is gaunt, her green eyes mere hollows in a skull. But it's not the thinness that makes her knock over the basin, screaming.

It's her lips.

They are as white as snow.

ACT THREE:
CONSPIRATOR

Let him that would move the world first move himself.
—Socrates

Chapter Fifteen

ALEXANDER SWEEPS SEVERAL SCROLLS FROM the table to the floor. A servant springs from the corner to pick them up but he says, "Leave them!" and starts to pace around his father's office. *His* office for now. Compared to the rest of the palace, which Olympias has overdecorated with florid frescoes and fussy furniture, it's refreshingly masculine with simple chairs and tables and war trophies—swords, axes, spears, and bloody flags—adorning the walls.

His favorite trophy is the ripped flag of Crenides—a black eagle on white linen—which Philip personally captured when scaling the city's walls the year of Alexander's birth and renamed Philippi after himself. As long as Alex could remember, he dreamed of naming captured cities Alexandria.

He has always liked being in here—at least, when his father was in a good mood—just the way he liked sleeping beneath the stars when hunting or in a tent before a skirmish. He likes being away from his mother's painted cupids and Persian carpets and all the smoking amber and perfume in the incense burners that irritate his nose. But lately it seems nothing can calm him, not even this room.

Lately it's more than the troubles of a growing nation that have gotten under his skin. He can't stop thinking about his abilities, about what he reads in men's eyes, and about what Kat told him. Snake Blood. The idea both thrills him and makes him shudder. He doesn't understand it, how he could have come by it…but it stands to reason that if Kat has magic blood and is in fact his true sister, then he might, too. With his mother gone from the palace until yesterday, he has been unable to get the satisfaction his mind needs. He's torn between the intense hunger to explore this power, and wariness. He already has too much to concern him.

The morning has only just begun—the gentle light streaming in through open windows gives the room a warm, rosy glow—and Alex wonders how he will make it through the day. He crosses his arms and looks at the documents littering the floor. Pirates intercepting Macedonian merchant vessels in the Aegean. Protests in Athens about Macedon's growing power. So much news, and still no word of Cynane or Arridheus, despite dozens of spies and messengers fanning out across Macedon and nearby countries.

Individually, each troubling report would be a normal occurrence for the ruler of a country to deal with. But together they are a maddening burden.

And the latest message: confirmation that Persian troops have slipped inside Byzantium to fight off Philip's invasion and its navy has closed the Bosporus Straits. That means none of the grain from the rich lands around the Euxine Sea can sail out. Grain feeds armies. Buys mercenaries. Keeps the people happy and paying taxes.

It's just like the Persians to offer Macedon a treaty on the one hand in the form of a bride, and on the other to fight against them in Byzantium, Alex knows. Aristotle told him that Persians would see nothing inconsistent in inviting a guest to a dazzling feast—savory meat, Chian wine in golden cups, beautiful dancing girls—and poisoning him.

He can't afford to send his men to Byzantium until the Aesarian Lords have paid their compensation to Macedon and left the country, but he also can't afford *not* doing anything and risk defeat in Byzantium.

"Cleitarchus!" Alexander calls, and the door from the hall swings open. A soldier enters.

"Yes, my lord?"

"Send for Captain Palamedes. Tell him it's urgent."

"Yes, my lord," the soldier says, bowing, "but I'm afraid that when the queen arrived yesterday, she sent Captain Palamedes and the Olympians on a special mission. They are not here at the moment."

Irritation rises in Alex like a cobra in a basket. His mother has her own unit, the Olympians, skilled not only in warfare but in espionage, deceit, poison, and all manner of treachery. They may not be the strongest nor most impressive unit in King Philip's army, but they are slick and fast and perfectly equipped to deal with Persia's slippery smiles. And his mother has sent them away.

Now his irritation coils around his chest, squeezing hard and spitting. Though Olympias was within her right to direct her own unit, protocol dictated that the king be informed to avoid just these circumstances. His mother has been back only one day, and she is already undermining Alex's authority.

"Send for the queen," he says, slamming his hand on the desk so hard that quills jump and several scrolls join their comrades on the floor. "Tell her it's urgent."

In a few minutes, a smiling Olympias enters on a wave of delicate perfume. Turning from the window, he sees that her bright eyes seem overlarge in a sunken face and her brows are heavily filled in with kohl. Her lips are painted blood red.

"My son, the war hero!" she says, her voice light and tinkling. She opens her arms to embrace him, and her wide sleeves fall back, revealing tiny wrists. He puts up a hand to stop her.

"Not now, Mother," he says. "I must ask you to recall the Olympians from whatever task you've sent them on. I have need of them."

The light falls harshly on her face. As she artfully arranges a bangle, he notices that she looks unwell, older than she did when he last saw her—was it ten days ago? Twelve? So much has happened since then it seems it was another lifetime.

"I'm afraid that's impossible," she says. "I need them where they are."

"Which is where, exactly?"

Olympias sweeps past him, settles in Philip's chair, and crosses her dainty ankles on the king's desk. She is wearing silver leather sandals in the shape of snakes with emerald eyes. "My Olympians are being *useful*, sweetheart. Are you worried about the pirates in the south Aegean?" She shakes her head. "They are getting forward. I will dispatch—"

"I didn't call you here to do my job for me!" Alexander says, rubbing a hand against a sore spot in the back of his neck. She's sitting in the king's chair, in his chair. With her feet on his desk. How can he get his own mother to move? "I have been managing well, while you disappeared. *Where* have you been?"

She sighs heavily and twists the loose rings on her fingers. "I went to deal with a threat to the realm."

Alex looks at her coldly. "If by threat you mean Katerina, you can be assured that she is no threat. Neither was the potter family you murdered."

"Oh, my darling." His mother smiles at him with pity, and Alexander suddenly feels like he is six again, when a thunderstorm rattled the palace so violently that everyone took refuge in the wine cellars. *It is just the gods practicing their swordsmanship*, she said then, holding him close. *Oh! That was loud! That must have been Zeus whacking Mars on his shield. They will not harm us, though.*

Now Olympias wags her finger at him as if he is a cute but naughty little boy. "If you let every pretty pair of eyes turn your head," she says, "then it's good that I've returned to the palace. The family needn't have died, but they wouldn't tell me her location. They defied the queen of Macedon so I had no other choice."

She sighs, a long sigh, then picks up an open scroll on the desk, scans it, and throws it back down. "You know as well as I do, Alex, how things must be done in order to maintain power and respect. Already, Hagnon's quarters have been emptied and men vie for the treasurer's position."

Heat pools in Alexander's stomach as he remembers the execution. He killed Hagnon, just as Olympias killed Kat's family. Is he *like* her? As a child, he wanted to be a warrior like Philip, but with his mother's grace, sophistication, and good looks. Now he wonders if they are alike in ways he doesn't want to acknowledge, and the thought chills him. But no, she killed innocent people, and he killed the guilty.

"They are completely different circumstances," he snaps. Suddenly, he is aware of his heart pumping hard. He must ask. Now. "Mother, I know."

"Know what, my darling?" She picks up his favorite dagger, forged in the blood of the last living phoenix, and rubs her fingers over the image of the bird on its hilt, wings and beak raised skyward, its eye a glowing ruby.

Alex takes it from her and places it back on his desk. "I know Katerina is my twin, your own flesh and blood." He can't quite bring himself to say the other thing: Kat's theory that they both share Snake Blood.

Olympias inhales sharply. For a split second Alex sees something unfamiliar flicker across his mother's face, but it vanishes before he can name it.

He pushes on. "Why did you separate us at birth?"

"That old tale," she says slowly, pulling her feet from the desk and rising in a cascade of shimmering scarlet robes. She starts pacing around the room, her hands clasped behind her back, and Alex realizes he must have inherited this habit from her, the need to move when conversation—or even thoughts—prove too burdensome.

"Years ago, Alex, when I was carrying you, I had a hand-maiden, Helen, who, though unmarried, got herself preg-nant and ran away. I heard rumors, over the years, that she was trying to pass off her child as mine."

She stops pacing and turns to face him. "Alex, think about it. Why would I send my daughter away with a handmaiden? It simply doesn't make sense. I've always wanted a daughter, and Philip would have loved another girl to barter on the royal marriage market. Helen must have told Katerina this story before she died."

His mother seems so angry, so sincere, that for a moment Alex doubts Kat's story. It is a strange one, after all. He wants to enter through his mother's eyes and learn the truth. He's never been pulled into her before, as he has with so many others over the years against his will. But if he concen-trates—does again what he did with Hagnon and Theopom-pus—could he enter Olympias's mind, access her memories? Somehow he doubts she would allow it. Would she know what he was trying to do, avert her gaze?

He doesn't even get the chance to try. When he approaches

her, she walks away. He puts a hand on her arm and she shakes it off and moves forward. She won't look at him.

He strides across the room and pours himself a cup of watered wine.

"Katerina didn't know any of this when she first arrived in Pella," he says, raising the cup to his lips. He drinks deeply. "When she escaped from the cell you put her in on false charges, she went to Halicarnassus and met someone who knew Helen. That's where she learned what happened at my birth."

Alex can see the gears and pulleys of his mother's mind working, moving and straining. Her wide eyes flit up to him. "Who?" she asks sharply. "Who did she meet?"

He noticed she doesn't bother to refute the false charges bit. "It doesn't matter," he says.

"You're right, it doesn't," she agrees, a little too swiftly. "What does matter is that under Macedonian law anyone pretending to be a member of the royal family is a traitor and must be executed. Katerina's mother was a traitor, and the girl herself is a traitor. Where is this peasant princess now?"

"Far from here," Alex says, and lines appear around his mother's mouth. "I sent her on a diplomatic mission. She boarded a ship almost a week ago."

"If you loaded her down with gold and gifts you will never see her again." Olympias snorts. "Your first diplomatic mission will be a failure." She sighs and reaches out a skeletal hand to tuck a stray lock of his hair behind his ear. Her hand is dry as leather. Alexander flinches.

"Really, Alexander," she says disapprovingly, "after all that time you spent studying with your precious Aristotle, you are still as gullible as a little boy."

"Yes, I'm just a gullible little boy who, in his first real battle, beat the most lethal fighting force in the world," he says, his voice as tight as a catapult spring. "Women from the palace—including Kat and your sixty-year-old mistress of the maids—helped me win that battle, Mother. But not you. You weren't here to help. You were off killing a harmless potter and his children."

A painful mingling of emotions moves across her face: regret, longing, even the faint curl of a rueful smile. He's shocked to see tears well in her eyes, spill over, and leave a trail of bone-white skin as they slide through her heavy makeup. "You may not love me, but I am still your mother, Alexander. All my love is for you. My heart's desire is to see you succeed." Her voice drops lower, softer. "Trust that all I do is for you."

Alex watches in shocked dismay as she takes a handkerchief from her belt and dabs carefully at her cheeks. As she pulls away the white cloth, color comes with it. But before he can ask his mother what has happened, she turns and slips away, as silent and mysterious as a plume of smoke.

Who should he believe, Kat or his mother? If Olympias speaks the truth, then what does that mean for his unusual ability, his suspicion that it could be magic?

What should he do? If only Aristotle were here to advise him and not off in Samothrace studying natural history.

If only Heph were here to help him parse his mother's words. Then they could spar in the training ring. Burn off energy. That was always a sure way to center him, remind himself who he is. Alex's gaze slides from the closed door to the piles of scrolls on the floor. He needs to find a new sparring partner.

An hour later, Kadmus breaks from Alex's grip, twists and, catching him by the waist, throws him to the ground. But not very hard.

And he doesn't pounce on Alex to end the match as Heph would have, glorying in his win. Instead he makes a lame attempt to knock him backward as Alex scrambles to his feet. When Alex lunges at him, he doesn't feel the taut resistance he should, the arms and shoulders repelling him, the sneaky feet tripping him. True, Kadmus is shorter than Alex is and probably weighs less, but he has had several years more battle training and fighting experience. Yet he goes down like a felled tree in the sand of the round training pit, his muscular, lithe warrior's body just lying there like a defeated little girl.

Alex runs a hand through his sweaty hair. He just wants to feel muscle against muscle, strength against strength. And it's not happening. Kadmus is letting him win, Alex is sure.

Distrust radiates through Alex like pain. He demands honesty: on the battlefield, in the council chamber, and in the training arena.

"You don't need to coddle me," Alex says, standing over the general and offering his hand to help him up. "You're not fighting me with all your ability."

Kadmus pushes his dark hair out of his eyes as a slow grin breaks across his neat, lean face. He lunges at Alex, twisting away from Alex's outstretched hands and gripping him around the waist. His right foot curls around Alex's right leg, and suddenly Alex finds himself hurtling through the air and slamming hard into the ground.

Alex grins. "Better," he says, rising and dusting the dirt from his tunic. The two circle each other, arms outstretched.

"My mind is elsewhere, my lord," Kadmus says, feinting a lunge as Alex dodges back. "I've heard your people are upset that you have only one council member—me."

"Go on."

The two of them slam into each other as hard as battling bucks and pull quickly apart.

"They say Macedon cannot continue to be run by a sixteen-year-old, no matter how brilliant. Even Philip, an experienced general and king, had a full council."

"They're right," Alex says, throwing his arms around Kadmus. His neck smells like leather oil from the stables and citrons rubbed on skin for a pleasant scent. His long dark hair has its own fragrance: smoke, probably from the barracks kitchen fire.

"I need a council," Alex agrees as they grapple, testing each other's strength and flexibility. Leonidas: dead in the fire. Hagnon: executed. Gordias: in prison. Theopompus: retired in anger to his country estate.

"Experienced people advising me with many voices," he continues, "and then I can choose what is best for Macedon. As it stands, I am frustrated on all sides—even by my mother."

Kadmus twists from Alex's grip and dances a couple of steps back. "Your mother?" he asks, raising his left eyebrow high. "That might be a tougher dilemma to solve than pirates or Persians. What has she done now?" He dives for Alex, puts one hand on his shoulder and the other behind his back, and tries to throw him backward. Alex resists him, aware of his tense muscles, sweaty tunic, and beating heart.

But Alex keeps his balance and knocks Kadmus's arms away. "Mother sent the Olympians out on personal business without asking me," he says, catching his breath. "And insulted my education. She was the one who insisted I study at Mieza. My father says kings should wield swords, not quills, and fire missiles at the enemy, not pretty speeches."

Kadmus lunges for Alex's left side, which Alex turns to protect, only to find it was a split-second feint. Kadmus now grips his right arm. He twists it, sending Alex to his knees.

"Well, what are you going to do about it?" Kadmus asks while simultaneously pulling Alex into a tight headlock.

Alex relaxes completely, knowing his adversary will loosen his grip. Then, he twists with all his weight. One arm grabs Kadmus's right elbow; his other arm grips his back. Throwing his years of built-up strength into the move, Alexander lifts the struggling man and throws him face-first onto the ground. Then he straddles his back and pulls Kadmus's hair so that his face is off the ground.

Now he knows exactly what to do about his mother, the council, and all his problems. "Thank you, my friend," he says. "You've given me an idea."

"What's that?" Kadmus asks, spitting sand out of his mouth.

Alexander carefully climbs off Kadmus's back and lets the general stand. "As soon as the Aesarian Lords leave Macedon, my friend, you and I will have a journey to make."

Chapter Sixteen

CYNANE HEARS THE THUNDERING OF THE horses' hooves first, a deep rumble that seems to come from the bowels of the earth. Then she hears the men's shouts and sees their torches advancing toward her. A cloud slides away from the three-quarter moon, and its silver-white light falls on the horns of their helmets, causing them to glow.

They cannot see her, curled up atop a tall, leafy tree. Nor can they see her tracks at night. But even if they don't find her tonight, if she stays in this tree, she is sure to fall from its branches from either exhaustion or starvation. She needs to get as far as she can before the sun comes up.

When the Aesarian Lords have dwindled into the distance, Cyn slowly climbs down. Every bone in her body aches. Every muscle is feeble. She realizes she must look like a wraith. A skeleton with matted hair. Her left shoulder and arm throb with pain where the bowlegged Scythian Lord tattooed a magical design of a stag deep into her skin with needles and lamp soot—to make her a real Amazon, he said. Her body emanates a fusty smell like a wool cloak left too long in a trunk. It's not the healthy sweat of fighting but the mustiness of going too long unwashed and unmoving.

The fact that Cyn is not hungry at all worries her. It's as if her body is giving up and food has no place inside it anymore. She needs to find safety, and soon.

She forces herself to put one foot in front of the other. It's dangerous to stick to the road, but she is too weak to climb over fallen trunks and push her way through bushes in the safety of the forest. And it's easier to walk on the road since she is barefoot. The best protection she has is the hope that she will hear the Lords' horses in enough time to duck into the woods.

The moon slides slowly across the arc of the sky, and Cyn wonders how many miles she has walked. Maybe not that many since she's going so slowly. Exhaustion hangs just as heavy as the metal chains Jacob melted from her. It had to have been Jacob who did it. If it had been her Smoke Blood, she would have done it sooner. And the smoke man who visited her in the cell—in her dreams—said he could not break shackles. Then again, if she has begun believing her dreams are real, can her own mind be trusted to decipher the truth?

Fingers of golden-pink light streak across the purple sky as if writing her death sentence. Morning. She has found no safe haven, and the Lords will be back soon. In fact...she hears the low rumble of horses' hooves coming toward her, growing louder, ever louder. She looks for a tree to climb, but she's moved too quickly and now dizziness slams down on her.

The world spins. Her knees collapse, hitting the rock-hard dirt, and they splay, sending her face forward. She puts out her hands to prevent her face from smacking the ground, but her legs are not as cooperative. They lie there, like dead things. Cursing them, she tries to drag herself to the nearest bushes, but her arms, too, have lost their last vestige of strength.

From the sound of the hooves, she knows a large troop of soldiers approaches. The Aesarian Lords have found her. They will take her back to the fortress, back to that hideous embalming. She won't allow it. She'll die first. Perhaps she can make them so mad they will kill her here, cleanly, in the clear rising dawn, not a bad death. Suddenly, the noise halts, and she doesn't know if they have left or have dismounted. She cannot see them clearly because gold sparks dance and pop before her eyes and dizziness holds her in its swaying grip.

"Princess Cynane!" She hears a voice call her name, sounding very far away. An enormous bulk surges toward her like a furious bear and as he gets closer, she makes out that it is a man. But friend or foe? He isn't wearing a helmet—horned or otherwise—so she can't be sure. But she was never one to take chances.

He bends over her and she punches him in the face. But her fist doesn't connect with flesh, only air. As he picks her up in strong arms, she tries to scratch him, kick him, bite him, but then realizes that she only fights in her mind. Her hands are flopping uselessly in the air, like two beached fish. She is still powerless. She is weak.

She is thrown on a horse, and before she can fall off the other side, her captor leaps up behind her, his huge muscular bulk preventing her from sliding.

With tremendous effort, she raises her head, and says, "May all three heads of Cerberus bite off your balls, you turd-eating, goat-humping sonofabitch." Then she slips into a safe, black place without pain, and is glad.

Her mother, Audata, is waiting for her there, washing her burning forehead with cool mint water, telling her to be strong.

"Mother!" Cyn calls out. But when the woman opens her mouth, Audata doesn't sound like Audata. Almost ten years after her death, her mother's sharp features have faded in her memory like wax under water, but her mellifluous voice remains clear, like an insect preserved in amber. The voice coming from her mother now is deeper. More masculine.

"Remember your legacy," Audata/not-Audata says. "You are a princess of Illyria."

Finally, Cyn places the voice. It's the same as the one that spoke so often to her in captivity. Yes! It is back. She is not alone, captured again by the Aesarian Lords. This powerful spirit will protect her. Hope rekindles. This is—

Audata places a cool hand on the top of Cyn's head, and agony engulfs her, drowning her hope in a jagged embrace. Just when she thinks she will die from the torment, she feels the first whispers of relief. The intensity fades. She looks up at her mother, who smiles down at her and says, with the ghostly old man's voice, "Sleep now, child."

Cyn wakes in her bedroom at the palace. Late-afternoon sun streams through the slatted shutters, making bars of golden light on the floor. She had been swept into a complex adventure by Morpheus himself, it seems. Her mother, the Lords, the disembodied voice, the melted chains—all explained by a dream.

She stretches, and as she does her left shoulder begins to ache and an earthy, pungent odor of healing herbs rises from a carefully wound bandage of fine linen strips. Her eyes fly open and she pulls off the bandage. There, beneath a thick smear of salve, is an intricate pattern of a Scythian stag with wild curling horns. Her time as a prisoner with the Aesarian Lords thunders back to her. No dream, then.

Carefully, she pulls back the sheets and examines her arms

and legs. She is covered with insect bites, but someone has washed her and put her in a clean shift. Even as she looks at them, she can see her bruises fading. Returning health and strength pulse through her veins.

She doesn't understand. How can she *not* have Smoke Blood? But the man of smoke who'd appeared to her had said she did not. And the Aesarian Lords, too, proclaimed that whatever protected her was an enchantment—not something that came from Cyn herself but from something *other*. What, then, is she?

The question consumes her, driving away every ache and pain and shard of self-pity. Cynane needs to know. She cannot rest until she finds the answer.

As she starts to slide out of bed, there's a knock at her door, and a moment later Alex enters. His face lights up when he sees her, as if he's truly happy to have her back. They've never been close. She assumed, during her endless days and nights in Aesarian captivity, he would be glad she was gone. But now...

"Cyn, I can't tell you how happy I am you are safe," he says, sitting on her bed and—great Zeus—he's actually hugging her. Her nose is buried in his pale gold hair, which smells of wind and grass and sunshine. Have they ever embraced before? She can't remember. He pulls away and looks at her, the sparkle in his eyes rapidly dulling. "What happened?" he asks, his voice as flat and hard as an anvil. "You're so thin. And what did they do to your arm?"

Haltingly, she tells him of her capture in the library and of her imprisonment and daily torture sessions in the fortress. She does not tell him about the extent of the torture, her miraculous healings, and the smoke man who visited her in the tower room. Alex's eyes grow wide when she embellishes her escape: she wrapped her chains around the guard's neck, strangled him, and took the keys off his belt. With each word, Alex seems to settle into himself more, growing hard and bright and fierce.

She finishes by adding the part she knows will matter most to Alexander: what she overheard the Lords saying about Supreme Lord Gulzar and his regiment of troops headed their way bringing not reparations money, but another, much stronger attack.

Alex nods, stands, and says, his voice tight with anger, "This changes everything. I had plans to bring Kadmus with me to…well, that doesn't matter just now. The Aesarian Lords lied to us in our treaty negotiations. I asked them repeatedly if they had you. I offered them a huge ransom. But they swore they did not have you. This means our treaty is null and void. And now they're awaiting reinforcements all the way from Nekrana? This means…"

He stands taller, straighter, and his strange-colored eyes burn with a preternatural fury.

"War."

He turns on his heel and storms from her room.

War. Cyn inhales her first true feeling of strength since her capture. She only hopes she has enough time to recuperate so she can join the battle. Surely Alex won't refuse her this time. She imagines cracking the skulls and slicing off the limbs of the men who tortured her. The tall Ethiopian with the soothing voice who oversaw her torment. The little laughing Scythian who stuck needles and hot soot in her arm. The enormous Celt with the blond braids who smashed her bones with an iron bar.

But right now Cyn has another task at hand. She wraps a robe around herself and slips into sandals. Silently she pads through the familiar corridors, encountering only Olympias's personal laundress, her head almost obscured by a pile of neatly folded towels. In the far corner of the residential section of the palace, she climbs the winding staircase and opens the door to the top tower room. Her mother's room.

It's dark in here, and musty. She flings open the window shutters, letting light and air into the circular room. Thick linen sheets drape the furniture. She plucks off the sheets covering the pigeonholes lining one wall and starts unrolling scrolls. They were part of Audata's dowry from Illyria, and her mother prized them above all her possessions.

Cynane unrolls maps of Illyria, histories of Illyria, drawings of Illyria. She's never been there, but her mother used to describe the seawater clear as rain, the round stone huts in mountain villages, the ancient songs—with the clapping of hands and the stomping of feet—and the spirited line dances of the people.

Audata would have become queen of Dardania—a kingdom within the Illyrian tribal lands—if she hadn't married Philip. When she did, her father made his grandson, Amyntas, his new heir. Cyn knows little of him, only that he is seventeen and somehow unfit to rule. And that if he died, *she* would become queen.

Queen. In her own right.

Not as a broodmare consort sitting decoratively on a small throne next to a husband with all the power on a big one. She looks up from the dusty scrolls, wondering what it would be like to rule a country. Lead armies to battle. Make life-or-death decisions. Gaze out over a sea of faces alight with fear and respect, envy and loyalty.

But right now she needs to keep looking for anything about the smoke man. She unrolls dozens more scrolls, sneezing and coughing as dust flies up her nose and tickles the back of her throat. Finally, Cyn finds a reference to a great magician whose name has been lost to time; one who could walk inside people's dreams. A man whose physical body dissolved slowly, fading day by day, until he was visible only as smoke.

Her heart skips a beat, then races with excitement. Goose bumps form along her arms. Yes, this is it! This is the spirit who visited her in the tower room of the fortress, who said he put a powerful protective spell on her the day her mother died. She didn't hallucinate it. It was real. The smoke spirit—

Cyn is so wrapped in thought she doesn't notice the door opening. When she sees movement out of the corner of her eye, she turns around to face a gliding, white-veiled figure. For an instant, she wonders if it is a ghost, her mother's ghost. When the figure raises its veil, she knows it's an apparition. The face is as white as an unpainted statue. Immediately, she reaches for the dagger she always keeps strapped to her thigh before she remembers that it's not there.

The apparition laughs, a tinkling, silvery little sound. A sound that makes Cyn grit her teeth. "Surely you're not thinking of stabbing your beloved stepmother?" it asks.

Olympias. Cyn looks at her uncomprehendingly. Her face is sunken, her eyes huge, and she's swimming in an ocean of blue robes instead of the sleeveless, tightly belted gowns she usually wears. The veil she has tossed back from her snow-white face does little to hide thin, stringy hair still damp from a bath. Why would such a vain woman leave her chambers looking like this? And then Cyn knows. Her laundress must have told Olympias she had seen Cyn in the hall. And Olympias, without waiting to do her makeup or fix her hair, threw on a veil and raced after her.

"By the gods, I thought you were a ghost," Cyn says rising. "Are you? What happened to you? You look horrible."

"I could ask you the same thing," Olympias says smoothly, and Cyn is annoyed by the queen's calm demeanor. "Have *you* looked in a mirror yet? When my guards brought you back, you were not even fit for the Augean stables. If you were an animal, I would have had you put down."

She sighs, a condescending sound that makes Cyn bristle. "I can only imagine how difficult it will be for Philip to arrange your marriage. He's in negotiations this moment, you know. But between your looks, your unfeminine tastes, and your low-ranking status…" The queen wrinkles her nose. "Let's just say it's been difficult."

Cyn's body goes rigid. *Marriage.* At eighteen, Cyn is getting quite long in the tooth on the marriage market; most princesses are married off as soon as they bleed at twelve or thirteen. She's successfully avoided it until now. It is something she simply cannot allow.

"My queen," she says, and she notices that Olympias looks momentarily startled as Cyn addresses her by that title. She has never done so before now.

Trying to hide her desperation, Cyn pushes on. "I wish to regain my stolen birthright, the kingdom of Dardania in Illyria. I don't want to stay in Macedon. After Philip, Alex will be king and there is no place for me here, just a spot on the royal marriage market, as you say. I don't want to marry, not even to become a queen consort. Everyone knows they don't have any power."

The last bit slides out before she can stop it, and Cyn almost flinches at her mistake. Olympias herself is only a queen consort.

Olympias rounds on her, green eyes glittering dangerously in her white marble face streaked with delicate veins of gray-blue. "What, exactly, are you suggesting?"

Cyn is suddenly very tired, either from her journey or from these games, she can't tell which. She rushes on. "What I'm trying to say is that in order for me to rule in my own right, my cousin Amyntas, the king, must die."

Cyn looks the queen straight in the eye. "Give me his head, and I will do whatever you ask me to do. I know you have plots and plans and lovers. Surely you could use someone with my skills. I can skewer a man twice my size with a sword, or seduce him and get him to tell me whatever I want."

The queen takes a step away from her, and she walks slowly around the room, snatching sheets off furniture, and running her fingers over tables and chairs as Cyn's blood boils. Olympias has no right to be in here, touching these items. This was and will always be Audata's room. Never hers.

The queen finally stops before a window and looks out over the city of Pella and the purple-blue hills rising in the distance. Then she seems to make a decision. She turns and studies Cyn with interest. "I *could* arrange for Amyntas to have an accident," she says slowly, "or have him drink something that disagrees with him...."

Hope sparks inside her. Olympias—with her rumored networks of spies and poisoners—could easily do it.

"But," Olympias adds, and Cyn braces herself for the price she knew would come. "I will want something from you, first."

The queen smiles, and for a moment Cyn wonders if her hard white face will crack. What *happened* to her? Her teeth, which were always blazing white from sanding them with pumice stone and rinsing them with vinegar, now seem oddly yellow in her chalklike face.

She quickly looks away from the queen's teeth. "Tell me."

"Last week Alexander sent that peasant friend of his, Katerina, on a secret mission," the queen says. "You must find out where she is, go there, and bring me back *her* head on a platter. Then I will arrange for you to go to Dardania as queen."

Olympias's eyes—molten green lights in that ghastly white face—are boring into Cynane as if daring her to protest, to ask questions. And though she has a thousand questions, Cyn realizes she doesn't really care why Olympias wants Kat dead. If that's what it takes for her to become ruler of Dardania, she'll do it. No answers needed.

"Agreed," she says, nodding. "I'll find her, kill her, and bring her head back to you. But you must make an oath that if I do this, you will make me queen of Dardania."

Olympias raises both arms and bows her head low. "I promise you, Cynane of Macedon, if you do as I ask, I will deliver Amyntas's heart to you on a golden platter. And I swear on all that I hold holy, by the vengeance of the Furies, and on the sacred mysteries of Dionysus and the Kabeiri, that I will ensure you become queen of Dardania."

Cyn searches the queen's face, looking for the lie. She can't find it, which disturbs her. There has to be a lie there *somewhere*. Her stepmother pulls the veil over her face before Cyn can interrogate her.

"You must hurry," Olympias says. "For if Philip signs a marriage contract before you've accomplished this task, not even I can sway his mind."

Cynane does not reply. There is no need. She picks up the scroll containing the story of the man of smoke and heads for the door. Already she has a plan. She will search her father's office, and if there's nothing in there about Katerina's whereabouts, she will bribe servants or charm soldiers until she knows the mission.

In the hall she turns back and sees Olympias standing in the center of the room, a heavily veiled, unmoving figure, like one of Hades's shades. A shudder runs from the top of her spine down to its base as if a blade had slit it open.

Cyn opens the door to Alex's office and silently slips inside. She is not alone. There is a girl already in there.

Cyn recognizes her from somewhere, though the waterfall of golden spangled veils cascading from the top of her head down to the floor seems new. Cynane tilts her head and sees her rubbing a small item with one of her veils. Little pieces of something—wax?—fall onto the desk. She gathers these up in her hand, sprinkles them inside her robe, and places a golden object in a drawer—Alexander's regency seal, his profile inside the sixteen-pointed gold star of Macedon. The seal that, impressed on wax at the bottom of a document, proves that he wrote it.

When the girl turns slightly, Cyn sees the distinctive cat-like profile and knows; it's Sarina, Arri's nurse. In two strides Cynane is at the desk, her hand like a vise around the girl's slender, golden-brown wrist. "What documents have you just affixed my brother's royal seal to?" she hisses. She tightens her grip on the girl's wrist so that she winces.

"I've just—I didn't—" Sarina stammers. With her free hand, Cyn opens the drawer and pulls out a large, round gold seal on the end of an agate handle. She runs her thumbs over the carved flat surface on the bottom. The gold is faintly warm. The red wax taper beside it is soft, melted.

"Please," Sarina says, her throaty voice shaking, as she looks down and bites her lip. "I am only trying to release my brother from prison in Egypt. The prince regent is so overburdened with cares, I didn't want to ask him to do it. It is such a little thing, a letter to the Persian satrap in Memphis asking to let my brother out so he can join me here. He is all the family I have left. The Persians killed everyone else."

"And how is it you have access to Alexander's office?"

Sarina tugs a veil. "With Arri…gone…Alexander has made me his personal attendant." She holds out her hand, and Cyn can clearly see the silver signet ring engraved with the sixteen-pointed Macedonian star that marks her as a member of Alex's household. Interesting…and possibly advantageous.

"Writing letters as the prince is forgery," Cyn says, drawing herself up to her full height. She towers above Sarina, who takes a step back. "A crime punishable by torture and death." The girl opens her mouth, but Cyn holds up her palm to silence her. "However, I won't tell Alexander so long as you give me the information I need."

"Anything, my lady," Sarina says, dropping a curtsy. "If I don't have it, I will find it for you, I promise."

Cyn relaxes, leans against the edge of Alex's desk, and folds her arms. "Last week the prince sent Alex's friend Katerina on a mission somewhere. I need to know where. By tomorrow."

"Ah," she says softly. "That I already know." She clears her throat and her black, liquid eyes look at Cyn. For a second, Cyn is mesmerized by their bright depths. "She did not go alone, my lady. Lord Hephaestion accompanied her."

Heph? Cyn feels a small, hot spark of…something. "Where did they go?"

"They went to Egypt to find the palace of Princess Laila of Sharuna along the Nile. There is talk of a marriage between Alexander and Laila, or at least a treaty with military assistance."

How curious, Cyn thinks, and she narrows her eyes. "If you're lying…"

The girl shakes her head. "No lie, princess."

"Good. Because if you are, I shall kill you." Cyn heads for the door before she can see how Sarina reacts to the threat.

She doesn't have time for nursemaids-turned-mistresses. She doesn't have time, either, to worry over how a lowly slave girl has learned to write.

In the hall, torches throw moving shadows on the dark red walls, making the frescoes of Hercules killing the Nemean lion with a club seem to move. Cyn, too, needs to move, but ships to Egypt are always leaving from Pella's port. Olympias will give her money, and she will pack lightly, riding to the port at dawn. It's a pity she'll miss the battle against those bastards, the Aesarian Lords, but—

"Did you find what you were looking for, my lady?" Cyn turns to see the guard who let her into the office addressing her. Torchlight glints off dark eyes on either side of a bronze nosepiece, and Cyn allows herself a moment to take in his height and shoulders that have no problem filling out his scarlet cloak.

She wishes she could see his face, the shape of his nose and the angle of his jaw, all hidden by the bronze helmet. But perhaps the face doesn't matter. The body is perfect, and unlike most warriors he's in possession of a full set of white teeth.

She wonders if she should invite him for a cup of wine in her room once his watch is over. The last man whose company she enjoyed was Hephaestion, almost a month ago, and that hadn't ended well... Cyn studies the guard again. His biceps are so huge, he could crush her, and the idea excites her. But, alas, she must rise early for her journey to track Kat. And her entire body still aches from her ordeal.

"I might have," she says, her gaze slowly scanning up to his face.

White teeth flash at her from the shadows of his helmet. "Am I really a turd-eating, goat-humping sonofabitch? And are you really going to...um, bite me where it hurts?"

She stops. "What?"

"That's what you said when I picked you up from the road," he says.

"You?" All she saw was something like a bear hurtling toward her with outstretched arms.

"Me," he replies. The part of his face she can see behind the helmet crinkles into a smile. She decides that the face must be handsome, too.

"What is your name?" she asks, arching her back slightly so that her breasts strain against her smoke-colored shift. They are not as full as they used to be, but they are still shapely.

His eyes travel down to her chest, and he smiles. "Priam."

"Priam." She allows herself to draw out his name a beat too long so that her voice drapes on the air like perfume. She turns her back and begins to walk toward the queen's chambers, conscious of how her hips sway with each step. She'll have to find soldier Priam again when she returns to Pella. He might make a nice plaything as she awaits news of Amyntas's murder and makes her way to Illyria as queen.

But first, she must find and kill that peasant-bitch, Katerina.

CHAPTER SEVENTEEN

HEPH LEANS ON THE RAILING OF THE NARROW, flat-bottomed riverboat and realizes once again that he was wrong. He has always thought of Egypt as a parched place of unending sand, but this is a land of sweeping, roiling water. It spreads out east and west as far as he can see, an ocean of rippling lapis blue, bustling with boats. Heph knew from his time in Mieza that the Nile floods for half the year, leaving behind rich, black alluvial earth for crops, but he never imagined a flood like this.

In Caria, it had taken them three days to find space on a boat bound for Egypt. Every available spot was taken up by Persian soldiers headed to quell rebellion. Finally, just when he thought he was going to lose his mind from impatience, they bought passage. Poseidon granted them a stiff following wind and fine weather on the two-day sail to Naucratis, an old Greek trading port on the westernmost branch of the seven mouths of the Nile.

And yesterday, Heph hired the most experienced riverboat captain he could find to navigate the dangerous Delta, a land of twisting canals, sucking swamps, and high, feathery-tufted papyrus reeds that routinely swallows entire invading armies who've lost their way. Their boat, the *Hathor,* glided past large villages built on stilts and negotiated around thin fishermen on the flimsiest of boats made of papyrus reeds.

Sudden winged explosions of geese and ducks surging from the reeds made Heph jump more than a few times. Kat laughed when she caught him grabbing for his sword, but it was his turn to laugh this morning when a hippopotamus rose next to their boat. Water poured off its flat brown head as it opened its enormous pink maw and emitted a roar that made Kat, the professed animal-lover, shriek on deck.

Finally, the boat emerges from the meandering forests of reeds onto the Nile proper, and now a stiff north breeze fills the huge rectangular sail, pushing the craft toward what looks like three snowy mountains in the distance. Heph's pulse races. He thinks he knows what they are.

Kat slides out of the cool shadows of the long canopy in the middle of the boat and puts her hand over her eyes. "What's that?" she asks, squinting.

"The pyramids," he says, his voice soft with wonder. "Tombs of the ancient Egyptian kings."

Soon they are gliding past three gigantic pyramids coated with white limestone and capped with gold that burns like fire in the bright afternoon sky. Aristotle said the pyramids were big, but the word *big* hardly begins to describe these mountains filling the sky in front of him. He finds it hard to credit men with building them. Gods, maybe, but not men.

In the distance, he sees a city glimmering white, its gigantic walls painted with colorful animal-headed gods. A broad channel wraps around the walls where part of the Nile has been diverted, making the city a fortified island. From its center, gold-tipped obelisks rise like divine fingers pointing heavenward.

"The white walls of Memphis," Heph says, "the capital of Egypt."

"Are you sure?" Kat says. "I thought maybe it was Mount Olympus come down to sea level. It doesn't seem real, somehow." She laughs. "And to think, when I first saw Pella I nearly swooned. But this…" Her words peter out, and wind wraps gently around her hair, tugging strands loose.

He, too, feels a surge of joy to experience the unfathomable wonders of Egypt with her. Though they disliked each other heartily at first, he now realizes they are alike in many ways: fiercely loyal, defiantly courageous, and constantly nagged by the feeling they never quite know where they belong.

For a moment, he can almost forget the urgency of their mission. That if they don't return with a military alliance for Alexander, Macedon could be in danger of falling to Persia. That if *he* doesn't satisfy the prince's request, he may fall from Alex's grace forever. For a moment, he can almost forget his love for Alexander, the best friend he ever had. And the horrible prophecy that predicts Alex's death at the hands of his own sister.

Kat flashes Heph a dazzling smile, which sends a jolt of prickling heat through him. Heph quickly looks away. He made a promise—to her, and to himself.

"What is the name of their king?" she asks.

"They call their king a pharaoh, and there isn't one at the moment," Heph says. "When the Persians invaded three years ago, he ran south to Ethiopia, and no one has heard of him since. The Persians have a satrap ruling now, a kind of general-governor."

The port of Memphis spreads out along the river as far as he can see. The *Hathor* passes shipbuilding facilities, a naval arsenal, and enormous silos that must serve as warehouses for

Egypt's abundant grain. As the boat's rowers angle the craft toward one of the piers in the bustling port, they nearly collide with an Egyptian funeral boat. Female mourners, faces caked with white mud, gather around a gilded mummy case, shrieking and beating their bare breasts.

"Egypt is so very *different*," Kat whispers, as the rowers stow their paddles and throw ropes to the pilings. "Caria was much more like home."

The *Hathor*'s captain bustles up beside them. His potbelly, hovering over two spindly legs, reminds Heph of one of the fat swamp birds he saw in the Delta waiting for fish. "We dock here for the night," he says in badly mangled Persian— the language he must assume they speak as the region is under Persian control. "Will you stay on deck or go into town?"

Heph glances at Kat. The skin below her eyes is tinged slightly with cobalt. He knows she hardly slept last night. There were river monsters—the captain called them crocodiles—churning the water beneath them and Kat shuddered, saying the beasts had no thought but one: *hunger.*

They both kept their swords at the ready.

"We'll find an inn," Heph says, and translates for Kat, who looks relieved. "We'll be back early tomorrow morning."

They push their way down the pier, past sailors unloading goods: curved elephant tusks longer than a man, iron ingots, animal hides. In the harbor, merchants loudly hawk their wares: sandals, incense, colorful birds and a mind-boggling array of other things that blend into a bright-hued blur. The air smells of salt and hot stone, of aromatic spices and sour sweat, of fresh bread and roasting meat.

"Let's find an inn!" he yells over the noise.

She opens her mouth, but he can't hear her. She cups her hands to his ear and tries again. "Away from the harbor, please!" He nods and gently takes Kat's elbow so that they won't be separated by the crowd and become lost among the stiff-limbed statues of pharaohs twenty times the height of a man.

A beautiful young woman with thick black hair and bright red lips smiles seductively at Heph as she passes. As he turns back to watch her, she pauses, takes off her wig to reveal a bald head, and scratches it before slapping her wig back on. His mouth drops open as he remembers Aristotle's lesson on Egyptian customs: everyone shaves their heads to prevent lice infestations.

Kat suddenly stops walking. "Did you see—?" She looks around at the dozen or so scribes sitting against walls, writing trays on their knees, then shakes her head. "Never mind."

"See what?"

"Nothing," she says, "It's just there are so many strangely dressed people here, aren't there? Look at them." She gestures toward two men chatting by the temple gate. They are bare-chested, and heavy kohl lines their eyes while their hair is a mass of tiny black braids. Wide turquoise faience collars adorn their otherwise bare chests, and pleated white kilts hug their slender hips.

She flashes another grin at him, and his heart rolls in his chest. "I'd like to see you dressed like that," she teases.

There it is again, the jolt like strong wine surging hotly through his veins.

"And I'd like to see *you* dressed like *that,*" Heph says, nodding in the direction of two young women talking animatedly to each other in the street. Their sleeveless, sheer white gowns seem glued to their curves, leaving almost nothing to the imagination.

He expects her to banter back, to tease, to play. Instead he sees a blush rise on her cheeks as she stares at the ground. He shouldn't have said it. Why did he say it? But she started it, didn't she? Saying she wanted to see him with his shirt off? The hot surge drains away, and he's left with cold dregs.

That evening, torches light the courtyard of the small inn they found on a relatively quiet street. Though this inn is laid out like the inns he's visited in the Greek world—rooms on two levels accessed by a courtyard, with the stables and latrines at the far end—it's wildly more colorful. The walls are painted turquoise, and life-sized red-skinned men in strange headdresses stalk panthers and lions in profile. Even the short, fat columns are painted with human-headed beasts and magical markings. Around the courtyard, lanterns of red and blue glass give off a brighter light than he has ever seen from the ox-horn-paneled lanterns back home. Heph makes a note to bring some back to Alex.

The night breeze off the Nile has cooled the entire city, and an enormous full moon and dazzling glitter of stars paint the black sky above. The roast duck in front of him is lightly spiced with coriander, and for the first time since they've left Pella, he feels relaxed. Capable. Confident.

He takes a swig of wild yeast beer. The taste is fizzy, musty, and full-bodied. "Four days, maybe five, according to the captain. I wonder— Kat, what's wrong?"

Katerina has suddenly sat up, dropping her bread in the bowl of cinnamon sauce. "Do you see?" she breathes, her eyes darting to the corner of the courtyard. "There was a man. A tall man in a black cloak with a scarf wrapped around his face. I've seen him a few times, ever since we got off the boat."

The beer suddenly weighs on his stomach. It is possible that the mercenaries onboard the *Prometheus* talked about meeting well-trained peasants with spectacular swords out at sea and sold this information to the highest bidder.

They might be known. Either way, they can't risk it. Too much depends on this mission.

"Stay still," Heph says, taking another sip of beer. It burns down his throat. "In a moment, we will both go to your room, but don't give away that we know."

Kat nods stiffly and scoops up some more sauce with flat bread.

"We're probably just imagining things, after everything we've been through on this journey," Heph says reassuringly. "Cheer up, Kat. You look as if you just knocked over King Philip's Nikosthenes amphora."

Kat smiles, but her shoulders are high, narrow, and tense. "I've broken too many pots in my foster father's workshop," she says, "to go anywhere near rare masterpieces by long-dead artists."

A few moments later, he gives her a slight nod, and she puts down the bread. They quickly make their way to Kat's tiny room. There's only one bed, but since they will each keep watch this night, it doesn't matter.

Heph volunteers for first watch and leans back against the wall, sword by his side. He left the door open two handsbreadths, and now a bar of soft starlight filters in. The only sound, other than intermittent voices in the courtyard below, is Kat's regular breathing. Lying there so peacefully, her pink lips slightly parted and strands of golden-brown hair resting across her cheek, she looks so very young. Her fire, her intelligence, her courage are nowhere to be seen. She reminds Heph of Alex sleeping. The prince had the bed next to Heph's at Mieza, and often they shared a tent on campaign with Philip or out hunting. Alex, too, looks like a sweet child when he sleeps.

The moment Alex and Kat first met, when Heph was trying to have Kat arrested for cheating on the Blood Tournament bets, he knew there was something between them. The very air seemed charged, like right before Zeus throws a thunderbolt to split a tree. When Alex countermanded Heph's order and rode off with Kat to the palace, Heph assumed it was physical attraction. But now he knows that these two share a special bond, a blood-magic bond that makes them much closer even than normal twins. Something he can never share with either of them, or with anyone else either, for that matter. The thought leaves him feeling that the night is very vast, and he is very alone in it.

A clatter reverberates through the room, and Heph leaps to his feet, pulling the leather cover off the lantern. Perhaps not so alone, after all. The new light illuminates a tall figure in black robes standing in the doorway, hopelessly caught in a fishing net. The bucket of pebbles that he and Kat placed on top of the door has fallen, bringing down the carefully draped net with it.

Heph tries to grab the figure, but even though he is caught in a net, the man is strong, twisting out of Heph's grasp and knocking his sword hand so hard that the weapon skitters across the wooden floor. Heph launches himself forward, puts his foot between the intruder's feet and swings his leg in a half circle, causing the man to lose his balance and fall hard on the floor. Suddenly Heph feels a hard kick to his knee and comes down like a sacrificial ox knocked unconscious by the hammer of a priest. Now the intruder, net and all, straddles Heph, but his hands, hopelessly caught in the net, can't reach for a weapon or Heph's throat. Heph pushes him off and sits on his abdomen, his knees squeezing the hands against the body.

Kat appears next to him holding the lantern, and Heph notes with approval that she has two swords in her other hand. She hands him his.

"Who are you?" he pants. "Who sent you? Tell me or I'll cut off your head."

"Heph, please! It's me!" The voice is female. And familiar. Somewhere deep down inside, it stirs up a cauldron's brew of guilt and desire. Heph climbs off and looks at Kat in surprise.

Kat stays back, frowning. "What is your name?" she asks.

The figure chuckles, a low throaty sound that reminds Heph of soft nights and whispering sheets. "Am I so forgettable?" the voice replies. "It's me."

Heph sucks in a breath. *Cynane.*

His body tingles a little as he remembers a passion the likes of which he never shared with any Mieza village girl. Afterward, he was surprised that his sheets hadn't turned to ash. But what is Cyn doing here, in Egypt? No one had seen her since the night nearly three weeks ago when the Aesarian Lords invaded the palace and set fire to the library. Briefly, he wonders how she could have possibly caught up to them so quickly, but of course: if he and Kat hadn't been delayed at sea and stranded in Caria for several days, she probably wouldn't have.

"Get this net off of me!" she says, flailing in it as pebbles fly off her and hit the floor with little pings. The loud orders certainly *sound* like Cyn. Tucking his sword into his belt, he pulls the net off, and together he and Kat stare down at the lost princess wrapped in a black Badaween hooded robe. She sits up and impatiently pushes back the hood.

"What are you doing here?" he asks, slowly pulling out his sword. Her cheekbones are razor-sharp, the curve of her jaw severe. Has she lost weight, or is it just shadows from the lantern?

"Jacob sent me," she says, sitting up and rubbing a lump rising on her forehead where the heavy bucket hit her, "to make sure Kat is safe."

Heph groans inwardly. *Jacob.* The one who beat him in the Blood Tournament in front of all Pella, using tricks and nets rather than hand-to-hand combat. The one Kat does not believe would ever harm her, despite the fact that Heph saw him crouching over her on the battlefield with a bloody sword. Their enemy, an Aesarian Lord, the merest mention of whose name makes Kat all misty-eyed because they grew up together, sharing memories Heph knows nothing about. Jacob, haunting him even here, in Egypt.

"That's ridiculous," Kat scoffs, keeping her sword pointed at Cyn sitting sprawled on the floor. Even in the warm golden-brown glow of the lantern, she looks suddenly pale, and her voice shakes a bit. "Why would Jacob send you anywhere, much less to find *me*?"

"The Aesarian Lords captured me in the library," Cyn says, pushing herself up from the floor. "They tortured me for weeks, trying to get me to tell them things about Pella. They chained me, starved me..."

Heph frowns at her. On the one hand, she looks like the Cyn he's known: tall, lithe, and beautifully wild. But on the other hand, her voice has notes of pain in it, softening it, adding weight to her story.

"You look fine to me," Katerina says. "Did they let you go once you agreed to be their spy?"

Cyn shakes her head, and her black hair flows across her shoulders. Heph notices that the lump on her forehead is rapidly turning a nasty shade of dark blue. "It was Jacob. He gave me water when he wasn't supposed to. He snuck me food. He...he helped me after..."

Her breath catches, and she turns her head. A darkness seems to descend on her like a raptor dropping from the skies. She flings off her black robe. Beneath it, Heph sees, she's in her usual outfit of leather breastplate, skirt, and boots. But she's much thinner than she was, her muscles like cords of

rope. "After what the Scythian Lord did to me." She turns
and raises her left arm to the light.

Heph sees a tribal tattoo of a stylized stag covering her
entire upper arm. In the Greek world, only slaves wear tat-
toos. Now Cyn will have to bear the humiliating mark the
rest of her life. How will she hide it?

"He didn't give me poppy juice before he started," she says,
her voice thick with the memory of it. Heph knows it must
have hurt like a harpy's talons. He imagines the hot needles
digging into flesh, the bloody wounds rubbed with soot as
Cyn whimpered in her chains. He feels something twist in
his gut. To do that to a woman. Those bastards.

But his sympathy goes only so far. Heph looks at Kat out
of the corner of his eye and grips his sword hilt firmly. He
doesn't know what to make of Cyn's story. She's too good a
manipulator, too good a liar, to be trusted. He, of all people, should know.

An image of her tanned body, glistening with a sheen of
sweat in the lamplight of his room, comes unbidden into his
mind. The black tangle of her long hair in the white tangle
of his sheets. He shoves the memory away.

"Well, what do you think, Katerina?" he asks, more
harshly than he intended.

To his dismay, Kat's jaw relaxes and she lowers her sword.
"Yes," she says softly. "That sounds like Jacob."

In the flickering lamplight, Cyn's eyes glow with something like triumph. "I made a deal with him," she says, seat-
ing herself on the low chair of woven river rushes. "He'd
help me escape if I swore I would find you, Katerina, and
make sure you were all right." She looks down at her tattoo and traces the curling blue-black patterns of horns and
legs with her finger. "And I kept my word. I went back to
Pella, but you were gone. Alex didn't want to tell me where

you were—he said it was secret—but after I told him I had to find you and keep you safe, that I had *promised*—he told me where you were going. He said he wanted me to keep you safe, too. Especially now, since the Aesarians have gone against the treaty, and he is planning to go to war. Macedon is vulnerable."

The words send a chill through Heph, reminding him why he's here in the first place. To protect Macedon. To protect Alex.

"Did Jacob escape with you?" Kat asks, and the tension in her voice is palpable. Her longing, tangible. Heph's chest constricts at the sound. Cyn shakes her head in answer, her black hair swaying.

"But when the Lords realized he let you escape, what would they do to him?" Kat demands, sitting on the bed directly in front of Cyn, and laying her sword across her knees. Heph moves to stand next to her, sword at the ready.

Cynane shrugs. "He said he had a plan. That's all I know." She raises the palms of her hands in a gesture of innocent ignorance. Her shoulders are white in the lantern's light. He's seen them bare before.

He clears his throat. "How do we know Jacob sent you? I think Kat's right. It seems much more likely that the Lords sent you to spy on what we're doing for Alex."

Cynane smiles, her teeth straight and strong. "Jacob warned me you might say that," she says, unpinning something from her breastplate, "which is why he gave me this to show you as proof."

In the soft orb of glowing lantern light, Cyn shows them a crudely fashioned iron pin with a smooth green stone flecked with gold set in a frame of iron on top. Kat inhales sharply. As she takes the pin and runs her fingers over the smooth stone, a look of wistful longing appears on her face. She holds it like it is something holy—something sacred. Something beyond Heph's reach. Kat is clearly overcome with the belief that Jacob still cares about her.

He feels as though she has just plunged the long pin into his heart. At the look on her face, he knows that he has been foolish to hope, to dream, to even think...

Kat looks up at him, her green eyes bright. "It's his," she says, unaware that her eyes have already confirmed this.

Heph shakes his head and tries to keep his voice level. "Things still don't add up." He looks at Cyn. "Why didn't you reveal yourself immediately? Why did you sneak into Kat's room?"

The princess looks at the ground, and Heph blinks in surprise. Cyn has never shown remorse or humility or fear before. Perhaps, then, she has truly been broken by the Lords.

"I was afraid," she says, "that you wouldn't trust me. That you would pull swords on me. I finally decided I would write a note explaining everything, and have a boy deliver it with the pin."

She looks at Kat now, brown eyes meeting green, smiling apologetically, and leans back in the chair, her hands on her thighs. "But then I noticed the door to Katerina's room was open, and I was afraid some harm had come to you. I was coming to check."

After everything Cyn did earlier in the summer to cause a rift between him and Alex, Heph would rather trust a rattlesnake's promise not to bite him than any story she tells them. He learned the hard way that Alex's half sister is a master manipulator with a secret agenda. Their mission for the prince is too important to let her try to ruin it, if that's what she's up to. She has always harbored a burning jealousy of Alex for being a boy destined to command armies and rule, while she was destined to marry a foreign king.

Yet she does have Jacob's pin. And Alex must have told her where Kat and he had gone. How else would Cyn have known? Indecision weighs heavily on him. He prefers fighting pirates in a storm. At least there he recognizes his enemies clearly—heaving waves, filthy men waving swords—and knows how to deal with them. This is all so unclear.

He looks at Kat. "Should we let her go?"

Kat turns toward Heph, and he feels her gaze as though a sword has pierced him. Kat knows about that night Heph spent with Cyn. Knows—and has judged.

"She's a hard person to trust," Kat finally says, "but I trust Jacob." A snort escapes Heph before he can stop it, and Kat narrows her eyes at him. "I trust Alexander, as well," she adds loudly.

"Alex is worried that the Aesarian Lords will try to harm you," Cyn says, looking straight at Heph now, her eyes not wavering. "Since Arridheus has been kidnapped, Alex feels that everyone he *loves* is under threat."

Only the slightest stress marks the word *love*, but to Heph it feels as though she shouted it. He looks at her on the low chair, her hands on her knees, every gesture designed to appear unthreatening, every word aimed at eliciting sympathy or stirring up emotional memories.

But the choice to allow Cyn to join them does not belong to him. It belongs to Katerina—a fellow princess. Cynane's *half sister*, he realizes with a start.

Heph sighs and sits back on his calves. The combination of Kat, Cyn, and him has to be a recipe for explosive disaster, something like naphtha, quicklime, and sulfur mixed in a barrel, set on fire and catapulted against a wall. But if Alex sent her, and Kat wants her…

"All right," he agrees, his shoulders sagging. "You can come."

★ ★ ★

The Nile is alive with boats of all shapes as the *Hathor* sweeps past more pyramids, the rising sun painting them pink and reflecting off their gold tips. Soon, the pyramids are lost in the distance, and they rush past fields of wheat and orchards of fig, date, and pomegranate trees, past temples and palaces, obelisks and grand estates.

As they glide through the hot afternoon, Cyn takes off her boots and stretches her long, tanned legs out on the deck, flexing her toes. Her head is back, the curling tips of her black hair grazing the wooden planks as she closes her eyes and drinks in the sun. The lumpy black bruise on her forehead where the bucket hit her has, oddly enough, disappeared. As she inhales, he can see the rise of her breasts.

"Heph?" she says, opening her eyes and smiling. "Why don't you lie here beside me and get some sun? It feels wonderful with the cool river breeze—and you could use the color. You seem a little pale."

Heph can't help staring at those legs, remembering... He feels a blistering gaze upon him and turns to see Kat looking at him, her arms crossed, her lips pursed. She storms as far away from Cyn as she can. But it's a narrow boat, so she can't get very far. Only to the bow, behind the large square sail which now shields her from sight.

"Maybe later, Cynane," he says, enunciating her full name with formality. He joins two of the crewmen on break who are sitting cross-legged under the long awning in the center, throwing dice.

As he holds the small, cool cubes of carved ox bone in his hands, he sees Kat's unmoving shadow behind the sail. If only she could feel for him the way she does for Jacob. But when he made the huge mistake of kissing her in Ada's palace, she cried. At that moment he felt more humiliated than the very public embarrassment of losing the Blood Tournament. To finally get the girl he desired in his arms, to feel his blood throb and his pulse race as he held her tightly, inhaling her scent, exploring her mouth with his tongue, and then have her burst into tears, push him away and run from the room—the memory of it causes the back of his neck to burn as hot as if someone has poured boiling water on it.

Why does Heph always long for forbidden fruit?

He throws the dice and gets one Nun—a man carrying a boat on his head and symbol of chaos—and one Anubis—the jackal-headed god of Death. The two crewmen laugh at Heph's bad luck. Hearing them, Cyn rises and joins them, her black hair tossed by the breeze. She, too, is forbidden fruit. Though she never cried when he kissed her. She liked it. Very much.

"May I play?" she asks.

Dinner that evening is extremely uncomfortable in the courtyard of the main inn of Henen-Nesut, a walled city of limestone rising out of the Nile floodwaters. Kat barely touches her food, while Cyn drizzles honey from a flagon onto her lips, licking it off and intentionally spilling some between her breasts. Heph, feeling the tension tight as a drawn bowstring, drinks more wine than he should, even though he knows he will have a headache in the morning. Wordlessly, Kat leaves the table as soon as she's done eating, stomping up the wooden stairs to the covered balcony that leads to her room. But Cyn lingers.

"You know," she says, pouring more fragrant golden wine into his cup, "the sound of footsteps on stairs will forever remind me of being in that tower room, chained and starved, knowing the Lords were coming to get me for a new torture session. I had to think of happy things so that I would not fall apart."

Heph can't even imagine what it was like for her. He studies her as he sips his wine. He should put it down, not have any more. But it's good wine, different from anything he has had in Greece, with a biting tang to it. It would be a shame to waste it.

"What did you think of?" he asks Cyn.

"Well," she says coyly, tucking a loose tendril of black hair behind her ear, "I often thought of you."

"Me?" he repeats, jerking his arm so a bit of wine sloshes out of his overfull cup.

"We only had one night together. But it meant so much to me. Again and again I told myself I would get out of that prison. And then I would have another chance with you. It's what helped me survive."

She thought of him in the prison. Memories of him helped her survive. An image of Kat flashes through his mind, red-faced and blotchy, upset by his kiss. He looks now at Cyn, her eyes shining with desire, her smile playful. He should put the wine cup down and go to bed. Alone.

Why can Heph never seem to stop himself from doing something he knows he shouldn't? As he ponders the question, he raises the cup to his lips and drinks.

Heph sits up in the lumpy bed as waves of nausea pour over him. He's going to be sick, and soon. He scrambles over Cynane, searches desperately for his tunic on the floor, throws it over his head and, with one hand clenched over his mouth, races across the courtyard toward the latrines. There, in the reeking stench, he empties his guts repeatedly. Each time he thinks he's ready to leave the foul place, his insides twist again, sending everything upward. Finally he staggers into the courtyard, the night air cool on his sweat-soaked skin.

He didn't drink all that much. Just enough for a headache

the next morning. This is something different. Was there something wrong with the duck? It smelled and tasted fine.

A short scream pierces the silence. He turns toward it, unsure if he should get involved. Is someone having a nightmare? Has a woman gone into labor? It slices through the night again, and this time it sounds like Kat, and it came from the second floor. He doesn't have time to retrieve his sword so he staggers upstairs and clatters down the long balcony. All the doors are shut. Which room is Kat's? He listens. Something falls to the ground. He throws open a door. In a room dimly lit by the glow of a lantern he sees two figures struggling. Cyn is holding a long, serrated knife, and Kat's hands are clenched around Cyn's wrists, pushing them away from her.

"Stop it!" Heph says, the room tilting and blurring as he races toward them and pulls Cyn off of Kat. "What are you doing?" He wrenches the knife from Cyn's hand and she bends over, her hands on her knees.

"I'm sorry," she says. "I had to do it. Olympias wants her dead." She looks up, imploringly. "When she learned Alex was sending me to find you two, she took me aside and threatened me. I didn't want to do it, but I don't want to die. You know the queen is evil and will make good on her threat, don't you?"

Heph looks at Kat. Her mouth is a hard line, her arms rigid at her side. She can't take her eyes off Cynane.

"Heph," Cyn says, standing up straight. "You've known me all these years. We grew up together. You've known Kat for a few weeks. You and I have made love, twice, now. Surely that must mean something to you. You must believe me."

Heph glances at Kat, whose face has closed up like a tightly rolled scroll.

"You're not going to choose her over me, are you?" Cyn asks, taking a step toward Kat and gesturing. "She's nothing to you."

"You should have told us, Cyn, about the queen's threat," Heph says, choosing each word carefully, though every part of him would like to threaten her with her own knife. Threaten, but not kill. He knows he could never willingly hurt her—they grew up together—but he'd like her to think he might. "We could have come up with a plan to keep you safe," he goes on, keeping his voice steady, even as he continues to bite back the foul taste of bile and old wine still lingering in the back of his throat. "We could have hidden you outside Pella while we talked to Alex about dealing with Olympias. But now, we can't trust you. If you choose to stay with us we will have to keep you bound day and night."

"Heph, please," Cyn says, her voice cracking. She bends forward again, as if she can't get her breath. Then she grabs the low chair beside her and throws it—hard—at Heph. He is so surprised he doesn't raise his arms to protect himself as quickly as he should, and it hits him in the temple with a horrible crack. Lights explode behind his eyes and pain radiates through his skull as he falls to the floor.

He needs to get up. Cyn is going to try to hurt Kat.

When he pushes himself into a kneeling position, he sees, in the middle of a wildly spinning room, the writhing shadows in the lantern light of two girls fighting. In a blur of motion Kat kicks Cyn in the abdomen and, as Cyn doubles over, punches her in the jaw. Howling in rage, Cyn throws Kat on the floor, straddling her. She raises a knife—he can see its razor-sharp blade glinting in the low light. As Heph cries "No!" and lurches toward them, Cyn brings it down toward Kat's throat.

But Kat has twisted to her left, and Cyn's blade comes

down hard on her hand. Kat screams, the two scuffle, and Cyn raises the knife again. But now, Heph is behind her, violently dragging her away by her hair. She turns to slash at him but he yanks her arms hard behind her back, and the knife clatters to the floor. As he moves to grab it, Cyn breaks from his grasp and, laughing, bolts from the room. He would chase after her but sees Kat sitting stunned on the floor, blood gushing from her right hand, which she is clutching in her left.

"Let me see. Kat, let me see it," he insists, kneeling beside her, gently forcing her to let go.

The entire fingertip of her right index finger is gone, the stump a raw, pulsating wound. Heph tries not to grimace. He's certainly seen far worse in battle and he knows Kat will heal if he helps clean the wound. But a sickening shame spikes through him and he almost throws up again. Cynane cut off Kat's finger. It's the horrible disgrace and humiliation of it that he can't quite believe. And, from the looks of it, he realizes while scanning the floor, she took the finger with her.

Why? For what foul purpose?

It doesn't matter. The only thing that matters is that *he* let this happen. It's all *his* fault. He can't believe his own passion has once again allowed a disaster to occur. He looks around the room in the darkness, panic ticking in his veins, filling him with a resounding sense of doom. He holds Kat tighter, ripping off part of his tunic to help stanch her wound. But he cannot look into her eyes.

Because if he can't trust in himself, who *can* he trust?

CHAPTER EIGHTEEN

JACOB STANDS SHACKLED IN A SMALL CLEARING in a kind of natural amphitheater, one side ringed by rock ledges, the others by trees and bushes. Seated on folding camp chairs in the center of the second ledge are the five members of the Inquisitorial Council, the group that judges members of the Brotherhood who are accused of crimes.

High Lord Gideon is at the center. Jacob has the feeling his judgment may be harsh, but he will, at least, seek for justice. On his left is Bastian, his face a hard sneer, and Melchior, the Persian, who has always seemed to look down on Jacob for his peasant background. To Gideon's right are Aethon and Ambiorix, former peasants themselves, who have always been friendly.

His life rests in these men's hands.

Around them, other Lords sit cross-legged on the ground or let their long legs and black boots dangle over the sides. Some of them are already perspiring, for it is the time of day when men's shadows hide inside themselves, the time of golden heat and white light.

They are farther up the mountain from the old fortress of

Pyrrhia, with guards posted in all directions to warn them of any invaders. High Lord Gideon is preparing for a Macedonian attack, Timaeus told Jacob when he visited him in his cell yesterday. Cynane has probably made it back to Pella and told Alexander about her capture and torture. The treaty that allowed the Lords to stay in Pyrrhia unmolested is no longer valid.

Tim also told Jacob that according to ancient tradition Aesarian Lords interrogate their own by sitting on boulders or rocks, in imitation of the primal spring of divine life, source of the Lords themselves, though neither he nor Jacob could make any sense of it.

Several feet away from him, Jacob's Aesarian armor— shield, helmet, leather pants, boots, breastplate, sword, and spear—lies in a heap. At the end of the trial he will either put it on again as a free man, or see it burned right before he is executed.

Lord Melchior rises from his chair, climbs down the ledges, and stands before Jacob. He unrolls the scroll and reads.

"The Inquisitorial Council of the Aesarian Lords does hereby charge the prisoner, Lord Jacob of Erissa, with several offenses, each one meriting death." His rich voice cascades over the assembly with the delicate lilt of the east. Melchior makes even the word *death* sound oddly pleasant.

"Charge one: that he did collaborate with a prisoner to effect her escape from custody. Charge two: that he allowed a prisoner to escape with Aesarian secrets. Charge three: that he let loose foul magic into the world."

As Melchior reads the charges, Jacob wonders how his life has gone downhill so fast. Just days ago he was on his way to becoming the best of the Aesarians, and now this. But one thing gives him strength. He's innocent. He didn't let Cynane escape. Sure, he thought about it. He even promised her he would. And who knows what he might have done if she had continued to beg and plead with him instead of attacking him? But he did not remove her chains.

At least...not intentionally. Over the past days in his dark cell, he relived the moment when heat rolled through him, from his hands into her chains, and the links melted and popped open.

Melchior looks up, his handsome chiseled face a mask of judicial impartiality. "Lord Jacob, how do you plead?"

Finally, this is his chance to speak, to explain. The first night in the filthy, pitch-black cell he yelled for someone to just listen to him until his voice was hoarse and his throat swollen and throbbing. Without watching the sun rise and night fall, he's lost track of time. The long stretches of thick black silence were broken only by guards bringing food and removing his slops bucket. When Jacob was arrested, High Lord Gideon had said the trial would be held in seven days, but it seems more like it's been seven weeks.

Then shortly after dawn this morning, Lords Aethon and Eumolpus hauled him out of the pit and into the light of a courtyard that almost blinded him. They led him up the spiral staircase to Cyn's old tower room with its arrow slit window, just wide enough to let in a ribbon of light. He pushed his face against the window, sucking in the light and fresh air as if they were a feast.

More delights awaited him: a bucket of well water for bathing—had he ever appreciated being clean before?—a laundered tunic, hearty food, and watered wine. When he asked Lord Aethon about this sudden bounty, the barrel-chested Lord replied that an Aesarian's appearance should not prejudice his brothers against him at his trial. It was the Aesarian way.

Now, standing in the bright light of a noontime sun,

Jacob throws his shoulders back and lifts his chin. "I am innocent, my Lords."

Melchior nods and returns to his spot on the ledge. High Lord Gideon rises, holding in his right hand the White Staff of Truth, an ancient ivory rod intricately carved with animals and human faces and topped by a jeering ivory skull. In an Inquisitorial Council, any Lord may speak as long as he holds the staff.

"Lord Jacob," he says, "explain."

Jacob clears his throat. "I did not let Princess Cynane go, High Lord. Magic brought about her escape." That much is true.

Bastian springs up and takes the White Staff. "Lord Jacob is lying!" he says, his gaze sweeping across the dozens of faces turned to look at him. "We spent many days determining the princess did not possess magic. You let her go in return for…what? Riches and favor from Macedon, perhaps?"

Hatred floods Jacob's every fiber. Bastian, that sneering, arrogant scum who tried to kill Kat.

He had a long time in the dark to think about Cyn's story of the queen calling out to Riel in her secret altar. And the more he thought about it, the more likely it seems to him that the queen herself told Bastian about the god.

And Jacob can think of only two ways one could pry information from the queen: either Bastian had turned traitor— something that seems unlikely, for all that Jacob loathes him—or else he had some *sway* over Olympias.

Sway that only a lover could have.

And there was more, something else that told Jacob that Bastian was intimate with the enemy queen. In the courtyard, Bastian had spoken of the queen in the past tense, as if he thought she was dead when no one else did.

What if…what if…Bastian met with the queen after the

battle? What if he even tried to kill her to cover up their af-
fair once he got the information he wanted from her? Jacob
doesn't have the necessary evidence, but the timing of events
seems to line up. And yesterday Timaeus told Jacob that Aesarian spies in Pella reported that the queen had been missing and returned ill and strangely marked, as if by poison.
Ever since he joined the Lords, Jacob heard rumors that Bastian has always been fond of poisons, concocting mixtures
to make himself immune to many.

Lord Turshu rises and calls, "The staff, please." Bastian
reluctantly passes it down the line of seated men.

"Bastian speaks the truth that Princess Cynane did not
possess Blood Magic," Turshu says in the singsong cadence
of Scythia. "However, we also determined that someone—
or some*thing*—was protecting her. She was clearly under a
powerful spell that healed her burned flesh and broken bones.
If Lord Jacob was embalming her as we instructed him—
and we found the hardened pieces of the ash mixture on the
floor—it is also possible that the spell interrupted the em-
balmment and melted her chains."

Jacob is glad to see many of the other Lords nodding at
Turshu's sensible words and feels a warm surge of gratitude to
the bowlegged little warrior for helping him yet again. The
first time, when Jacob was cleaning the Pyrrhian stable, a
spooked horse almost stomped him to death. Jacob saw flailing hooves sharp as knives trying to pummel him, and could
only raise his arms above his head. A moment later Turshu
was there, clucking and whistling in his strange, Scythian
way, and the horse immediately calmed.

"The staff," calls Timaeus, rising, and Turshu passes it
down to the row of Lords sitting on the ledge below him.
Jacob feels another little flush of relief. Timaeus, too, will
support him.

Taking the staff, Timaeus says, "When we heard the disturbance, I ran into the embalming room before any of you and found Lord Jacob standing there in shock, his face a bloody mess, the chains gone but a strange smell in the air like molten iron. Surely those Lords that entered the room immediately after me noticed that smell, too."

Jacob looks around the faces, and to his relief, he sees Gideon, Ambiorix, and several other Lords nod.

"If Lord Jacob had merely broken off her chains," Tim continues, "why would the room smell of melted metal? Where did the chains go? We never found them." Thankfulness surges through Jacob like the rich warmth of mulled wine after an icy day of hunting. In the cell, Timaeus said the chains went missing and winked quickly. Jacob isn't sure what his little friend did with them, but he trusts that they will never be found again.

"The White Staff!" Bastian calls. Timaeus, whose mouth was open to continue speaking, shrugs and passes it back up to Bastian. Jacob groans silently. Whatever Bastian has to say, it won't be favorable to him.

"She could not melt off her chains while we held her the past weeks," Bastian points out. "Why then did she have the power to do so when she was alone with Jacob?"

That question has been bothering Jacob all during his long, dark imprisonment. The ludicrous thought that came to him in the moment before Timaeus burst through the door was exactly that: ludicrous. Impossible. Insane. He had pushed it into the furthest recesses of his mind. And even when another memory—a memory of red fire flaming from the Hemlock Torch as he held it—flickers into his mind, he always ended up shaking the idea away like a wet dog shaking off water.

Because…because if he were the one responsible for healing his arm at the palace, healing Katerina on the battlefield, making the torch go crimson, and melting the chains, it could mean only one thing: that he has what he has sworn as an Aesarian Lord to eradicate. That he is not a hunter of magic, but a bearer of it.

And the irony is too much to stomach.

"And how could a woman," Bastian continues, "weak from hunger and torture, overpower an Aesarian Lord? Especially the *hero* of the Pellan palace break-in? The *victor* of the Blood Tournament?" Bastian feels he's winning. He's practically licking his chops. He reminds Jacob of the hyena that stole baby lambs and goats in Erissa. When he and Kat tracked it down, its maw was red with fresh blood and it seemed to be grinning at them insolently, daring them to stop him.

"No, my Lords, what we have here is not magic but treason. And the punishment of treason is death."

Jacob knows that the scarred Lord wants him dead. If it wasn't clear before, it is clear now. Even if he survives this trial, Bastian will make sure he dies in a training accident or gets stabbed in an ambush.

It's Jacob or Bastian.

It has always been Jacob or Bastian.

Jacob inhales deeply. "There was magic, I assure you," he says, trying to quell the notes of fast-paced, squeaky panic begging to slip in. "As I was stirring the mixture, the embalming ash I had already placed on the princess cracked and fell off. Her chains disappeared in a blaze of light, leaving that odd tang of metal lingering in the air that several of you smelled."

He sees several faces nodding and continues as hope burns hard in his throat. "She stood before me, laughing at my surprise. I made ready to throw her to the ground, but then she told me something so shocking that I hesitated a few seconds.

During that time she grabbed my pin and stabbed my face." His hand touches the crusted scab on his cheek. "It was a scratch only, but... My Lords, it was her words that pained me far more than the wound."

Silence descends as the Lords digest this. A warm wind ruffles the leaves of nearby trees, and the buzz of the cicadas rises and diminishes.

A laugh cracks the momentary peace. "What news did this *girl* tell you that shocked you so badly you weren't able to fight as an Aesarian?" Bastian scoffs.

Jacob's heart beats in his ears. *He's got him.*

"Interesting that you, Lord Bastian, should be the one to ask," Jacob says, loudly and clearly. Taking a deep breath, he's ready to take his fate into his hands. He's ready to guess at the truth. "She said that you are the lover of Queen Olympias of Macedon."

Shouts of surprise echo across the rock ledges as council members sit up straighter and lean forward. Bastian's face is alight with feral anger. "Liar!" he says, pointing at Jacob with the White Staff. "Traitor!"

He turns to High Lord Gideon. "We must cleanse our brotherhood of this vermin. Allow me, High Lord, to execute him. Now."

It's true. Bastian's blind fury has erased the last shadow of doubt regarding Jacob's theory. As a hunter, Jacob has seen the spitting, snarling fury of a cornered animal. He's trained to know what an animal thinks. And all the signs are there in the panicked anger of the cornered animal called Bastian.

"My brothers," Jacob says, drinking in Bastian's outrage as if it were the finest Chian wine, "have any of you noticed how often Lord Bastian has gone missing from our ranks with no explanation? Have any here received useful information from Bastian about the Pellan palace, yet wondered why he refused to tell you how he obtained it?"

High Lord Gideon stands, as Jacob knew he would, and takes the staff from Bastian. "I have." His voice rolls out, muting the other whispers. "Ever since we entered Pella for the Blood Tournament, Lord Bastian has often gone missing from our meetings, training sessions, and even the bedroom he shared with Lords Melchior and Aethon." Gideon reminds Jacob of a thunderhead, toweringly high, dark as night, ready to unleash its unfathomable fury.

"When I asked him about it, he replied that he was conducting reconnaissance into possible magic wielders in the palace. I did not question him further as his rank grants him some freedoms."

As Gideon speaks, Bastian stares at Jacob, and Jacob tries to stop a shiver that runs down his spine. Bastian's eyes are unblinking, filled with a cold and merciless rage.

Gideon turns to Bastian and asks, "Lord Bastian, what have you to say?"

Bastian flips his long curtain of dark hair out of his face and raises his chin proudly. "We have long suspected sorcery in the Pellan palace, and we have endeavored to get our hands on their magic archives," he says, his fingers rubbing the hilt of his sword. "While we were in the palace, I conducted my own investigations. After we left, I returned to discover the source of magic that destroyed the Hemlock Torch. I didn't want to waste your time, High Lord, with the details of my efforts until I had valuable information to report."

"Lord Bastian, Lord Jacob has not accused you of spying on our enemy to assist our cause," Gideon says. "He has accused you of taking the queen to bed. Any Aesarian Lord sleeping with a witch, a soothsayer, or a possessor of Blood Magic is punished with death, no matter what the underlying reason. As a member of the Inquisitorial Council, you know this."

"I have done no wrong!" Bastian turns his defiant dark eyes on High Lord Gideon. "I deny having any such relationship with the queen." He almost spits, as his fury rises to a crescendo. "I challenge you, Lord Jacob, to a Gods' Duel!"

Jacob's mouth drops open. A Gods' Duel is an Aesarian tradition where the man who draws first blood is acknowledged to be the one telling the truth, as it must mean he has the gods on his side. Jacob senses Bastian won't stop at first blood, though. He will try to kill him as quickly as possible, and he has years more expert weapons training than Jacob. But if Jacob refuses, everyone will think it's because he's guilty. And then he'll die much more slowly than a sword thrust, tortured to death, probably.

"I accept the challenge!" he says, his gaze sweeping boldly across the ranks on the rock ledges, trying to meet each man in the eye if only for a split second. They all lean forward, enthralled.

Gideon nods, his large obsidian eyes sparkling with interest. "It has been a generation since there has been a Gods' Duel," he says. "The Aesarian way is for brothers to resolve their differences through mediation and negotiation, not duels. But in this case…" His gaze falls on Jacob, who feels as if Zeus himself is judging him, and then on Bastian.

"Release Lord Jacob from his chains!" Gideon says. "The opponents will be given time to prepare for the duel."

Lord Aethon, whose face is redder even than usual, takes the shackles off Jacob's wrists and ankles. Timaeus leaps nimbly down from the ledges and claps Jacob on the back. "I'll help get you ready," he says, then pulls on his neck to whisper, "Is it true? About Bastian and the queen?"

He hands Jacob the black leather pants. Jacob hastily pulls them up, tucks his tunic into them, and laces the front.

"Yes," Jacob mutters, as he sits on the dirt and catches the boots Tim flings at him. "It was a guess, at first, but if I had any doubt before, his response—to call a Gods' Duel!—is proof enough. He's desperate to keep the others from prying."

He finishes tying knots in his boot laces then stands up. *That might be the last time I ever lace up a boot*, he thinks. He spreads his arms wide as Tim throws his thick leather breastplate over his shoulders and laces up the sides. *And that might be the last time I put on a breastplate.* Tim claps on his helmet, and Jacob pulls the leather chin strap through the bronze buckle on the side, making sure it's tight. In any battle, an unhelmeted head is a blazing target just begging to be cut in half. *And that might be the last...* He throws away these pessimistic thoughts as if they are wormy pears. The gods must be on his side. They can't be on Bastian's.

He picks up his cowhide shield, gripping it firmly by the inner leather strap. But High Lord Gideon, who has been huddled with the other Lords, looks up and says, "No shields in a Gods' Duel!"

Jacob blinks. No shield to protect his left side—his heart side. His sword alone must keep Bastian's vicious hacking and slashing at bay.

He hands Tim his shield and unsheathes his sword. On the other side of the little clearing, Lord Melchior hands Bastian his sword and claps him on the shoulder. Bastian runs toward Jacob and stops a few feet away. His left cheek twitches, making his zigzag scar pulsate as if it were alive.

Jacob quickly sums up his opponent just as he did with all those bears and wild boars he hunted in Erissa in the seconds before they charged. Just as he did with all those

Macedonians on the battlefield running toward him with swords raised—a split-second analysis of advantages, weaknesses, differences.

Bastian is the same height as Jacob but leaner, quicker, more agile. Jacob is stronger but slower. He can't hope to outdo his opponent with speed or better swordsmanship. But he has one quality Bastian has always lacked: patience.

The imperturbable patience of a hunter.

A fine sheen of sweat gleams on Bastian's pale face. "How dare you, you vile, slimy piece of scum," he hisses, his dark eyes shining with malevolence. "A potter's son. A big, lumbering pile of peasant crap."

Even though his heart is pumping wildly and his arms tingling with anticipation of the fight to the death, Jacob decides he has two additional advantages over Bastian.

One: His mind is free of anger.

Two: Bastian is lying.

Lord Gideon raises the White Staff high in the air. "Are you ready?" he asks.

"Ready!" Bastian yells, as if the sheer volume of his voice will convince the gods he is right when he is wrong.

"Ready," Jacob says softly.

They slam their right fists on their hearts then extend them straight out from their chests. They turn and face each other.

"May the Gods enlighten us," Gideon intones. He abruptly lowers the staff. "Begin!"

Jacob and Bastian circle each other slowly. Bastian feints with his sword, jabbing and poking then springing back. Jacob raises his sword to deflect, but doesn't attack, letting Bastian think he's afraid.

"Coward," Bastian cries. Suddenly he is spinning, wheeling, leaping, though Jacob has time to block with his sword, crouch down to avoid a blow to the head, leap up to miss one aimed at his shins, twist right and left out of the way.

Jacob's moves are intentionally defensive, allowing the enraged Bastian to exhaust himself before Jacob moves in for the kill. The minutes—or is it hours?—crawl by. Sweat flies off Bastian's face. Poking beneath his helmet, his shoulder-length black hair looks like a twisting nest of wet baby serpents. Dark stains spread across the underarms of his tunic above the breastplate.

Jacob focuses not only on Bastian's sword, but also on his eyes, his shoulders, his legs. Where will he strike next? How tired and angry is he? But as time wears on, Jacob finds himself tiring as the sun pounds down on his heavy helmet. Dust coats his parched throat, and sweat rolls down his cheeks. Behind Bastian, he sees a blur of faces under horned helmets.

As he and Bastian circle, Jacob notices a huge crow, wings outstretched, landing on a tree branch beside a dozen other crows. It reminds him of the night the Hemlock Torch exploded, when hundreds of crows wheeled through the air and attacked the spectators. A gathering of crows, the Lords said, was a sign of magic. And Cynane isn't here. If they are here because of magic, then it's because of Jacob's magic, even if he doesn't feel the strange heat that filled his blood the night of Cyn's escape...

Bastian takes advantage of Jacob's distraction by springing forward so quickly that Jacob has no time to block him with his sword and merely jumps backward. Bastian's sword scratches a long mark on Jacob's leather breastplate, but it doesn't reach his skin.

They back away from each other, circling slowly, and Jacob smells something pungent, bitter, like burning food at the bottom of a cookpot. A wisp of smoke rises from his breastplate. He looks down and sees the leather scratched by Bastian's sword puckering and sizzling. Poison. Bastian's sword has been dipped in poison—in direct violation of the code of a Gods' Duel. And this is the kind of poison that even Bastian, with all his antidotes, cannot be immune to. If this poison burns leather, it will melt flesh.

The other Lords notice the sizzling breastplate, too. "Stop!" High Lord Gideon cries out, his dark form rising from the bench, his massive hand outstretched. Three Lords clamber down onto the field below to stop the fight. Turshu, Ambiorix, and Timaeus, who Jacob fears may start somersaulting through the air to grab Bastian's sword—a famous trick he does to entertain the other Lords in their daily weapons practice—and end up cutting himself with it. But a wild spirit seems to have possessed Bastian as he swirls his sword in a poisoned arc, preventing them from coming near.

"Fight me, you whore's bastard!" he shrieks, diving toward Jacob with his sword. Jacob blocks the sword and twists. The sword flies out of Bastian's hand and sticks deep in the sand, swinging back and forth crazily. As Bastian stares at it wildly, Jacob swings his sword and cuts his left biceps. Startled, Bastian looks down at the thin line oozing red.

"First blood," Jacob says.

Jacob's won—there can be no question. Bastian's cheated with poison and Jacob drew first blood. But it isn't just winning the duel that floods him with satisfaction; it's the knowledge that he was right. Bastian has been sleeping with the queen. The gods have proven it to everyone now.

Jacob looks at the ledges and sees the Lords murmuring and shifting, some of them standing up and pointing. On his left, Timaeus shouts, "Jacob! Behind you!"

Bastian pulls a long serrated knife from each boot and charges.

Several Lords cry out in protest, and two more climb

down to the field, swords drawn. One of them is Gaius, the Roman, perhaps Bastian's best friend.

"Bastian! Stop!" Gaius cries, striding toward him. But Bastian runs straight at Jacob. Jacob's sword is much longer than the knives, but Bastian has two weapons, and as Jacob swings his sword against one of them, the same acidic smell fills the air as the other one drives toward his bare sword arm. Even the slightest nick, Jacob knows, will kill him.

"Stop the fight!" Gideon calls again, but Jacob and Bastian ignore him. The five Lords on the field hoping to intervene fan out in a broad circle around them, but Jacob knows none dare draw too near this dance of death. For that is what is going to happen now: Jacob is now entirely certain one of them must die.

Jacob leaps, twisting the left side of his body away from the knife flashing toward him in Bastian's right hand, and strikes a hard blow on the knife in his left hand, sending it flying. Bastian lunges for it, but instead of grasping the hilt, his hand closes around the blade.

His eyes widen in horror as a faint plume of foul smoke rises from it. Within moments, flesh bubbles and sputters like fat in a cookpot, the putrid odor making Jacob's eyes water and his stomach lurch.

Bastian screams, eyes tightly shut, mouth wide open. Holding his smoking arm, he lurches toward the Lords standing in shock on the rock ledges, bellowing like a wounded boar.

Wheeling to face Jacob, Bastian gasps, "I can't... Not like this..." His face looks more surprised than pained and the skin on his hand has turned black as tar, the top layer curling up like charred meat. Then chunks of seared flesh fall, exposing white bone.

Bastian shakes. His glazed eyes meet Jacob's. "You," he

whispers, flecks of black foam on his lips. And then he falls to the ground. For one moment, Jacob stays as still as a gazelle, then he crouches down to check the Lord's heartbeat.

Lord Bastian is dead.

Chapter Nineteen

SITTING CROSS-LEGGED ON THE FLOOR OF THE old mine shaft, Alex sees dim lantern light glinting off the bronze helmets and iron swords of the fifty other soldiers squeezed around him, waiting. The thrill that always comes to him pre-battle surges through his veins now. But one thing is different: he's never gone to battle without Hephaestion by his side.

Still, the Lords are anticipating reinforcements all the way from Nekrana, in the Eastern Mountains. He can't afford to wait for Heph's return. He can't afford to wait until his council has been rebuilt. He can't afford to wait for anything. He must strike hard, and early. He must strike *now*.

At least he has Kadmus—his last remaining council member and, in the absence of both Katerina and Hephaestion, his most trusted friend. Catching Kadmus's eyes just before dawn this morning as they hiked into position, Alex felt that old exhilaration he used to feel with Heph, whether sparring with one another or working in tandem against a greater foe.

Alex had been certain Cynane would insist on joining the battle; he had seen her face light up when he told her he was going to war. And he would have given her the opportunity to slay her tormentors. Surprisingly, she had left the palace almost as soon as she had arrived, leaving him a hastily scrawled note about making sacrifices at some obscure temple as thanks for her escape.

The strong fragrance of peppermint oil, mint, and citron pulp tickles his nose; he and his men have smeared the thick, sticky paste on their necks, faces, and hands. Luckily, it's cool in the tunnel, much cooler than the late summer weather just outside, so his long-sleeved buckskin tunic and pants aren't too hot, though they do feel strange rubbing against the skin of his arms and legs.

As if reading his thoughts, his friend Phrixos, sitting next to him, scratches his leg as his wide, homely face creases in a smile. "I hate wearing these tubes on my legs," he whispers.

Beside him, Telekles grins, his long golden hair fanning out below his helmet and shimmering slightly in the gloom, pale against the dark buckskin.

What was that? Alex raises his palm for silence and strains to hear. There it is again, louder. One long, ghostly wail of a ram's horn: the Macedonian signal to light the greenwood fires. Though the main signals are given a quarter mile away, near the front gates of the fortress of Pyrrhia, Alex stationed a relay horn near the mouth of the mine shaft so he would know what's going on outside.

The Aesarian Lords—snug in their high fortress nestled against cliffs and well prepared for an attack they must have known was coming when Cynane escaped—can fire arrows and catapults down on Alex's men with impunity...unless their vision is obscured. Alex had every man bring two packs of wood with him up the slope last night, one green and the other dry and well-seasoned. They built fires around the fortress, the green wood on top of the dry, to be lit just before dawn. The thick white smoke wafting upward will obscure the Macedonian men climbing the hill. The Lords will be forced to fire blindly, wasting their arrows and stones.

Two blows from the ram's horn. Now Kadmus is launching flaming catapult stones and fire arrows at the fortress's walls and parapets, concentrating on the area of the wall about eighty paces east of the main gate. Last night, the general pointed out to Alex that the Lords, when dousing the limestone walls and wooden parapets with vinegar as a fire retardant, had poured too much on that particular spot. When limestone and vinegar are exposed to consistent high temperatures, the limestone crumbles. That will be the best spot to make a breach in the walls, Kadmus and Alex decided.

Three haunting cries from the ram's horn. Now Diodotus and his men must be pushing the battering ram cart toward the gate, hoping the smoke obscures them so arrows don't whistle into their necks from the tall towers just above. Yesterday, leaving the oxcarts and horses on the plain below, the men carried up the twisting mountain path the pieces of the cart, its main support beams, the ropes and pulleys and wheels, and the protective canopy of cowhide panels, soaked in water and vinegar. It took eight men to carry the ram itself, a log twice the height of a man and nearly as wide, tipped by an iron ram's head with curling horns.

In the darkest part of the night, Diodotus and his team assembled the battering ram in the protected curve of the path as close to the main gate as they dared. The past few nights in Pella, he and Alex made the men practice again and again in the dark until he knew they could do it blindfolded. Once in position directly in front of the gates, the men will jump inside the canopy and swing the ram, using the momentum of the ropes for maximum impact.

But the Lords won't be too concerned about the battering ram because, Alex suspects, both the Macedonian attack and the Aesarian defense are pretenses. The main action will probably occur here, in the wide sloping tunnel. The Aesarians must be planning to send their crack troops down through the shaft to swing around behind the Macedonian line and pin them against the walls. At least, that's what Alex is praying for.

He had never heard of this tunnel, a silver mine that gave out long ago, when Troy was young. But while planning the strategy for the attack, one of Kadmus's men, who had lived on a farm near Pyrrhia, told the general he used to play here with his brothers, until the Lords, on their periodic visits, chased them out. Phobidas knew the exact location of its mouth, hidden by saplings and bushes. Halfway down the shaft, it forks, one path going deep into the bowels of the hill, the other leading upward to empty into the chief courtyard of the fortress, though a heavy iron gate usually bars the entrance.

But that gate will be open when the Lords stream into the tunnel to attack Alexander from behind. And even if they lock it behind them, Alex has a feeling it will open up for them again quite soon.

It's so quiet now—the heavy silence is broken only by breathing and the periodic gentle cough—he hopes his men can't hear the pumping of his heart. He's not nearly as afraid as last month when he led the charge downhill and across the field at the Aesarian cavalry. Fighting at close quarters isn't as dangerous as on a battlefield, where an arrow launched from half a mile away can whizz into your forehead before you know what happened. Still, he could die in the next few minutes. Suffer terrible pain. Lose a limb. Lose a friend.

A friend. Alex feels a twinge gnawing in his chest. If only Heph were here, sharing this moment with him—the rush of excitement spiced by fear that courses through soldiers before the action. And then the ringing clash of swords and shields and battle cries—the best sounds to a man fighting for his country and his honor.

Up ahead, around the bend, he hears the tromping of boots, the rumble of shields against scabbards and spears, and the echoes of men's voices. Silently, Alex and the men stand and raise the damp cloths tied about their necks to cover their mouths and noses. His six handpicked archers rise and nock their arrows in their bows.

Alex nods to one of his lieutenants, Herodes, who puts a taper to the bone-dry wood soaked with olive oil in the specially constructed brass oven just ahead of them. Then Herodes sprinkles in a variety of bird feathers and puts the lid on. He and another soldier, Kriton, each grab a bellows connected to the rear of the oven and start working them. Immediately, thick black smoke and an unbearable stench blow out the pipe soldered to the front of the oven, toward the tromp of booted feet coming toward them.

"Lord Gaius, what is that horrible smell?" asks a voice.

"There's smoke coming our way. Men, raise your shields and draw your swords! I think we're not alone."

Alex hears the scraping of swords emerging from scabbards just as torchlight gleams on the walls and the first horned helmets appear. He raises his hand and brings it down swiftly. Arrows fly into the first row of Aesarian Lords, most of them thumping into shields. Then four men kneeling behind the oven remove the stoppers from the beehives they have been holding, stand, and launch them toward the Lords.

Furious at their captivity, enraged by the smoke, the bees fly in buzzing waves toward the Lords, stinging savagely where they find flesh. Some bees fly back toward the Macedonians—Alex is aware of three hovering angrily in front of his face. But they don't like the aromatic mixture he applied, and buzz off. Another tries to sting his buckskin sleeve. Alex feels nothing.

The Lords, however, scream from the countless stings and retch from the nauseating stench and choking smoke.

Alex waits. Give the bees time to sting them. Give the smoke time to choke them.

"Attack!" Alex cries. He and his men push past the oven into the smoke. Immediately his eyes start to sting, but the damp cloth around his nose and mouth keeps out the worst of it. Beside him, Telekles, aping his fearless hero Achilles, leaps past Alex into the Aesarians, screaming the ancient war cry, "Alala! Alala!" Other Macedonians rush behind Telekles, but Alex's way is blocked by something—someone—looking down at him.

When the smoke clears a bit he sees a horned helmet perched on top of one of the largest warriors he has ever seen, a head taller than Alex and twice as wide. But this giant of a man is at a disadvantage here: stung, coughing, and ambushed. He begins to swing his sword so wildly Alex isn't sure who he is trying to kill—him or the bees.

Alex pushes forward, knocking his opponent's sword back again and again as more Macedonians rush past them up the tunnel and some others—are they Lords?—race back down. The torches the Aesarians were holding nearby are gone, and in the smoky darkness Alex can't see. He hesitates. His worst fear is killing one of his own men.

"Telekles! Phrixos!" he calls, over the din of war cries and men's screams of pain.

"We're up here!" one of them cries. "We're beating them back!"

Just then light appears from behind him. He snatches a glance back. Through the swirling smoke he sees that two

Aesarians are fighting two Macedonians. One of the Macedonians has dropped his sword but waves a lit torch in his opponents' faces, parrying their sword blows with his shield. Alex wants to help them but can't turn his back on the giant, if he's still there.

With a roar, the huge Lord hurtles himself through the smoke at Alex. His eyes are almost swollen shut from bee stings. He snarls, baring black and broken teeth, and advances. Alex uses all his strength to push his shield hard against the man's sword in the hope of driving his own sword into his belly, but the Lord uses his considerable weight to drive Alex back.

Alex knows what's going to happen as soon as he sees the six or seven bees hovering between them, as if deciding which one to sting. Sweat streams from below his hot, heavy helmet down his cheeks, but the aromatic ointment still smells strong. The bees seem to decide as a unit to sting the Aesarian. Two fly down the loose neck of his black leather tunic, another lands on his neck, the rest on his face. He screams, dropping his sword and swatting at them. Alex drives his sword into the soft, fat belly beneath the breastplate and up, toward the heart, as the man gasps in pain, his brown eyes wide. Blood trickles from his mouth as he pitches over.

Behind him, Alex hears a scream. The Macedonian soldier with the torch has caught an Aesarian Lord's long bushy beard on fire. This Aesarian, however, isn't about to drop his sword; raising his shield, he rubs the fiery beard against the sleeve of his leather tunic, smothering it. But it's enough of a distraction that Alex can jump out of the smoke and stab him in his left armpit. The man howls and collapses.

Now it's two Macedonians fighting the single remaining Lord, who defends himself admirably. He dodges and parries and feints. Alex notices he has cleverly forced his opponents around in a half circle so that his back is now toward the tunnel entrance on the hillside. All at once, the Lord spins around and runs. The Macedonians start to follow.

"Leave him! Come with me!" he calls to them. Up ahead he hears the grunting and clanging of a pitched battle, or as pitched as it can be in the enclosed space. Every man is needed. He picks up the sword of the giant he killed and slides it across the floor to the man with the torch.

Two long blasts followed by a short one echo through the tunnel. It must be an Aesarian signal; it's not one of his own. "Retreat!" cries a voice. "Retreat!" other voices repeat. Alex leaps over the body of the giant warrior and races up the incline, followed by the two others.

Through the lingering smoke, he sees horned figures running away followed by Macedonians, and all of them seem to be yelling in fear or victory.

The Lords at the rear of their pack jog backward, swords, spears, and shields facing the Macedonians as they close in. Then everything stops and Alex can't see why.

"Make way!" Alex says, pushing his way through the Macedonians, who squeeze against the walls to let him pass. At the front of his men now, he sees that the Lords are piled up against a door.

"Open up! For the love of the gods! Open up!" several cry, banging on the door with their swords. "Hunor! Hunor!" which Alex takes to be a password.

As the door swings open, the trapped Lords topple forward into the bright light of a courtyard, gasping for breath and swatting away bees that continue to dive down and sting. The Macedonians are hot on their heels. After so long in the tunnel, the brightness hurts Alex's eyes, but the fresh air invigorates him. Fresher than the tunnel, anyway. Blue-gray smoke from his green fires wafts over the battlements, but the courtyard is only slightly hazy. He yanks off the wet cloth over his nose and mouth and squints.

The courtyard is ringed with Lords with drawn swords, gaping at the sight of their brothers' frenzied, howling rush back out of the tunnel, most of them without any apparent wounds other than large red welts on their faces, arms, and legs. Archers line the walls and peer out of windows, and now they are aiming at the Macedonians spreading out of the tunnel like an incoming tide. An arrow whizzes past Alex's head, another lodges in his shield with a thump. He raises it to cover his head and chest, and blows two short blasts on the ram's horn around his neck, the signal to the men outside to stop aiming catapult stones inside the fortress where they could just as easily kill Macedonians as the enemy.

Then Aesarians and Macedonians throw themselves against one another in the center of the courtyard. A wiry, olive-skinned Lord rushes straight for Alex, sword outstretched. Alex rushes to meet him and their weapons ring out. This is more like a normal battle with air and light and room to maneuver, but also with danger coming from unexpected places. At least now in the jostling skirmish it must be hard for the archers to make sure they don't kill their own. On his periphery he sees them, squinting one-eyed as they aim, jerking their bows this way and that, hesitating.

Suddenly the wiry Lord peels off and disappears in the melee and Alex is faced with a taller, broad-shouldered Lord who looks vaguely familiar. But as the two clash, he can't quite remember who he is and it bothers him. He should know. It's important for him to know. But it's hard to rack his brains when parrying the Lord's blows with sword and shield. The man is strong, his brown eyes radiating a quiet ferocity. They are well-matched, the two of them, and could probably go on like this for hours, circling, dodging, feinting, parrying, then coming together in a loud clash like two angry rams vying for a female.

That's it! This is Jacob, Kat's Jacob. Her foster brother, the one she loves, who won the Blood Tournament and became an Aesarian Lord. Alex curses his luck. Of all the men in the fortress, why does he have to come face-to-face with Jacob? Kat has lost the rest of her entire family. How can he kill Jacob? Alex leaps away, Jacob follows, and an arrow that must have been meant for Alex hits him in the arm. He cries out in pain and drops his shield.

Now, Alex tells himself. *Drive the sword into him now.* But he hesitates. And a moment later his sword is plucked from his hand by a tiny person somersaulting through the air. He doesn't have time to wonder what just happened. He needs to survive the next few moments. In front of him stands Jacob, an arrow sticking out of his left biceps, blood pouring down his arm, holding a sword in his right hand, hard fire in his eyes. And Alex has only a shield.

"Alex!" cries a voice at his side. It's Phrixos, handing him a sword. When Alex looks back, Jacob is picking up his shield and racing back into the thick of fighting.

The gate. They need to open the gate to let in the hundreds of Macedonians outside. But he sees smoke rising from the top of the gate towers, darker smoke than that of the greenwood fires. Boiling pitch perhaps. He needs to keep moving or an archer will fire at him.

As he zigzags through the fighting, he blows three short times on his ram's horn. This is the signal for Diodotus and his men to move the battering ram out of the way and for the bulk of Alex's forces to prepare to storm the gates. But before they do, Telekles and his team must secure the east tower, Phrixos and his team the west.

A lithe, golden-haired warrior races through the confusion, sword raised, followed by several men. Telekles. It's a tough job slashing your way up a winding staircase, but it must be done. For two days, Phrixos, Telekles, and their chosen men practiced with Diodotus in a narrow turret in the Pellan palace. But where is Phrixos?

An arrow whistles out of nowhere and impales a nearby Macedonian in the thigh, its ridged head poking out of the back of his buckskin trousers. He drops his weapons and crumples in pain. A Lord rushes over, spear raised, to finish the job. Alex's sword flashes, and the Aesarian's spear—and his hand—drop to the ground. Blood spurts obscenely from the stump as Alex, sword tucked under his arm, drags the wounded Macedonian out of the thick of the fighting. Another Aesarian marches toward them, intent on wounded prey, but two Macedonians spring to either side of Alex and shield him as he pulls the man behind a staircase.

Alex slices off the man's trousers and quickly examines the bloody wound. The arrow has torn through muscle, but not bone. He removes from his pouch the long strip of bandage all soldiers carry and wraps it tightly around the thigh. "I will send a medic as soon as I can," he says gently.

It's time to return to the fight. Alex emerges from behind the stairway just as two bodies fall from the top of the east tower, and Telekles leans down and blows five short times on his ram's horn: the signal that the tower is clear.

Alex never saw Phrixos enter the west tower and worries he is wounded or worse. But Macedonians are certainly in there now. Alex hears screams and curses, the clatter of metal against metal, the thwump of metal against ox-hide shields. Yet no one has given the signal that the west tower is clear—four short blasts of the horn. Still, if the Lords in that tower are busy defending themselves, they may also be too busy to pour boiling oil down on him and his men. He can't wait any longer. He must try.

Alex blows on his horn again—one long and two short blasts. Six handpicked men disengage from fighting and join him in the passageway to the gate, as six more form a wall behind them, battling any Lords trying to prevent them from opening the massive oak and iron-bound doors. Five large logs lie horizontally in brackets, a clever way to absorb the force of the battering ram.

He looks up. Telekles is leaning over the battlement aiming an arrow at someone on the other tower, someone ready to pour something boiling down on Alex and his men. The arrow flies directly over Alex, then Telekles waves down, smiling.

Quickly Alex and his men pull the logs out of their brackets and swing open the gate. The first man to hurtle in, not surprisingly, is Diodotus. Alex grins to see the burly, hairy body, the broken nose and scarred face. He spots Alex and grins back, waving his sword and screaming wildly, followed by dozens of Macedonians. Arrows whizz into them, some men screaming and falling. But most make it into the courtyard unscathed, looking eagerly for helmets with horns.

On Pellan Fields last month, Alex wished heartily for a bird's-eye view of the battle. Here, at least, he can get something comparable. He marches into the west gate tower and takes the narrow winding stairs three at a time, stepping over three bodies—two Aesarian and one Macedonian.

"Macedon!" he cries as he nears the top so his men will know it's him, rather than a Lord intent on pushing them from the battlements.

The two men guarding the doorway relax when they see him. "Good job," he says, clapping them on the back. He waves to his men on the other tower. Where's Phrixos?

But in between the towers, something is going wrong at the gate. Aesarians have rushed the incoming Macedonians and managed to close the gate, though the fighting is heavy around it. Alex storms over to the side of the tower overlooking the hill below. Through the shifting smoke, he sees his men trapped outside.

"Sir, we have their pitch," Telekles says, gesturing to the cauldrons of a foul, bubbling black brew over open fires.

Alex looks down at the vicious battle for the gate and sees Macedonians and Aesarians in equal numbers. "No," he says. "I can't do that to my own men."

Some eighty paces away, rocks explode into the courtyard like an avalanche as part of the wall crumbles. A nearby wooden parapet lurches sideways and falls as the two Aesarian archers in it scream. Alex's heart skips a beat. As the dust settles, he sees a red-crested helmet push through the breach in the wall, followed by the rest of Kadmus, a wide grin on his tan face, his sword gleaming in the sun. Behind him more Macedonians rush through cheering wildly and head straight for the gate, which they soon open once more to let the rest of their comrades stream in.

He's winning. Yes, *again*. He's winning against the Aesarian Lords. The greatest fighting force in the world. Joy surges through him. Men the world over have praised his father's victories, but Alex will have so many of his own he will make them forget Philip.

Already the plan forms in his mind. He will execute Lord

Gideon and his Elder Council for their treachery. The rank-and-file men he will imprison and hold for ransom. The Lords are known for always taking care of their own and should be able to raise much needed funds for Alex's treasury.

Somewhere a horn is blown—two long and one short blasts, Alex counts. Aesarian. And the Lords back away from the fighting, some of them dragging wounded comrades. Clearly, it's the signal to retreat. Alex wonders where they can retreat to in this squat, crouching fortress. If they try to escape through the mine shaft, they will fall right into the hands of the regiment he stationed outside the entrance.

An explosion rips through the air, then another. Heavy smoke wafts through the courtyard. Alex sees horned helmets racing into it and disappearing. What is happening?

"Lord Prince, they've set fire to barrels of olive oil in the next courtyard," says a Macedonian, in between heaving coughs.

"And barrels of pitch and resin in those buildings over there!" says another. More explosions. The fortress and even the hill itself tremble as smoke billows everywhere.

Now the enemy is using smoke against *him*. Alex can't see.

Anger pulses through him. Alex missed capturing High Lord Mordecai because of Heph's prideful rage. He will *not* miss again.

"A sack of gold and a farm to anyone who captures High Lord Gideon!" Alex shouts. "He's not easy to miss!" Some of his men nearby laugh. Gideon is the only black giant they've ever seen. "Search the entire fortress! We have men posted on all sides. They'll signal us if the Lords try to escape."

But when the smoke clears and the fires are put out, Alex finds not a single Aesarian Lord who isn't dead.

All the rest of them, with their weapons and even their horses, have disappeared into thin air, like smoke.

CHAPTER TWENTY

AS SHE FLIES OVER THE PITTED ROAD ON THE stolen horse, Zo's arms ache from their tight grip on Ochus's waist. She has lost track of the days since they found the princesses' decomposing bodies in the woods. At first she thought Ochus was intent on putting as much distance between them and the corpses as he could. Then she wondered if he was circling around in an effort to confuse any pursuers. She thinks they approached the same craggy hill three times from different directions. There's an air of panic in Ochus's concentration, in his intense silence, that strangles her questions about their journey in her throat.

She has tried talking to him about the murdered princesses and the bloody Xs on their chests. But whenever she brings it up, he waves his hand as if swatting a fly and says, "Robbers."

Robbers, leaving all that gold.

And then there's the way he handled the farmers—killed them discreetly and swiftly, without a second thought. Especially after one of them stared too long at Zo and seemed to guess she was from Sardis...

For most of their journey, Ochus irritated her to no end. But even then, she thought she understood him. He was her prideful and prickly captor, determined to prove himself to the Great King. Or so she believed. Now, this Ochus of the last few days frightens her. Who is he, really? She can't help but feel that their initial quest of finding a Pegasus has changed into something else, something more sinister. He hasn't mentioned the mythical horse in well over a week, and her doubt that he actually believes in her story keeps getting stronger. She is suddenly very afraid of this man and of the mysterious journey they're on. Where is he really taking her, if not to the Flaming Cliffs to find the Pegasus?

And now today, in a land of starved and stunted trees on dry hills, the pounding of the horse's hooves jolts up through every bit of Zo's aching body. She feels like a piece of tough meat that an enraged cook has beaten to tenderness, beaten to…

Her hands start to release their clenched grip around Ochus's waist. She tells them to hang on, but they no longer listen to her instructions.

She tumbles backward in slow motion. She sees sky—searing turquoise sky—as she falls.

She feels Ochus try to grab her before she hits the ground but he isn't fast enough. He stops the horse and leaps off, gently lifting her to a standing position. He keeps his arms wrapped tightly around her so that she is pressed up against the warmth of his body. She looks up, and sees his glinting amber eyes drilling into her.

For a moment, she feels safe. He leans down, as if he is going to kiss her, and in her thirsty daze, she half wonders what it will feel like when their lips touch. But then he is whispering into her left ear: "It's time we part."

She can't have heard him right. Dizziness threatens to

make her fall again. She stumbles toward the horse, shaking her head.

He grabs her shoulders. "Zofia." He hands her the goatskin of water and she simply stares at it, confused, wondering why she heard him use her real name when he doesn't know it. "You must go," he says.

"Go?" What does he mean? She must be hallucinating. They are in the middle of a no-man's land of near desert, and she's supposed to take a goatskin of water and…go? Go where? She can barely stand, let alone walk. He pulls away from her and takes the reins of the horse.

She staggers forward and grabs at his back. "What—what's happening? Are you insane? You're not leaving. We're, we have to—" But at the look of his face, it's clear he's not interested in the Pegasus. Maybe he never was. She tries to clear her parched throat. "If you no longer want to look for the Pegasus, why don't we go back to the Royal Road and you can leave me at a posting house?"

"We have to part, Zo." Ochus's voice is the rich timbre of a drum, pounding and insistent. "It is the only way." He's avoiding her eyes.

They've come this far and now, out of nowhere, *in the middle of nowhere*, it's over?

"Only way for what?" She looks around at yellow grass on crumpled hills. She has no idea where the nearest village is, nor any idea of which direction. Her heart starts thumping hard in her chest. Panic swells like a dust storm within her. "If you leave me here," she says hoarsely, almost like a whisper, "you're sending me to my death." Her whole body shakes. She is still clinging to his ragged, torn tunic.

This can't be happening.

This isn't happening.

He finally looks at her, his face hard, his eyes shrewd.

"Remember where we found water yesterday? Look for thick clumps of trees. It's a sign of a pool."

"What?" she practically shrieks, and the sound scratches her throat. This is real. He actually means it. "You're—you're leaving me here to die. Why?"

Ochus gently pulls away from her grasp, and where she was once hot, she now feels like ice. "I'm not leaving you to die. I'm leaving you to live. You *will* die if you stay with me," he says, getting ready to remount the horse. "This is the only way."

"The only way? Have you lost all reason?" she says, pushing him hard in the chest. Fury, desperation, and confusion swirl around and through her in rapid gusts. "Who are you? Where were we going? What really happened with the dead princesses? You *knew* they weren't killed by robbers! You never cared about the Pegasus, did you? You've had me *chained*! You've been lying to me! What's going on? What did those bloody marks on the bodies mean? Why did you kill those farmers? Why—"

He claps a large hand over her mouth. Fury blazes in his eyes and hardens the lines of his face. His next words are quiet but threatening, like the slow scrape of a knife over stone. "I know who you are, Princess Zofia of Sardis."

Her heart stops. Time moves slowly and her lips part—he knows? He's known all along?—but nothing comes out. Suddenly, her heart kicks back in, beating as rapidly as the patter of raindrops in a summer storm. *Why?*

Ochus drops his hand. "And I *should* have killed you before now."

"K-killed me?" Her voice is back, but it's weak. He isn't making any sense.

"I couldn't. I couldn't do it. I couldn't—" he begins, fumbling for words for the first time since she's known him.

He is staring not at her but at the horse, looking almost like he will break. "I couldn't kill you." His voice drops lower, softer. "All those nights when you were sleeping. It would have been so easy to snap your neck. I should have—it was my duty to do so—but I couldn't, I *couldn't*, and I can't." He looks at her, his eyes burning. "And I won't."

"But why?" she croaks. "You need to tell me *why* you were supposed to kill me."

"You were marked for death the moment your marriage to Prince Alexander was announced," he says, his voice so low it is almost a whisper. "If you had set off for Macedon, you never would have made it. Your caravan to the coast would have been attacked, like the one we found. Or your ship to Macedon sunk. Or perhaps something more subtly Persian—you would have eaten or drunk something that disagreed with you. Whatever the case, you would most certainly be dead by now."

Zo feels as if all the breath has been sucked out of her. Finally, her lungs draw in a huge, gasping breath, and she tries to clear her head to think about this logically. Living in a palace all her life, she knows this isn't about her. This is about politics. About the ancient rivalry between Persia and Greece. She would have been a civilian casualty like the three princesses in the *harmanaxa*. She pictures their bloated, maggot-ridden bodies, and bitter bile rises in her throat.

She swallows it and straightens. She can't get sick. She needs to think. To figure this out.

King Artaxerxes himself has sanctioned the alliance between Persia and Macedon by marriage. Was it a trick to lull Macedon into complacency while Persia planned an attack? Or is there something going on that even King Artaxerxes doesn't know?

She racks her brains to remember the Persian history lessons the old eunuch, Bagadata, taught her and the other well-born girls in the palace. She wishes fervently she had paid attention instead of passing notes to friends and doodling on her wax tablet.

"Your foolishness in running off to find that soldier saved your life," Ochus adds, almost spitting the words.

Her eyes widen. Cosmas—how does Ochus know about Cosmas? Does everyone—the Great King of Persia and his ministers—know she was meeting Cosmas in the palace cellars? She feels a hot blush of shame tingle on her neck and rise to her cheeks.

"We have spies everywhere," he explains, reading her thoughts.

"We?" she whispers.

He shakes his head. "I could never tell you," he says. "But I will tell you this much. When you disappeared, I was sent to find you, to kill you so you couldn't return from the dead and head for Macedon."

"What?" she says, her voice almost inaudible.

He looks off into the distance. "When I first saw you, climbing out of the cage, I knew who you were. I had been given a good description of you. But I couldn't kill you in front of the entire regiment. Not all of them knew of my mission. So I decided to pretend to believe your story about being a horse breeder's daughter and knowing where a Pegasus lived. I was going to leave the Royal Road and kill you in the woods the next day with two men loyal to me."

Each word is like a punch to her gut. Javed and Payem, the amiable companions of the road those first days. Javed, with his big horsey white teeth, whose stomach had been ripped open by the mountain lion. Curly-haired Payem, bleeding to death as Zo held his head in her lap and sang a lullaby. She had mourned them both and blamed herself for their deaths.

But they knew of Ochus's mission and would have gladly seen her die and molder in a secret grave.

Part of her wants to push her fists into her ears so she can't hear any more. And yet she needs to know, to understand, to...

"But I postponed it," he continues. "Not yet, I said. It doesn't have to be today. Days turned to weeks and it became harder to even think about. Now I know I can't do it."

"Why *didn't* you?" she retorts, feeling as though she might snap, might fall facedown into the dried grass that goes on endlessly and die right now, alone, of pure exhaustion and confusion. It would have been better, maybe, to be dead already. "Why can't you?"

"Because I—because..." He stops himself. His arrogance seems to be dissolving like salt in water. Finally, he whispers, so close to her that his hot breath brushes softly against her cheek. "You must know."

Suddenly, she can't swallow. Can't think. Can't breathe. Heat floods back through her body, and the vast yellowed landscape around her swims in her vision as she realizes with a flash of clarity: of course. She *does* know.

She felt it from the beginning, the way he looked at her. The way he liked to tease her, infuriate her.

And she knows, now, too, that he is not alone in this feeling she refuses to name. That she—she, too—has felt it pulling her toward him, despite the fact that she carries another man's child in her womb.

And all this time, Ochus needed to kill her. Now she understands. Now it all makes sense.

She stares at him. "And yet you plan to leave me to my death out here."

He shakes his head. "It's your only chance to live. Follow the track east until it meets a road. Take that road south, and in three days you will be back on the Royal Road. But do not go back to Sardis. Never tell anyone your name. Start a new life."

He turns back to the horse and pulls a small sack out of the saddlebag. "Here's the gold we found near the *harmanaxa*. Take it. The last of the dried beef is in a cloth inside."

She just looks at him, her arms like lead weights at her sides. He ties the sack to her belt and then removes his knife from his own belt and ties it to hers.

"Never mention my name either," he says, knotting the leather thongs securely. His voice sounds raspy, almost desperate. "I cannot appear to have let you live." He takes the reins of the horse.

"You're taking the *horse*?" she asks, her voice a frantic squeak. "If you actually do care about me, why don't you let me take it? That way I would have a better chance finding my way back to the road instead of stumbling through the dirt and heat and..."

"If anyone tries to track us," he interrupts, "a horse is much easier to follow. Those who killed the princesses might not be far. Please, Zofia. Run. Run now—for I cannot stand to let you go, and I don't know what I will do if you stay."

Zo's eyes sting with anger and fear. And what she refuses to name bubbles up to the surface, overpowering all other thoughts. She is drowning in an emotion that can no longer be suppressed:

Love. For Ochus.

Love for his fire and energy and the heat that sizzles between them. Love for his keen intelligence, for his smoldering amber eyes that take in everything at a glance, that know everything with a fierce and immediate wisdom.

Love that is stronger than anything she ever felt for Cosmas, who now seems to her like a schoolgirl crush. A love that suddenly blazes through her body, deliciously consuming her for a few seconds before she snaps back to reality. What a fool she has been to deny it. And now it is too late.

The horror of the situation descends upon her like a black, wet blanket, suffocating her. The moment she realizes she loves Ochus is the last time she will ever see him.

He drops the reins and steps toward her. She can hardly see him through the hot tears in her eyes. But she feels his muscular arms encircle her, feels the strength of his chest pressing against her. And then, he is kissing her. Softly at first, but then deeply, urgently, as though their kiss might save him. One of his hands is on her waist and the other he moves up to her neck, and then into her hair. He tilts her head back and keeps kissing her, biting her lower lip, then trailing his own to her ear, then her neck, even as tears spill onto her cheeks. She feels his need and her own, and for a moment thinks he will pull her onto the dirt and make love to her right here and now. And that she will welcome it.

Instead, he thrusts her from him with both arms. Though she always thought she had no memories of her mother before she left Sardis for Bactria, Zo has a sudden, soul-wrenching memory: the beautiful Attoosheh rudely pushing her away to climb into the litter that would take her three thousand miles east to become queen.

Now this rejection, this abandonment, this sudden loss of love and possibility.

She drinks in the angle of his jaw, the flare of his nostrils, the amazing honey-gold color of his eyes blazing with a dangerous intensity.

"Go!" he says.

She doesn't move, can't move. Her heart has gone to stone.

He swings gracefully onto the horse, a single fluid motion that reminds her of a haunting poem in flesh and muscle. He kicks his mount and tears across the field, golden-brown hair streaming behind him, an ever-diminishing figure, until he is a smudge on the horizon.

And then, he is gone. And she is alone.

CHAPTER TWENTY-ONE

BREATHING IN THE FRAGRANT SCENTS OF HIS private garden, Darius admires the thick foliage and vibrant blossoms. The riot of color and wild vines are contained on all sides by the rooms of his palace apartments. This garden—the Garden of Life and Death—is for him alone.

Life is all around him in the thick, rich foliage, the splashing of his two pet crows in the small fountain intricately carved with snarling monsters of the underworld, and the buzzing of bees hovering over brightly colored flowers.

But Death lurks, too.

He strokes the spade-shaped leaves and purple bell-shaped flowers of the deadly nightshade bush. Two to five berries—or a single leaf—will take down a warrior.

Squatting, he examines his rhododendron bushes, only two handsbreadths high. Their yellow petals like crooked fingers are gone now, having bloomed earlier in the summer. But bees from his hives in the corner of the garden continue making honey from the nectar and pollen—delicious honey that in small quantities intoxicates and, in large ones, kills.

The hellebore flowers—white and roselike—will not bud until early spring, but Darius is not interested in the blooms. When crushed, the plant's seedpods can burn through a man's clothing and blister his skin. Ingested, they swell the throat closed, blocking off air completely. He carefully pinches the seedpod between finger and thumb. They are ready to be harvested and brought back to his workshop.

Holding the place of honor in his garden is his masterpiece, the rose he has spent years cultivating. It's the palest pink—almost white. And in the center, two red veins cross, creating a vibrant, bloodred X. The Assassin's Bloom, he has named it.

He strokes the velvety petals with a lover's caress before snapping off a withered bloom.

He senses the presence of someone nearby, a new energy coming into the garden on silent feet. There's a shift, a disturbance in the usual feeling of the place, like waking up in the dark and knowing for a certainty that someone is in the room. Bending over his roses, he quiets his thoughts to examine the feel of the visitor, almost like handling an object while blindfolded. Male, though perhaps not entirely. Vicious beneath a polished veneer of refined elegance.

"Yes, Rostam?" He turns and sees the surprise in the younger man's heavily lined eyes. Rostam is still new and unused to his master's skills.

Rostam recovers, though his dark eyes remain wide. "It is done, sir."

Darius turns back to his Assassin's Blooms, humming a little tune a bard played at last night's banquet. He sees a jewel beetle on the underside of the leaf, named for its shiny shell of gold, green, and red. He picks it up. It's as innocent as a Persian princess...or three. As dazzling as the jewels he sent them off with, to wear for a prince they would never see.

With a swift movement, he crushes the beetle between his thumb and index finger before its spangled wings can even flicker.

With a true smile now on his face, Darius turns back to Rostam.

"Good."

ACT FOUR:
THE CURSED

False words are not only evil in themselves,
but they infect the soul with evil.
—Socrates

CHAPTER TWENTY-TWO

WHEN KAT SLIPS ON THE CRUMBLING STAIRS carved into the bluff, rocks tumble down the hundred-foot drop. Her sword bangs into the cliff wall—why didn't she wear it on her back, by all the gods? And she grabs a jutting rock with her injured hand—preventing herself from falling, but causing her finger to ache more than ever.

Worst of all, Heph twists around and looks down at her, eyes wide in alarm, as if she's a helpless girl about to fall off the cliff.

"Are you all right?" he asks, coming back down a couple steps toward her.

Everything's fine except her dignity. "Yes," she says casually, trying to smile despite the throbbing in her finger. She looks behind her.

They are at the narrowest part of the Nile, with cliffs rising high on both sides, and eddies and whirlpools swirling in the dark waters below. Already, she can see that the *Hathor*'s crew has removed the sail and stowed the mast. The four crewmen plunge their long oars into the sand, and the boat turns as slowly as an old grandmother. But as Kat watches, the currents take control of the vessel, and it is as though the waters have given the *Hathor* new life. In moments, the ship has skimmed the Nile toward Memphis, then rounded the bend and disappeared. She suddenly feels very small and alone.

Heph, too, has paused to look at the disappearing boat. "How will we get back?" she asks.

He wipes sweat from his forehead, but it's the only sign of exertion. She's constantly surprised at how clean his tunic is, how the curls of his tousled dark ringlets fall beautifully without benefit of a comb, while she's a bedraggled mess no matter how many times she rinses out her clothes and tidies her hair.

"Beg or buy a ride, I suppose," he says, his gaze lingering on the foam-flecked river. "There will be plenty of pilgrims coming back from the temples of Luxor and Karnak. Come on—we're almost there."

Palms and acacias, the branches hovering horizontally like clouds, greet them at the top of the cliff. Out of the narrow gully, the wind is free to whip through her hair, and she welcomes its light touch on her hot face. She hears quiet laughter and turns to see Heph watching her, amusement in his eyes.

She hastily grabs her wayward hair and braids it down over her shoulder. "What?"

"It's nothing." He shifts his pack to pull out a thin leather cord. "It's only—well, when I see your hair like that, I can't help but think of the fields of ripe grain outside Pella this time of year. All golden brown and wild, swaying in the breeze, just begging you to run your fingers through it." He blushes at the last statement, and Kat knows he wonders if he's gone too far.

She tilts her head quizzically, not about to let him have his compliment. She won't accept flattery from a man who so recently allowed Cynane to get him drunk and...whatever else happened between them just before her brazen attempt to kill Kat. "So you're saying my hair looks like plants. Like food," she says flippantly.

"No," he says, his eyes widening. He exhales sharply. "That was supposed to be a compliment. I guess it fell flat."

She suppresses a smile, though her mouth twitches a bit to the left. "I suppose it did. What if I said your hair reminded me of...of lentil stew?"

She expects him to come back with a quick retort, but instead he frowns. "That's not what I meant." He is suddenly serious, and for a second, Kat thinks she sees the man he will become. A man of deep thought and resting laugh lines. "I only mean that your hair is the same beautiful, waving amber in some lights."

Kat's cheeks warm again, and this time it has nothing to do with the climb. Heph hands her the leather cord, and she ties it around the braid's end.

"Come on," she says, "if we move quickly, we can reach the city before the sun is too high." She walks past him, and she feels him follow close behind.

It's cool here, an oasis of silence after the heat of the climb with the roar of the river below. They walk beneath a canopy of trees, patches of sunlight falling as if through fretted screens. Kat listens for birds. With so many trees, there should be at least a dozen different songs trilling the air. But there isn't even one. No creatures dart out of their path to plunge into piles of leaves. There are no buzzing cicadas. No lazy fat flies. Not only does she not hear anything, she doesn't *feel* anything. She looks right and left, suddenly desperate to find something alive.

There is nothing. No life.

She stops so suddenly Heph almost bumps into her. They have emerged from the trees into a field and in the distance, gold-tipped cupolas and spires rise above gleaming white walls like the points of a crown. Between two high rectangular towers, a golden gate winks in the sun.

"Sharuna," Heph says. His shoulders relax but Kat is suddenly nervous. There's something not right here.

"Heph," she says slowly, searching for the words to make him understand. "I have a...a bad feeling."

"A *bad feeling*? We've made it this far and you have a *bad feeling* now? Perhaps it's just the exhaustion of the journey."

"I'm *not* tired," she says, though it's not quite true. "There's something else. Or rather, *not* something else. Doesn't the forest seem eerily quiet to you? Empty? I haven't seen a single bird or—"

Heph makes a little *tsk*-ing sound and points heavenward. "Kat, there's an eagle." She looks up and spots it, a white body with dark brown wings, tilting and soaring on air currents.

"But there's nothing down here," she insists, unable to shake the suspicions itching her skin like insects.

Heph shrugs.

"Remember what the captain said?" she persists. "As soon as he let us off, he left because everyone says this place is haunted."

"Oh, for the sake of almighty Zeus, Kat," Heph says, rolling his eyes. "You believe that old man's ghost stories? Besides, what choice do we have? We've come this far, battled pirates, survived a storm and Cyn trying to kill you, and you want to turn back around? Without helping Alex?"

He's right, of course. But still... Every hair on her body seems to stand on end. Every part of her being screams to leave. *Now.* She looks back up at the eagle.

She's never tried to use her powers to reach out to an animal so far away. Gripping her lotus necklace in her palm,

Kat closes her eyes. Taking note of her breath, she begins to count the beats of her heart. They are slow, steady...but if she were to fly, it would need to be beating fast.

She would need to feel life coursing through her veins as she stretches her wings, feathers gently pricking the hidden skin beneath as the currents push her along.

Her stomach would be empty, light after hours of hunting. The need for a warm liver and soft entrails drives her forward, and the eagle opens its eyes.

The world is color and motion. With its wings held straight, the bird swivels its head, searching for the tremble on the ground that means food. A strong draft pushes down on its wings, and it shifts its tail, tilting slightly until the wind moves under. The eagle soars through the vast empty *up*, looking at the solid, crowded *down*.

Another gust throws dust into the air, but the eagle only blinks clear eyelids and continues to hunt. It never stops searching. And yet—even though the eagle can usually spot dark specks crawling on individual leaves or the slightest bend in the bush that indicates life, there is nothing for it to spot now.

Frustrated, the eagle cries out—not in anger, because an eagle does not understand what it means to be angry—but in exhaustion. It will have to fly farther, search longer.

The eagle knows that if it keeps flying away, back toward the great rushing *wet*, it will find food. But something makes it want to turn back to the place of small mounds and stone trees, even though it doesn't like going that way. No matter how much the eagle strains, it's as though some invisible force pushes it toward the walls.

The eagle banks hard in the sky and turns, changing its course to the two-leggers' nests.

As the eagle flies, its eyes still sweep the ground, but

this time it is searching for something other than blood and breath. Well, not *only* blood and breath. The primal needs remain, but a new, *human want* smothers them all. It's a want to explore and understand.

As the eagle circles the stone trees, it looks down on small square valleys filled with tiny springs and colorful rocks with the patterns of butterflies' wings.

Courtyards. The word pops into the bird's mind, unbidden. *Fountains. Murals.*

As the bird looks below, knowing washes over it.

Not *stone trees,* but *towers.*

Suddenly, names come to everything: large squares and fountains, marketplace, temple, courtyard houses. And in the center of the city a royal palace, surrounded by high walls.

The eagle doesn't like to be inside the walls but still it remains, dipping toward a sparkling pool among carefully cultivated flowers.

A moment later, the bird spots movement: the movement of a two-legger—no, *woman*—lying next to a long lake in the center of the main courtyard. Gleaming golden-brown in the sun, she lies naked, looking plucked, soft and easy to tear into, though the long black hair would be difficult for a beak. The eagle is uninterested. This woman is not a meal for her. The bird will need to keep seeking.

But as the eagle circles the city, the woman is the only source of movement. There is not the slightest stir in any of the buildings. There are no four-leggers—donkeys or horses or cats or dogs.

And now the eagle senses something else in the air, something it knows all too well: a low throbbing ache of… Words come into its mind: *Loss. Loneliness. Sadness.* When it left its nest of hatchlings for food, it returned to find an owl devouring them. The eagle was forced to live on. Alone. Always with the feeling of emptiness, a kind of hunger that no amount of soft flesh and bleeding livers can assuage.

The eagle screams.

It's falling.

And with the bird, the girl Katerina falls, too, lending her voice to the eagle's cry. She's too aware of herself—of human fingers trapped in talons, and human thoughts overcoming eagle instinct. Kat/eagle has forgotten how to fly. She needs to get *out*.

But she's stuck. She doesn't remember what it means to be a human girl. They're going to hit—

"Kat!"

A shout shatters her concentration, and Kat finds herself in the dirt. She has not fallen hundreds of feet, only collapsed onto the ground, wholly human.

"Katerina!" Heph's voice is loud and angry. It makes her head hurt. "Kat! What *happened*?"

She opens her eyes and they slowly focus on something silver and shiny on the red earth just beyond her nose. She rolls over on her back, exhaustion claiming every corner of her being.

"I—the eagle," she croaks out, her tongue thick and clumsy in her mouth. Did the eagle make it? She tilts her head back, and though nausea rises, she's able to see a black speck soar into the sky. The golden eagle recovers its height and flies north, away from her and the silent city. She doesn't blame it.

Suddenly, Kat feels water coursing down her face. She blinks. Heph has poured water from her goatskin onto his hands, and he's gently rubbing the refreshing liquid over her face, tracing her cheekbones with his thumb, and wiping away the grime from her fall.

His eyes meet hers, and she's pulled in by their rich, warm

depths. They are the only things that seem to have color after leaving behind the extraordinary eyesight of the eagle.

After a moment, she whispers, "Thank you," and pushes herself up to a seated position. Across the field, the golden city of Sharuna shimmers in the heat.

"Kat," Heph says again, stroking her hair before suddenly pulling his hand away. "What happened? Are you all right? One moment you were standing, and then the next, you were falling. Your eyes were open but you weren't *here*."

"I'm all right," she says. "All is well."

What she doesn't say is that she needs more training on how to use her magic. Ada of Caria had warned her that without the proper knowledge, she could get trapped in an animal's body and die with the creature. Then her human body, without a spirit, would also die.

She instinctively grips Helen's silver six-petaled Flower of Life pendant and brings it to her nose. Ada taught her to rub lotus oil on the pendant and inhale it deeply when her Snake Blood experiences raced out of control. Now she inhales the rich, exultant smell, a kind of intoxicating wine for the nose that lifts her out of herself immediately to a place of perfect peace.

By the grace of Tyche, goddess of fortune, she collapsed in such a way that the pendant fell near her nose. Though it has been many days since Kat was able to apply lotus oil to the amulet, the fragrance is still there.

But what about next time? She has no more oil to replenish the scent, and she might not have Heph shouting her name, anchoring Kat to her human body.

"Where were you?" he asks again.

She shakes her head. "I got a bird's-eye view of the city. And Heph—it's beautiful."

The images that had been so confusing to her as a bird

come back to her. Buildings with thick columns, each crowned with a capital in the shape of a lotus flower or a god's head. Everything painted with magical signs and the figures of people and gods in red and blue, green and yellow.

It was so beautiful…and so horrible.

"There's something wrong with the city," she says, gazing at its walls.

"In what way?" Heph rummages in their pack and hands her a pouch of dried figs. She accepts gladly, and the sweet, sticky thickness bursts on her tongue.

Kat chews, considering his question. "There are no animals. None at all." She spits out the date pit. "There are no donkeys or horses, or dogs or cats. The chickens or goats that roam every village, town, and metropolis are nowhere to be seen. There is not a single mouse or fly."

Her body starts to shake involuntarily, but she can't tell if it is from exhaustion or fear. She forces out the next words. "There are no *people*, save one—a single woman sunbathing nude in the main palace garden."

"So the legends Sarina told Alex are at least partially true," Heph says, running a hand through tangled curls. "But, Kat…" He hesitates, and she follows his eyes toward the massive gate. She doesn't immediately grasp what he's saying, but then she sees a flicker of movement. She squints—her eyesight seems so dim after the eagle's—and sees that behind the crenellations, soldiers pace back and forth.

She inhales sharply—they were not there moments ago. At least, she thought they weren't. She shakes her head slightly, but the soldiers remain—muscular, armed, and very real.

"Could you have been confused?" Heph asks. "As a bird, I mean."

"No." She frowns. "An eagle's eyesight is much better than ours."

"Maybe they were all inside?" Heph suggests. "The heat of the day…" But he stops talking when he sees Kat tilt her head.

"I don't think we should go in there."

Heph raises a black eyebrow. "What?"

"None of this makes sense!" Kat says, waving her hands about her. She regrets it immediately as her hurt finger sends shooting darts of pain up her arm. She winces and cradles her right hand in her left palm, holding it close to her heart. "Why have all the animals gone?"

Heph stands up, then offers her a hand. Though the dates helped, she still feels weak. She allows him to pull her up.

"I don't know, but we knew before that it is a city of powerful legend and magic." Heph ties his goatskin to his belt. "It's not a normal city like Pella or Halicarnassus. And Alex needs us to go there. This is bigger than either of us."

Kat knows he's right, but she still can't shake the fear of being trapped within those thick, high walls, trapped with the eternally aching sadness pulsing through the place.

A thought occurs to her: perhaps she isn't really scared at all. Maybe the fear flooding her heart is left over from the bird's terror. But before she can explore this idea further, a yawn overtakes her. She is so very tired, despite her protestations otherwise.

"The sooner we go, the sooner you can rest," Heph says, grabbing hold of her arm and supporting her.

Sleep. She nods.

He wraps his arm behind her back, and she lets him. "Let's go and see what the princess has to say about Alex's proposal."

Before they are even halfway there, though, the massive gate swings open and dozens of soldiers line up forming a solid wall. They are gigantic, broad-shouldered and olive-skinned, each wearing a leopard skin tied over the left shoulder. Their tall, figure-eight-shaped shields are made of zebra skin, and they each hold an impossibly long spear. They wear red-and-white striped headdresses, low and tight across their foreheads, with folds of cloth hanging down their chests.

As Kat approaches them, she sees they all look nearly identical, and she wonders if she has ever seen people so beautiful in her life—the flashing dark eyes, the straight noses, the strong cheekbones and square jaws, the bulging biceps and legs like tree trunks. Oddly, incised into their arms and legs, shoulders and chest—on every bit of skin below the neck—are rows and rows of magical symbols many shades lighter than the surrounding skin. Kat makes out birds and snakes, hands and feet and eyes.

She doesn't know what to say. She never learned how to greet soldiers as a visiting ambassador, and Alexander didn't have time to teach her before he sent her away. Luckily, Heph seems to know.

"We bring you greetings from the prince regent of Macedon, Alexander, son of the great King Philip," Heph proclaims loudly, bowing slightly. "We are the prince's emissaries on a diplomatic mission to meet Princess Laila. I am Lord Hephaestion of Pella, and this is the prince's sister, Princess Katerina."

Kat almost laughs. *Princess Katerina.* She glances down at her patched, travel-stained, dun-colored tunic and wonders if the guards will laugh, too.

A soldier steps forward, even taller and more formidable than the rest. "I am General Wazba, commander of the city," he says in heavily accented Greek. "You may not pass in daylight. Return shortly before sunset, and we will escort you inside."

Kat's stomach lurches as if a horse has kicked her. Why would they not let them in while the sun shines?

"We will be here," Heph replies, gripping Kat's arm, and she's more than a little grateful for his support. Her traitorous legs would not be able to hold her up just now.

The soldiers turn and reenter the city, leaving Kat and Heph outside to stare at the massive gate which has closed without making a sound. Only then does Kat finally realize what is so wrong.

She hears no tromp of booted feet.

No creak of leather shield grips.

No gentle clanging of scabbarded swords against shields.

It is a silence that belongs to the dead.

"It's time, Kat."

She opens her eyes. She barely remembers Heph spreading out the blanket under an old carob tree. She doesn't feel refreshed, but at least she doesn't feel like she's about to fall over. She looks down at her hand and is surprised to see that her wounded finger has been attended to recently. She must have slept so deeply that Heph was able to change the bandage without her waking.

She sits up. Now the golden streams of light through the branches have become soft, gentle: the rosy silver glow of sunset. Time to go. But she does not want to. Every part of her wants to head back to the cliff and scramble down the stone steps as quickly as she can without falling.

"Heph?"

"Yes?" he says, rolling up her blanket and stashing it in his pack.

"We can't go back to the gate."

"What?" He looks up, startled. "Why?"

She shrugs, not knowing exactly what to say.

"So what do you suggest, then?" he presses. "That we stand down by the river and find a boat to take us back to the coast? And then go home to Macedon and tell Alex we failed him because you had a bad feeling?"

"Y—maybe." She hesitates. "I'm not saying—"

"Kat, did you get a look at those soldiers? They make the Aesarian Lords looks like children! Those men could squeeze a Persian's neck with each hand and not miss a step marching. Whether the princess agrees to marry Alex or not, we still need to negotiate for some of these warriors to be added to Macedon's army."

Kat sighs. He is right. They've come too far and survived too much to just turn around now. She firmly tells her stomach to stop doing its nervous flutter. Alex needs her. She picks up her pack, and together, she and Heph walk toward the gate.

The Sharuna warriors are waiting for them, lined up as if for battle in the light of the setting sun. General Wazba steps forward holding a torch which, Kat supposes, they will need very soon. In Egypt there is very little twilight. There is day, and suddenly night. "The princess bids you welcome, visitors from Macedon," he says, unsmiling. "Follow me."

They enter the city beside the general as the fifty or so soldiers fall in behind them. For a second time, Kat does not hear the thud of the gate. As they walk down a street of impressive buildings, she feels a cold breath on the back of her neck and shivers.

She keeps her eyes open, missing the eagle's sight. The Egyptian buildings seem heavier, more solid than those in Macedon, with their low, fat columns and boxlike shapes. The Greek public buildings she's seen in Pella and Halicarnassus emphasize tapering height and pleasing proportions. But these are brightly painted, all the figures with thick black wigs and heavily lined eyes and shown in profile, one shoulder and one leg in front. She sees a goddess with enormous cow ears. A god with the head of a jackal. Paintings of people baking bread, farming fields, fishing from reed boats.

Kat starts to feel her heartbeat skipping. Something is wrong here. Very wrong. The empty buildings. The odd, nearly identical guards. The lack of sound. Even the air feels wrong. It's all she can do not to turn around and run back to the gate.

Ahead of her is a fountain of a woman, arms and wings spread wide, water spewing from two horns on her head surrounding a full moon. It is masterfully carved, but that's not what catches her attention.

There is no slap of water as the droplets hit the rock, and as the last ray of the sun touches the fountain, it illuminates the spray, making it seem as though it is a fountain of embers. Then the sun drops below the horizon, and everything changes.

In the blink of an eye, the fountain collapses with a thundering crash. The goddess is on her side in the street, her wings and head broken off. The stones are charred, the basin cracked and bone-dry.

The formerly pristine buildings are burned and broken, crumbling to ash around her. The eerie silence is replaced with wails, moans, screams, frenzied prayers, crashing thunder, exploding lightning, crying babies who suddenly stop crying, shrieking animals, crackling fires...

And all around her, there are bodies.

At her feet, a mother wrapped in rags shields a child, bones protruding from her legs and arms, her eyes black, empty sockets. And there's a horse, its moldy flesh pulled back from large, yellow teeth as if it is grimacing in agony, every rib exposed.

This is a dream, Kat thinks, trying to quell the scream bubbling up inside her but caught in her tightening throat.

In dreams, scenes shift from one to another in the blink of an eye. Not even in Ada's enchanted fortress did Kat experience anything like this. Her spine has turned to ice, her legs to jelly.

Kat sees two long bundles lying right in front of her in the street. *Don't look*, a voice inside her head commands. But she can't help herself. With an increasingly heavy sense of dread, she bends down and lifts some rough-spun cloth to see what is inside one of them. It is a human head, its eyes yawning cavities, its nose eaten away, maggots writhing in its blackened cheeks. She leaps away from it and stands behind Heph, shaking, wondering if she will throw up.

Silently cursing, she tells herself to remember who she is. A princess. A Snake Blood. Twin sister of Prince Alexander. A sixteen-year-old girl whose cleverness and bravery turned the tides of Alex's battle against the Aesarian Lords. But right now she would take on a whole regiment of Lords by herself rather than face the enchantments of this doomed place.

Heph, too, has paused in shock and fear. "What treachery is this?" he demands of Captain Wazba's back, outrage in his voice. "What have you done?"

"Come, honored guests," says Captain Wazba in a deep voice, though the giant soldier keeps his back toward them. "We will not allow you to be late."

"No," Kat says, finally finding her voice as she grabs for Heph's hand in the growing dark.

The captain pauses. Then slowly, he turns around. And that's when Kat's scream finally comes.

For the captain is no longer the handsome man of moments before. He is a giant figure of flaking brown clay, covered with magical symbols, his huge eyes two fiery orange lights glowing in a cracked and crumbling face.

Whirling away from the awful sight, Kat sees the soldiers

behind her have undergone a similar transformation. They are ancient, living statues.

The eagle was right; other than Princess Laila, there are no living things in the city. Because the soldiers standing all around Kat are not the army of an Egyptian princess, but the diabolical regiments of sorcery.

CHAPTER TWENTY-THREE

JUST OUTSIDE THE BEACH COTTAGE, WAVES pound the shore like the angry drums of an invading army. Inside, the air tastes like salt and wind, and a fine coating of sand lies on clay jars, metal instruments, and scattered scrolls...items that look like ancient artifacts but which are, Alexander knows, the tools and writings of his former teacher.

"He's not here," the prince says, impatience dampening his mood even as the moist island air soaks into his cloak. He had wanted to come to Samothrace much sooner, but the Aesarians had forced his hand. Now that they've been temporarily driven back—completely off Macedonian soil, according to reports—he is eager to return to troubling matters closer to home.

"Are you certain we're in the right place?" Kadmus takes the lid off a jug, bends over it, and quickly replaces it, his lean handsome face a mask of disgust. "Something dead in there," he says. Then he points at a bronze contraption on a table and raises an eyebrow in question. Balls of different sizes can be moved around one another on an elaborate network of thin curves of metal.

Alexander smiles. How many times did he and Heph and the other boys work with the astronomer at Mieza, predicting eclipses and the location of planets in the night sky? The center ball is the earth, around it are the sun, the moon, and the six other planets.

"Yes," he says, suddenly missing his old tutor—and those boyhood days, which seem so long ago—with a physical ache. "This is definitely his home."

A dark silhouette blocks the low doorway and a woman enters, carrying two jugs.

"Are you looking for Master Aristotle?" she asks in the harsh accent of Samothrace. "He's not here today, but I expect he'll be back this evening or…" She casts a glance out the window at towering dark clouds rising from where the sea meets the sky and adds, "Perhaps tomorrow."

The woman pushes aside some scrolls and sets the jugs on the table. "If I didn't bring the man food, I think he would forget to eat."

She wipes sweat off her face with her apron and tucks a stray black tendril behind her ear.

"Do you know where he is?" Alex asks. "He was my teacher once, and I have traveled far to see him."

The woman eyes Alexander and then Kadmus. Alex realizes that to her, they could be any two high-ranking soldiers in the prince's army. "He's on the islet, doing research," she says, gesturing out the open window. Alex looks out and sees a green-gray blur of rocks and trees across the choppy water.

"Can someone take us out in a boat?" he asks, turning toward her. She has grabbed a broomstick of twigs and started sweeping the floor.

"On this side of the island you would have to ask the Wave Dancers," she says. "They have all the fishing boats."

"Wave dancers?"

"The Wave Dancers of Poseidon," she says. "They fling themselves into the arms of the sea when it's rough as a way of worshipping the Trident Bearer. And today, with the storm coming, they will be dancing, not fishing, I imagine. Go left outside the door and along the beach until you round the bend where the cliff comes down to the water. You'll find them there."

When they round the cliff, they see that waves thunder toward shore from a half mile out. Alex doesn't know what he expected from the Wave Dancers, but he is surprised to see human heads, dozens of them, poking out of the rolling foam. The swimmers seem to be flying on the waves. In between the swells he sees naked men and women studying the breakers, swimming out to meet them or ducking below them to wait for others. Alex is amazed. Usually even the best swimmers run from such seas.

But none of them is willing to take Alex and Kadmus to the islet. "Look at those waves," one bandy-legged graybeard says in awe, gesturing to the high foaming breakers. "Now is the time to worship the god by embracing him, not take fish from his waters."

"Perhaps we should just wait until this evening, when he comes back?" Kadmus suggests, shading his eyes with his hand and staring at the islet. It's hard to judge exactly how far out it is; it looks to be the size of a man's sandal, and sometimes large swells hide it entirely. But Alex doesn't want to wait. His teacher is so easily distracted by stars and birds, plants and tides, it is possible that he will focus on some new observation and stay on his islet for the next several days.

Alex needs Aristotle's advice now. The Aesarian Lords

could come thundering back with reinforcements at any time. War wages in Byzantium. And something else sits heavy on his shoulders like the golden parade armor Olympias made for him, weighing him down, constricting him—something that maybe only Aristotle can help with.

The sea wind blows Kadmus's straight dark hair back from his face as he studies clouds that seem to get darker and angrier by the moment. Alex bends down and takes off his sandals. The hard rocks of the beach push into the soles of his feet as he unties his belt.

"My lord?" Kadmus says, snapping to attention. "What are you doing?"

Alex lifts his tunic over his head and knots the garment around his waist. The unbleached cloth just covers the snake-shaped scar on his thigh and the slightly smaller muscles. "I'm going for a swim."

"But, my lord!" Kadmus protests. "The clouds are heavy with rain and the surf is dangerous—a storm is coming."

The wind pricks at Alex's chest, causing goose bumps to ripple over his skin. Breathing in the fresh salty air, he feels like he's woken up from a long sleep, and now he's ready to live.

"You don't have to come with me," Alex says, looking Kadmus straight in the eye—a challenge—and then he is sprinting toward the sea, his feet slapping against the shallow water as wet sand sucks and tugs at his ankles. He hears slapping behind him—Kadmus—and laughs as he used to years ago when he had nothing to worry about except displeased tutors.

A foamy wave slams into his knees, and he pushes through it. Another hits him in his abdomen and suddenly he's lifted, weightless, floating in water the pale translucent green of rare Egyptian glass. He looks down and sees an entire world swaying below him—sea anemones and swimming crabs with pincers outstretched and schools of tiny silver fish.

Straightening his legs, he keeps his head and shoulders high. He kicks, and in the water his left leg is just as whole and strong as his right. He is strong. He is powerful. He is soaring in the hands of the god Poseidon. He propels himself through the water toward the islet, rising and sinking on the rolling waves, Kadmus to his left, though sometimes he loses sight of him when a wave slides between them.

At first they make good progress, and the islet grows larger, ever closer with each stroke, but then the wind picks up, shrieking like a wounded animal. The waves rise higher, crested now with bubbling foam, and dip so low Alex wonders if he will hit sand. He sees the islet growing smaller on his left and corrects course, pulling with all his strength toward it.

Suddenly, the waves are so high Alex can't see anything but water. It seems as if the sea has swallowed the island, the islet, and Kadmus. This is like riding Bucephalus for the first time, he thinks, remembering the jolting, heaving, twisting mass of angry horseflesh below him, only now the challenge is a beast of water. Alex laughs, and a wave slaps him hard in the face like the girl in the tavern outside Mieza when Heph pinched her butt and she thought Alex had done it. He coughs and sputters as he laughs some more. Here he is, riding out a storm in the sea. Shouldn't he be afraid? Yet he has never felt so alive.

There's a roar and he looks over his shoulder. A wave the size of a small temple crests behind him, curling and twisting, and tosses him high. He tucks in his arms and looks ahead but the wave slams him down hard and spins him around. As he somersaults beneath surging water, he doesn't know what direction is up. Then he's dragged against the sandy bottom, scraping his chest and legs.

For a moment Alex wants to open his mouth and cry out in protest, but he needs to save every bit of air in his lungs. The wave will pass. If he doesn't panic, the air inside him will lift him to the surface. He rolls, tossed back and forth in the gray-green twilight world, his chest ready to explode. And then he starts to rise.

Suddenly a pair of arms surrounds him. It's Kadmus with a large piece of driftwood. "Put your arms on it and kick hard with your feet," he says. Together, slowly and painfully, they make their way toward the islet, finally catching a large swell that swings them toward the beach and hammers them into the shallows.

Gasping, Alex staggers out of the water, Kadmus just behind him. They collapse onto the beach. His entire right side is an angry red mark where the sea has slapped him, and blood pours from a gash in his left shoulder he didn't know was there and still doesn't feel.

"Congratulations," Kadmus says, leaning on an elbow and grinning. "Poseidon has just initiated you into the cult of his Wave Dancers!" An unexpected laugh bursts from Alex, surprising him and hurting his scraped sides. And then Kadmus laughs, too, his ice-colored eyes shining with mirth.

Alex sits up and realizes that the sea, like an impatient lover, has yanked off the tunics both Kadmus and Alex knotted around their waists. The general's tanned chest is strong, his stomach flat and hard as a tabletop. Even the battle scars soldiers proudly display as marks of honor—white lines on golden-brown skin—are sprinkled over his body artistically.

Suddenly, Alex realizes that his scar is completely visible. *The* scar. The one he was born with like a mark of shame, marring his left leg. His laughter dies out before Kadmus's, and then the general falls silent, too.

They are completely alone on the little beach, a thick screen of trees behind them. Kadmus stares at him.

No, Alex realizes with sudden shame. *Stares at his leg.*

Shifting it, he tries to hide the scar in the sand. The movement seems to startle Kadmus, and the general quickly looks away. No one knows about Alex's scar except for his parents, his old bath attendant Hestia, Kat, Heph, and Sarina. And now Kadmus.

For a moment, Alex wishes he could grab his sword and cut it out, separating himself from the weakness.

"True strength is not hiding who you are," Kat said once when he was complaining about his leg. "It's accepting it, and working to improve it if you can. And you'd be surprised how many people don't even care about the thing you're working so hard to hide." He had nodded in agreement but said to himself that Kat would never understand. Her body was perfect.

But now he can see that she was right. He doesn't want to keep hiding himself from his friends. He wants Kadmus to really *see* him—and still find him worthy.

Alex opens his mouth to speak, but a shout breaks through the silence. He twists around to see a man coming out of the tree line, his dark hair liberally streaked with silver, his rough-woven gray robe clearly spotted with dirt and sea spray even from this distance. A smile spreads over Alex's face as the man draws closer.

"Well," Aristotle says, coming to a stop next to them, his gray eyes crinkling. "Just look at what the tide washed up!"

Alexander sits on the sand, a poultice of vinegar and calendula leaves bound on his injured shoulder, and a salt-stiff tunic of Aristotle's making his back itch. With a battered basket over one elbow, the philosopher wades through a tidal pool, a small lagoon protected by two rocky arms from the choppy waters beyond. Suddenly he squats down, the tip of his long beard hanging into the water.

"Look at this!" Aristotle calls, and though Alex looks, the darkening sky makes it too hard to see what Aristotle is holding up.

"I can't see it!" he shouts back. "What is it?"

Aristotle shakes his head and, instead of answering, flings a mass of slimy black tentacles interspersed with what looks like fat black beans. It lands with a wet plop next to him.

During his three years at Mieza, Alex grew used to his teacher's eccentricities—watching spiders build webs by candlelight or studying thunderstorms from the roof of the tallest towers. Throwing around seaweed is unusual, but not unexpected.

Nor was it unexpected that Aristotle waved away Alex's questions when he found them on the beach, saying there would be time to talk later. High tide was coming in on the breath of a storm, he pointed out, filling the tidal pool with new treasures. After Aristotle bandaged Alex's shoulder in his hut, he directed Kadmus to find firewood and left Alex sitting on the sand as he went wading, his tunic hiked up over his belt, exposing knobby legs.

Now Alex looks at the slimy tangle next to him as his teacher walks toward him until the water comes up only to his ankles.

"This seaweed is very rare here," Aristotle says. Seawater drips from his beard and creates a dark damp patch on his tunic. "It thrives only in the north of the Black Sea and rarely makes it through the straits down into the Aegean."

Alex picks it up. "Rare though it is, some of it will make

it past the Pillars of Hercules into the endless sea. Nature's nature is to disseminate."

Aristotle grins, his lined, weathered face looking almost youthful. "So you *were* paying attention in class. And I thought you were always daydreaming about your next hunting trip with Hephaestion and new moves to try out in your wrestling lessons."

Alex smiles back. "Well, that, too."

"Though I do wish you had managed to do more than memorize facts. I wish I had taught you to think. But perhaps I was simply not up to the task."

Alex sits up straight. "What do you mean?"

Aristotle squints down at the water sliding back and forth over his feet. "I know you want me to join your council. That's why you're here, isn't it?"

Alex doesn't know how Aristotle knows, but he rises and slaps the sand from his tunic. This is a formal request, and he shouldn't be sprawled in the sand when making it. "Yes, teacher. My father has mired himself and most of our army in war with Byzantium. Pella was attacked by the Aesarian Lords. I need your wisdom, your advice. The people of Macedon would be delighted to know you were helping me." Delighted is too soft a word, but Alexander doesn't want to admit that he needs something massive, something persuasive, to make the people trust him.

He finds it incredibly annoying that Aristotle isn't looking at him but at something in the water, and doesn't appear to be listening. He's the prince regent of Macedon now, not a student. "And it would calm Athens," he adds, "which is getting nervous about my father's expansion into other kingdoms." Though born in Macedon, Aristotle has spent most of his life in Athens. Maybe this will sway him.

"Aha!" Plunging both hands into the pool, Aristotle pulls

out a golden whelk shell as water drips from his beard. "I've been looking for one of these. Do you see how the opening is on the left side instead of the right? Isn't it fascinating that seashells can be right- or left-handed just like people?"

Alex wonders if his frustration will burst right out of his head. "Aristotle, please listen to me. I need you on my council," he says, and his voice is sharper than he intended.

Aristotle turns the shell over and over in his hand, then holds it up to his eye. "No, no, no," he says, frowning and peering inside. Alex isn't sure if he is saying he won't join the council or if he's talking to himself about the whelk. He crosses his arms and waits.

Aristotle places the shell in his basket and raises inscrutable eyes to Alex. "I will not join your council," he says.

"You're refusing?" Alex can hardly believe his ears. "Why?"

"I don't want to witness your transformation into Philip of Macedon."

He feels as if his former teacher has punched him hard in the gut. "How can you say that?" he spits, thinking of his father, drunk and staggering at a banquet, cuffing male cup bearers on the head and fondling servant girls' breasts. Most palace servants keep a wide berth around the king when he's in his cups, carrying dishes and chamber pots twice the distance to avoid him. Everyone knows Philip to be barbaric, pompous, and uncivilized, both at home and afield, and Alex has endeavored for the last sixteen years to be *nothing* like his father.

Aristotle looks at Alex with solemn gray eyes the color of the storm clouds churning overhead. "I know *why* there are openings on the council."

Alex bristles. "You don't understand—I *had* to do it. I cleansed the council of treachery. Gordias confessed. Hagnon was guilty, and Theopompus is, too, though I didn't get a confession from him. When I return I will send him into exile."

Aristotle looks at Alex thoughtfully, as though Alex were responding to a question in class. "And where do you think Theopompus will go?"

"What do you mean?" Alex asks. What kind of a question is that? Who cares where Theopompus goes?

"Carry out the scene, Alexander," Aristotle says, pushing past his former student to sit on damp sand. He grabs a towel and dries his feet. "Once Theopompus leaves, he will go straight to the Persians and do the exact thing you have accused him of. This time, he'll *actually* sell all the information he has, in exchange for a comfortable lifestyle under the Great King. No, no. It's far better to keep him close at hand. As long as he is comfortable in Macedon, he will never betray you."

I wish I had taught you to think. Alex wants to slap his forehead. Of course. Whenever the Athenians, jealous of one man possessing too much influence, exiled their most successful generals, the exiles usually took their knowledge and experience to a grateful enemy. Themistocles went to Persia, Alcibiades to Sparta. Alex should have anticipated that a man like Theopompus would probably do the same. He feels a blush rising up his neck.

Still, Theopompus is guilty of something. Why else would the Athenian in Alex's vision have given him the Praxiteles statue? And Alex is no longer a little boy sitting on a bench scratching notes on his wax tablet with a stylus as his teacher lectures. "You've been to his country estate," Alex says. "The furnishings, statues, jewels, tapestries. And a Praxiteles from Athens. It can't all be ambassadorial gifts."

Aristotle barks out a laugh as he ties his sandal strap. "Oh, poor Theo! If you were older, Alexander, you would know he runs the most expensive brothels in all of Greece. He buys the finest young slaves of both sexes when he travels as ambassador. Black-skinned Ethiopians. Golden-haired Gauls…"

Aristotle shakes his head, still chuckling. "That Athenian gave Theo that statue from his private collection in return for a gorgeous Persian hermaphrodite. The poor man couldn't decide if he liked boys or girls better, so he got two at once for an enormous price. It was all the agora could talk about two years ago."

Alex feels his stomach clench into a coiled knot. While running brothels is distasteful, it isn't illegal. It certainly isn't deserving of capital punishment.

"And…Gordias?"

"A true priest of the gods," Aristotle says, placing his rolled-up towel in his basket. He looks up and Alex flinches under his teacher's hard, gray stare.

"So incorruptible, in fact, that he confessed to a crime he didn't commit in order to save Theopompus, who, let us admit, you would have executed even if he *had* told you about the brothels, just to show the people how strong a ruler you are at sixteen."

Alex feels something tighten in his throat. He *would* have executed Theopompus. And Gordias, too, if he hadn't been protected by priestly law. He would have killed two men innocent of treason.

A memory rolls through him with the force of a punch: a kneeling body, blood spraying the scaffold like the first hard, fat raindrops of a storm, and a head rolling into the crowd like a children's leather ball. Alex doesn't want to ask the next question, but he must. "Hagnon?"

"Oh, Hagnon deserved death, don't worry about that." Aristotle stands up, puts a hand on Alex's shoulder, and starts guiding him down the beach toward his hut. "Everyone knew that Hagnon was corrupt. He arranged it so that foreigners docking in Macedon's ports wouldn't have to pay duty on cargo. The ship owners paid him half the price they would have paid Philip."

That explains exactly what Alex saw. The Persian plunking down a sack of gold, Hagnon giving him a small scroll. A duty-free certificate.

"But I saw such pure hatred in Gordias's eyes," Alex says, remembering how the dark eyes smoldered with loathing.

"I'm sure you did," Aristotle replies. A jagged bolt of lightning illuminates the sky over Samothrace, and thunder spreads out in silent waves, practically rattling the little islet. They quicken their pace. "Hatred for what you were doing. Hatred for the brutal ruler you so quickly and readily became. Those who are truly strong don't need to make a public show of strength, you see. True strength often calls for walking away from a situation even if you might look weak or foolish."

Alex shakes his head. "No. Now the people respect me." He thinks of the beautiful story Sarina told him, of the god who demanded loyalty of his subjects, made them choose death to prove it to him.

"They fear you," Aristotle says gently. "That is different." He bends down and grabs a fistful of gray powdery sand. With his index finger, Aristotle sifts through the grains in his palm, examining tiny pieces of shell ground down by waves and rocks.

For a moment, Alex wonders if he, too, is but a shell in the ocean of tumultuous political winds and tides that will wear him down to grist. Is there any other end for him than being crushed between Persia and the Aesarian Lords, between Byzantium and Athens?

"Is fear not equal to respect?" Alex asks, hating that his voice rises like an angry child's. He takes a deep breath. "How can there be respect if there is no fear?"

"Fear leads to more treason, not less," Aristotle replies coolly, picking a shiny pearlescent shard from the sand, examining it, and throwing it down. "Some people will want to kill you before you can kill them. Others will submit, becoming sheep, meekly obedient without thoughts of their own."

He looks at Alexander, his eyes calm now, like the placid waters of a mountain lake on a cloudy autumn day. "We are not Persians, Alexander, too cowed by the whip of the Great King to utter a word or think a single thought he might disapprove of. You would grow to despise your own people if they were like that. When you possess power over those whose lives, whose minds, you do not value, all you will have…"

Aristotle opens his hand slightly and sand slides out in a steady trickle. "…is an empire of dust."

The words hit Alexander hard, like a physical blow. Aristotle is practically accusing him of being stupid enough to destroy Macedon. Hot anger rises in him and he knocks Aristotle's hand, spilling all the sand at once. Aristotle's eyes open wide in surprise. This is not the usual behavior of students or former students with the man many consider to be the wisest person in the world. But his hard gaze immediately softens. While Alex's other teacher, Leonidas, routinely disciplined with beatings and starvation, Aristotle always said bad behavior contained the seeds of its own brutal punishment so he didn't need to lift a finger.

Alex runs a hand through his hair and rubs his sore neck. Clearly, Aristotle thinks he behaved unwisely in dealing with his council. But what else could he have done? "An empire of treachery, you mean!" he says. "If the spy wasn't Hagnon, Gordias, or Theopompus, then who was it? Because whoever it was is still in the palace in a position to spill secrets to my enemies."

Aristotle smiles ruefully. "Indeed," he agrees. "When you return, you must look more closely at those you didn't suspect of treachery. Look at them very closely indeed, Alexander." Their eyes lock, and Alex feels a frisson of something. An understanding that hits him with the force of an arrow tearing through flesh in the heat of battle.

He hears the rain before he feels it, a soft patter of shimmering sound all around them. They should run back to the hut, he knows, but he can't move. He studies his teacher. The weathered face is mapped with the lines of time, wisdom, and humor. The gray eyes peering out from under bushy eyebrows spark with a hidden secret.

He knows.

Aristotle *knows* about Alexander's ability to read men's eyes. He knows about Snake Blood. He *knows* about Alex—and he's kept it from him. Always taught him to revile magic.

"Why—" The betrayal has lodged somewhere in his throat, making it hard to speak. Rain falls on his forehead and he impatiently rubs it off. "How—"

"Alexander." Aristotle says his name so gently, that the anger building within Alex is suddenly extinguished, as though the older man smothered the burning sparks with the liquid kindness of his voice. "Do not be angry. Do not let this keep you from seeing reason—for *reason* is why I have never told you what I have always suspected."

"Explain," Alex croaks. "Tell me why you kept my magic hidden from me."

The philosopher scowls, and silver raindrops pool on the tips of his gray-streaked dark hair. "Magic such as you mean

does not exist," he says. "The only true magic is human in-
genuity. Search for answers to your problems within yourself, Alexander. For in yourself all problems and all answers
lie. Not outside." He turns and starts walking quickly as the
rain falls now in silver sheets, sticking Alex's tunic to the
skin of his back.

"When did you know?" Alex asks above the rising hiss
of rain, his injured shoulder nearly touching his teacher's as
they walk.

"Do you remember," Aristotle says, "the first time we
ever met?"

"Of course," Alex says. When he was five he often liked
to stand outside his father's office and try to listen at the
door, while the guards on duty rumpled his hair and gave
him honey cakes. One day he overheard Philip arguing with
a man about becoming Alex's tutor.

"As for me, I don't give a cracked obol whether you do
or not," Philip was saying, "but my wife insists, and it's not
easy to keep that one happy."

"Highness," the other voice came wearily, "many kings
have begged me to instruct their spoiled princelings, and I
always give them the same answer: no."

Finally, the man reluctantly agreed to at least meet Alex
before deciding. Alex ran back to his nursery, only to have
a guard fetch him moments later and take him back to the
office.

"Good day, Prince Alexander," Aristotle said, and Alex
had the odd feeling he was being treated as an adult. The
man bent down to peer at him more closely. For the first
time ever, Alex felt himself pulled into someone's eyes, going
through the tunnel of white light, and out the other side. He
saw this man as a child, not much older than Alex himself,
standing next to a funeral pyre laid out with mother, father,

sisters, and brothers. All around him, mourners wore cloth masks pinned with parsley and cloves of garlic. Plague.

When Alex returned to himself, he looked around at the familiar furnishings—the battle standards and torn shields—and wondered briefly where he was. Then he looked up at the dark-haired man bending over him, and remembered. A tear slipped down Alex's cheek. He looked up and saw his father's face turning red.

When the man asked him why he was crying, he said, "Because you lost your whole family in the plague. I can see you standing there as the pyre was lit, see you throwing your plague mask into the fire."

"What nonsense are you prating there?" Philip said angrily.

"No, it's all right," Aristotle replied, holding up a finger. He turned to Philip and said, "I am too valuable to teach reading, writing, and figures. Anyone can do that. Send the boy to me when he is thirteen and needs to learn how to think."

Now, they turn left on the narrow footpath from the beach through the trees, and in the clearing ahead Alex sees smoke rising from the roof of Aristotle's hut and hears a comforting clatter of pots. Kadmus must be attempting to prepare dinner. But he's not ready to go in. Not yet. He needs to finish this conversation in private.

"Are you saying magic is evil, then? That it's wrong to use?" he asks, drawing Aristotle beneath the leafy branches of an elm tree.

Aristotle shakes his head. "Not necessarily. But neither is it inherently good. It's neutral. It can be a boon to you or a curse. You have benefited from your vision into men's souls, judging whom to trust. Then again, you almost killed Theopompus because you misinterpreted what you saw."

He hangs his head as Aristotle continues, "There is another kind of Blood Magic that can heal: Earth Blood. That, too, can be beneficial, or it can be used to destroy."

Alex sighs. "I wish I had that one," he says, rubbing his left thigh.

"Do not ever wish for what you are not—you will always be disappointed," Aristotle reprimands. "You have strengthened your leg with clever exercises. You have run with weights on it in the face of tremendous pain. Would you have tested yourself so, mentally and physically, if I had uttered an incantation and miraculously healed it?"

Alex remembers that when planning the attack in the tunnel on the Aesarian Lords he had wished Kat could be there. She could have easily used her magic to infuriate the bees into stinging the enemy. But then he had come up with the idea of building the portable oven with the bellows to burn the bird feathers. He hadn't needed her magic at all. Does he even still need to find the Fountain of Youth and heal himself?

Yes. Aristotle doesn't understand what it's like. "I'm the prince regent," Alex says, shaking his head. "Everyone looks at me. I am imperfect."

"Magic," Aristotle cuts in, "is an illusion. So is perfection." He wipes rain off his cheek with the back of his hand. "So is power, unless it is the power an individual wields over himself."

Perhaps, but Alex knows that what an empire needs is a ruler who can manage the illusions of magic, power, *and* perfection. Only that kind of ruler can bring together people of different languages, cultures, and gods.

Aristotle continues, "Magic is shifty and unreliable, Alexander. It corrupts more than gold and the pleasures of the body. Think of Hagnon selling tax exemptions, of Theo sell-

ing girls and boys. Do you want to be like them? It will cause
you much more damage than just a weak leg. It will weaken
your heart and your mind. I only withheld the knowledge
until you were strong enough to survive the world without it."

He's right, Alex thinks. History is bursting with examples
of kings and queens, warriors and heroes, grasping for riches
and power, love and fame, setting the world on fire and ending up in a heap of ashes of their own making. The Trojan
War, which consumed all of Greece and Asia for a decade,
started because of lust and revenge. The thirst for magic—to
be strong and powerful, healed and perfect—must be something like that.

"Where does magic come from?" he asks. He wants to
believe Aristotle that magic is dangerous. He *does* believe
him. And still, a tickling curiosity—an urgency—courses
through him.

"The gods," Aristotle says, gesturing to the wind and rain
and dripping trees. "No one knows the exact source, though
it is believed that in the Age of Heroes—the times before
Troy—two gods left the heavens to live among mortals, and
it is their descendants who exhibit Snake Blood or Earth
Blood. You are a direct descendant of one of those gods."

"A child of the gods," Alexander repeats, weighing the
words and their meaning. Given his mother's reputation as a
witch, his divine blood must come from Olympias, though
many have said Philip must have magical powers to build
up Macedon from a backward group of rebellious chieftains
into a world power so quickly.

"You must know, then," Alex says, picking off a leaf and
rolling it between his thumb and forefinger, trying to calm
the eagerness that thrums within him. "Does my Snake
Blood come from Philip or Olympias?"

ELEANOR HERMAN

Aristotle stares at the rain just outside the dripping shelter of the tree, slamming hard into the ground and running in boiling rivulets past their feet. The line like a vertical needle between his eyebrows deepens as it always does whenever he is working out a problem, and in the gloomy light, his eyes look like large, dark holes. He is silent for so long that Alex wonders if he has heard him.

"Teacher?"

Then the man turns to Alex with a gaze that pierces him like iron nails.

"Neither."

CHAPTER TWENTY-FOUR

"SO," TIMAEUS SAYS, HIS BREATH CATCHING AS he hurries to keep up with Jacob's long strides down the hilly path, "it's really happening."

"Yes, Tim. It is. Don't tell me you're jealous," Jacob says with a half grin, turning to face his friend, who is usually a source of entertainment, but lately… Lately he's been looking at Jacob the way he is now, with an intensity in his big bright blue eyes that Jacob can't read.

"Jealous?" The eyes spark with dark amusement. "No. Not jealous. That would not be the word," Tim says, once again inscrutable.

Jacob shrugs off the bad feeling Tim's voice has left echoing around him, and adjusts his new helmet. Every time he moves he feels as if it might tip right off his head.

Just this morning Lord Ambiorix handed it to him, crowned with the many-branched stag horns Jacob chose to replace the nubby cow horns of a new recruit. He has, in the language of the Aesarian Lords, earned his horns. The Gaul also handed him a bronze lightning bolt to decorate his black leather cape, a symbol of divine power, for having slain the lying, cheating Lord Bastian.

Today Jacob will become a member of the Elder Council, the youngest one ever, privy to all Aesarian secrets, taking the place of the traitor he exposed. The attack by Macedon's army, the day after the Gods' Duel, delayed the rituals. And then the Lords were forced to retreat. But now, finally, the day he's dreamed of for the past months has arrived. And once he has officially become an Elder, he will pursue his hunt for the god, Riel. He knows now that if this secret was something Bastian would kill—and die—for, it *is* the quest that will make Jacob more than just one of the Elders. It will make him indispensable.

And he needs to be indispensable. He needs the Lords' utmost trust. They need to know and believe that he is one of them through and through.

He needs to know and believe it.

Otherwise, the dark doubts will creep back in again. The ones that have been haunting him ever since Cynane's shackles melted at his touch... The suspicion that it was he who caused the metal to twist and pop open. That it was he who caused the Hemlock Torch to flame red in Timaeus's makeshift forge. That it was he—not Kat and her healing salve—who made his arm heal inexplicably after his trainer for the palace guards, Diodotus, had slashed it in sword practice. That something more was happening when he kissed Kat on the battlefield, and the shuddering sensations of joy and sorrow moved through his body. That *he* was the reason she survived that fatal wound.

The suspicion that he, Jacob of Erissa, a nobody who has risen through the ranks of the Aesarian Lords to become *somebody*, has, all along, possessed Blood Magic.

It's baffling. It's horrifying: that the one thing he has

sworn against could be brewing within him. The Brother-hood's entire mission is to rid the world of such magic. It is an evil that cannot be abided. That's what they teach. And he agrees with them.

And yet… His mind wanders as he picks at the stitches in his left biceps suturing the wound from the arrow that sliced through him at the battle of the Pyrrhian fortress. He knows it's healing because it itches.

The sky is a brighter blue than any he has ever seen, the clouds so white they hurt his eyes, belying the dark thoughts swirling within him. Each morning at dawn a glowing fog sweeps up from the Bay of Corinth far below like a violent incoming tide, churning over fields, rolling up hills, and throwing itself against the spur of craggy gray cliffs before burning off in the heat of the sun.

After escaping the Pyrrhian fortress through abandoned mine tunnels, after a long march and a choppy sea voyage, they finally reached the estate of a retired Aesarian Lord outside Delphi. But the luxury of the palatial house—hot baths, soft beds, fine wine—and its incredible view of the lush emerald valleys and shimmering bay below, were worth it. Plus, as Gideon explained, Delphi and its surrounding area is neutral territory. No one—soldier or civilian—can harm another person under penalty of death for breaking the peace of the god Apollo who owns these sacred lands. There will be no worries about Macedonian armies here.

He hasn't been to Delphi itself yet, though he has seen the merry caravans of pilgrims coming and going on the road outside Lord Imbrus's estate. High Lord Gideon has said they will go to sacrifice there and receive advice from the oracle at some point in the future.

"I just wonder…" Tim goes on, still short of breath, "if this is really what you want. Really what's best for *you*."

"What exactly are you implying?" Jacob snaps. He can't help but recall the way Tim looked at him when the torch burned red. The way he covered for him about Cynane's escape. For all his silliness, Tim is clever, and sly. Is it possible he has guessed the same thing that Jacob has guessed about himself?

"Oh," Tim says nonchalantly. "I never like to *imply* anything. It's just that as an Elder, that girl Katerina and her luscious, er, assets—" here he nudges Jacob playfully in the ribs "—will be even further than ever from your grasp. Elders aren't supposed to marry, you know…"

The back of Jacob's neck prickles with anger. "It's best not to speak of things you don't know anything about," he says, more harshly than he intended. He can't think about Kat. Not now. Maybe not ever. That is a wound that will never heal.

"Don't I? Because I think I'm the only one who does…" Tim has stopped walking and cocks his head at Jacob like a curious dog.

And in that instant, Jacob realizes he's right. *Tim knows.*

And if Tim thinks Jacob is hiding Blood Magic, then Jacob has even more to worry about than he thought. Because despite his often annoying antics, Tim is almost never wrong.

"Jacob, I am your friend. I only want to help you," Tim says, resuming his merry looks.

"I'm sorry," Jacob says, his throat hoarse.

As they pass between the narrow pine trees, Jacob sees High Lord Gideon rowing toward them in a small boat. Beside him sits a goat, grunting quietly.

"Well," Tim huffs, "we're here. Have fun, Lord Jacob." He bows elaborately, turns on his heel and goes, leaving Jacob with an uneasy feeling.

Gideon pulls up next to a small pier and Jacob clambers in. "Greetings, High Lord," he says, taking the oars from him.

"Greetings, Jacob," the older man says, eyeing the new helmet with approval. "Very impressive horns."

Jacob grins and starts rowing. The bulge of his muscles against the strain of the oars soothes his disquieted mind somewhat. The brown-and-white spotted goat chews its cud and looks at him curiously, and it reminds Jacob eerily of Tim. He almost laughs.

The narrow river winds through meadows ripe with grain and orchards of gnarled, gray-barked olive trees with silver-green leaves. Jacob breaks out in a sweat as the sun beats down. He feels it tickling the back of his neck, moistening the tunic beneath his leather breastplate.

"Up ahead," the High Lord says, standing so suddenly the tiny boat rocks wildly for a moment, and pointing to a granite outcropping around a bend. "Take us inside."

Jacob angles the boat inside the large cave mouth where he is swallowed by a blessed coolness.

The High Lord bends over his flint and tinder set, pulls a resin-soaked torch out of a leather bag and sets it ablaze. "Back there," he says, gesturing to a yawning opening in the back of the cave. Jacob obediently grips the oars and pulls, sliding the boat deeper into the cavern's belly. It smells wet in here, the dank kind of wet never exposed to the cleansing effects of sun or fresh air. As he maneuvers them into a narrow corridor, the dipping and rising of his oars echo strangely, and Gideon's torchlight slides like liquid gold across moist stone walls. Jacob wonders briefly if the River Styx is like this.

Up ahead are two passages and he pauses, oars outstretched like a bird's wings, listening carefully to the sound of rushing water. Is there a waterfall somewhere back here? Are they going to tumble over it? Will his initiation be contingent on surviving the fall?

"Continue down the passage to the right," Gideon commands. After a time, the corridor opens up to another cave on their right. Gideon hops off on a sandy beach, reaches back, and grabs the goat. Jacob pulls the boat onto the sand. In a few moments, Gideon has set several blazing torches in iron wall sconces. He takes a large wineskin out of his pouch, turns to Jacob and says, "Drink this," in a voice that permits no refusal.

Jacob hesitates only a second. He drinks deeply and tastes something that reminds him of the wild mushrooms he and Kat used to collect in the forest outside Erissa. Mixed in with honeyed wine are lumps of something chewy, like gristle, that taste of rich earth and dark places and summer rain.

Jacob waits, his heart stuttering a bit. The sweat on his body has chilled in the coolness of the cave, and he tries to suppress a shiver. He doesn't want Gideon to think he's afraid, even if he is.

Something strange is already happening to his body. He feels as if he's floating, hovering, no longer bound by the weight of flesh and bone. The enormous shadows of the two horned men seem to leap and move on the torch-lit walls like wild animals, and for a moment, he forgets that *he* is one of them.

He's only vaguely aware of Gideon, chanting loudly in a language Jacob doesn't understand, and then a pitiful protesting bleat. Gideon has slaughtered the goat. Jacob hears the sound of its blood gushing into a bowl in the shadows. He tries to focus his vision.

Gideon rises, dips his finger into the bowl of blood, and starts to draw figures on the smooth cave wall, large human forms towering over small ones.

"In the beginning of all time," Gideon says, the cave adding a new timbre to his already deep voice, "the gods created the world and filled it with mortals. This we all know."

Jacob stares at the figures. A trick of the torchlight makes them appear to be moving. They seem to march across the vast expanse of rock. In wonder, Jacob stretches an arm out, and with the tip of his finger, he brushes the still wet lines of blood. The liquid is hot, but not the heat of a recently stilled heart. Hot like a pot brought to boil.

Jacob cries out—but he has no voice, no throat, no breath in which to make sound. He is a stick figure drawn of blood flickering on the cave wall. The world is a palette of reds, grays, and browns, bumpy and cracked and glistening wet in patches. And still, Gideon's voice continues, though Jacob no longer hears him with his ears. The words seem to well in his chest, sewing him into the story—and then the world cracks open.

He is in a fertile mountain valley crowded with people, and in front of them a blinding light blazes like a thousand setting suns. Jacob instinctively closes his eyes, but the light barely dims. From somewhere within the radiance, he hears a voice of bronze, and thunder reverberates through his body.

HOW GREAT THE WICKEDNESS OF MAN. HOW GREAT THE EVIL OF THEIR HEARTS. IMPIOUS. SELFISH. CONTEMPTIBLE IN EVERY WAY. WE WILL WIPE FROM THE FACE OF THE EARTH THE HUMAN RACE WE HAVE CREATED—FOR WE REGRET THAT WE HAVE MADE THEM.

The voice is not comprised of one, but of many, each one perfectly harmonizing with the next to create the hammer of sound that pounds down on Jacob.

There's a white flash, and the air around him is filled with a sharp smell—similar to the smell before a summer storm.

He knows without knowing how that a bolt of lightning has struck the rocks in the valley below. A rushing roar fills his ears, and water gushes up in a towering fountain.

The spray of water continues to grow, and Jacob wonders if it will eventually rise all the way up to the stars and never return to earth.

As he stares into the sky, a wave hits his knees. Looking down quickly, he sees the fountain flooding from its base, its thirsty fingers stretching across the valley.

Jacob turns to run, but it's too late. A jet of water hits him on the back, pushing him down. He struggles up, fighting the swirling waters. The last thing he hears are the screams of panic-stricken people around him cut short as the deepening waters leap over them all in a fatal surge.

Suddenly Jacob is next to Gideon again in the cave, though the wall before him has disappeared, and the flooded plain stretches out to meet the horizon. "And so," the High Lord intones, "the gods created a deluge to wash the world of evil, and with it, the Age of Heroes ended. This all nations remember."

Jacob watches as the cavern ceiling morphs into a sky, where the moon and sun circle dizzyingly. When he looks around, he sees the flood from before rapidly receding to reveal an earth barren except for a small geyser at the spot from which the column of water gushed. A moment later, the earth bursts into bloom, then snow, then bloom again, as the night flickers in and out, in and out. The geyser becomes a spring in the center of a pond, and a village begins to be constructed around it.

"At first," High Lord Gideon continues, "the people of the Eastern Mountains remembered that the fountain's waters had once washed away an entire Age, and humans were forbidden from drinking it. They knew it to be the remnant of the gods' anger, knew that it still had the power to kill all that is human. But as time went on, man forgot that no mortal should touch the fountain, and they began to drink."

Jacob watches as the people inhabiting the village begin to stand taller. They become more muscular, healed from all pain and illness, healed even from the ravages of age. Children run and laugh near the pond, and at one point, Jacob sees a man with a flowing white beard pick up a boulder that ten Olympians would have been unable to lift.

An ache begins to ripple through Jacob from the sheer beauty of the people and their village. It all seems so good. Watching the inhabitants swim through the fountain's crystal waters, a thirst tickles the back of his throat.

"But the water, no matter how clear, remained cursed." Gideon's voice drops, and Jacob is surprised to hear a note of sorrow. "The water instilled its drinkers with a terrible, unquenchable thirst. A hunger for the divine."

Now Jacob's throat is as dry as kindling, rough from thirst. He feels a hunger clawing in his guts, in every muscle of his body. He never knew emptiness could bring such pain, but pain is what he feels as his need overpowers him. His hunger, with nothing to turn to, sinks its teeth into his soul. He no longer feels human.

"The villagers began to hunt for something that would satiate their hunger." Gideon's level voice brings Jacob back to himself, and the hunger vanishes as suddenly as it came.

Now Jacob can once again concentrate on his surroundings, and he sees that he is still on a cliff, but it's higher than the one before, and the village below is harder to make out. From here, he looks down at black figures moving among the reddish-brown of baked clay houses and the yellow of thatched roofs.

Jacob feels his stomach clench. "Those shadows… Are those…?"

Gideon nods gravely. "Yes, those are villagers."

"But they seem to have grown bigger…as large as their homes." He squints, half wishing he could see more clearly, half wishing there was nothing to see at all. "And they don't move like humans."

"Watch," Gideon instructs.

As Jacob looks, the black figures surround a tall pulse of light that seems human in form, but nearly twice the size of any person Jacob has ever seen. In the center of the light, he can make out the figure of a woman with long black hair. By some trick of this strange dream, he can see the silver irises of her shining eyes even from this great distance.

The light surrounding the woman flickers like stars behind clouds, then vanishes completely. From somewhere far, far below, Jacob hears the thread of a scream, and then crunches and slurps.

He squeezes his eyes shut and puts his hands over his ears. "Make it stop," he moans.

And suddenly, it does. Jacob is just a disembodied thought in the dark, but before he panics, Gideon's voice floats around him and Jacob clings to it like a drowning man gripping a rope. "The gods never meant for humans to drink from the Fountain of Youth, and so humans cannot stomach the water without giving up their humanity. Over time, those who drink repeatedly from the fountain are not healed— they are turned into creatures that must live on the divine spark within others. They become terrible monsters. They become…Spirit Eaters. And so," Gideon continues, "the war between gods and their creation began."

Slowly, light begins to brighten the dark around Jacob the

Thought. Something solid appears—a cave wall for Jacob the Stick Figure to cling to.

"In the war, most of the gods were consumed, and the few that survived fled the mortal realm, never to return."

Sparks of light appear around Jacob. And as before, within the light he can make out glowing humanlike figures. They begin to rise upward, away from the earth, fleeing into the sky. Jacob marvels. It is like a shower of shooting stars—only in reverse. The lights stream by him and past him and away.

"Though many fled, at least two gods remained: Riel the Snake and his brother, Brehan of the Earth."

As Gideon talks, two radiant beings stride toward the spring, their long capes made from dragon wings billowing behind them and their silver eyes gleaming. They extend their arms, chanting and praying as black clouds gather and lightning crashes around them. The air is green and smells fresh and sweet. The storm increases in intensity, and the scene in front of Jacob blurs until he cannot tell if there are two gods at the fountain, or three. He tries to blink water away from his eyes, but since he is not really there, the water does not clear.

Suddenly, a lightning bolt hits the spring, throwing the gods far away. The rain stops. The clouds scuttle away, revealing blue sky.

When Jacob looks back at the brother gods, he sees they have changed. Light no longer surrounds them. And though they are tall, they are no taller than any soldier in the Macedonian army. When they open their eyes, Jacob notices that their irises are no longer the silver of divinity. One god has emerald eyes, the other sky-blue. They stumble back toward the spring, fall to their knees, and search, their hands patting the ground. But there is no water there. Only scorched dust.

A low burn begins to prick at Jacob's muscles. From somewhere deep inside him, he realizes that he is again growing aware of his body—his flesh and blood body, not the two-dimensional lines of the Jacob on the cave wall. Solid ground appears beneath his feet, and once again there is *down* and *up*, and Jacob the man. The pricking continues, growing in intensity as Gideon speaks again.

"Though the Spirit Eaters were defeated, the very act of drying the Fountain splintered the last gods' magic. Riel and Brehan were forced to remain trapped in the mortal world, as they were no longer true gods, but somewhere between mortal and immortal, each carrying but a strain of his former divine power. And from these two gods—and their relationships with mortal women—Blood Magic came to humanity."

Jacob stands perfectly still, afraid to breathe, terrified of what Gideon will say next. Has Tim mentioned anything? Has Gideon brought him here and drugged him to render him powerless…to kill him?

But then the story begins to sink in. Blood Magic is inherited from the last two gods. How can this be bad? Confusion overwhelms him as forcibly as the experience of the flood.

Gideon seems unaware of Jacob's rising panic. "The descendants of Riel possess what is called Snake Blood," he explains, "and those of Brehan are Earth Blood. Snake Blood is a magic of the mind, Earth Blood a magic of the body. At the height of their powers, those who possess Snake Blood can enter the mind of an animal—or another human—sometimes even taking over the other's form entirely. As for Earth Blood, the greatest wielders of it can have near divine strength. They may melt metal, cause the earth to quake, heal wounds, and even bring life back to the fatally injured."

Jacob gasps as his lungs expand. It's almost as though he'd been holding his breath since he drank the elixir, but that was unlikely, as entire ages seemed to have passed in front of him. But as he looks at the body of the goat, the blood still dripping from its throat, not yet congealed, he realizes the entire experience must have lasted two or three minutes, no more. A shiver traces its way up Jacob's neck as if an icy finger caressed him.

Those with Earth Blood can melt metal. Heal wounds. Bring life back to the fatally injured. Now there is no doubt. *He* healed the festering wound Diodotus had given him in the Macedonian training pit—not Kat. *He* melted Cyn's chains. And *he* saved Kat's life on the battlefield, with a single kiss. Without him, Bastian's sword thrust would have killed her.

His stomach heaves, and he vomits.

"Here." The tall figure of Gideon leans over him, holding out a goatskin. Jacob accepts it and slurps the cool, pure water noisily.

"Many react to the elixir that way," the High Lord says. "And though you might feel weary, it should clear up in a day or two."

Jacob hopes he's right, even if he knows it wasn't the elixir that made his stomach turn. *Do you know?* he wants to ask. *Do you know that I am Earth Blood?* But that question would be the beginning of the end.

Instead he asks, "Why show this to me?" He rubs his throbbing forehead. "How does this pertain to the Lords' affairs?"

"It pertains to us," Gideon replies, "because though the Spirit Eaters retreated into the depths of the earth, they did not, in fact, die out."

Horror chills Jacob's bones as those words sink in. The Spirit Eaters. The terrible monsters who fought the gods…

"And though the last gods obliterated the fountain," Gideon goes on, "it was not completely destroyed. From somewhere deep within the earth, the fountain's waters seep out of the rock walls of a cave in the Eastern Mountains."

Jacob tries to control the trembling in his body. "These Spirit Eaters—they still exist?" He remembers the black figures surrounding the light—remembers their devastating, unquenchable hunger—and revulsion fills him.

"Yes," Gideon says matter-of-factly. "Though it is a great secret, one that has been protected for many centuries. The village that once surrounded the fountain no longer exists. Their descendants, the Hunor, moved to the bottom of the mountain to try and contain the beasts and to prevent anyone else from drinking. Living so near the fountain, they remain stronger than the average man and are said to be able to see into the future and spot the turning points in a man's life. Now, people sometimes think that the Hunor are the Spirit Eaters—but they are wrong. They are only the monsters' keepers."

Gideon loosens his helmet strap and removes the helmet crowned with enormous notched ram horns curling back on themselves so as to be circular. He runs a large hand over his closely cropped hair.

"For hundreds of years, the Hunor have made sure that the Spirit Eaters' hunger is satiated with the flesh of magic creatures," he says. "A Pegasus, a siren, a hellion, a soothsayer, or a bearer of Blood Magic will ease the hunger enough to keep the Spirit Eaters isolated to their mountain. If they do not have magic to feed on, then they will turn to mortals, though the mortal souls are but a grain of wheat compared to the feast that is the soul of a centaur."

Gideon's head glistens in the torchlight as the hypnotizing voice continues. "The first Lord, Lord Aesario, and his four brothers were from Hunor. You—and every Aesarian—wear their symbols over your heart—the five flames, along with the crescent moon, which represents the swallowing up of magic."

Jacob's hand lightly touches his breastplate over the scar. He had undergone the branding ritual in front of Pella's elite—with Kat watching—and wasn't permitted to cry out or flinch despite the excruciating pain.

Gideon continues, "Those Lords left the village to seek out souls brave enough to do what must be done."

"And what must be done?" Jacob all but whispers. The darkness of the cave seems to close around him. He wonders if he is going to faint and breathes deeply to steady himself.

"We must search the world for magic and bring the wielders of it to the monsters. For if we do not, the Spirit Eaters will leave their mountains and devour the world."

He looks at Jacob, and each word rings with resounding weight. "This is the true reason behind our brotherhood. In order to seek out magic and roam unfettered across the known world, we had to become the best fighting force ever, acquiring warriors from all nations, bringing law and order to lawless lands. To insinuate our way into positions of power as advisors, ministers, counselors, and generals. Then, having proved our usefulness, we decreed magic a great evil and were permitted to take magic wielders away."

Jacob realizes there is a horrifying logic to it. "We tell people we burn them in secret," he says, looking at the dancing flames—blue and red and gold—of the nearest torch. "But that's not true, is it? We embalm them to take back to the Eastern Mountains…" He recalls the quickly hardening mud he was asked to lather across Cynane's body.

"To feed them to the Spirit Eaters, yes. They need to eat magic flesh while it is still alive. They must drink magic blood fresh from a beating heart and still flowing with vigor."

Jacob shudders, knowing this should, by all the Lords be-

ELEANOR HERMAN

lieve, be his own fate. To be alive as monsters feast on his
flesh, snap his bones, and suck out the marrow.

"Is there no way the Lords—as strong as we are now," he
begins, his voice cracking and his throat dry as ashes, "could
destroy the Spirit Eaters, High Lord? Why should we—who
are, as you say, the greatest fighting force in the world—remain at the beck and call of monsters?"

A wave of something like sadness washes over Gideon's
face. Is it a trick of the light and shadow in this cave, or has
he really aged noticeably in the three weeks since taking over
the position from High Lord Mordecai? There are gray hairs
near his temples that Jacob never saw before, and the lines
around his mouth seem deeper, harsher.

"In the past, there were those of us who tried. The Spirit
Eaters, having drunk so long from the Fountain, are immortal, Jacob, or nearly so. Every attempt to eradicate them
resulted in the loss of thousands of human lives. And so we
sacrifice the few to save the multitudes."

Jacob looks at the cave wall and discovers that the few
stick figures Gideon drew seem to have multiplied and now
cover one entire wall. If he had never left Erissa for the Blood
Tournament, if he had never tried to make himself someone
Kat could be proud of, right now he'd be helping his father
stoke the kiln and lift out the pots, the breeze in his hair,
the sun on his face. His little brothers would be chasing each
other around the kiln, his mother calling them to come in for
fresh baked bread. He would never know of these horrors or
how strange the world is. He might never have learned what
he truly is. He wonders if his father knows. If his father is
magic, too. One of his parents must be. Did they hide it for
his protection? He has so much to ask them now.

He is not sure how to feel about it all. Happy that he has

come so far and seen so much, proven himself time and again? Sad that he has lost not only Kat but his innocence? He puts his fingers gently on the drawings as if hoping they will give him the answer.

Gideon follows his gaze.

"We have been, perhaps, too successful in finding magic wielders and magical beings," Gideon says. He reaches out a blood-smeared finger and touches the figure of a winged horse. A thoughtful, almost wistful look, passes over his face, but it leaves quickly, and his demeanor is as stern as ever. "It has become increasingly more difficult to find them."

Gideon drops his hand. "There are new reports every day that the Spirit Eaters grow hungry, restless, and some have even left the mountains. The Lords in Hunor are worried they will not be able to contain them much longer."

He looks over at Jacob. "That is why it is so unfortunate that the princess Cynane escaped. Though she is not Snake Blood or Earth Blood, the powerful enchantment on her would have bought us more time."

Jacob feels torn. If he brought Cynane back, it would mean honor, influence, and keeping the devouring horror of the Spirit Eaters at bay for years. But to subject her to the abomination of being eaten alive... Perhaps there is another way, one that will solve Jacob's biggest problem.

"If she has made it back to Pella," he says, concentrating, "I doubt we could easily take her again. But in the cell when I was watching her, she often told me how proud she was of her Illyrian heritage. That she was a princess of Dardania and I wasn't fit to wipe her boots, that sort of thing."

Gideon raises an eyebrow questioningly.

"What I mean is, one of us should go to Illyria to look for the source of her magic. The Lords have no presence in that wild region. I suggest we send someone as a spy to learn about Illyrian magic, about a protective spell that heals broken bones and gashes. Perhaps we could find others like the princess or learn about the root of her magic to keep the Spirit Eaters sated."

"It is a good idea," Gideon agrees. "But whom should we send? Should we ask for a volunteer? Or were you thinking of volunteering yourself, Lord Jacob?"

Jacob waves a hand. "No, High Lord, I am a terrible liar and would make an equally terrible spy," he says. "I was thinking..." Here his mind races ahead, to an idea that may help *both* of them. "I was thinking of my friend, Lord Timaeus. He seems so friendly, so harmless. He's a skilled acrobat who can backflip as easily as walk and, perhaps, could go from town to town in that disguise. Maybe he could even find work in the palace as an entertainer. No one would suspect funny little Timaeus of being an Aesarian Lord." *And*, he doesn't add: sending Tim to Illyria will keep him far away from their regiment, and the temptation to reveal what he knows about Jacob.

"I remember him in the Blood Tournament," Gideon says slowly. "We were impressed that such a small man could beat the fiercest warriors in the Greek world, and with a slingshot, no less." His mouth slides into a wide grin. "Do you remember how he hit the noble Macedonian champion in the forehead with that pebble?"

Jacob nods. "And he can get anyone to talk about anything over a cup of wine," he says.

"It's agreed, then," Gideon says. "We will send Lord Timaeus disguised as a wandering acrobat to Dardania to see what he can find."

Jacob feels a wave of blessed relief wash over him. He

will miss his friend. But with Timaeus far away, Jacob will stay safe.

His relief must show on his face because Lord Gideon scowls. "This is no time to celebrate, Jacob. It is not a matter of whether the Spirit Eaters will eventually grow too large and too hungry to contain. It's not a matter of whether they will one day devour the world as we know it. It is only a matter of how soon."

"But if we brought them one of the last gods, Riel or Brehan?" Jacob asks, suddenly excited. "Would that satisfy them?"

Gideon pauses, staring at Jacob in the dim torchlight. He has never mentioned Riel before to any of the Lords, but he recalls how Gideon reacted when Bastian brought up the name. "Feeding on such divine power," Gideon says slowly, "the Spirit Eaters would be sated for centuries... It is possible—faintly, but distinctly possible—that they could fall into a deep sleep during which we might slay them. But at this point, it is foolish to believe the last gods may still be among us."

He removes two torches from their sconces and dips them in the water as Jacob follows suit. Steam rises as they hiss in protest. "The secrets I have shared with you here are known only to the Elder Council," he says, fixing Jacob with dark eyes glittering in the glow of the remaining torch.

"I swear by all the Furies to tell no one of this," Jacob says. Emotions course through him, and he feels himself trembling from head to toe. There's fear that the Lords will find out about his abilities. Relief that Timaeus will be leaving tomorrow for Illyria and taking Jacob's secret with him.

But he also feels an upward surge of pure, raw ambition. Because the Lords won't worry about *him* if he brings them something greater even than an enchanted princess to quench the Spirit Eaters' hunger.

There is no longer any question in his mind. If he wants to save his own life, Jacob will *have* to capture the god Riel himself.

CHAPTER TWENTY-FIVE

AS CYN ROUNDS A BEND OF THE TUNNEL BE-neath the ruined palace of Knossos, a whirlwind of bats flies at her, screeching and flapping, one of them hitting her squarely in the face. She drops to the floor, letting them pass. Perhaps it would be best to wait for Olympias outside, in the court-yard of fallen columns and toppled walls, which look to Cyn like foaming waves frozen in stone.

When Cyn left Alex's office after talking to Sarina, she had marched straight to Olympias and told her Katerina was in Egypt. A strange green gleam came into the queen's eyes, and she replied that Cyn should meet up with her on Crete, an island three days' sail from Macedon with good winds and only a day or two from Egypt.

"Why Crete?" Cyn asked, surprised.

"I will be performing rituals in the Labyrinth of Knos-sos," the queen said, a slow smile spreading across her face, "in preparation for a more important ceremony. Don't you know? The Labyrinth is revered by sorcerers from across the known world because of its history of evil and madness."

Cyn knew. Long ago, Poseidon, the god of the sea punished the king of Crete for disobedience by making his wife fall in love with a bull. She bore the bull's son, who had the body of a man and the head of a bull, a crazed creature so vicious the king kept him in a labyrinth of tunnels below the palace and sent him victims to feed on. The Athenian hero Theseus slaughtered the creature, whom he called a Minotaur, and soon after, Poseidon sent earthquakes and gigantic waves to kill the people and destroy the entire civilization.

Olympias said she and her guards would be staying at the main harbor inn of Amnisos, the port nearest Knossos. As soon as Cyn disembarked this morning from Egypt, she visited the inn, and the innkeeper handed her a message from the queen: *Meet me at the Labyrinth entrance three hours after sunset.* And so she came to this sinister place.

For Knossos, though long deserted, is alive with ghosts. Whether Olympias is planning on sacrificing puppies, babies, or doing strange things with snakes, Cyn doesn't know and doesn't want to know. Because there's only one thing that matters: that Cynane obtain what she has wanted her whole life. Power. Real power. Ruling over a nation. Commanding armies. Not sitting in the shadow of a brother. Not waiting around, fat and pregnant, to give birth to wailing babies for a king. If only she can convince Olympias that she has killed Kat and the finger is proof.

She had promised Olympias Kat's head. But even if Cyn had killed the annoying peasant girl, surely the queen will understand that a human head is heavy and awkward to travel with, and dangerous when meticulous Persian customs officials open up every bag and crawl over every ship leaving Egypt like ravenous ants at a royal picnic. The queen is desperate for Kat's death; Cyn could see it clearly the night before she left for Egypt, in the intensity of her eyes and the convulsive clenching of her hands. She will want to believe

Cyn's explanation, but she will also want to save face by threatening revenge if Kat turns up alive later. At least, that is what Cyn is counting on.

If it works as planned, Olympias will remove the ruler of Dardania, one of the Illyrian kingdoms, ensuring his death so that Cynane might take his place. She even said she'd cut out his heart and give it to her on a golden platter. And then Cyn will have what she has always wanted. Tonight.

She hears a low rumble from the road outside the ruins. The thunder of horses' hooves grows louder, then stops. Boots hit the ground heavily and a male voice issues orders about tying up the horses. She sees the orange glow of torches as several cloaked and hooded figures pick their way over rubble. Automatically, Cyn puts her hand on her sword hilt.

"Princess Cynane?" asks a deep voice. "Is that you?"

"It is," she says, eyeing the figures carefully. There are seven of them, of varying heights, three holding torches. She cannot see their faces.

The one who spoke to her, tall and broad-shouldered—clearly a warrior and vaguely familiar—draws near and holds out a hand. "Give me what you promised to deliver to the queen, Princess."

Cyn doesn't like this. The secluded meeting place, the hooded riders—she can tell the ones in front are wearing swords because their cloaks stick out strangely by their left knees—and no Olympias. It could be a trap. A plot. Was she foolish to trust the queen?

"No," she says, standing up to her full height and taking a step toward him to show she is not afraid. "What I have is too important to give to anyone but the queen herself. Know that the thing you seek is hidden. If you kill me you will never find it."

A small figure holding a large basket pushes its way

through the others and stands before her. It sets the basket down and pale hands pull off the cloak, revealing a smiling Olympias, her shimmering dark red gown falling to the ground like a waterfall of blood. Her thick silver-blond hair—a wig, Cyn realizes, remembering how shockingly thin her hair had been that day in the tower room right after her bath—glistens in the torchlight.

"Greetings, stepdaughter," she says. Cyn steps closer for a better look in the shifting torchlight. Olympias is exquisitely made up, her eyes heavily lined with kohl, her lips painted scarlet to match her gown.

"I have done as you requested," Cyn says. "I have killed Katerina."

"Where is her head?" Olympias asks, arms out, palms up in the timeless gesture of questioning.

Cyn shrugs. "I could not bring back the head."

Beneath the heavy makeup, Olympias blanches. "So you have brought me no proof—"

"You misunderstand," Cyn cuts in. "I do not have her head, but I do have proof." She removes a tiny leather wrapping from the pouch on her belt. Olympias takes it and moves beside a man holding a torch, where she opens it curiously.

"What is it?" she asks, frowning at the small, sticky mass.

"Her fingertip," Cyn replies. "Smeared with honey to keep it from decomposing. Small enough that the customs officials in Memphis didn't pay it any attention."

Olympias stares at the fingertip, then wipes the honey off with her own and looks closely, squinting.

"Yes," she says, almost to herself. "I see a fingernail." She looks up. "But how do I know it's hers? It could belong to anyone."

"It was the best I could do," Cynane retorts. "You try smuggling a human head out of Upper Egypt."

"It's *not* what I asked for," Olympias says, her face folding in irritation.

But Cyn has her own suspicions of what Olympias wants the head for, and it isn't just proof of Katerina's death. The darkest magic spells always call for human blood or a human body part. If that is what the queen wanted the head for, the fingertip should do just as well.

"Then I shall feed it to the wild pigs I saw rooting around here earlier," Cyn says, making as if to grab the finger and its oily wrapping from the queen.

Olympias clutches the bundle. "No."

Cyn smiles. "Ah, stepmother, I see the finger has some value to you, after all."

Olympias tosses her head. She turns quickly to Cyn, fire flashing in her green eyes, and grabs her wrist with her surprisingly strong, bird-claw fingers. "Swear," she says, "on all the Furies and their eternal vengeance, that this is Katerina's fingertip."

"I swear," Cyn says without hesitation. She is thankful Olympias didn't make her swear she killed Katerina. That was luck.

The queen's eyes, locked on Cyn's, seem to sense the truth in her, and the talons release their rigid grip. "Very well," she says. "I will choose to believe you. But, Cynane, I will know if you are lying and if so, I will punish you, even if you are the queen of Dardania. In the meantime, I will fulfill my part of the bargain."

Cyn's heart pounds in excitement. *It's working.* Working just as she thought it might. This is it. Her entire future, everything she ever wanted, is here, right in front of her.

Olympias snaps her fingers and a guard walks up holding a gold platter. On it lies a scroll.

A warning enters Cyn's heart with the suddenness of an

arrow. Something is not right. This is too easy. The queen is too pleased, especially considering all she got was a finger-tip. And the golden platter is a bit dramatic… Cyn grabs the scroll from the rider, unrolls it, and walks over to her torch.

The royal house of Macedon does formally agree that a union shall be made between its blood and the noble house of Illyria, through the marriage of the young King Amyntas Cleitus of Dardania and Princess Cynane Audata Illona of Macedon…

"What is this?" she cries out, a tightening pain rippling over her chest, constricting her lungs.

The queen smiles cruelly. "It is the fulfillment of my promise. I promised you the *heart* of Amyntas. On a platter. And that is what I have just given you. He shall be your loving husband. Your overlord. The father of your many, many children."

A red fog obscures Cynane's vision. Her heartbeat pounds loudly in her ears. She flings the scroll on the ground and leaps onto the queen, knocking her down and wrapping her hands—her strong, warrior hands—around the queen's dainty neck. A clean knife thrust to the heart is too good for this bitch. She will choke off her air slowly.

Strong hands pull Cyn up and away from Olympias. One soldier holds her right arm behind her, another her left, while a third holds a sword so that its tip barely scrapes against the bottom of her chin. Another soldier takes her sword. She cannot fight her way out of this. Not yet, anyway. But still she struggles.

Coughing, Olympias rises from the ground with the help of a guard and claps the dirt from her hands. "A ship awaits you in Amnisos harbor," she says, straightening her wig, which has fallen sideways. "It will take you directly to Dardania's port. No one can accuse me of not doing my duty as your stepmother, darling. I have provided trunks and trunks of beautiful gowns for the bride—all of them pink and embroidered with the loveliest flowers."

Cyn's rage congeals. It is no longer red and hot, pumping through her veins. It is cold and white and sluggish as ice. At least she can think more clearly. She stops trying to pull her arms free and lets them hang loosely in the guards' grip as if she has completely yielded. She turns her head away from the sword tip and hangs it as low as that of a beaten cur. Then she remembers finding her mother that day in the bathtub and coaxes out tears, which slide slowly down her cheeks.

"What?" Olympias sneers. "I never thought I'd live to see you cry."

Cyn makes a little noise in her throat that she hopes sounds like a stifled sob. "I'm not crying," she says. "I just don't want to ever marry. I want to ride to war like men do."

The guards around her chuckle. She feels their grip on her arms relax ever so slightly.

"Check her legs for knives," Olympias commands. The tallest guard kneels, feels the tops of her boots, and removes two knives. Then, smiling up at her, his hands travel up beneath her leather skirt. There he finds the knife strapped to her thigh, which he slowly unties, as if it was a garter and she a bride. His hands go back up, his fingers warm and strong against her skin. "Anything else up there I might find?" he asks. She knows she could break his jaw with a blow from her knee but decides to wait.

"Perhaps," she purrs, staring down at him.

"Enough," the queen says. "Diocles, Erastos, Jason, and Euphron, take her to the boat and lock her in the cabin. My men onboard will take over from there. Make sure it sails, then return." She flashes a wide smile at Cynane and adds, "Don't trust her. Always keep your sword on her. If she tries to escape, kill her." She grabs her basket and walks with the two remaining guards into the tunnel that leads to the Labyrinth.

Cyn has always bristled when soldiers laughed at her, looked down at her, underestimated her fighting ability. But now their derision is a weapon she will use against them.

When they yank her over fallen walls and broken columns, she tries to look as if she wants to comply but is having difficulty without the use of her arms. Twice she asks the guard with the torch to shed some light on her path. The two at either side of her slacken their grip even more. And then, when they approach a huge fallen column, the guard with the sword concentrates on scrambling over it, holding his weapon carelessly. This is the moment.

Cyn wrenches her arms free, grabs the careless guard's sword, and swings it right and then left in one fluid motion, cutting down to the arm bones of the guards on either side of her. They scream and fall writhing to the ground. The one who lost his sword pulls a knife from his belt, which she kicks out of his hand. Her sword cleaves into his neck and his head falls back, opening like the lid of a jewelry box, kept on by a single muscle.

The remaining guard throws the torch into his left hand and with his right draws his sword. Their weapons meet and sing the ancient song of battle, Cyn's favorite song. For the first time in weeks—ever since she killed two Aesarian Lords the night of the library fire—she feels completely and utterly alive.

But this is no normal battlefield. She must concentrate, not only on her opponent's sword and torch, but on where she places her feet on the uneven ground. Luckily, she's far more agile than the soldier, who is so stocky she can't imagine he's able to bend at the waist. She leaps gracefully onto a pile of rocks as he tries to scramble up behind her, but it's hard with both his hands full. She wants to use the advantage of being uphill from her enemy—one of the most basic battle strategies. But if she dives at him, he could thrust the sword or the torch into her face. If only she had one of her knives, she could throw it into his neck.

She stares at the sharp, jagged rocks below her feet, switches her sword to her left hand, picks one up, and flings it at him. He turns his face and tries to block it with his torch but it hits him square in his cheek. He cries out in pain and she advances, aiming to stab him in the stomach. Blood flows freely down his face as he jabs at her head with the torch, singeing one of her long black tendrils. Cyn swings and cuts off the torch's head. The resin-soaked stump of wood falls flaming to the rocks.

"You little…" He drops the useless base of the torch and springs at her. But Cyn dances through the darkness to the other end of the rock pile as he loses purchase, the rocks tumbling under his heavier, clumsier weight. He claws at the rocks, climbs up a bit, then slides back down, spread-eagled. Cyn jumps down and stabs him through the back of his breastplate, feeling her blade hit the rocks beneath. The man groans and is still.

With each life she takes, she feels stronger, more vibrant, more powerful. Her blood hums. Her heart beats like a battle drum.

Cyn jumps to the bottom of the rock heap and sees one of the wounded guards, his left arm bleeding heavily, stumbling toward her with his sword outstretched. She hits his weapon hard, sending it flying, kicks him hard in the groin and, when he's doubled over in pain, yanks a large paving stone from the ground and crashes it down on his head. Then she darts over a pile of orange roof tiles to pick up his sword. Now she has one in both hands.

She stands there, panting. Done. Free. But she can't just slink away. Where would she go but back to Pella? Olympias would return, too, and try to kill her.

She's not free yet. She cannot let Olympias live. She must kill that lying bitch of a queen.

Like a shadow in the moonlight, she returns to the crumpled courtyard and once again enters the Labyrinth. Without a torch, she feels as if she has been swallowed by a Titan and wanders lost in his bowels. She tests each step with her toe to make sure she is not going to pitch headlong into some hole and, like a blind person, feels her way along with her left hand, one sword clutched firmly in her right, the other tucked into her belt.

The tunnel slopes downward into the cellars of the legendary palace, and the farther she goes the more the cloying smell of ancient dampness bothers her nose. She feels as if she is in a tomb headed straight for the Underworld, with all its terrifying monsters.

Suddenly her left hand touches nothing. Feeling around, she realizes there are three choices she can make: left, right, or straight ahead. Which one should she take? When she docked in Amnisos and asked the way to the Knossos palace, the locals warned her not to enter the Labyrinth at any cost. Most people who go down there exploring never return. The ghosts take pleasure in blowing torches and lanterns out, they warned. Either the trespassers get lost in the dark and die of starvation, or something worse.

She hesitates. It would make more sense for her to wait outside, just beside the tunnel entrance, for them to leave. The guards will not have their swords in hand, and before they know what is happening she will kill them. And then the queen. But her she will kill more slowly.

As Cyn turns, she hears something. A low voice coming

from the right-hand tunnel. Silent as a ghost, she follows it. About thirty paces away she stops short of the opening to a large storeroom well-lit with wall torches. On all four sides, enormous round-bellied grain amphorae as high as a man's breast nestle in storage holes.

In the center, she sees the queen. Olympias is kneeling before a hideous, larger-than-life-sized statue of the Minotaur, its human body stocky and grotesquely muscular, its bull head full of hate and hunger. Olympias wears around her neck a large green snake as if it were a scarf, its emerald eyes glowing in the warm brown light. The queen holds her arms out in front of her, palms facing the statue, as she chants in a tongue Cyn does not understand. The guards seem to have vanished.

She creeps behind Olympias, sword raised.

"Bitch, prepare to go to Hades," she cries, raising her sword. Olympias turns around, red mouth parted, clutching the snake as if it were her child. The two guards spring out of a dark opening. Cyn engages them both, lunging, parrying, thrusting with both swords, whirling and jumping. One of the guards, the shorter one, raises his sword so that his underarm is exposed, that soft, white area unprotected by armor. Cyn thrusts her left sword deeply into it as the man screams and keels over. The other guard, the one who seems familiar, keeps up with her two swords and cries, over their metallic din, "Princess! Stop this. I do not wish to kill you."

A trembling voice comes from behind the statue of the Minotaur. "Kill her! I will not mind."

Anger boils in Cyn's veins and she redoubles her efforts to wound the remaining guard. In some positions Cyn has a clear view of her opponent, the twitch of his neck muscle, the glint in his eyes, the movement of his sword. Then they circle a pace or two, and he is plunged in the black moving shadows cast by the torches.

He lunges but she can't quite see where his sword is—

Cold metal and blood-curdling pain enter deep in her abdomen, right below her navel, and she gasps, dropping a sword. The guard opens his mouth in surprise, pulls his sword out of Cyn and looks with horror at the red mess on it. She slides her hand down her skirt and feels blood, warm and sticky, gluing her leather skirt to her skin. It seems that the jolting spasms of an earthquake rupture her every organ, every muscle and bone, followed by a rolling, violent tidal wave of torment.

Concentrate. She needs only to wait this out.

Doing her best to ignore the agony, Cyn uses her remaining sword to twist the guard's weapon out of his hand, sending it flying across the room. He dashes for it, and Cyn, realizing the guard is between her and the queen, grabs a torch and runs down the nearest passage, which is not the one she used to come in. Her abdomen throbbing unbearably, she turns right and left and left again, then right and right— or is it left and right?—passing room after room full of fallen ceiling stones, cracked amphorae and festoons of cobwebs as blood continues to pour out of her heinous wound, soaking her leather skirt and gushing down her legs.

Perhaps she can hide her torch and herself in an amphora until Olympias and the guard are gone and she is healed. Surely they can't check all the hundreds—perhaps thousands—of storage vessels down here. She stumbles into another storeroom and drags herself toward the giant jugs in the corner. She lays her torch across a jug and grips the thick-lipped opening of its neighbor, intending to heave herself up and into it.

But before she can, she keels over from pain and vomits, then lies down on her chest, tearing ancient dirt in her clenching hands. Something sharp digs into her chest. She pushes herself off and sees she's lying on human bones, but whether they are those of a recent lost wanderer or a palace resident killed in the earthquake two ages ago, she does not know.

She must wait, that is all. Wait until the wound heals. Then she will stalk Olympias and the guard if they are still in the Labyrinth and kill them both. But for the moment, she is weak from blood loss and must rest. Should she throw the torch into the amphora so Olympias and her guard don't see its glow? If it goes out, will her life eventually be snuffed out along with it if she can't find her way back in the utter darkness of the Labyrinth? The smoke man—the vision from her dream—told her there were some things even his protective spell couldn't save her from.

But she cannot move. She can only hope her enemies run down another passage.

Torch smoke curls in front of her, lengthening. Soon it is the height of a man and has the head of a man with broad shoulders and arms in wide sleeves. It shifts in the torchlight so that she is not sure if it is an illusion brought about by her wound or if it is him. The man of smoke. Come to help her kill Olympias and her guards.

"No, my girl," he whispers in his misty voice. "I am not here to help you kill them. In fact, I am come to ensure the opposite occurs. You must let them capture you."

"No!" Cyn cries as she feels the unbearable throbbing in her gut finally start to lessen. "Never!"

"You must go to Dardania, my child. That is where your fate awaits you."

Cyn pushes herself up to a seated position. The pain is draining rapidly, and the reduction of pain feels like the greatest physical pleasure she has ever known. "I will not be sold like a broodmare," she says, spittle flying through the smoke standing before her. "Tell me who you are. Tell me why you protect me. Tell me how to become a great ruler and general."

The figure bends over her and whispers, almost like a lover, "Very well. I will tell you how to become a great ruler and general."

Cyn leans forward, feeling the wispy insubstantial body wrap around her. It reminds her of sitting around a fire pit in winter when a gust of wind comes tumbling down the roof hole and wafts smoke all over everyone. But this smoke doesn't make her cough or sting her eyes.

"Go to Dardania." Suddenly the smoke dissipates. She reaches for it, trying to clutch it in her hands, but she grasps at nothing.

"Over here! I think I see a light!" calls a male voice. Cyn freezes, contemplating the smoke man's words. Two figures enter the storeroom.

The tall guard skids to a halt before her with a torch, kneels, and stares at her face. "Princess, are you gravely wounded?" he asks. He almost sounds like he cares.

"No, I am not wounded at all," she says. He pulls up her bloody, dripping tunic and stares at her abdomen. There is only the faintest pink line where her wound had been. He looks into her eyes, questioning. And suddenly she remembers him. The guard outside Alexander's office the night she found Sarina in there using the royal seal. The soldier who picked her up from the road when she had collapsed after escaping the Aesarian Lords. The one she called a turd-eating, goat-humping son-of-a-bitch. The one with the white smile and perfect body. Priam.

"I thought…" he begins, frowning.

"Chain her," says a sharp female voice. After a moment's hesitation, Priam takes manacles off his belt. His hands are strong yet not unkind on her arms as he pulls them behind her back. His breath is hot on her neck as he snaps the manacles on her wrists. "I thought I had killed you," he whispers.

"Take her to the ship, Priam." The imperious coldness of that voice cannot chill the warmth of the man's strong hands on Cyn's arms. "Go with her to Dardania. Stay with her there to make sure she does her duty or I will have your head."

"Yes, my queen."

Cyn twists around to look up at him, knowing Olympias can't see her smile.

Safe from the queen's glance in the shadows, Priam smiles back.

CHAPTER TWENTY-SIX

HEPH DIGS HIS KNIFE INTO THE HINGES OF THE dungeon door, trying to force open a small crack in the iron. They've been here for three days and nights now and have eaten all their food supplies. Every evening at sunset a guard opens the door to set a bucket of water inside, seemingly unaware they might need food. When they begged him to take them to Princess Laila, or at least bring them something to eat, he ignored them. Heph knows they have to do something to get out of here or they will starve to death.

Kat draws her sword from its scabbard and admires its reflection in the sliver of moonlight coming through the high, barred window. She has been practicing with it the past days, attacking imaginary warriors in the cell, and sometimes Heph sparred with her. Just to have something to do.

"Beautiful," she says, running her hand over the glistening iron. "And in this place, utterly useless."

Her words sink into the cool, humid air around them. They both know that their weapons won't do them any good. Not against an army of darkness. That's why the guards allowed them to keep them. This afternoon, Heph and Kat discussed attacking the guard the next time he opened the door to set down the bucket, but a few hours ago, when they gazed at his enormous creaking clay muscles and flaming eyes, neither one made a move.

The city of Sharuna is damned, cursed, alive and dead at the same time. Though Heph can hardly comprehend the horrors they witnessed in the city's streets—at first seemingly abandoned and then suddenly echoing with the anguished cries of the dying and the stench of the dead—the images refuse to stop swirling through him, making him feel sick somewhere deep in his gut. This time a few months ago he was still a schoolboy who hardly put any stock in the notion of magic. And now here he is, inextricably caught up with a girl who can accomplish wondrous feats of the mind, in a city that is clearly under the spell of a very dark magic the likes of which he's never imagined.

With each hack of his knife at the stubborn hinge, he thinks of the irony. Less than a month ago he was breaking Kat out of Pella's damp and moldy dungeon in a rush of righteousness. He believed she was innocent and, just as Alexander always claimed, he acted first and thought later. He doesn't regret it, of course. Then again, he still can't shake the foreboding prophecy from his mind—Leonidas's hastily scrawled words in the margins of the Cassandra scroll… That the moon would blot out the sun; the girl would kill the boy, and the world would come undone. Kat, Leonidas wrote, was the girl, the moon; Alex was the boy, the sun.

And now, here he is, attempting to break her out of another dungeon—only this time, from within.

Though he hates himself for thinking it, he wonders if Kat really *is* doomed, if somehow the magic in her has brought about this terrible turn of fate. If the powers in her could ever become as dark and corrupt as the magic of Sharuna.

He pictures Pella like Sharuna, corpse-strewn and ruined at night, Kat sunbathing in the Poseidon garden during the day.

And that's when he drops his knife and turns to look at her.

Her big eyes stare back at him. "What is it?" Her voice comes out like barely more than a breath.

"Forget escaping. I have a better idea."

Kat looks at him suspiciously. "Which is?"

"We'll offer them something extremely rare and valuable instead, something that might particularly interest a legend-ary, enchanted princess."

"But we have nothing..." Kat surveys the darkness of their chamber, and in the shifting moonlight he can see how vul-nerable she looks, despite her courage, despite her strength. After all, she is just a girl, no older than him, who until re-cently had never left her small village. Who hadn't known she was sister to the prince, and who *still* doesn't fully know the extent of her power, nor the power she has over *him*. Which is why he can hardly believe what he's about to say.

"But we do," he says softly.

He continues to look at her, the mixture of sweetness and fire in her eyes. And then, slowly, understanding.

"Me," she says, a tight edge to her voice. "You want to give her *me*?"

"No," Heph says quickly. "That's just an excuse to get her to agree to meet with us. To keep us from dying of starva-tion in here. If we can just see her, maybe we can convince her to let us go, or find what it is she wants and promise to get it for her."

Kat lowers her eyes. "But what if the thing she really wants *is* me? What if she makes you leave me here?"

Heph runs a hand through his dark curls. "You're right,"

he says. "It was a stupid idea." He picks up the knife and re-turns to chipping at the door hinge.

After a moment, he feels the weight of a calming hand on his shoulder. "I'll do it," she says.

"No, really, you're right," he says. "We'll find another way."

"Heph, listen to me," she says, her breath warm on the back of his neck. "I've lost my entire family. Alex is all I have left. I'll do anything to help him, even if it really does mean staying here. If the princess agrees to see us, and if she wants me to stay—bear in mind, that's two very big ifs—you can return to rescue me." Here she smiles, just slightly. "But first let's see if we can convince her to help Alex. You've said all along that this trip isn't about either of us. It's about him."

Heph turns. A shaft of moonlight makes her hair glow silver. How can this girl, so willing to give up her life to help Alex, be the one prophesied to kill him? The prophecy must be wrong or, at least, Leonidas's interpretation must be incorrect.

His gaze sweeps the four walls and lands on their packs, empty of even a scrap of food. He feels his stomach rumble. Despite the darkness, he can see a gleam of eagerness in her eyes. Even if he has to leave her here, she will be better off in the palace with the princess than starving with him in this filthy cell.

"All right," he says. "Scream."

Kat's shrieks pierce the air as Heph twists her arms behind her back and holds her in a tight lock. "I won't!" she cries. "I won't tell her!"

"You will!" Heph grunts, surprised at how strong Kat is, and how readily she has put on the act. If she really wanted to break from his grasp, she probably could. "It's our only way to get out of here!"

"Guard!" Kat wails. "Help me!"

"Guard!" Heph repeats. "Come and see what I have for the princess!"

Heavy footsteps echo down the corridor. A key scrapes in a lock. The door opens. The guard's eyes are as orange and fiery as the flames curling from his torch. Heph feels a shiver of revulsion creep up and down his spine.

"What is this?" the guard says, entering, his bulk completely blocking the door.

"This girl has Blood Magic," Heph says, as Kat struggles against him. "She is a great enchantress. Perhaps the princess can use her magical abilities."

The guard steps forward, holding the torch close to Kat's face, and stares at her with a terrifying, burning emptiness in his eyes. "The princess will know of this," he says in a deep monotone voice. As quickly as he appeared, he's gone again, almost melting into the darkness beyond their cell with a click of the lock.

Heph lets go of Kat and she turns to face him. "Do you think this will work?" she asks, searching his eyes. A cobweb is caught in her hair, and a streak of dirt covers most of her right cheek. How can anyone be so filthy and yet so incomparably beautiful?

"I don't know," he says honestly, his pulse thudding through him. This *has* to work. He is too far down this road. He is too committed to the prince to fail. Without Alex, Heph would be nothing. As for Kat, he realizes with sudden, simple clarity that he is in love with her. Without this wildly exciting, quicksilver girl, so strong and brave and *noble*, his life would be flat and gray and empty. Not a life worth living. But he cannot ever express his love, cannot commit himself to both her and Alex. Not with the prophecy weighing on him like it is. Not with the chance that one could do harm to the other.

And on top of these miserable contradictions, there's the fact that he promised her he'd never kiss her again. Not after the way she reacted. He can't stand the idea that she doesn't want him. Even with her rejection, he can't cut the hope out of his chest.

He studies her from across their chamber, trying to memorize everything about her. The way she bites her lip to steady her nerves. The way she stands a bit on her toes, as though she's always just on the brink of running. He looks at her until he can't look at her anymore without her guessing the truth of his feelings.

After a time, Heph hears boots marching toward them and sees a glow of torchlight outside the door. Kat jumps up. The guard unlocks the door and says, "The princess will see you now. Come with me. Bring your things."

Kat flashes Heph a look that reflects his own emotions back at him, somewhere between terror and victory.

They march up a long spiral staircase and through a room with several silent, motionless guards, who truly look like crumbling ancient statues except for the flames coming from their eyes. Together, they stand and fall in behind Kat and Heph.

The door to the street opens, and for a moment Heph is glad to be out of the filthy cell, out in the night air—until the stench of rotting flesh stings his eyes and makes him want to retch.

"Follow me," the guard says, leading the way down a street lined on both sides with charred, roofless buildings.

Heph steps over sooty copper pots in front of one door and heaps of scorched leather sandals at the next. This was a street of colorful shops once. Lying in front of the third door is the bloated, blackened corpse of a very fat man, stiff fingers wrapped tightly around a half-burned sack of gold. His head spins at the thought that all this could even be real. He had been taught—both before he came to Pella and after with Alex's tutors—to rely on logic and his own perseverance. That the gods existed—or at least they had centuries ago—as well as a few witches and fortune-tellers who dug up bones and sold spells. But he had never considered any enchantment like the one in Sharuna could exist. He feels the horror of it crushing him, grinding him down like the heel of an enormous boot.

Heph puts an arm around Kat and finds she's shaking. Even though she's Snake Blood and trained with Ada in her enchanted fortress, Kat, too, has evidently never experienced anything as gruesome and ghastly as this.

They turn at the next corner and Heph sees a street nearly blocked with the broken golden statues of gods three times the size of a man, arms crossed over their chests. Behind them, temple columns painted lapis blue have fallen in orderly rows.

Then he sees it. The royal palace. Not burned and broken; it has obviously been spared from the enchantment that falls over the rest of Sharuna at sunset. The windowless walls sloping outward to the ground are covered with colorful paintings of war: Egyptian kings in chariots fire arrows at fleeing enemy soldiers who leap into the air in panic or fall beneath horses' hooves. Soldiers launch spears and wave knives as winged gods fly calmly above. Huge cressets—iron fire baskets on long poles filled with logs—burn brightly around the base of the walls, casting enormous shadows of the actual soldiers standing guard there.

As Heph and Kat enter the gate, these soldiers fall in behind them. They walk through a courtyard with pillared porticoes on all four sides and enter the double doors in the portico ahead. In the corridor, life-sized paintings of Egyptian gods seem to move in the torchlight, turning their profiled heads to gaze at them full-face. Heph recognizes Anubis, the jackal-headed god of the afterlife, and his consort, Bast, the mother goddess with the head of a cat, and wonders if they will jump off the walls and attack him and Kat. He is glad when they emerge in a fragrant garden with a long pool.

At the far end of the garden stand two pillars—one seems to be of solid gold, the other of emerald—and both gleam in the light of cressets with an unearthly radiance. The guard motions Heph and Kat to enter the door between them.

What will they find inside? Has the princess, too, become a rotting corpse? Heph's heart thuds in his chest.

They enter a throne room with ceilings six or seven times Heph's height, the walls and countless thick columns brightly painted with figures of kings and queens and kneeling captives. Set into sconces on the columns are dozens of priceless alabaster bowls, the oil lamps inside lighting up the colored striations—white and cream, yellow and orange—and casting the entire chamber in a soft glow.

Heph has a sudden pang of longing for the comparative coziness of King Philip's throne room, the simple stone benches on all sides, the plain iron wall sconces for resin-soaked torches, and the low ceiling designed to retain heat from the fire pit. It is a room where anyone—even the lowliest peasant with a grievance—can feel free to speak. Laila's throne room—so alien and extravagant—would make the greatest nobleman feel small and unimportant, as perhaps it was designed to do.

And then he sees her. Atop a tall dais, the princess sits on a golden throne, each arm a roaring lion. Her skin is the color of burnished bronze. Her nose is long and commanding, her full lips are painted a deep, bloody red. Her large eyes are of a brown so dark they are almost black, and a thick, shoulder-length, blue-black wig frames her face. She is fiercely, breath-takingly beautiful, but there's something icily cold about her.

She stands, and Heph sees that she is impossibly tall and slender, though perhaps it is the effect of her crown, a golden pillar rising from her head at least six handsbreadths high and flaring wide at the top. So liquid are her movements that Laila seems to pour herself down the dais steps rather than walk.

Kat, Heph notices, is massaging her elbow as she takes in the princess's robe of turquoise netting with gold sequins and carnelian beads, and a sheer, sparkling gold capelet around her shoulders. Even the princess's sandals are gilded, with thongs shaped like lotuses. It occurs to Heph that Kat, in her travel-stained tunic, covered with filth from the dungeon, must be comparing herself to Laila's regal splendor.

The princess stops at the bottom step and stands before them unmoving, scrutinizing them intently.

Heph must speak, despite the grisly sights of the city out-side, despite the terrifying beauty of the princess in front of him. He is suddenly very glad he studied royal protocol at Pella with all the fervor of an outsider who knows he doesn't belong. King Philip often granted audiences to foreign am-bassadors—the grim-faced Spartans, the charming Athe-nians, the bejeweled and perfumed Persians who prostrated themselves on the floor like slaves. When emissaries from the Wild Scythians rode into the throne room on short hairy horses, the king received them with the customary courte-sies, not even batting an eye as one by one the animals lifted their tails and relieved themselves on the marble tiles of the throne room floor.

"Esteemed princess," Heph says, bowing deeply, and trying to keep his voice calm and low, "we come before you as emissaries of the great prince regent, Alexander of Macedon, heir to the throne of his father, King Philip II. His highness the prince seeks an alliance with you, Princess, either through marriage, if you will do him that honor, or as a military treaty. He—"

"Silence." She raises her palm and takes a step toward Kat. "Tell me, girl," she says in lightly accented Greek, "how you came across such a rare and valuable item."

Kat curtsies awkwardly, her face serious with concentration. *She's nervous*, Heph thinks. *She knows how much is at stake, and a few weeks at the palace don't make a farm girl an expert in courtly customs and foreign affairs.*

"I'm sorry, Princess, but I have no item of value, just—" she begins, but again Laila interrupts.

"That." She reaches toward Kat's throat and Kat stands still as a statue. It's all Heph can do not to dive forward to protect Kat. But the princess's fingers brush Kat's collarbone and then lift the silver Flower of Life pendant she wears around her neck, before letting it drop again. *"This* is what I desire. You are only here because my guard spotted this amulet."

"This?" Kat asks, as her hand flies up to touch the pendant. A shadow passes over her face. "What would a princess of your fame and wealth want with such a plain trinket? It is hardly worthy of your beauty, my lady."

"And still, it belongs to me." The princess deftly unclasps her capelet and throws it on the floor. There, above her heart, is a white mark in the shape of the six-petal lotus, lightly indented into her flesh.

Heph hears Kat suck in a breath. The mark looks like an exact match to the pendant.

"Your necklace," Laila says, "is a token of the gods. It is a reminder of the source of the world's magic."

Heph's heart skips a beat as Kat grips the amulet. He tries to remember what she told him—he has never seen her without it.

"Tell me, please, what you know of this pendant," Kat says, lifting her chin. "It was my mother's, and I took it off her body after she was murdered. I would not part with it."

The princess turns her head to the left and stares down at the floor as if considering what to say. Now Heph's heart skips another beat—not out of fear, but from the impact of her gorgeous profile. Strong and majestic, wildly exotic. Yet he finds her beauty too intense, blinding almost, like looking straight into a noonday sun. The moon—softer, unpredictable, and mysterious—never blinds, only washes her admirers with magical silver light. His gaze slides to Kat.

Laila, too, is staring at Kat now, her dark eyes hard and flat as obsidian. "The Flower of Life pendant is the symbol of a forgotten god," Laila says.

Kat blanches visibly. "Are you—?"

"No." The princess shakes her head. "I am not immortal, but neither am I mortal. I am trapped in an endless curse, doomed to exist somewhere between life and death."

She stares at Kat a long moment, and Heph is suddenly afraid what this princess's interest might mean. Will she harm Kat? Insist on keeping her forever in this haunted city of living statues and never-ending death?

But the princess says, "As bearer of a Flower of Life pendant, you have a right to see. He can come, too."

They follow her to an alcove between two columns where alabaster lamps glow brightly. In the center is a tall bronze tripod filled to the brim with water, and floating on the water are three large lotus flowers, the long, pointed petals white at their base, purple at their tips. In the center of each burns a tiny oil lamp.

Laila moves the blooms, and the water ripples. "Look into the water."

Heph and Kat peer into the basin, and for a moment, he sees only ripples. But then the lines on the water seem to arrange themselves into images—distorted faces, buildings expanding and contracting—and then he clearly sees the throne room. Laila is on the throne, just as beautiful but with the pale skin of palace beauties who scorn the sun and bathe in milk.

"I was quite proud of my beauty," she says quietly. Heph pulls his gaze away from the water to her face, which is solemn, almost repentant. He glances at Kat, who still stares at the water. "And I loved toying with men's affections, driving them wild with desire for me. Look." She gestures to the water.

In the water, Heph sees the image of two men striding into the throne room, both tall and powerfully built, with shoulder-length blond hair. The men are handsome, one with eyes as blue as lapis lazuli, and the other with eyes like polished emeralds.

"It was long after the great battle of gods and monsters when the brothers arrived," Laila says, and Heph starts slightly, surprised to hear her voice so close to his ear. He glances up to see that the princess has leaned over the basin as well, her black hair draping forward to hide her face.

"They were powerful sorcerers, or so I thought, and looking back on it, I think I enjoyed playing with fire, setting one against the other, wanting to discover just how far their passion for me would drive them, though at the time it felt like pain, not vanity. Riel, the one with green eyes, promised me eternal life, but Brehan, his brother, offered me eternal love."

She looks up at the ceiling as if searching for answers, then back at the water. "In the end, I made the wrong choice.

The scorned brother marched through this city, driven by a murderous rage."

Princess Laila gives the lotuses another nudge, and the water ripples again. Heph sees a dark street. Wild-eyed horses gallop by whinnying in terror as lightning bolts blast buildings apart and strike panic-stricken people dead.

"He killed every living thing within my lovely city," Laila says. "Every living thing, except for me."

"But...the soldiers," Kat says, gesturing to the unmoving dark shapes in the throne room.

Laila nods. "*Ushabtis*—a final gift to serve and protect me. Formed from the earth, with magic spells carved on their bodies."

Ushabtis. Heph learned about them from Leonidas: small clay statues with magical markings that Egyptians put in tombs to serve the dead spirit, baking, cleaning, and preparing food. He and Alex had laughed at the silliness of Egyptians believing the statues could actually grow to human size and serve as commanded. Of course, the *ushabtis* in tombs and those he saw in the marketplaces of Memphis had been created by human potters, not sorcerers.

"I've been trapped here ever since, permitted to enjoy my city as it was during the day but doomed to watch it return to its destruction every sunset."

Laila holds up her brown hands and examines them critically. "I must bathe in the sun all day long, soaking up its life-giving rays, or else I, too, start to look like a corpse."

Her beauty suddenly strikes Heph as ghastly. "What sorcerer has such power?" he asks. "I have never heard—not even in the time of Troy when magic was much stronger—of such evil spells as these."

Laila traces her finger along the edge of the basin. "You

are right, Hephaestion," she says. "These brothers were no mere sorcerers, but the last of the gods."

"I have never heard of these gods," Kat says. "Zeus and Apollo, Athena and Poseidon, all of those and many others, yes. But Riel and Brehan?"

"You only heard of those who wanted to be worshipped, to receive sacrifices at temples," Laila says, leaning against the tripod and staring at the water. "Not all gods desired that. Riel used to say that he wanted real power, not slaughtered goats and mumbled prayers. But those gods you mentioned, in fact all of those you know, were either killed by monsters or fled the earthly realm for safety."

"No one has seen the gods for centuries," Kat says, her voice trembling. "They used to walk among men, fight with them on the battlefield, disguise themselves as beggars to test the charity of people they visited. People say the gods fell asleep. But you're saying that's not true. They are…"

"Gone. Not on earth anymore. The age of Gods has ended, Katerina. A new age is coming, though whether it will be an Age of Men or of Monsters, I do not know."

"Why did those two—Riel and Brehan—remain on earth?" Heph asks. "Why didn't they flee like the others?"

"They fought a great evil and used up most of their divine power, remaining trapped in mortal form. Riel told me that they had sired many mortal children with many women. Brehan's children possessed Earth Blood, and Riel's offspring Snake Blood." Her flashing dark eyes rise to meet Kat's. "Your pendant, Katerina, is a symbol of Earth Blood."

"But, Princess," Kat says, wrinkling her forehead, "are you sure this is a symbol of Earth Blood? I don't know my pendant's history, other than that my mother gave it to me. But Ada of Caria told me it was used by Snake Bloods when we—when they—go into a trance."

Laila nods, the many golden rosettes in her wig glittering in the torchlight. "That is correct. As Brehan's token of Earth Blood," she says, "the pendant balances the effects of Snake Blood. Without it, those with Snake Blood can become trapped inside an animal or inside someone else's mind. They can succumb to insanity. The scorned god said my curse would last until I found a pendant to match the scar."

Laila stares hungrily at Kat's pendant, and the air between them pulses with tension. Heph's hand moves slowly to his sword hilt. "And now," Laila purrs, "after five hundred years, you are here."

Kat steps back from the princess, and her hand flutters again to her necklace.

A short burst of laughter comes from Laila, but it contains no mirth. "How will you prevent me from having my guards cut you down so I can take it?" She takes a step toward Kat.

Without thinking, Heph draws his sword and steps in front of Kat. His sword is heavy and feels right in his hand. In a single movement, the *ushabti* guards draw their own swords—swords of glinting iron, not clay—and circle him.

Laila tilts her head, revealing her long, slender neck. "Are you really thinking of sacrificing yourself for her? I cannot die. You must know that if you make one move toward me, you and she shall both be dead one heartbeat later."

Heat rushes to the back of Heph's neck at the princess's mocking tone. "I know it's foolish, lady, but I cannot stand by while Katerina is threatened."

Laila reaches out a long, tanned arm, and traces Heph's jaw with her finger. He is paralyzed by a touch like freezing metal.

"Such a handsome boy," she says quietly. "I can feel your love for her, and it warms my heart, something that hasn't happened in a long, long time."

Though his body is rooted to the floor, Heph's mind reels. Did Kat hear the princess? He wants to look at her, but he can't seem to wrench his eyes away from Laila, who holds him in a long stare. She seems to be looking not just into his eyes but directly into his heart.

Laila pulls her hand away from his face and sighs, a sigh that whistles through the throne room and makes all the oil lamps flicker and almost go out.

"There has been no love in this city for five hundred years," she says. "You, Hephaestion of Pella, look as Brehan once did at the end—willing to die for me."

The princess twists her gold signet ring inscribed with magical symbols. Heph sees a bird, a star, and an eye among them. Then she seems to come to some decision.

"I will be merciful to honor the memory of love," she says, her dark eyes bright with tears as she stares first at Heph, then Kat. "If you give me what I require, I promise that when this city is but ash under the sun, you will find the pendant among the ruins. Do you accept?"

"It is not my decision to make, Princess," he says, looking at Kat, who still grasps the pendant in her hand. "The Flower of Life belongs to Katerina. Ask her if she will do as you wish."

Kat doesn't look at Laila but at Heph when she replies, simply, "Yes." The word sends a powerful thrill through Heph's body, and he realizes he will likely never know all the meanings contained in that yes.

Laila's entire body relaxes and a true smile spreads across her lips for the first time. "Make sure you take good care of it, Katerina of Pella. I have a vision—unclear, though it is—that in your hour of need, it shall save you, too."

She runs a hand gently through Kat's golden-brown hair and closes her eyes as if searching for something with her mind. "What's this?" she asks, her eyes opening wide. "You are wounded. I feel betrayal, pain, almost murder. Where is this wound?"

Kat raises her right hand, the bandaged forefinger much shorter than it should be.

"Ah," the princess says softly, carefully taking Kat's hand in hers. "And in return for the pendant, Katerina, I will give you something in return. Remove the bandages."

Katerina's eyes dart to Heph. Though Laila seems to tolerate their presence, he does not entirely trust this bewitched and bewitching princess.

"Peace, young lordling," Laila says, surprising Heph again. "I shall not hurt her—much."

Kat unwraps the bandage, revealing the oozing, scabbed-over stump. The maimed finger looks stunted and ugly on her otherwise graceful hand. Heph's stomach lurches. If he hadn't been with Cynane...

The princess takes off the gold signet ring on her left hand and slips it onto the top of Kat's stump. Then, chanting loudly, Laila pulls her hand among the floating lotus blossoms, and the water begins to bubble. Kat screams and tries to pull her hand away.

Heph pushes in between the women, but Laila hits him with her free hand so hard, he tumbles backward across the room and slams onto the floor, sliding across the marble. When he tries to stand up, he finds himself pinned down by an invisible force.

"*Menat-iqbit-nerek-hetep,*" the princess calls, "*keper-pernu-sesheb-djane...*"

Steam rises from the basin, and Kat's knees give way. She sinks to the floor, her eyes closed and her mouth open in a guttural moan, but Laila still holds her hand in the boiling water.

Heph feels as if a giant foot is pressing down on his abdomen. Like a beetle on its back, he can raise his head, arms and legs, but he cannot stand. "Stop!" he yells. "Don't hurt her!"

But the princess ignores him, and Kat's wail increases.

"Akbet-sinoth!"

The princess lets go of Kat's hand and Kat crumples to the floor. After a long moment, she groans, pushes herself up to a seated position, and opens her eyes. She doesn't seem to be in pain any longer, but she is clearly weakened and gasping from it. She holds up her right hand and murmurs in wonder. At that moment, Heph feels the crushing weight lift from him. He scrambles up and races to her side. Something flashes on her hand, and when he looks, he sees that her right forefinger now has a golden fingertip, fused to her flesh, with a perfectly shaped nail.

"Are you all right?" he whispers in her ear.

But before Kat has time to answer, Laila grabs the pendant and yanks it off her neck. She strides over to the dais and mounts the steps. "Come, my faithful servants," she cries, arms extended. "It is time for rest."

Dozens of soldiers crowd into the throne room, pushing toward the dais, swords bumping against long shields in a clattering roar that sounds like rushing water.

Heph and Kat watch as Laila, chanting again, presses the Flower of Life pendant over the mark on her chest until it sinks into her flesh. He knows they should turn around and race from the room—something perilous is coming, of that he's sure—but he can't move, and neither, it seems, can Kat. They are like people on a beach who watch in horrified fascination a wave as tall as the sky thunder toward them, but remain rooted to the spot.

"Ush-ab-ti nen-en-pur en-tek-abkwarda wasset…"

Her chanting grows louder, filling the throne room, bouncing off the tall columns and high painted roof beams.

The pendant starts to glow until it blazes silver-white like a full moon inside Laila's chest. Heph, who has been studying the princess, looks around for the soldiers but finds they are gone, replaced by tiny blue-glazed figurines, maybe two handsbreadths tall, arms crossed over their chests like mummies, the long lappets of their headdresses falling to their breasts. Like the soldiers, every part of the figurines is covered with magical symbols except the heads.

They are really *ushabtis*. Heph feels pinpricks of fear on the back of his neck. They need to go.

Kat doesn't seem to share his mounting horror. She stares down at the figurines curiously. "Alex sent us here to get soldiers," she says softly, looking up at him. "Heph—"

"Ma-twa kar-kam-nen-en jemset..."

The fiery glow brightens and expands to the coffered ceiling high above Laila and out to the walls, swallowing her tall form.

"We've got to get out of here," Heph says, "Come on!"

He races to the door and pauses, realizing Kat isn't beside him. She is still in the middle of the throne room, bent down, scooping up armfuls of *ushabtis* and throwing them into her pack. The white light expands from the dais, filling the entire throne room with a blinding brilliance, engulfing Kat.

"Katerina!" Heph shouts and races into the light.

He can see nothing but a silver-white blaze. Wildly, he casts his hands about until they find her. He grabs her arm, pulls her toward the door, and they sprint through.

Outside, it is mercifully dark except for cressets, and they run alongside the rectangular pool. But still the light follows them, streaming across the garden like a rapidly spreading flood.

They race through the connecting corridor, across the entrance courtyard, and out of the main palace gate into the street. When they look back, the light is still behind them, washing into the cursed city.

"We've got to get out of here, now!" Heph says. "To the gate!"

As they run through the rubble and corpse-filled streets, Heph can only hope he knows the way to the gate. There's no time to think about it. He nimbly jumps over charred roof beams, broken walls, and decomposing bodies with Kat at his side. They run past the collapsed fountain of the winged goddess, and there, just beyond, is the gate, wide-open.

They tear through it and keep going across the field and into the safety of the trees, where they stop and turn. The city's walls are glowing now, so white it hurts Heph's eyes to look at them, and then a huge ball of light erupts from the city, rising heavenward. Without thinking, he throws Kat to the ground and covers her as the earth roars and waves of searing heat roll over his back.

As the sound subsides and the heat cools, he rolls off her. As Kat groans and pulls herself up, Heph finally looks back. Moonlight illuminates the smoldering rubble of what was once the City of Sharuna.

ACT FIVE:
RESURRECTED

Fear is pain arising from the anticipation of evil.
—Aristotle

CHAPTER TWENTY-SEVEN

WAVES LAP AS GENTLY AS HEARTBEATS AGAINST the harbor piers just outside the inn, and a cool salty breeze drifts through the window slats, yet Alexander cannot sleep.

He turns onto his right side. Then back to his left. It's not that the Samothrace inn is uncomfortable—the linen sheets are of the finest weave, the soft mattress is stuffed with down, and the ropes below the bed are stretched taut. But his mind is troubled, tumultuous.

After Aristotle told Alex that neither of his parents possessed Snake Blood, Alex pressed him to reveal more, but his teacher said he knew nothing else. He knew only that Snake Blood passes from parent to child, and he did not understand how Alexander came by this birthright. He refused even to guess.

Alex twists to the other side of his mattress.

His Snake Blood points to one truth. That at least one of his parents isn't, in fact, his parent. And if that is true, then it's actually possible—outlandish as the notion at first seems—that he may not be the rightful heir to the throne.

The very thought makes him feel so ill he wants to retch.

He has spent all his life training to become king—what would he do if he weren't?

If he is not the heir, then that would mean Arridheus, the missing boy doomed to be forever slow, *is*. And without a capable heir, the country will tear itself apart on Philip's deathbed as a vast array of distant royal cousins tries to claim the throne.

The rising panic within him surprises Alex. Even when battling the Aesarian Lords with flaming arrows and spears whistling past his head, he was calmer than this.

He flips onto his back and tries to treat his concerns like a battlefield: observe, plan, strike. Breathing deeply, Alex examines his options.

He can't ask anyone about his lineage—that is, he can ask only one person who would have as much to lose as he does if the information were to spread: Olympias.

If Olympias is not his mother, she will not want people to know she is not the mother of the prince regent. It would drastically reduce her station.

And if instead Philip is not his father…well, Olympias could not have that information come out, either. The king would likely banish or even execute her for treason.

Finally, if Alexander is a foundling, son to neither Olympias *nor* Philip, then enemies and friends alike would mock Olympias for being incapable of being able to perform her most important task, and they would question Philip's manhood. Life in the palace would be made unbearable for her.

It's an easy enough solution, then. He must return to Pella and question the queen. As soon as they get up—which, Alex realizes, will be *quite* soon, given the silvery light coming in through the wooden window slats—he will ask Kadmus to make arrangements to sail on the next ship to Pella.

That settled, Alexander tries to relax, hoping at least to rest comfortably for a few minutes. But even rest is like a wriggling slippery fish that he can't grab hold of. His gut is telling him he's overlooking something big, something important.

It could be nothing. But it could also be a Snake Blood warning, an effect of the magic in his blood, which he is only now beginning to accept. *Blood Magic.*

Alex tries to ignore the writhing suspicion, but the longer he lies in bed, the more the urgency builds, simmering in his blood until there is no point in denying the need to act. Something is very, very wrong.

"Kadmus," he calls to the door, open a handsbreadth or two. There, in the little antechamber, Kadmus sleeps on a pallet, keeping his sword at the ready. But there is no answer, no sound of gentle breathing or shifting of weight. Alex throws off his covers and in two strides throws the door wide open. The sleeping mat is rolled up and stacked neatly next to the exterior door.

Has Kadmus gone outside to use the latrine? Or has the general deserted him, thinking that Alex is a deformed weakling and that he'd rather serve King Philip?

Alex finds his sandals on the floor and hastily buckles on his sword and dagger. Yet uncertainty chains him to the spot. Frantically, he tries to remember whether Kadmus told him anything that would explain his disappearance. With a rising sense of panic, he remembers last night in the tavern. Kadmus gave his best tunic, belt, and pair of sandals to the waiter, who couldn't have been more delighted if the general had given him a sack of gold. Alex thought it was merely compassion for the skinny, threadbare youth, and jokingly asked Kadmus if he was going to live in the cliffs on the north side of the harbor as a hermit. What had Kadmus said? Alex strains to remember his exact words.

"Those cliffs would indeed be a fitting place to meet the gods."

When Alex races outside, the sun is a blur of dazzling gold lighting up the horizon, streaming through rose-pink clouds, and reflecting orange on a sea the color of iron. Creaking ships bob against piers as sleepy sailors yawn and stretch.

Alex squints at the cliffs to the left of the harbor. It's hard to tell in this soft early light, but he thinks he sees a small, straight figure on the edge of the cliff, the sea breeze tangling his dark hair.

Heart leaping into his throat, Alex races around the harbor and up the steep path of the cliff. His left leg throbs in protest as he scrambles over rocks, digging into sandy soil that seems almost vertical in patches. In some places, Alex grabs hold of bushes to pull himself up; in others, he leaps from boulder to boulder like a billy goat. Maybe his misgivings are all wrong. Maybe Kadmus is getting some fresh air. Watching the sun come up.

Gasping for breath, Alex makes it to the flat top of the cliff just as Kadmus takes a step forward.

And then Alex knows. He intends to jump.

"Kadmus!" Alex cries. But the general doesn't react, and Alex wonders if the sea wind has whipped his words away.

"Stop!" Alex screams again, rushing forward. This time, he knows Kadmus can hear him. He sees the general flinch, but still Kadmus does not step back from the edge. Alex pumps his legs even harder.

He stops several feet behind him, not wanting to make Kadmus panic. The general is only one step away from tumbling onto the jagged rocks below. Breathing heavily, Alex bellows, "As prince of Macedon, I command you to step back!"

And—thanks be to Tyche, goddess of fortune—Kadmus

does. A loyal soldier never disobeys a direct order from his prince. Kadmus always obeys.

Still, Alex doesn't make any move toward him. Only a desperate man would want to kill himself, and desperate men are ultimately loyal only to themselves.

"Stand here, beside me," Alex says. Hanging his head, Kadmus complies. "Explain yourself, General." He wishes he sounded more royal and powerful, but it is hard to do so when he is out of breath from the climb.

"My prince, release me." Kadmus keeps his head turned from Alexander. "You are doing me a great unkindness."

"And you are doing me a great disservice," Alexander says, his voice growing more commanding. "Who are you to take away my one remaining counselor? Who are you to abandon me when I'm surrounded by danger? You are my best soldier. I need you, Kadmus."

Kadmus cringes as if Alex had given him a painful blow instead of a compliment. "Oh, my lord, I wish you would not say such things."

Alex is startled by the depth of anguish in the man's voice. When Kadmus finally turns to face him, Alex doesn't recognize the handsome war hero with the confident swagger and cocky white grin. This man is ashen-faced, his eyes red-rimmed, his back bowed.

"If only you knew," Kadmus says. "If you knew, you would not say such things."

Alex is about to ask what he means, but suddenly he stops himself, the truth flowing into him with sudden clarity.

Of course.

It's as though a giant fist has just punched him in the gut, leaving him completely breathless.

"You are the spy."

Kadmus falls to Alex's feet and lies prostrate on the ground.

"My prince, I wish that it were not so, but I cannot change what is. I beg you, take your sword and cleave my head from my shoulders, for I am not worthy to remain."

Alex hardens his heart. He must ask. "Arri found an extremely valuable cameo brooch of the Great King. Was that yours?"

"It was mine," Kadmus admits, his cheek pressed against the dirt and his eyes squeezed shut, "one of their unwanted gifts for my services that I threw in the bottom of my trunk. One day last month I caught your brother playing in my room. After that, I couldn't find the cameo. I was glad it was gone. I hoped he had thrown it down the latrine as I should have done."

He twists his head around to look up at Alex. "But I don't work for Artaxerxes," he says, a haunted look in his eyes. "I serve the true power behind the Persian throne, the Envoys of Death, the brothers of Daeva, god of wrath and revenge."

Realization dawns fully now. "You work for the Assassins?"

"Yes, my lord." Kadmus's voice is but a whisper in the dirt. "Unlike the Great King, they do not wish to see a union made between the Empire and your kingdom. They see Macedon as a threat to be wiped out before it grows stronger."

Anger overwhelms Alex, pulsing in his veins, pounding in his head. Most of his anger isn't directed at Kadmus, but at himself. How stupid could he have been? Why did he let his liking for the general overrule the need to investigate him more closely? How can Alex ever rule wisely when he makes so many idiotic mistakes?

"Do you need gold so badly?" Alex asks, almost spitting the words. "You seem to live simply enough."

"It's my family," Kadmus says so quietly that Alexander has to lean down to make out the man's words. "I was born into poor circumstances, joined the Macedonian army at fifteen, and rose quickly. I have only one surviving relative, a sister, who married a Greek merchant from Apasa. I visit them whenever I get leave. I love her three children as if they were my own."

Here Kadmus is quiet, lost in memories. It takes him a moment to collect himself. "The Assassins were looking for a spy on your father's council and used my family in Persia to their advantage. If I do not obey their orders, they will murder my sister, her husband, and the children. They had hoped King Philip would take me with him to Byzantium so I could give them his battle plans. But since the king left me behind, my orders are to spy on you, my prince."

"Stop calling me, 'my prince,'" Alex says through clenched teeth. "*My* family—*my* little brother—has been taken from me so that yours might be safe. You are no man of mine."

"I know," Kadmus says miserably. He pushes himself up to a kneeling position. "But know, prince of Macedon, that it was not I who kidnapped your brother. Nor was it the Assassins. Some other party is responsible for that atrocity."

"It was your suggestion that I arrange the kidnapping!" Alex flings at him.

Kadmus winces and hangs his head. "I did," he admits, "because I honestly thought it would protect Arridheus and relieve you at least of that burden."

He looks up at Alex, his gray eyes smoldering like embers. "I have given word to the Assassins only of minor things: bad behavior in council meetings—of Gordias falling asleep and Theopompus drinking too much and Hagnon's miserly refusals to spend an obol on anything. I told them of your reluctance to marry. Things of that nature only. Harmless things to keep them entertained. I would never..." Kadmus trailed off, struggling to find words. "I would never share anything that would endanger you, or your relatives, or Macedon. But their patience with me is running out."

Alexander cannot stop the relief that sings through his body at Kadmus's words, but he must remain guarded. A traitor is at his feet...and a question remains to be answered.

"Why did you not share more pertinent information?"

"I am a most reluctant traitor," Kadmus says, with a little choking laugh that sounds like a sob. "Not only do I not want to betray my country, but..." He trails off. After a time, he says stiffly, "It's you. You see, I have the utmost regard for your well-being."

Alex sees the unasked question shining in Kadmus's eyes, and he finally understands. The realization is both flattering and confusing. He knows what Kadmus has left unsaid. And it's not that Alexander has never entertained the idea of a male lover. It is certainly not uncommon. However, though he admires both the general's lean muscles and brilliant mind, he does not want what Kadmus seeks—the *intimacy* his eyes are asking for, even if his words are not. At least, Alex doesn't *think* he wants it. Especially not now, when he is still trying to understand who he even is.

"If you believe me," Kadmus says, sitting back on his haunches and staring at the dirt, "then I can die a happy man. I will not beg for my life."

"You still plan on dying today?"

Kadmus looks up, surprise mingling with dust on his face. "Prince?"

Alexander offers a hand, and Kadmus looks at it as though it were a viper. He shakes his head.

"There is only one way both my family and you can remain safe," Kadmus says firmly. "I must die."

Alexander grabs Kadmus's hands and, ignoring his protests,

pulls the general to his feet. He places his hands firmly on Kadmus's shoulders. "If you died, the Persians would force someone else to become their spy, and I wouldn't know who it was. You can help me far more by staying alive, *pretending* to spy for them."

What he says is true. It would be unwise to allow Kadmus to die, even if it's what the general wants. And yet... Alexander wonders if there is any other reason he is being so lenient. He *doesn't* love the general—not like a lover, nor like a brother, nor, he thinks with a sudden pang, like he loves Hephaestion, with an intensity that goes beyond friendship, that knows no bounds. All Alex can reason is this: he can't live with Kadmus's death on his shoulders. He can't live without him, period. In this short time, he has grown to need him, and whether that's a political or personal need doesn't matter. It is as undeniable as the rage of the sea churning below them or the warm rays of the rising sun.

"I will give you information," he goes on, "of the interesting yet harmless sort—which you can feed them. It will be a dangerous job, convincing the Assassins that you remain loyal. If they have the slightest suspicion, you will drop dead at the next banquet. But I can help you. We just have to remain one step ahead."

Kadmus considers this, and Alex sees hope kindling amidst the despair and self-hatred in his face.

"Will you stay with me?" Alex asks, looking into Kadmus's eyes but not, this time, to try and read what's in them. Only to convey what is in his own heart.

"Yes," Kadmus says softly, "I will."

Sarina places the diadem of gold olive leaves on Alex's head and smiles. "Ready, my lord," she says, tweaking the shoulders of his tunic—rich Tyrian purple, bordered with a wide gold key pattern.

Alex spent most of the one-day journey from Samothrace and the ride from the Pellan lake port thinking about what Aristotle said. Though it stung to learn that his teacher did not want to return with him and claim a coveted spot among his council, his wisdom has shown Alex the path to take.

When he and Kadmus dismounted at the palace this morning, Alex sent word immediately inviting leading citizens to meet with him. He was so eager to get started that he didn't want to take the time to bathe and dress. But if his people are going to agree with the radical changes he wants to make, they need to see the majesty of a prince, not the carelessness of a bedraggled boy traveler.

Now Alex looks into Sarina's eyes—he could drown in their warm, dark depths—and nods. He grabs her hand—it's slender, with long, tapered fingers—and says, "I want you to come with me."

She blinks in confusion. "But you have called this meeting in the temple, my prince. You will not have need of wine and cakes."

"It is appropriate for the regent to have a personal attendant with him at all times."

She frowns slightly, as if not fully trusting his answer, but nods.

Accompanied by six bodyguards, Alex, Kadmus, and Sarina walk from the main palace gates to the nearby central marketplace, where the temple of Zeus the Father is located. The crowd in front of the temple parts as Alex's party arrives. Word must have spread that the prince has something momentous planned.

It's a cool, cloudy afternoon, little bursts of wind toying with cloaks and shawls like invisible kittens. An old man's straw hat rolls in front of Alex like a wheel. Smiling, he picks it up and throws it back to the man.

"Long live Prince Alexander!" the man cries. "May Zeus bless our prince!" cries another, as more and more people clap and cry out blessings.

Ahead of Alex is the temple, freshly painted bright yellow, its four dark red columns topped by bright green acanthus leaves curling around the capitals. He pauses halfway up the steps to the porch, raises his hand in acknowledgment, and smiles. The faces in the crowd light up at this small mark of respect from their prince. His gaze falls on a teenage girl who looks like she's ready to swoon with love for him, a silver-haired matron whose dark eyes glow with admiration, and a pauper beaming a gap-toothed smile.

Inside, the temple is dark and cool, light filtering in the high open windows in slanting bars. This crowd consists of invited guests: wealthy merchants, top palace officials, important priests, major landowners, and leaders of various craft guilds—blacksmiths, armorers, leatherworkers, and jewelers. Most of them prosperous, Macedonian, and male, of course, though there are some widows who have taken over the roles of dead husbands, and several foreign-born individuals.

At the far end of the *naos*, a gigantic statue of Zeus sits on a red marble throne, a sunbeam lighting up his smooth ivory face. His eyes are lapis and onyx, his beard and hair pure silver, his tunic and the lightning bolt in his right hand pure gold. In front of him, at the altar, the priestess Orythia holds the rope of a large white goat, its horns gilded, a garland of blossoms around its neck. Dark gray hair frames the priestess's strong, smooth face, and in her other hand glints the silver blade of a knife.

"Loyal subjects," Alex says, stepping in front of her. "You must wonder why I am holding this meeting here, in a temple, rather than in the palace throne room or council chamber." Several heads nod.

"I am proposing changes to our traditional way of governing, and before I do so I must be sure that the gods approve."

Eyebrows lift in question. Heads turn as people look at one another in surprise.

Alex nods, and Orythia slices the goat's throat. The creature falls immediately, bleating, its front legs sprawled out, and its blood gushes into a silver basin. Two young priests lift the still-bleeding carcass onto the altar and slit it open. The liver is placed in a golden bowl and handed to Orythia, who pokes and prods it.

Alex holds his breath, remembering all the stories of kings who ignored omens and suffered disaster as a result. The king of Troy, who refused to hand Helen back to her husband Menelaus. The Great King Xerxes of Persia, who stubbornly invaded Greece. King Croesus of Sardis, who attacked Cyrus of Persia.

The worst thing that could happen is for the goat's liver to be missing—that would signify such an immediate catastrophe everyone would race home and bar their doors. But if the liver is misshapen, or deformed by a black growth, or even if it is the wrong color—a pale and sickly pink instead of a strong reddish-brown—he will have to pretend he was going to alter the rules of ambassadorial appointments and do this another time. But he doesn't want to wait.

Orythia comes forward, smiling, her startlingly ice-blue eyes almost glowing in the soft light of the temple. "My lord," she says, and he knows before he looks in the bowl that the omens are good. "Never before have I seen such a healthy liver. The color and shape are perfect. But more than that, my prince," she adds, and Alex feels a shiver of antici-

pation run through him, "the liver bears an unusual mark."
His heart skips a beat. *What kind of mark?*

She places the bowl in his hands and Alex sees a pale jagged mark in the flesh that looks just like a lightning bolt.
"Whatever it is you aim to do, my prince, Father Zeus himself has given you his special blessing."

Alex lowers his head in gratitude and respect, wondering if Father Zeus really approves of the shocking change
he is going to make, or if this could be a coincidence. He
quickly decides to believe the former. Whatever the case,
the omens will make this a lot easier for him, because many
here will not like what he's going to do. He places the bowl
on the altar for anyone who wants to come and look after
the meeting is over.

"My lords and ladies," he says, "as you are aware, the
Macedonian royal council has suffered depletions recently."
Someone in the crowd sniggers. "With my father's attentions
turned to war, it is up to me to form a new council. I have
invited you here today to make known my wishes."

Many men in the crowd draw themselves up to their full
height and lift their chins.

"General Kadmus, who so ably helped defend us against
the Aesarian Lords, will remain my minister of war." Heads
nod. This was expected and hardly controversial.

"My new minister of religion," he says, and several white-
robed priests puff out their chests, "will be Orythia." Her
eyes fly open as a rumble of discontent echoes through the
temple.

"My lord?" she asks.

Alex turns toward her. "You have spent your life since
childhood serving Zeus the Father devotedly," he says.
"Moreover, you are known to have more of the Sight, priest-

ess, than any priest in Macedon, which will help me to rule." She lowers her eyes in obedience as the murmurs stop.

He goes down the list, naming a mix of Macedonian-born males, foreign-born males, and Macedonian women, all known for their wisdom, fairness, and business acumen, to the positions of an expanded council: minister of provisions, advisor of the guilds, advisor of foreign trade, minister of finance, counselors for agriculture, armaments, and judicial affairs, and general counselors.

Finally, he beckons Sarina forward from her spot against the wall. She winds her way through the crowd. "This woman, raised to be advisor to pharaohs, has given me council when I needed it," he says. "She has seen things I have not. She knows things I do not. I name Sarina of Egypt, too, to be a counselor."

The crowd in front of him is utterly silent, each face marked with a frown, outrage, or puzzlement.

"She's not only a woman, but foreign-born," says a plump merchant at the front of the crowd. "Worse than that, she's a slave."

"She is free now," Alex says, averting his eyes from Sarina's gaze. Her eyes seem to burn with fury.

Alex hears whispered words. *Mistress. Prostitute. Witch. Spy. Macedon will be a joke.*

This goes too far.

Kadmus stands next to Alex and, in the same clear, carrying voice he uses calling out commands on the battlefield, announces, "Sarina of Egypt was one of the three palace women who risked her life to fight the Aesarian Lords last month. She worked the catapult to launch the jars of snakes and scorpions at the enemy, turning the tide of the battle. She is not only intelligent, but as brave as any soldier." He turns toward her and says, "It is an honor, Sarina. We will welcome your wisdom and insight."

The mutterings cease. Alexander strides outside to address the people in the marketplace, as those inside crowd behind him on the temple porch.

"People of Macedon," he says, "as we look ahead to our future, we must ask ourselves what kind of nation, what kind of people, we want to be. When we cast our gaze just a day's sail to our east, we see Persia. Its culture is rich, we know, its army powerful. Yet everyone there lives in fear of the Great King. Do you wish to live in fear of your king and his counselors?"

Heads shake. Voices murmur.

"As for me, I have no wish to rule over a flock of stunned, scared sheep," he continues. "I want our culture to thrive, our *people* to thrive, to believe not only in me, your future king, but in Macedon, and in its rightful place in the known world. I want my advisors to come from all segments of Macedonian society, bringing me different kinds of knowledge and wisdom. I want every citizen to take pride in our nation and to support its expansion. And in fact, I have realized something more—we will never win new lands without understanding *their* cultures."

"Long live the prince!" cries a male voice from somewhere in the crowd. "We will not live like Persian sheep!" cries an old woman, lifting a cane. They clap and cheer as Alex and his entourage return to the palace.

At the main gate, a guard takes Kadmus aside as Alex and Sarina return to his room. She says nothing, but he can feel a hot, pulsing anger pouring from her. The click-clack of her sandals on the floor reminds him of a hand repeatedly slapping a face. As soon as he closes the door she rounds on him, nostrils flaring and dark eyes sharp as flints.

"With all due respect, Prince, you have done me no favor."

He puts his hands on her upper arms. "Don't pay attention to what those people said in there. You have already served as my advisor—"

"Your *unofficial* advisor," she cuts in, fury surging thickly in her voice as she shakes off his hands. "Now I am a public laughingstock. Everyone will hate me. They might even try to kill me! How can I bear the shame of it?"

Alex takes her hand, and though she tries to pull away from his grip, he holds fast. "The shame of what, Sarina?" he asks softly.

Her mouth parts, but she says nothing. There is a heat between them so strong, it is a kind of invisible fire pit, radiating outwards, warming Alexander's skin.

"That you've chosen me because, because…" Her smooth dark cheeks refuse to blush, but she looks away. "Because you desire me."

Surprise stabs through him. *Does* he desire her? He cannot help but take in the stunning curves of her lithe body, the gloss of her hair, the intensity of her gaze, the feeling he gets around her. And yet…

"Sarina, listen to me," he continues. "You have helped me unofficially already. You have given me invaluable advice in dealing with treachery. That is why I trust you. Not," he says, pausing to check within himself, to confirm that this is in fact true, "for any other reason."

How can he make her understand? And Kadmus, too, for that matter. That Alex can love and yet not love, desire and yet not desire. That all of his decisions, and loyalties, are of the mind, not the body. That the body is but an imperfect vessel of the soul of a man: his ambition, his strength, his destiny.

"Prince Alexander!" a voice says.

Alex looks over her shoulder to see Kadmus himself in the open doorway, his hair unkempt and an open scroll in his hand.

"What news?" Alex asks calmly, masking the sense of foreboding creeping up the back of his neck.

Sarina turns abruptly and slides past Kadmus, leaving the room with her head bowed low.

"What news?" Alex prompts again, more loudly.

"Your father the king has fought a great battle at the walls of Byzantium and captured many men. But he has lost far more than he has gained. I fear—"

Alex bristles, holding up his hand. He knows already. His father's pride will never allow him to retreat, even though this war is draining the treasury and leaving Macedon defenseless against its enemies. How can Philip not see this? He finds his fists clenching.

"Fortunately," Kadmus says, "the king captured many men whose families could afford their ransom, and he is already using these funds to hire mercenaries. The men who were not ransomed were put to death—all except one."

Alex frowns. "What has this man done to spare him the fate of his brothers?"

"This Persian went into a building set on fire by our arrows and rescued those who dwelled there…even though the civilians were Greek. When he came out, our soldiers captured him. Philip wants to reward him with an honorable public death to show Macedonians the bravest of the Persians."

Alex shakes his head in amazement. What kind of Persian would risk his life to help Greeks?

"Where is this man?"

"He was taken to the palace jail," Kadmus says. "We're waiting for your orders."

"I wish to meet a soldier that so impressed my father. Take me to him."

The Persian sits patiently on fresh straw in a ground-floor cell of the palace jail—used for the occasional brawling soldier, misbehaving servant, and drunken palace employee. With a great clanking of chains, he rises as Alex and Kadmus enter, and continues to rise. He's half a head taller than Alex, with shoulder-length black curls and a face of almost feminine beauty, his eyes fringed with thick lashes. He has an aura of calm about him, despite being chained.

Kadmus pushes him to his knees. "Kneel before the prince regent," he says.

The prisoner bows his head and clasps his hands in respect.

"Rise," Alex says in Persian, and the man does so, rattling and clinking again.

"So, you rescued people from a burning building instead of retreating with your men," Alex continues. "Did you know the people you saved were Greeks?"

"Yes, lord," the prisoner says in rapid Persian. "That is the neighborhood of Greeks, near the western wall. All Greek people in Byzantium live there."

"But are Greeks not your enemy in this war of Byzantium?"

"Yes," he agrees. "But no one deserves to *burn* to death. These were mothers, fathers, children, all of them civilians." His face twists in pain so intense, it is as if Kadmus had kneed him in the groin. "Kings choose war, and we soldiers fight as is our duty. But civilians should not suffer as much as they do. Soldiers are strong, and it is our responsibility to protect those weaker than us, even the innocent enemy."

Alex stands thunderstruck. The man is right, of course. But what Greek king would ever consider such a shocking idea? Innocent enemies are routinely slaughtered, raped, robbed, or enslaved. Everyone shrugs it off as the price of losing a war. Alex suddenly wonders what it would be like if he, as king, granted clemency to innocent civilians, particularly from those kingdoms who surrender peacefully and make an alliance with Macedon. Wouldn't all the other countries in his path of conquest do the same rather than run the risk of war? It would be something like that children's game of standing roof tiles up in a long curving row and pushing over the first one; all the others behind topple neatly to the ground in turn.

He turns to Kadmus. "And this is the man Philip wants us to execute?" he asks, incredulous.

Kadmus nods. "The king recognized his courage and wants him to have an honorable death."

"There would be nothing honorable about executing this man," Alex snaps. He looks back at the prisoner. "As you have heard, my father wants me to execute you."

The man nods and raises sad eyes. "You must obey your father, lord."

"Do you not wish to live?" Alex asks impatiently.

The man shrugs. "I have no family. I did love a girl, but she is dead. When I die, I will swim the River of Ordeal and find her on the other side."

"Do you speak Greek?" Alex asks.

"Nai, oligon ti." Yes, a little bit. His lips wrap thickly around the Greek words.

Alex makes up his mind. He has already caused such an uproar this morning, what's one more bit of scandal? "Find your dead girl if you wish, but it won't be any time soon. Kadmus, unchain this man."

"Prince," Kadmus says urgently, "if we release him, he will go straight back to the Persian army and fight your father again at Byzantium."

Alex scowls. "As do those who are ransomed. This man

had no family to ransom him. What is the difference? A sack of coins?" He stares pointedly at Kadmus, who unlocks the prisoner's chains and removes them from his wrists. The man massages the sore spots where the iron chafed him raw and looks at Alex expectantly.

"What is your rank?" Alex asks in Greek.

"Captain, my lord."

Captain. A high rank given for bravery, skill, and intelligence.

"You obviously understand the Persian culture. Do you understand the Persian mind?"

The man sighs. "I know it, my lord, but I do not share it. The Persian mind has wheels set within wheels, secrets within secrets. Flowers and jewels conceal death. You Greeks are more..." He knits his brow, searching for the right Greek word. "Straight... Straight..."

"Straightforward," Alex says.

"Yes! That is the word," the soldier agrees.

"Then listen carefully, my straightforward friend." He stops in front of the prisoner and fixes his eyes on him. "I hear—" he glances briefly at Kadmus "—that there are powerful groups in Persia outside of the Great King, surreptitiously interfering with his policy. A guild of assassins. I need advice on how to deal with Persia—perhaps you can help me."

Kadmus is nearly spluttering with shock. He pulls Alex to the other side of the cell and says in a low voice, "Your highness, you cannot trust a Persian."

Alex smiles sadly. "You're talking to me about trust?" Kadmus lowers his eyes. "And," Alex adds, "this man has no family in Persia, no ties to be threatened in exchange for disloyalty. Still, we will keep an eye on him, keep him away from discussions of military planning."

Kadmus clutches Alex's arm. "You can't be thinking to make this man a council member?"

"No, not a full council member, yet. I am not as foolish as that." He studies the man, taking in his height and calm demeanor. "Let us call him our resident Persian expert."

"But—"

"That is all, Kadmus."

"Very well," Kadmus says, though he looks unhappy about it. "Though your father—"

"—will find out that in his absence I am doing things my own way. If he wants things done *his* way, he should stop making a fool of himself in Byzantium and come home to rule his kingdom. Now, get this man a bath, a room, a meal, and a tunic."

He turns to the prisoner. "Your name?"

"Cosmas, son of Borzin."

Alexander nods. "Welcome, Cosmas, to Pella."

He leaves the dank air of the prison behind, pleased with himself. His new council is composed of individuals with wildly different backgrounds, cultures, and experiences. He will have many viewpoints, strategies, and perspectives to choose from, helping him rule with wisdom and insight. The gods would approve, he imagines.

And so, too, he thinks with a smile, will his old teacher, Aristotle.

In the wide marble hall, a series of slave girls carrying buckets of steaming water pass him by, heading toward the queen's apartments. So, she's back again.

And now that his work restoring the council is done, there can be no further delay.

He must have the truth.

The guards outside his mother's room lower their spears

in salute as he pushes open the door to her chamber. She is setting items in a basket on her worktable, probably preparing for a bath, given the steaming water. Her favorite snake is wrapped around her neck, a living, writhing shawl of shimmering green coils with a pattern of gold. A small black snake is coiled around her upper arm like a bracelet, and several others peer curiously into the basket.

She looks up startled, and then her face softens. "Oh, Alexander, you should really knock, you know. I've just been called to my bath." Her diaphanous violet robes give off a delicate fragrance, he notices.

His gaze falls on the items in the basket. A silver bowl, a strange red flower, a knife, a small leather pouch, and what looks like a handkerchief with dried blood on it.

"In your absence, dear, I sent Cynane off to get married," she says as if that's some sort of explanation for the strange items. She strokes the large snake around her neck, "She will wed King Amyntas of Dardania."

Cynane, a wife. Alex has a hard time wrapping his mind around the idea and wonders how his mother got his sister to agree. And isn't there something wrong with King Amyntas? Isn't he a half-wit or something? "You should have waited for me to return before bundling her off," he says.

"Your father approved of the match," she says airily.

"My *father*?" he asks softly. The word feels like flint on his tongue. His heart hammers in his chest. Now is the time. He must have answers.

"Yes, your fa—"

"Mother, I know."

The air hangs heavily between them.

She stares at him.

And then suddenly, she laughs. It's a silvery, tinkling sound that conceals more than it conveys. "Know what, my darling? That he's as glad as I am that your ill-tempered sister is gone?"

"I. Know." The words dangle in the air like a pair of knives. "You've been keeping a secret from me my entire life."

Olympias places her hands on the basket, but remains silent.

"I'm not Philip's son, am I?"

The queen's face is impassive, as quiet as a lake on a windless day. And—try though he might—he cannot see beneath her surface. The green snake lifts its large head and stares at Alex with inscrutable eyes, and he has the strangest sense that the snake is blocking him from seeing into his mother's memories.

"There are many kings in the world, Alexander," she says quietly, stroking the snake again. "It is not so unusual to have a king for a father. Even my pathetic father was a king."

What is she trying to say?

"But you, my heart's treasure, flesh of my flesh—*your* father has far greater power than you could ever imagine. Soon my love, soon."

Alexander is entranced, mesmerized by her words as she steps out the door in a whisper of robes, and he is left behind, alone in her bedroom.

But even though he is alone, his mother's words still echo in his head.

Your father has far greater power than you could ever imagine.

CHAPTER TWENTY-EIGHT

ROXANA CLAPS HER CHUBBY LITTLE HANDS and cries, "Pegasus! Pegasus! Give me a ride and fly away with me!"

Laughing, Zo bends over and her sister climbs onto her back, throws her arms around her neck, and kicks her gently in the waist. Zo gallops down the long, cool blue corridors, waving her arms as if they were wings as Roxana squeals in delight. Through the open windows, the scent of roses wafts in, clinging to sunbeams. Neighing loudly, Zo turns the corner to see a plump eunuch carrying a silver tray piled high with fresh bread, a crock of golden butter, and roast lamb with parsley, and Zo wants to stop to eat. She's starving, but Roxana is on her back, and that is more important. Food will be there later, but Roxana... There's something troubling Zo about Roxana.

"Pegasus knows its way by the stars!" her sister cries, and Zo joins in. "Pegasus knows the way of fate! Pegasus is never lost!"

The scene shifts, and Zo finds herself in her uncle's throne room, looking around in desperation for Roxana. A tall, hooded figure glides toward her down the dais, and she is terrified that King Shershah will punish her, because she has done something horrible, though she can't remember exactly what it was.

When the figure throws back the hood, she sees it is Cosmas, and his dark eyes are sad, disappointed. "Love is duty," he says, shaking his head. "You have failed your duty in so many ways. Better if you had died as I believed, instead of running away like a fool."

Maybe she is a fool, she wants to say, but love certainly isn't *duty*. How can anyone believe that? How could she ever have loved him? She looks at him standing there, slouched in front of the throne. He has no spirit. No fire. He's just a good-looking, sweet guy with shoulders too wide for his body and impossibly long eyelashes that fluttered their way right into her heart. How stupid was it to love a man for his eyelashes?

Another figure approaches, a little shorter but broader, gait swaggering. He rips the cloak off impatiently and throws it to the ground. Ochus, his golden eyes gleaming fiercely in the torchlight, wearing the skin of the lion he killed with his bare hands when she tried to escape.

"He's the fool," Ochus says, smirking at Cosmas. "Love is passion, the spark between a man and a woman that drives them both mad with desire."

She remembers the feel of Ochus's mouth, moist and hungry, against hers. And then her thoughts drift to the fact that he had been sent to murder her by the Assassins, the secret group operating outside even the power of the Great King Artaxerxes. Ochus recognized the X marks over the hearts of the girls in the *harmanaxa*. He knew his brothers had fulfilled their assignment to murder Alexander's new brides, and were probably fanning out searching for him and Zo.

Perhaps the Assassins were hot on their heels when he abandoned her. To save her. Or to let her die out in the wilderness, for all he knows. How can she love him now?

Licking her dry, parched lips, she wants something to drink more than anything in the world. Cosmas, staring at her with all his sincerity and seriousness, reminds her of a cup of water: pure and refreshing...but for the first time she wonders if she would have eventually become bored by him. Ochus, on the other hand, arms crossed and eyeing her intently, is a cup of fire mead, dangerous and fierce and exciting.

Yes, Zo agrees. Ochus is right, not Cosmas. And it is Ochus she wants now. She goes toward him, arms outstretched. He grabs her wrists, twists her around, and cries, "Guards! Lock her up for lying."

Faceless soldiers tromp into the throne room and drag her away. She's so hungry. Why didn't she eat that lamb? Where is Roxana? She trips and her head slams down on the marble tiles. No, not marble. Dirt. A dirt floor. Wearily, she sits up and rubs her eyes. Light streaming in through the holes in the roof is the color of tarnished silver and falls on split wooden logs piled high against one wall. Is it dusk? Or just before dawn?

Now she remembers. She's in a firewood hut. She found it by the light of the moon last night outside the wooden palisade of a hillside village and curled up in it. Now, with the sun coming up, the gates will be open, the villagers heading out to their fields and orchards.

Somehow she has survived the past... How many days has it been since Ochus abandoned her? Eight? Ten? She never found the road he told her about, but he was right about finding pools of water near clumps of trees. One day she found a clutch of bird eggs in a nest and devoured them raw. And then, a few days ago, she had the amazing good luck to stumble upon a hunter's tent with skins full of olives and dried meat, though the hunter was nowhere to be found.

Now those provisions are gone, and her goatskin is empty. Her throat feels as if she has eaten dust. She stretches. Despite her deep sleep, every bone in her body throbs with fatigue. But for the first time since Ochus left, she feels hope bubbling up in her chest, boisterous and irrepressible. The gold jewelry in her pack will buy food and drink, a place to rest, and probably a horse to find the Spirit Eaters and the Hunor village to change her fate.

Her body is frustratingly slow at following her command to walk. She trips over a rock in the gray light and stumbles, nearly falling. Outside the palisade are a few nicely tended olive and fig trees. She's tempted to search the branches for fruit, but wonders if she could even swallow it without water. No, there's something better just moments away. Water, fortified with wine. Fresh milk. Bread. Meat. Herbed cheese. She's almost there. She just has to put one foot in front of the other, climbing the rocky path up the steep hill.

Now that she's close, she realizes it's less of a village and more a collection of thatched huts behind a wooden wall. But right now she finds the huts more beautiful than the gleaming palace of Sardis.

As she suspected, someone has unbarred the wooden gate with the advent of morning. She swings it open and enters the settlement. There's an empty paddock to her left—have the villagers already taken the horses and oxen out to the fields? Just a short way down the dirt path between huts—thanks be to Anahita and all the gods—is a well. She races toward it and with trembling arms cranks up a bucket of sloshing water, which she places on the stone rim. Just as she's about to cup her hands in it, she realizes there's something wrong with the water. It doesn't look clean. There are bits of…something floating in it, like little pieces of raw meat. It smells bad. As thirsty as she is, she backs away from it.

It's only then that she notices the stillness of the village. In Sardis early in the morning, wells are crowded with women gathering water to brew tea and boil eggs, to wash in and rinse out night pots. Jugs balanced elegantly on their heads, the women go home satisfied with new gossip and off-color jokes.

But at this well, on this morning, there are no women. Zo narrows her eyes and looks toward the roofs. There is no friendly furl of smoke signaling baking bread and simmering stew. Unease prickles her scalp. Perhaps some wild animal has chased the villagers—and their animals—away.

She remembers the rumors she and Ochus kept hearing along the Royal Road, of entire villages vanishing. Of horses disappearing and bones left behind.

She pulls Ochus's knife out of the sheath on her belt and stands perfectly still, not even breathing, listening for a growl, a roar. There's nothing but the soft sigh of the wind across the plains and, it seems, the buzzing of flies. She walks to the closest cottage and sees that the door is lying on the dirt floor, deep scratch marks gouged in its surface. A wooden bar, which the inhabitants evidently slid into place to keep the door secure, lies broken in half beside the door.

She doesn't want to go inside, but her situation is desperate. Pausing a moment to offer a prayer to Mithras, she steps past the threshold and looks around. In the early light, everything is painted with shades of gray and black. There's a fire pit in the center of the cottage with rolled-up sleeping mats around it. She sees a bread oven in the corner, a table and benches on the side. Her heart leaps. There's food on the table. Whatever happened, the villagers were not expecting it.

One hand still grasping the knife, she picks up the circular loaf of bread and bites into it, almost cracking a tooth. Hard as a rock—but not moldy, which must mean the attack happened not more than a couple of days ago. Four cups are tipped over and flies rub their legs in the dark splotches on the dirt floor. The wine amphora is cracked and drained, the water buckets tipped over. There is nothing to drink here. She grabs a handful of olives from a bowl and pushes them into her mouth but they stick in her dry throat. She wraps the rest in a napkin and stashes them in her pack for later.

Though she sees no danger, she knows she needs to get out of here as soon as she can. Two knives glint a dull silver on the table. She picks them up and tucks them into her belt. On her way out the door she grabs a little ox-horn lantern. That might come in handy.

Silently, she enters the cottage next door. Its door hangs off the hinges like a grimace, and on the ground, there are long, dark streaks. In the full light of day, they would almost certainly be red. It's almost as if someone horribly wounded had been dragged through the broken furniture and dragged outside...

Run! The thought hammers at her mind. *Run, now!*

She steps back into the dirt path between the cottages, almost falling in her haste to leave the abandoned village. As fast as she tries to run, it feels as if lead ingots have been tied to her legs, which are weak and awkward. She trips over something and tumbles into the dirt. Pushing herself up, she looks back and sees the pale shiny bone of a human skull minus its lower jaw, teeth marks over its shiny surface as if something has chewed on it.

She scrambles up and runs wildly. But this isn't the way

she came in. Is there another gate? Or is she trapped inside the village with the wild animals that did this? Looking over her shoulder, she races ahead until she realizes something is blocking her path, a huge heap of...stones. No, not stones.

Bones. Long leg bones. Rib cages. Skulls—not just of humans, but horses and oxen. A scattering of vertebrae like white coral sea creatures. Flies buzz and hover and land on the bones, hoping for a meal, but almost all of the skin, the flesh, and muscle have been sucked clean.

And the bones—every one of them that Zo can see— have deep teeth marks gouged on them. Someone—some *thing*—has devoured this entire village and sucked the marrow out of the bones.

Heart hammering, she races around the pile, past a forge, its furnace cold and dead, and flings herself out a little gate. The sun is rising now over the distant hills, the light strengthening.

She runs across a dry, rocky expanse, no idea which way she's heading, no sense of how far she may be from the nearest road. She could swear she has reached the end of the world. Maybe she has. But she keeps running, knowing that if she stops, she might never move again. She might collapse forever. Her lungs are aching, her throat filled with dust. She knows she must stop at some point, must find water, but where? Nowhere seems safe. And so she runs, until, in the haze of dry heat before her, she suddenly sees that the ground seems to stop.

She slows down, coming to the edge of a steep hill. A short way behind her, towering white cliffs rise heavenward.

The view of the canyon below takes her breath away. At her feet are rocks of every shape and size, fallen from the cliffs. But farther away, shades of yellow grass mix with gray-purple underbrush, bone-white dirt and gnarled, stunted black trees. More untamed land, on and on and on as far as the eye can see. Down there, toward her right, is a clump of trees. Water. She will get water first, then run as fast as possible from whatever evil has devoured this village.

She finds what looks like a path and slowly makes her way down, clinging to rocks and twisted bushes. Loose earth crumbles beneath her feet, and she slips onto her back with a shock. Yet perhaps it's a good idea to stay low to the ground. She slides down the rest of the way on her rear end. At the hill's rocky base, as she stands up and dusts off her tunic, she smells something. Dampness. Water. And then she sees the opening of a cave. There's water inside the cave.

Quickly rifling through her pack, she strikes her iron on flint and sparks the oil lamp inside the ox-horn lantern into flame. Checking the knives in her belt, she walks inside the cave, holding the lantern high. It's cooler in here, the air refreshingly moist on her sweaty skin…but she has to find water. She still feels like she's about to faint. She puts her hand on the cave wall for support and gasps.

Underneath her palm, she feels dampness. She holds up the lantern and sees that the wall in front of her shimmers with wetness.

Barely able to control herself, Zo sets down the lantern. Long shadows dance around her as she leans her entire body against the wall. It takes a few moments for the dampness to soak into her clothes, like lying on dewy grass on a summer's morning. The wetness wraps around her tired, fevered body.

A sound comes from the far end of the cave. She snatches up the lantern and holds it high, but the area is cloaked in blackness so intense the dim light cannot begin to penetrate it. She is not sure what kind of sound she heard. There is something like an animal movement, a turning, a digging of claws into earth. And then…whispers.

What animals whisper? None. She is imagining things. She is so thirsty.

Carefully, she turns back toward the sparkling wall, leans forward and gingerly places her lips against it, like a first kiss. The taste of earth and stone fills her mouth, but she doesn't focus on it. She focuses on the tiniest droplet of water that has fallen onto her tongue.

There is a blast of pure, refreshing cold, like opening a door in a gusting blizzard. It tastes like water from a virgin mountain stream tumbling wildly over crystal. It tastes the way music sounds when it grabs your heart so violently it makes your eyes sting with the beauty of life and love and loss. It tastes the way roses smell and true love feels. It tastes of things much bigger than human life, of ancient gods and brightly burning stars and endless oceans deep with secrets, of fate and death, courage and joy.

It is too much. She stands back from the wall, stunned. Is she ill? Dreaming? How could one drop of water be all those things?

Oddly, her burning thirst is gone. So is her hunger, along with her exhaustion. She feels as strong as she ever did after a good hot dinner and a long winter night's sleep in the palace, wrapped in blankets of soft Milesian wool lined with fox fur. But how can that be?

There's that sound again. She stops her breathing and strains to hear. Whispers. Or the scuttling of an animal. The rustling of snakes through a nest of leaves. The fluttering of wings. She is not sure. She swings the lantern in a wide arc around her and sees nothing except for a few drawings painted on the opposite cave wall. Drawings of men in horns pointing spears at what looks like the opening of a cave... and within the cave are eyes.

She moves the lantern, and as the light slides over to another section of wall, her heart thumps wildly in her chest. Long gashes—like claw marks—are gouged deeply into the rock.

A scratching sound comes from the back of the cave. Someone—no, more than one—is whispering in a language she cannot understand, a language of clicks and shushes. Claws drag across rock. She hears a crack, a footstep. Someone has stepped on a stick or…a bone. Someone is coming toward her out of the darkness ahead…

An animal scream breaks through the scraping sounds. Zo drops her lamp. It rolls onto the floor, and the flame shudders once, then dies.

Zo turns her face toward the bright light of the entrance and begins to stumble toward it. She lurches out of the cave.

As she scrambles across the rocky ground, ripping her nails and banging her knees, she hears something like whimpering, a small, plaintive cry. She freezes. It sounds like a child, like Roxana the time she tried to climb up the statue of Mithras and fell, hitting her head badly.

She looks right and left, up and down. Where is it coming from? Just then a ray from the rising sun pierces a cloud and falls like a heavenly spear on the ground, illuminating a tiny white horse head with dewy brown eyes, its body engulfed in fallen rocks. Sticking up from the rocks are feathers, veined and golden-pink in the dawn light.

No, it can't be. This, too, must be a dream, a hallucination, just like playing in the palace halls with Roxana and being in the throne room with Cosmas and Ochus. This image will vanish any moment. She has been through so much, this can't be…

But it is. The legend is real. She picks her way over jagged rocks and kneels beside the creature, touching the warm blood seeping out beneath the stones.

She puts a hand on the creature's head. "Hush, now," she whispers, and the pale eyelashes flutter. "I will help you. All will be well." Sheathing her knife, she starts pulling rocks off the animal, but some are too heavy to lift. She has to tip them up and wiggle them from side to side. Somehow freeing the colt calms her, gives her a sense of purpose, something to concentrate on other than her wild-eyed fear. She is going to free this little horse if it's the last…

The tiny horse shudders and sighs gently. Zo gasps. *No.* It can't. She can't let it. She can't let another thing die. Horror and sadness threaten to choke her. She is going to die out here, too. Just like Roxana. Her little, helpless sister. Just like this creature, this beautiful mythic creature. Real. She has found a Pegasus. A baby Pegasus. She has found one and it has died, and with it, the very last grains of hope Zo had been clutching, deep inside her heart. The hope keeping her alive—for herself. For her baby.

A huge shadow falls over her and the body of the colt. Zo tenses, feeling as though her bones have been locked together. Some distance behind her, something huge hits the earth with the impact of a catapult missile, and the pebbles and loose stones are thrown into the air like a reverse rainstorm and clatter down on Zo. Even though the colt is already dead, she hunches herself over it, protecting it from the worst of the rocks.

She does not want to turn around. If she's to die, here, now, she'd rather her last sight be the gentle, sweet face of the Pegasus, and not the gnashing of teeth and claws.

No, Zofia. The voice seems to come from somewhere far off, and it takes Zo a moment to realize it is not a voice at all, but her own mind.

She, Zo, knows what to do for the first time. She is not Attoosheh. She will not meekly accept a revolting fate like her mother did without lifting a finger in protest. She has come all this way. She has lost everything.

She has nothing else to lose.

She turns around.

The sun hits her in the eyes and she's forced to squint. A tall shape stands in relief against the molten light. And then the figure shifts a large, feathered wing, and she can see what it is: a white mare twice the size of any stallion in the Sardis stables, feathered wings sweeping out from her withers.

A Pegasus.

For a long moment, Zo stares at this promise of impossible things. A feeling that could be awe, or hope, or fear—or all three—rises in her chest.

The mare rears, and her neck curves like a crescent moon as she bares her teeth and screams to the rocky cliff, her large lips trembling with the force of it. The piercing sound echoes all around, and Zo feels the mother's cry reverberate in the chambers of her own heart. The front hooves hit the earth with the sound of thunder, and the ground beneath them trembles.

Then suddenly, the mare charges. The Pegasus is the powerful white roar of a waterfall or the violence unleashed by a snowy avalanche—dangerous and without thought. Zo realizes a second before the mare reaches her that the beast will not stop.

She hurls herself to the side, just missing the enraged mare's gem-hard hooves. The sharp rocks bite into her side as she rolls to a stop, and her arms feel hot where the ground scraped her.

Pushing herself up into a sitting position, Zo looks toward the Pegasus and sees the mother standing protectively over the body of her lifeless colt. The creature's large ribs heave and a sheen of sweat covers its marbled flanks. Her nose brushes over the colt's bristly fur, and a low nicker comes from somewhere deep within the beast—a sound as soft as rainfall and as sad as the closing door of a tomb.

An ache travels through Zo and she instinctively places a hand to her womb. A mother—be she human or horse or myth—is never meant to outlive her child. There's a flutter in her stomach, as if in response to her thought. Zo wonders if she will live long enough to meet her child.

Using a nearby rock to steady herself, she slowly gets to her feet. The movement startles the mare, and the Pegasus pulls back her top lip, baring her teeth again with a little warning grunt.

Zo stops. "I'm sorry," she murmurs, keeping her voice even. "I'm so sorry, my beauty." The taste of salt and earth fills her mouth, and she realizes that she is crying—her tears mingling with the dust on her cheeks. Loss is all around her on this eternal journey of the damned. It marked the beginning of her journey with her sister's murder, stalked her through the desert with the loss of Ochus's companions, and stays with her now, waiting to claim her within these mountains.

Zo puts her face in her hands, trying to block the image of her little sister. Roxana had been so proud when her front teeth fell out and two overly large adult teeth started pushing through her gums. A sob slides out of her mouth, and she lets the grief come. Roxana dancing around the room, holding her doll's hand. Roxana fresh from her music lesson sourly twanging the strings of her lyre, her small pointed face lighting up with delight. Roxana snuggling into Zo's bed at night, the sweet baby scent of her neck calming Zo to sleep.

A wind pushes against Zo's ear. Though it's warm, her wet cheeks feel cold. Her hands drop, and she's looking straight into the liquid eyes of the mare. She's so close that she can see the great feathers are not just white, but muted shades of gray and cream and the faintest blush of pink. A reflection of all the shades of the mountain.

Zo doesn't move—she doesn't want to startle the Pegasus and cause her to attack, but she's also mesmerized by the fierce beauty of the beast. She holds her breath, waiting for the creature to make the next move.

The mare slowly drops onto her front knees, the wings unfurled like sails. The feathers rustle together, a sound like a secret whispered between the moon and stars.

Roxana's voice floats to her from her memory. *Pegasus knows the way of fate. Pegasus is never lost.*

With a calm she does not feel, Zo reaches out a tentative hand and places it on the mare's neck. It's soft, like a newly shorn sheep. When the Pegasus stays still, Zo makes up her mind. Grabbing onto the thick woolly mane, she swings herself over the mare's back, just behind the winged shoulder blades.

Keeping one arm around its neck, she entwines the other in its mane. She leans forward to feel its solid body beneath hers, bringing her a sense of comfort and safety for the first time in many weeks. At that moment, sunlight streams through a break in the clouds, warming Zo's face. Out of the corner of her eye, she sees something flicker a bright orange-red. She turns. The cliffs above her look as if they are on fire. The Flaming Cliffs.

The creature lurches to her feet, and Zo leaves her heart and stomach on the ground as the Pegasus gallops across the rocky plain—and takes flight into the red eye of the rising sun.

CHAPTER TWENTY-NINE

OLYMPIAS CLIMBS UP THE LADDER INTO HER bedroom naked, dried blood all over her arms and torso. In one hand she clutches an enormous snakeskin, like a crisp, honeycombed netting, its papery mouth yawning wide open.

She crawls onto the floor, gasping and woozy from the venom. The bars of bright light coming through the slats of her shutters hurt her eyes.

Memories of the ritual she performed just hours ago swirl through her mind: the bone of the honey-glazed fingertip. The blood from the handkerchief she'd used to tend to Alexander's wound during the Aesarians' sword-fighting demonstration last month. The entire spell made more powerful by the cultic ceremonies she performed in that ancient heart of darkness, the Labyrinth of Knossos.

This wasn't the first time she tried the Blood and Bones ritual. Last time, though, she'd used the bones she thought belonged to the newborn Katerina. When Olympias finally tracked down her handmaiden Helen ten years ago, Helen had handed the queen the tiny bones in a box, swearing she had done the deed. *Liar.* Ten years the queen had kept them, cherished them, stroked them, as she waited for the great lunar eclipse to usher in a new Age when the ritual would finally work.

On that night of bloody sacrifices and orgiastic dancing, of drums and screams and chants as the sky swallowed the moon, Olympias performed the ritual and... Nothing happened. And when her snake bit her, the purple blood against the ivory skin inside her arm had formed the words *She's still alive*. That was how the queen learned that her daughter must still be alive.

But this time it was different. The snake had hungrily devoured her own fresh blood mingled with the blood of her son and the bone of her daughter. Then it raised its head, its eyes dilated, before sinking its fangs into her. She remembers the hidden chamber below her bedroom tilting sideways as she fell to the floor. The last thing she saw before blackness took her was a pair of glowing emerald eyes.

As soon as she came to, she thrust her arm next to the last sputtering lamp and saw a very different message. *I am free.*

Free! But what kind of free? Free of her?

Find him. She must find him. She struggles to her feet and throws on a long-sleeved robe. Staggering a bit, she opens the door and nearly collides with the guard.

"Your majesty," the man says, surprised, "are you all right? Should I call your ladies?"

"Nooot necesssssary," she says, her lips not quite working right. The guard tilts his head slightly, as though he is trying to figure out a riddle. She realizes he must think she's drunk, and the thought makes her laugh loudly as she adjusts the snakeskin tightly around her shoulders and makes her way down the hall.

Where has he gone? Panic grips her heart and begins to squeeze it.

She pauses before a fresco in the long hallway: Zeus, disguised as a huge white swan, beating forceful white wings as he ravishes the beautiful Queen Leda of Sparta. Olympias stops and stares at the painting as if she is seeing it for the first time. The father of all the gods got Leda pregnant with twins—one of them Helen of Troy—and dumped her, the way gods always dump their mortal women, even though Leda was still radiantly beautiful. Which Olympias is not. Not after what Bastian did to her. Not without her heavy cosmetics and wigs. Tears slide down her face, and she wonders if her makeup is running down her cheeks with them.

"What is wrong?" She hears Alexander's voice and feels a hand warm on her shoulder. A silent sob racks Olympias's body. She doesn't want Alexander to see her like this. No matter what, even if she is abandoned and ugly, he is her son, and through him she can remain relevant and powerful—but not if he sees her like this.

Olympias lurches away from the hand. "Leave me, Alexander," she says carefully, though the words sound thick and slow. "I am not feeling quite myself this morning. I…I didn't sleep well." Her fingers begin to nervously stroke the snake's skin hanging around her neck. It rustles slightly, like a dead leaf falling.

Suddenly, Alex's hand is on her again, trying to turn her around to face him. "Come with me."

"What do you want?" Olympias snaps, her eyes still stinging with salty tears, her mind still clouded with snake venom from the ritual.

"You, Myrtale."

Her heart skips a beat, then, and begins to thud rapidly. *Myrtale.* Her soul name. No one calls her that, except for…

Slowly she turns and looks up into Alexander's face.

The hallway swims around her.

She stares dumbstruck at her son's eyes.

They have *changed*.

Alexander no longer has one sky-blue and one dark brown eye. He has two emerald-green eyes. Eyes she knows well.

The prince before Olympias smiles slowly, and she feels an irresistible power drawing her in and a fiery heat that Alex never had.

"Myrtale, my queen," the young man says. "What has kept you?"

And then Olympias knows. She knows with the certainty of rock's hardness, the way water only ever flows toward the sea, that it has finally happened.

The man before her is *not* her son. Not at all.

Riel the Snake, the last of the last gods, has returned.

★ ★ ★ ★ ★

ACKNOWLEDGMENTS

MOST WRITERS—MYSELF INCLUDED—ARE FOR the most part solitary souls, hammering away at their craft in silence all hours of the day and night. But one of the real pleasures I have had as an author is working with such an incredible team of talented, fun, and supportive people, without whose expertise I would not be writing the Blood of Gods and Royals series.

At PaperLantern Lit, co-founders Lauren Oliver and Lexa Hillyer and editor Kamilla Benko will have my eternal gratitude for believing in me and teaching me so much. Seriously, if any of you ever needs a babysitter on New Year's Eve, someone to clean up after a violently sick pet, or money to bail you out of jail, just call me. Thanks also to Tara Sonin, marketing manager extraordinaire and a true Aristotle of social media, who taught this old dog the new tricks of facetweetogramming.

I am grateful to my agent Stephen Barbara of Inkwell Management for all his hard work selling and supporting the

Blood of Gods and Royals series, and to Jess Regal of the Foundry Literary Agency for all those exciting foreign sales.

At United Talent, thanks to Jason Richman and Howard Sanders for selling the Blood of Gods and Royals series to the WB Network. Let's keep our fingers crossed that hellions and Pegasi will be flying into millions of American homes via their TVs soon!

At Harlequin Teen, I want to express my gratitude for the warm support of my editor Natashya Wilson, especially for all her *Oohs!, Aahs!,* and *No, she didn't!s* in the margins of Track Changes. A heartfelt thanks to Natashya's editorial assistant, Lauren Smulski, to marketing manager Bryn Collier, and to my fabulous publicists Siena Koncsol and Shara Alexander.

AUTHOR'S NOTE

ALL WRITERS ARE, IN A SENSE, WEAVERS, threading words and ideas into a story. Authors of historical fiction work on a special loom, where the weft is history and the warp fiction. We must shuttle fictional action and character development around facts, tightening the threads and creating engaging patterns.

Alexander the Great's life, however, was so extraordinary that even the facts read like fiction. As *Empire of Dust* starts to explore the burning question of whether Alexander the Great's real father was a god, the reader might wonder if I made this up. I swear I didn't. In his youth, legends swirled around the prince of Macedon that he was not the son of King Philip but sprung from divine stock. According to ancient writings, on the eve of the consummation of her marriage to Philip, Alexander's mother, Olympias, dreamed that her womb was struck by a lightning bolt, causing a flame that spread "far and wide" before dying away. Many believed that the lightning bolt, symbol of Zeus, indicates that the king of the gods was Alexander's true father.

Some ancient commentators reported that Olympias told Alexander of his celestial parentage, instilling him with the belief of his own grand destiny—which, perhaps, turned out to be a self-fulfilling prophecy. Later, when King Alexander of Macedon visited a sacred shrine in Egypt, the oracle confirmed that his father was indeed a god. The rest of his life, Alexander either believed it, or pretended he did, as it was the best PR a young warrior king could get at the time.

Regardless of the nature of Alexander's genetic relationship to King Philip, the prince was greatly influenced by him. Alexander went with him on campaign and watched him ignore serious wounds as he flattened the enemy. The prince of Macedon grew up not just wanting to emulate Philip's battle tactics, but to outdo him wherever possible, hoping his divine blood would give him that needed extra boost.

It's not easy bringing to life one of the most influential people of all time as a teenager. Luckily for me, many ancient historians have written about Alexander, dropping plenty of important clues about his character. Plutarch wrote that Alexander's ambition "kept his spirit serious and lofty in advance of his years," a quality I have tried to endow him with in this series.

It seems that Alexander's intellectual abilities took precedence over his physical desires. While Alexander had an extremely close relationship with Hephaestion, there are no stories of the prince pursuing girls or boys the way most young men of his age and class did at the time. He had great self-restraint in "pleasures of the body," according to the ancient historian Arrian, and little interest in marrying and siring heirs. Many princes were married early—at sixteen or seventeen—because illness and battle culled them young, and when they died they needed to have heirs of their own old enough to wield a sword. But Alexander didn't take his first wife until he was twenty-nine.

According to ancient writers, Alexander could be stubborn at times and heartily disliked his father ordering him around (what sixteen-year-old does not?). Yet he was always open to reason. Though he could have brief outbursts of temper, usually he was calm, insightful, and shrewd. He loved reading, philosophy, science, and foreign cultures.

Alexander's interests must have been shaped by the man who taught him from the age of thirteen to sixteen, another of the most influential people in world history, the philosopher-scientist Aristotle. I greatly enjoyed bringing Alexander's teacher to life, if only for one chapter. If all brilliant people tend to be a bit eccentric, Aristotle, one of the most brilliant ever to walk the earth, must have been shockingly so.

Aristotle not only studied almost every subject possible at the time, but made significant contributions to most of them. He was, in some ways, the world's first great scientist, exploring, experimenting, teaching and writing about zoology, anatomy, embryology, physics, geography, meteorology, geology, astronomy, and botany. He was the first known writer to notice changing landscapes—dried-up lakes, shifting rivers, tectonic upheavals—and came to the shocking conclusion that the earth doesn't stay unchanging forever but, in fact, is always changing, something the ancients hadn't considered. In his spare time, he wrote about ethics, economics, logic, political science, foreign cultures, education, literature, and poetry.

I hope that I have captured the timeless mystery of Egypt in Kat and Heph's journey down the Nile. Egyptian civilization was already thousands of years old when the Greek city states emerged. A land of ancient traditions and unimaginable wealth, Egypt was a multicultural economic powerhouse. Its harsh deserts were home to gold, amethysts, emeralds, iron ore, and many other valuable minerals. The rich black earth left behind by the annual Nile flood made it the breadbasket of the ancient world, the place all other nations flocked to for grain when their own harvests failed.

Empires and dynasties rose and fell; Assyrians, Persians, and Nubians—and later Greeks and Romans—conquered Egypt and were driven out—but the Nile never seemed to notice, and the animal-headed gods still ruled serenely over the land of hot sand, abundant crops, and roiling flood waters. Because of its antiquity, young men from all over the known world traveled to Egypt to complete their education at the hands of its priests, considered the wisest men alive. In Kat and Heph's Egypt chapters, I wanted to make sure the reader knows they aren't in Kansas anymore—or Macedon—but in a vastly different place where most of what they know has little or no relevance.

I enjoyed digging a bit more deeply into the coldly glittering Persian Empire in the characters of the Great King Artaxerxes and his nephew, Darius. At its height, the empire comprised some three million square miles, from the Aegean Sea—uncomfortably jostling elbows with Greece—to the borders of India. But Persia was more than military might. It needed an extensive government bureaucracy to administer all those kingdoms. It was also the center of a rich and thriving culture boasting sophisticated poetry, music, art, and architecture.

Unfortunately, very few Persian records of this time have come down to us, though we do know that Artaxerxes, aged eighty-five in *Empire of Dust*, was a wily, still youthful ruler who murdered eighty of his brothers in a single day to win the throne, personally strangling infants in their cribs.

In Alexander's Greece, the word *Persian* was synonymous with poison, double-dealing, and effeminate luxury while Persians themselves thought Greeks were dirty, smelly, ignorant, and barbarous.

Every novel on Alexander the Great must include a breathtaking battle scene. In Alexander's attack on the Aesarian fortress of Pyrrhia, I have taken several tactics from ancient military history. I was inspired to have Alexander burn smoke-belching green wood to hide his men from Aesarian archers by stories I read about the Theban general Epanimondas, who died in 362 BC. He was famous for obscuring his army's maneuvers by burning green wood on top of dry, causing an enormous haze.

Siege warfare—an army attacking a walled city—often involved digging tunnels under the walls for the invaders to enter. As a city's defenders did everything in their power to stop a subterranean assault, many pitched battles were fought in dark tunnels. I was excited to write a tunnel battle and researched many that took place in the ancient world.

I modeled Alexander's burning of feathers on tactics used in 190 BC by the Greek city of Ambracia. Fending off the Roman army which had dug tunnels beneath their walls, the Ambracians brought portable ovens into the shafts where they burned feathers—apparently the world's most noxious stench!—and used bellows to pump the fumes toward the invaders who turned tail and fled. Nor did I make up the part about bees being drafted into the army. Mithridates VI (134–63 BC), King of Pontus (northern Turkey these days), lobbed hives of furious bees at attacking Romans in tunnels.

As an author of historical fiction, I always remind myself that human nature never changes, only the props do. The people of Alexander's time wore different clothing than we do, lived in different houses, and rode horses instead of driving cars. But every individual in this beautiful, frightening, and tumultuous world of ours—past, present, and future—experiences hope and worry, love and despair. Every one of us expresses anger and jealousy, courage, self-doubt and self-sacrifice. Every one of us climbs out of bed in the morning wondering what the day will bring and hoping it will be good. This is the most enduring and most magnificent thread in literary weavings both old and new—the indestructible bond of our collective humanity.

QUESTIONS
FOR
DISCUSSION

1. Prophecy was important to the ancient Greeks and to their mythology and literature. In *Empire of Dust*, Heph thinks, "The power of prophecies is not always in what they say, but in the fact that people go to such extremes to either avoid or fulfill them. Prophecies, real or false, are incredibly dangerous." Do you think he is wise to hide this prophecy from Kat and Alex? How might believing in a prophecy make it self-fulfilling? Discuss how the characters might act if they knew about the prophecy.

2. When Jacob realizes that he is an Earth Blood and is the source of the magic that causes the Hemlock Torch to explode, he decides to hide his true nature and make himself invaluable to the Lords. Would it be better for him to embrace his true nature even if it meant being an outcast and possibly hunted by the most powerful warriors in the known world? Or is it better to hide who and what he is to fit in? Why? Discuss in both the

context of the world in the book and if Jacob were in a similar situation today.

3. Olympias ages significantly during the time frame of *Empire of Dust*. Is what happens to her fair? What different choices might she have made, and what might have been the result? Give your group extra credit if your discussion examines her character development from the ebook novella *Voice of Gods*, through *Legacy of Kings*, to *Empire of Dust*. Compare and contrast Olympias's situation with that of Princess Laila. Consider Zo's goals and what Olympias's and Laila's actions and the consequences of those actions might predict about Zo's journey.

4. In literature, symbols have power and can evoke emotions in readers, sometimes without our being aware of that power. How does the author use water in *Empire of Dust* as a symbol of her characters' journeys and situations? How does she contrast the situations of the characters on or near water to those who are encompassed by land? Point to specific elements in the book to support your answer.

5. Kadmus is a classic example of an enemy turned potential ally. His mission to spy on Prince Alex becomes a double-edged sword as he comes to admire and ultimately love the prince. Based on what you have learned about Kadmus, do you think it is wise for Alex to not only forgive him, but to conscript him to be a double agent? What other enemies-turned-allies inhabit the book and in whose interests do you predict they will ultimately act? Point to evidence in the book to support your answer.

6. During his attempt to root out the traitor, Alex believes that his actions show his strength as a leader and will make his people respect him. Later, his mentor, Aristotle, tells him, "They fear you. That is different." What does Aristotle mean, and what does Alex learn about power over the course of the story? How does his view change? What is Aristotle's role in the book, and how does his character impact your view of power?

7. Why does Jacob help Cyn to escape, and what does Cyn choose to do with her freedom? Why will or won't she be successful in her goals? Compare and contrast Cyn's experience with captivity to Zo's. Why did each woman bond with her captor, and how, if at all, did each character—Cyn, Jacob, Zo, Ochus—change from the experience? How might those relationships inform how countries treat prisoners of war today?

8. King Artaxerxes wants peace. The Persian Assassins' Guild wants war. How does each go about seeking this goal? Based on the events in this book, do you think it is possible to attain peace when someone is determined to start a war? It is said that if we do not learn from history, we are doomed to repeat it. What comparisons can you draw between the conflicts mentioned in *Empire of Dust*, which are true to history, and later wars such as World Wars I and II?

Thank you for reading EMPIRE OF DUST!

As the end of an age approaches,
blood soaks the earth, twisted prophecies wield immeasurable power
and tyrants demand impossible sacrifices.

Return to the rich and fantastical world of Eleanor Herman's
Blood of Gods and Royals in book 3,
REIGN OF SERPENTS!

Will Prince Alexander become nothing but a vessel for the
last living god?
As Zofia travels from afar to unite their kingdoms
against the terrible darkness of the Spirit Eaters,
the deadly consequences of Smoke Blood magic loom.
Now magic rises and warriors clash…and the fate of all Macedon
rests in the hands of the unstable prince and those whose loyalty
can no longer be trusted.

Turn the page to read an excerpt from this next
breathtaking adventure.

CHAPTER 1:
ZOFIA

ZOFIA, PRINCESS OF SARDIS, LEANS FORWARD and digs her heels into the beast's sides. Vata strains, shaking her mane, each beat of her powerful wings launching them higher into the sky. Zo doesn't need to look back to feel the dark energy of the thing—the horrifying shadowy form hurtling toward her, gaining on her.

A roar splits the morning air.

Vata lets out a terrible whinny and banks hard to the left. Zo's heart plunges into her stomach as she begins to slip, frantically grasping tufts of cottony mane with both hands to steady herself. Far below her, the dry, crumpled hills stretch to the horizon.

The Pegasus veers again, her mane whipping Zo's face as the wind stings her eyes and tears blur her vision. A shadow falls on her and Vata. Something rakes her back. Sudden warmth floods through her tunic: blood.

She only has a second to register what has happened before white pain explodes across her body. In her agony, she is only vaguely aware that she has stopped holding on to Vata and that she's slipping, falling...

She slams into something brutally hard.

The pain goes numb.

Blackness drowns her.

Zo wakes in a sweat, flinging her arms and crying out in panic until she realizes that she is inside, lying on a little bed of straw and blankets. Panting heavily, she slowly understands that the flight and the chase were just a nightmare.

The Pegasus is not real—was never real.

Zo calms her breathing, taking in the moss-covered walls, daylight streaming in lazy diagonal shafts through the triangular cave openings. And for the third time that week, Zo forces herself to steady her heartbeat after the dream of flying and of falling.

Both the pain and the dreams are, Zo was told, the result of an avalanche that nearly killed her. Since then, she has lost her sense of what happened. Of what was real. She recalls images of a destroyed village, full of ash and ravaged bones and bright blood.

Red on Zo's hands, smeared on her thighs.

She tenses on her straw pallet, closing her eyes. No, those memories do not belong together. The blood was not the villagers' blood. It was *hers*. Her unborn child's. A moan falls from Zo's lips.

"My child?" Cool fingers suddenly trace her cheek, and Zo grabs for the wrinkled hand. Blinking up, she stares into the cloudy, violet eyes of her savior: Kohinoor the soothsayer.

Gradually, Zo's pulse slows, and her grief subsides. Being around Kohinoor eases her because each time she catches a glimpse of the old woman, she's reminded of miracles.

For it had to have been Fate that threw the two of them

together—first as captive slaves, then again, when the nearly sightless soothsayer had found Zo, battered and swollen, beneath the stones of the avalanche. Kohinoor had brought her to her home in the Eastern Mountains, allowing her to rest and recover from her wounds. She was there in the night when Zo screamed as her bruised body healed. She was by her side when Zo stood again, taking painful practice steps. And she was there to hold her when Zo had asked the terrible question. Kohinoor had been the one who'd gently informed Zo that her unborn baby was no more.

Now Zo leans into the old woman for comfort. The knowledge that she has lost her child still catches her off guard, making her feel as though a giant fist has knocked the wind out of her. The agonizing loss is like another avalanche of rocks crushing her chest, making it nearly impossible to breathe, or to think. Her sweet child would never see the world, never inhale fresh air or feel Zo's warm, loving arms. Long ago, in the slave cage, Kohinoor predicted that if Zo ever saw Cosmas again, she would cause his death. And now their child—her permanent link to him—is gone. So much is gone.

Kohinoor helps Zo sit up and hands her a warm mug of tea. Slowly, Zo sips the brew, which tastes like earth and roots and smells like fall leaves. Warmth curls inside her, soothing her and calming her heart.

"Better?" Kohinoor asks.

Zo nods but can't speak. An overwhelming weariness is settling upon her. For even when she sleeps, she does not rest. She battles the dark shadow of despair that threatens to engulf her when she thinks too much about all she has lost on this endless journey: her life as princess of Sardis; her five-year-old sister, Roxana, killed by the slave traders; Cosmas, the man she loves, and their baby. It is too much.

Before she can finish her tea, she lets sleep take her.

When Zo wakes, Kohinoor is gone. She's not sure how much time has passed, but from the absence of sunlight through the cave's roof, she guesses it is dusk. A tendril of fear rises within her—she hasn't woken up alone before. Kohinoor has always been here. She tells the fear to go away, that Kohinoor will be back soon, either from the fields where she picks herbs or the stream where she traps fish.

From somewhere far away, Zo thinks she hears a drumlike pounding. Sitting up, she frowns, wondering what it is and why she's never heard it before. Though steady, the sound is far away, like the world's heart beating in the center of the earth. Curious, she stands and is grateful that her legs can again bear her weight after a month of healing and training. They no longer ache with movement. In fact, she feels strong. Much stronger than she has in weeks.

She pours herself some water and drinks as the beat continues. What *is* it? Could it be the answer she seeks—the truth behind the dreams of flying beasts and monsters? Heart pounding with dread and hope, she feels around on the large table for the fire-starter kit as if she were as blind as Kohinoor herself. She strikes iron on flint and soon holds a blazing torch that illuminates the cave. Her pallet rests on one side, Kohinoor's on the other. In between are tables with crockery, jugs and mortars. Baskets of many different shapes line one wall.

She follows the sound to the back of the cave—nothing there. But through the solid wall of stone, she can still hear the rhythm. Turning her head, Zo presses her ear to the wall, and that's when she sees it. A small, dark opening in the shadowy corner, invisible unless you are looking for it.

"Kohinoor?" Zo calls. "Are you there?"

No response, but the beating is crisper now, louder, a

drumbeat calling her to action. Curious, she ducks her head and steps through the opening into the passage. It is so narrow she has to angle her shoulders, and even then she brushes against rock. She follows the passage for several minutes, the torch's light illuminating only a few feet in front of her at a time. Part of her says to go back to the cave, to lie down again before she exhausts herself. But a bigger part tells her to keep going. For the first time since waking in Kohinoor's cave she feels…alive. More awake. More herself. She's tired of days spent sleeping or pacing around the cave and is eager to see something new. To maybe even learn more about the Eastern Mountains and their dark secrets.

At last, the passage opens in another cavern, dark except for the torch she holds, and there, in the center, sits Kohinoor. She hunches over a wooden plank, hammering a peg into one end. Relief sighs through Zo, followed quickly by another emotion: disappointment. There is no answer here, no clues to ancient mysteries. Just an old woman building something.

The hammering suddenly stops.

"You're here," Kohinoor says. It isn't a question.

"I am," Zo says. She hesitates before drawing closer, feeling as though she's stumbled upon something private. The old woman has already done so much for her. She doesn't want to be more of a burden.

"I woke and you weren't there," Zo rushes to explain. "And then I heard the hammering and followed it. I'm sorry to disturb your work."

"No harm. Shall we return? I will make you some more tea."

"That's all right," Zo said. "Finish what you're doing. What are you making?"

"A table." Kohinoor suddenly slams her hammer into the

peg again, and Zo starts as the sound rings around the cave. She is constantly astonished at the soothsayer's ability to see without eyes, and at the strength which allows such a seemingly frail old woman to lift heavy pails of water or this weighty mallet. As the woman returns to her work, Zo raises her torch and sees paintings brushed onto the rough walls.

"What are these?" she mutters to herself, walking over to hold the light closer.

"Paintings from the Hunor," Kohinoor says without turning her head from her woodwork. The Hunor, Zo knows, are an ancient tribe here in the Eastern Mountains. Yet how can the old woman know what the paintings are without seeing them? She shivers.

With her fingertips, Zo traces a green snake curling around a lotus flower. A few paces away, she sees men with horns dancing around a blazing pyre. Serpents in tall waves racing toward a city of temples and palaces. Three old women weaving on a giant loom atop a hill.

Their colors faded, these images are clearly things of the ancient past, but for some unknown reason, they make Zo's heart pound. It's as though time has instilled a sense of weight to them, a thick patina of importance. Of truth.

The paintings curve around the entire length of the cave wall, and she follows it, her heart hammering in her chest. And then—

Zo gasps. There on the wall, in her flickering torchlight, is a Pegasus, white wings outspread, climbing into the sky. A girl with long dark hair, arms flailing in panic, has just fallen off its back and plummets to the earth. Falling. Falling.

Just like in her dream.

And next to the image of the Pegasus stands a walled city, Persepolis from the looks of it. There, next to the gate, is King Artaxerxes's famous Tower of the Sun and Moon, with its great horned battlements, cracked in two, soldiers tumbling out as flames explode in all directions.

Zo can feel her pulse in her throat now. These paintings are ancient, centuries old, at least.

But she knows that the tower was constructed within the past couple of years. Are these paintings some sort of prophecy...or warning?

She stares at the flaming tower in Persia's capital. The destruction. The ruin. The tiny figures of people fleeing. As if in a trance, she reaches the last image and holds the torch close. A winged child, its arms encircling a wax tablet, rises from the earth as darkness descends from above.

She doesn't understand what that last symbol represents, but she senses that it's important—that it shows the culmination of this...this prophecy. Of the fall of Persepolis.

"Kohinoor," she breathes. "What *is* this?"

The hammering stops. "As I said, pictures from the Hunor."

"Yes, but what do they mean?"

"You know what they mean, child." Kohinoor's voice is but a rasp. "Danger breeds in the heart of Persia."

Zo's blood turns to ice as she remembers the rumors she and Ochus heard at taverns along the Royal Road. Entire villages reduced to ashes. Missing couriers. Empty farmhouses. Vanished horses and oxen. And the village she herself wandered into the day of her injuries. Doors yanked off hinges. Bloody streaks on the ground. And below a shifting cloud of flies, a heap of bones—human and animal—gouged with deep teeth marks. She had thought, during these weeks of healing, that perhaps that memory, like the Pegasus, had been a dream. A fantasy born of rocks hitting her head.

But if these paintings are true, if they are a prophecy... could it be that there had been no avalanche? That Kohinoor had found her unconscious and bloody among rocks, assuming she had been caught in a surging tide of stones. That Zo's dream of flying and falling was no dream at all, but a memory. That the Pegasus was real. And the creature that raked her back with sharp talons… Had it been a Spirit Eater?

"But who…what is doing this?" she asks.

The old woman turns sightless eyes to Zo and croons eerily, as if singing a lullaby to a baby, "Spirit Eaters are doing this, girl. The Spirit Eaters' hunger is sharp."

Spirit Eaters. Months ago, on the slave cart, Kohinoor had told Zo it was fated for her blood to mix with that of Prince Alexander of Macedon. *The only way to undo the threads of fate that have been woven for you is to find the Spirit Eaters who can negotiate with those goddesses who spin out, weave and cut the threads of our fate,* she had said.

Where do I find these Spirit Eaters? Zo asked.

If they still exist, you will find them in the Eastern Mountains. That is where the Spirit Eaters sprang up from a fissure in the rocks, and there they still live. That is where you must go.

Zo had thought of these magical beings as gods, not monsters, and ridden east with Ochus to find them. Thinking once more of the pile of bones in the abandoned village, she realizes she almost did find them. Or, they almost found her.

Mouth dry, Zo licks her lips. "Then we must go and tell the king. We must tell him what is to come before there is more death and loss."

The old woman sets down her hammer and looks up, her smile revealing a few brown teeth.

"Must we? All right, child, let us return to our living quarters to discuss it."

Her calm response unnerves Zo. It's as though she thinks Zo is addled, that she doesn't believe her…and maybe she is right. Maybe there was no Pegasus, no falling from the sky.

Zo does remember something about an avalanche, doesn't she? *What happened the day Kohinoor found her?*

She shakes her head in frustration. There's so much in her mind, and though her thoughts feel sharper than they have in many days, they are still somewhat blunt at the edges, like a dull sword. It's as though she's been living life at the edge of sleep, as though she were downing a sleeping potion instead of water or...instead of tea.

A terrible thought crosses Zo's mind, and once she thinks it, it cannot be unthought.

"Come," the old woman urges. "The passage is over here." Her dry, gnarled hand grabs Zo's wrist. The skin is leathery, like that of a crocodile. It's all Zo can do not to pull away in disgust. But Kohinoor rescued her, nursed her back to health. In all likelihood, Zo would have died without her.

So she allows the soothsayer to guide her to the opening in the wall. Just before she ducks into it, Zo notices something glinting in her torchlight: a large cage.

"What's this for?" she asks.

Kohinoor blinks. "I see that soon a dog will come here looking for food, and I will make him my companion. That is where I will keep him until he learns that this is his home."

But the cage is taller than Zo. A dog wouldn't need a cage that high.

"Did you make this yourself?" Zo asks.

The soothsayer laughs, not answering her, and starts down the narrow, winding tunnel. As soon as they emerge in the cave below, Kohinoor sets about boiling water in her pot, throwing in leaves and powders, preparing the strengthening tea she has been giving Zo every day to ease her pains. But now the earthy scent makes her stomach roll.

When Kohinoor hands her the clay mug, Zo waves it away. "I...don't want any today."

Kohinoor pushes matted hair out of her face, and her bleary lavender eyes seem to stare at Zo beneath a furrowed brow. "You must drink. For your health." Her rasping voice suddenly seems as strong and deep as a man's.

Zo's discomfort grows. "Very well," she says, pretending to sip. After a time, the old woman goes back to the jugs on the table, opening them, sniffing the contents and exploring the insides with her bony fingers.

"You walked very far today, princess. Are you not tired?" the old woman croaks.

Zo stares into her mug. "Yes," she whispers. She rearranges the straw on her pallet as if to sleep and silently tips the mug into it. A moment later, Kohinoor's clawed hand is there, ready to take the empty vessel from her.

"You rest," Kohinoor says. "I will go and gather more rosemary."

Obediently, Zo lies down and closes her eyes. She can feel the old woman staring at her a long moment, and then she hears her slip out of the cave.

This is the first afternoon Zo hasn't had any tea, and her blood hums with energy. Her thoughts are clear. All sense of lethargy and disorientation is gone. So. Her terrible suspicion is correct; Kohinoor has been drugging her...but for what purpose?

Zo sits up quickly. She doesn't know how much time she has before Kohinoor will be back.

Grabbing the torch, Zo again goes to the back of the cave, into the narrow passage and back to the painted cavern. She first takes a closer look at the table Kohinoor was making. With her free hand, Zo pulls the wooden planks up and feels her heart tumble into her stomach.

It's not a table—it's a cradle.

And at that moment, she feels a flutter in her womb. A tiny tremble.

Zo's hand flies to her belly. Her baby… Cosmas's baby. *She's still alive.*

Zo almost sways with relief, happiness and…horror. Not only has Kohinoor been drugging her—which Zo might have dismissed as a well-meaning attempt to prevent her from overexerting herself—but Kohinoor has been *lying* to her.

A cradle and a cage. One for the infant and one, Zo realizes with rapidly increasing horror, for her. The cage is for Zo.

She lurches back, and as she does so, the torch sweeps an orange swath of light across the wall. The paintings are illuminated, and the winged child stands out in sharp relief. In the flickering light, the wings look like they beat the air. And as Zo stares at the prophecy, she feels her child kick.

Her heart now a hammer against her chest, her eyes flick quickly to the image beside it: the girl falling from the Pegasus—*her.* Her empire's capital burning. And a child destined to save it from flames.

Her child.

She needs to get out of here, away from destroyed villages and soothsayers, away from iron cages and drugged tea. She must get to Persepolis to tell the Great King about the missing villages and the warning on the wall.

To find answers.

To save her child.

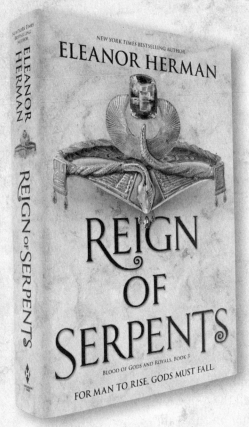

  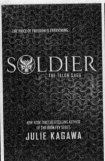 

DAUGHTER of the BURNING CITY

AMANDA FOODY

"Utterly original. If you enjoy your fantasy on the darker side, then you will love Gomorrah!"

—STEPHANIE GARBER, *NEW YORK TIMES* **BESTSELLING AUTHOR** **OF** *CARAVAL*

STEP INSIDE THE GOMORRAH FESTIVAL

COMING JULY 25, 2017

MAKE **HARLEQUIN TEEN** YOUR NEW BFF
BY SIGNING UP FOR OUR EMAIL NEWSLETTER!

DON'T MISS OUT, SIGN UP TODAY!
bookpages.harlequin.com/teen/

GET THE LATEST SCOOP ON
BOOKISH NEWS, EVENTS AND CONTESTS—
YOU KNOW, THE ESSENTIALS!

HARLEQUIN®TEEN
www.HarlequinTEEN.com

Find Harlequin TEEN on

HTNEWSTR